MW01204607

LAMA WITH A GUN

By Seth Augenstein

pandamoon
publishing

www.pandamoonpublishing.com

Jacket design and illustrations © Pandamoon Publishing
Art Direction by Lylah Williams: Pandamoon Publishing
Editing by Rachel Schoenbauer, Forrest Driskel and Tylee Ertel: Pandamoon Publishing

Pandamoon Publishing and the portrayal of a panda and a moon are registered trademarks of Pandamoon Publishing.

Library of Congress Cataloging-in-Publication Data is on file at the Library of Congress, Washington, DC

Edition: 1, Version 1.00
ISBN 13: 978-1-950627-64-6

Reviews

"Fiercely original, Augenstein takes you on an unforgettable wild ride through a slice of forgotten history with a searing, propulsive hero blazing the charge. All hail Lama with a Gun." — **Adam Frost, author of** *The Damned Lovely*

"This action-packed esoteric thriller set in the Buddhist areas of the Inner Asia is based on the true history of Ja Lama, a mysterious warrior-prophet who operated in the chaos of early twentieth century Mongolia. Entering the mind of this colorful warlord, Augenstein will simultaneously mesmerize you with the scenes of steppe and desert travels, showdowns, and tantra ritual. A must-read for those who love action, and also want to learn about the cultures of Inner Asia." — **Andrei Znamenski, author of** *Red Shambala*

Dedication

To my mother

LAMA WITH A GUN

Words of welcome to Innermost Asia:

This story is a work of fiction, but it is based on many real people, tangible places, and true events. It is culled from dozens of historical accounts spanning back centuries. The tales have been met where they live and the sources are honored with an account based on facts, reconstructions…and some outright falsehoods. This world you are about to enter differs entirely from the one in which this novel was conjured. Innermost Asia in the 19th and 20th centuries was a place of brutal miracles, beautiful violence, and everything in between. Your morality is not its morality. Unspeakable crimes are committed, where laws fear to tread. It was a place and time where anything could happen. And as you will see…it most certainly did. Enjoy its wonders—but tread cautiously on its trails.

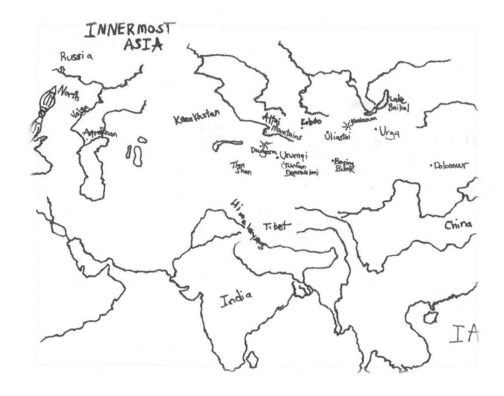

Yeah there's one born every minute
Oughta know 'cause here I am
Seems I'm always steppin' in it
But I finally understand
This whole world is full of takers
This whole world is full of thieves
This whole world is full of fakers
With the aces up their sleeves

Angry Johnny and the Killbillies, "Jawbone"

"On the way back Tzeren related to us the hundreds of legends surrounding Tushegoun Lama. One tale especially remained in my mind."

- Ferdynand Ossendowski, <u>Beasts, Men and Gods</u>

CHAPTER 1
A GIFT

I arose from prayer, opening my eyes to the darkness of the yurt. The scent of other men's blood, haunting each and every breath for so long, lifted. I had believed the ghastly odor had fused to my very essence once and for all. Suddenly it was gone. Yet it was no relief.

Because they were coming. They had finally converged on me, like vultures.

The candles were all extinguished on the shrine the troops had erected for their most holy Lama (me) after we robbed the last caravan. The sun seeped through a tear in the sheepskins over my right shoulder. The ray shone on the bronze sculpture of Amursanaa (also me). I bowed once toward it, offering my previous incarnation the respect I so rightly deserved through all these incarnations in this glorious slaughterhouse.

I stepped forward and knelt at the armory. The rifles were lined up in perfect order, just so, from the old Russian muskets to the larger German carbines, along the east wall. I ran my fingers over the hand grenades and fingered the pins of one of them, listening to that delightful little jangle—that tiny tinkling of metal presaging eruption, the screams. None of these would help in the battle to come.

Outside the small bell jingled—the warning that interlopers had discovered the secret side of my compound. The moments were slipping away.

I smoothed my traditional yellow deel and blue sash over the crisp European military uniform, making sure the bright monk's garb completely covered the drab green combat fatigues, my Colt, and the blade in my green scabbard. These had been my only armor, my only security, from the top of the highest peaks of the world, to the purest psychic depths of the paradise of Agharti, where the rivers and roads ran in golden currents. But all that was far in the past. From my washing bowl I splashed water on my face and stepped through the yurt's flap.

The sky was gauzy with light. The courtyard of the castle bustled with the men sweeping, herding cattle to the corner, some repairing their gear. Dozens conducted their normal business in this, my desert city of thieves and holy men. But some other bustle was amiss this day. Trusty Tömör, dead these last hours, was being buried in the softest soil on the western side of the courtyard. It was Tuesday, as far as I could tell. The calendar (at least the earthly one kept by men in this life) did not matter anymore, since the caravans had become so few and far between in the Black Gobi. We kept a constant lookout for the few fools left who thought they could approach the castle of the dreaded Ja Lama, the false lama, the conqueror and avenger of Dzungaria, the reincarnated scourge of Amursanaa, anointed on a mission to save Mongolia. The bandit with Buddha at his back.

It always made me laugh inside to consider myself in such grandiose terms. The warrior revenger from lives long past, the holy man highway robber, the Lama with a gun. How could people ever know the truth? Would they ever know the truth?

Ha.

The answer is that I would never let them.

Until now, of course—in this story you alone will hear.

The warning bells jingled again, tolling me back to my sole self, and what remained of this life. The two interlopers—both of them were indeed coming for me from the secret entrance to the compound. I sensed them.

Finally, the world had caught up with me.

The boy, Tömör's son, approached. He still wept, but he grimaced and wiped the tears from his face before he presented himself to me.

"Tushegoun," the boy said, his voice ethereal in the light of day after my long time in the dark. "The two interlopers are wandering the castle, saying they wish to offer a gift in tribute. Shall we proceed as usual?"

"Have you seen the face of the one who does not speak?" I asked, my throat raspy, my voice a croak horrible to even my own ears.

"Their faces are still covered," the boy said, shrugging. "They appear to be pilgrims. Still…you told us we can never be too careful with outsiders."

I reached out and patted his shorn head. Squeezing his shoulder, I turned him to walk with me back toward his father's grave.

"You are a born warrior, son," I said, as we walked stride for stride toward the man smoothing the last clods with a shovel. "Your father knew this."

At this he wept, shoulders shaking with sobs. I stopped and pulled him in close. I embraced him, but not tightly.

"Your father was a great follower. He gave us his life. And I don't need to tell you how important he was to our plans in Urga."

We reached the soft, dark dirt of the grave. The boy, who had procured the amounts of poison necessary for our failed assassination plot, nodded. I patted his head, and kept my hand there, like I did when I blessed the true believers. The faithful who put their lives at my disposal.

"Rest assured, when we are all living in the pious and perfect Mongolia of our dreams, an Agharti above ground, then we will construct a shrine to him right in the center of Uliastai. His statue will be the biggest of all, so that travelers, businessmen, and monks traveling the streets of our capital may never forget one who made our dreams a reality. Almighty Tömör. He was a true bataar, a real hero, and not just in name."

I removed my hand from his head. Beneath my heel, I crushed a clump of black dirt—the fertile earth of Mongolia—atop the grave of dear dead Tömör.

"But for now, let us tend to today—because that's the only time when we can make things happen," I said. "Can you fetch the two pilgrims? We must take in all the believers we can, especially if they bring us gifts to kill Bolsheviki."

The boy hesitated. But then he bowed, turned on his heel and trotted away. I marveled for the first time that day about the irrepressibility of youth—the energy reserves that could be drawn on by the faithful who had been educated correctly in our ways from the tenderest ages. I stepped once more on the grave. But this time my boot sank into the soft dirt until I nearly toppled. I caught myself, did a half-hop to the side, and brushed some of the clods from the yellow silk of my deel. A divot a foot deep was pocked into the ground. If I lived, I pledged to punish these gravediggers, those lazy shirkers, tomorrow. There was no telling what shoddy work may leave at our doorstep—contagious disease, vermin, or angry spirits. Perhaps all three. The last thing we needed was cholera, or Bolsheviki, or demonic possessions, or some other nasty outbreak.

The other fresh grave…I stopped over. I spit upon its rotten soil three times. It seemed insufficient; I considered pissing into that soft dirt, the stream soaking deep down to the traitorous corpse beneath. But I did not. Truly, you will be the judge of whether I should have let loose on the grave of that despicable traitor whose name you will learn, in due time.

The voice from beyond spoke to me, then. It came without form, and it intoned directly into my soul so none could hear beside myself. And it offered me revelations beyond this world, after so many years of haunting me with riddles and mysteries. My soul reeled.

Beware, said the otherworldly voice.

Thus, I was confused—and unprepared for the attack.

The ambush came in the blink of an eye. From afar, one of the strangers grappled my mind with his, choking my will to its utmost limit. Our souls struggled invisibly, from afar; I fell to the ground with the psychic pain.

3

My mind whirled.

The agony and ecstasy of battle were fought on an ethereal plane.

The fracas…it lasted for hours. My lieutenants watched my fits and curses and spasms with terror, as they veered between thinking I was dying of an illness or suffering from madness. Never did for a second did they think I was grappling with an invisible enemy in their midst.

But it was this battle of wills, at a distance, using only the unseen power of our minds, which revealed to me the mortal enemy who had dogged my entire journey of one million versts, and more. And I must say it was one of the last surprises of my life; this shadow of the Khenbish Khan which had fallen on my fresh tracks for so long.

This struggle of souls relented after the better part of a day. There was no use in denying the inevitability of what gift the strangers sought to bring me. It was nothing but death. I staggered back to the yurt to await my visitors, opening both flaps to allow light and air inside. I lit a single candle in front of my shrine and stood in front of the rows of rifles. I didn't wait long.

The pair entered to my left. Their forms were backlit, faces obscured. But they stood as tall as giants, shambling forward in a nauseating miasma. Of vodka. Russian vodka.

I knew my mortal enemy from more than just the scent. Our willpowers, our internal strength, our minds themselves locked once again in a deadly embrace, like they had over the last hours, years…utter lifetimes before.

The one in front held out the ceremonial scarf, red as blood and blue as the clearest eternal sky, with little flecks that looked like vultures soaring through the timeless infinities.

"Tushegoun, we have come for you…" the one started to say.

"We have come to kill you," said the mind of my nemesis, his face still covered like a coward.

I reached within my deel and drew my Colt. They reached for theirs.

Two shots cracked the stillness.

This tale thus has its ending. But as all followers of the Buddha know, endings do not exist.

In fact, epilogues are always prologue to the past and the future, all at once.

You do not have to call me Tushegoun. Call me Ja Lama instead—that's where you will find me in the fine print of the histories and encyclopedias. It's where you will find only the merest fragments of this story that you are now about to hear.

CHAPTER 2
A BOY OUT OF COUNTRY

Let me start at the particular beginning of this particular life, these particular failings in this, my last existence.

My first memory was riding across the rocky bridge over the Volga, the cart slamming again and again into ruts, clattering forward without pause as my father drove the horses on with his sharp whip, muttering cruel curses he believed I could not hear. But even then my senses were heightened from my previous incarnations, going back centuries.

"On, you bastards. Onward!" he hissed, and I heard every word. I also heard my mother, from beside him, sobbing—but this I heard only occasionally, far-off, like it was from over the horizon somewhere.

I saw every sparkle on the Volga, shining under the sun from a momentary hole in the clouds. I smelled the shitting chickens and the tanned hides from the baskets in the middle of the wagon. My parents held handkerchiefs to their noses for the dust, but I breathed in the last dirt of my birthplace, believing this stink of Russia—pungent and musky—would never again plague me so.

The odor of Mongolia is one I had never had the pleasure of breathing in. But it was coming.

I was eight years old, if you only count this lifetime. I could have been seven; it's hard to say exactly, because my parents were never good with the earthly calendars. They were too concerned with my future to worry much about my short accumulation of years up until that point.

The year was about 1870. The cart rumbled eastward. My father was absorbed with his plans for me; my mother consumed with her love for me. I can still feel her caresses on my cheek, a lifetime later.

My boyish heart swelled with pride at our return to the homeland, our rightful place in this world. From my earliest memories of my parents and grandparents and even to my many uncles and aunts, we all knew the stories about our exile from Mongolia centuries before. We heard the tales of the battles against the Chinese—broken swords, severed heads, and rivers of blood—forcing us thousands of versts down roads of fear to a place we would never truly call home: Russia. Our people had been living like the undead, never really alive at all, since our shame hung heavy on our shoulders, as we waited to die out along that final stretch of that filthy Volga. The Russian taxmen came to our doors every month to exact what they claimed was theirs.

So as our family cart forged east, bravely trekking across the plains and into lands I had never seen before, strength coursed in my still-spindly limbs, my strengthening heart. During the days, I watched the herds grazing on hillsides, the far-off mountains like the promise of a future already foretold. At night, we stopped the carriage by the flat side of the road, and we covered ourselves with the stinking hides to keep us warm against the western winds. My parents struggled, grunted, breathing hard under one skin in the dark, and I turned away on my side. Other times my father tended a fire, squinting underneath his hard bushy unibrow into the darkness for bandits who never quite materialized. The water we conserved stingily. The horses Chingis and Gerel were strong and hardy, and even as my father cursed and whipped them late in the afternoon as the sun set behind us, I heard the pride in his voice.

"Palden," my father said every so often, using my birthname, "come up here and take the place of your mother. She is weak. She must lay down."

My mother would kiss me on the forehead with the tenderest lips imaginable.

"You know you are the return of the great Amursanaa," she'd say. "The hero of our peoples. My dear boy."

We'd switch places in the cart, and now I could watch the whole future on the horizon before me. My father would hand me the reins when he wanted to drink from his skin of water, or when he preferred to doze for a few minutes on the trail. At such times I set aside the whip, and gently whispered to Chingis and Gerel, thanking them for returning us to where we so rightfully belonged. They trotted faster at my smooth words and my gentle pats on their manes.

We stopped in towns, but never for long. Especially in Kazakhstan. The children in their rags playing in their filthy streets stopped and stared at me quizzically. I turned up my nose at them, so they knew I was a Mongol returning back to the land of my ancestors, merely passing through their misbegotten land. My father traded some of his wares, the cured skins and maybe a chicken or two, for water and provisions. He showed me how to tie the quintuple underhand constrictor hitch knot, a family secret, to hold all the cart's cargo together. But my teeming mind was focused on other things. Higher things.

In the second month, misfortune struck. The rear axle of the cart snapped in a deep rut, and a rainstorm left our cart's cover ripped in two places. Our flesh was soaked to the bones. After the winds died down and we took stock of the damage, listening to my mother's insistent sobbing and my father's swearing at the sky and mountains, my thoughts grew light—confused, strange. The gray sky spun around me, I swooned…and fainted dead away.

The boy may not make it after all, my father said, harsh words piercing my fevered haze sometime later. The illness had ravaged my body quickly, devouring every morsel of my flesh, quaking it with chills and scalding it with sweat. Every breath was pain, every swallow of saliva or the rare splash of water was an effort. And every bounce of that infernal cart was like a fresh stab through my burning insides.

But even though the darkness tantalized me toward letting go, that ultimate relaxation ending this short and ill-fated incarnation, I forced myself to open my eyes. I had to at least glimpse my beloved Mongolia before settling for another cycle of existence.

That was when I saw it.

Far-off to the north, at the absolute limit of my range of vision, was the glittering of enormous shapes out in the foothills. Roads shining golden, flowing like liquid. Dark flecks floating in the current—tiny boats, with far-off figures paddling. The network of splendid flaxen thoroughfares stretched far beyond the horizon—because I peered into the hills, within the land itself.

I was gazing into the deep underground, to the center of the Earth.

I blinked, unable to believe my eyes. But the forms remained—the spinning prayer wheels and the ziggurats and the rising minarets sparkling with their own darkness deep within, like an eclipse of a light unknown to man.

It was the abyss…perfected.

The next day I was revived. Leaping from my makeshift bed, I threw the coarse blankets aside. My mother nearly fell out of the cart when she saw me. My parents stopped the horses and felt my forehead, examined my tongue, poked at my organs. They gave me ladles of water and inspected my eyes and ears. The disbelief in their faces told me they had already assumed they were transporting a corpse back to the motherland. The recovery was a miracle.

"My dear boy," my mother said, embracing me.

"Did we already pass the golden city, the glowing rivers, and the shining ziggurats?" I asked, glancing around the dry Gobi landscape.

Their jaws slackened, and they stared. They felt my forehead again for fever.

For a few hours, they treated me like a little madman, gently pulling me off my feet and down into the blankets at the back of the cart. I assured them I was much better and told them I was ready to continue our journey at full speed, urging them onward with a smile. My mother ran the backs of her fingers across my face, as she looked at me with her usual adoration.

We didn't have much longer to go. Two days later, we arrived.

The city, one my parents kept calling Dolonnuur, was filthy. The wheels of our cart stuck time after time in the muddy streets, and the buildings were all covered with a gray ash, like the crowded bustling city had been through a fire that consumed only the maids and mops.

And the faces—these were not my people. They could not have been, at any time or place. Compared to me and my family, these people had pale skin that seemed to delicately shrivel underneath the sun the day of our arrival. They stood much shorter than the Mongols I knew, but they moved quickly through all that muck underfoot. Their cheeks were soft, and they had wide noses which must have helped them filter that horrific stench of excrement and animals, worse than Russia, that wafted over and through our cart. Their eyes were big and accusing, staring at our cart as we slogged through the town. The few Mongol children in particular looked at me with such venom it took my breath away. What I had done to deserve such hateful glares I still do not know, even as an adult man who later came to rule one of their outer provinces.

"Who are these people, father?" I asked, shouting out toward the front of the cart. "Where are we? What are we doing here? Is this Mongolia at last?"

My parents ignored my many questions. They shouted over the bellowing of the strange tongues of the townsfolk. My father did not stop for directions, or provisions, though we had been days without clean water. Instead, we made right for a plot of land on the eastern side of the city, got down off the cart, stretched our limbs, and took our first few steps in this new land.

I was to be a monk.

That had been their plan from the very beginning, before we had even left the banks of the Volga, months and a half a world before. I was to be a great leader, to bring our peoples back to the respect and greatness we once had, when the haughty fell before our arrows, and our cavalry slashed across the whole known world. From my earliest memories, I remember my mother looking at me with such love in her eyes that I thought she would burst open, right there before me. She would run the backs of her fingers across my cheek, so slowly we seemed to be frozen in time. And she would nod, saying, "My dear boy will be the one who returns to Mongolia, and there he will raise up our once great people on a pillar of faith and peace. Not war." She spoke as if I wasn't there. And she talked this kind of claptrap even after I robbed several older kids of their clothes, which I burned in a fire outside their own house. I could do no wrong, and her assurances of my born greatness were what helped me understand from my earliest years the history of my own soul, and its place in the cosmos.

I was to be a monk.

But as we traveled to the monastery on the edge of this Dolonnuur, this Chinese outpost in Mongolia, this first step on the path to nirvana, there was pause. We stepped around the deepest puddles of mud and carefully avoided the slipping horses on the filthy streets—and then a one-armed beggar gave me a newfound form of enlightenment, in just seven words.

"Welcome to China, savages! Change to spare?" he said, coming close, tugging at the sleeve of my small threadbare tunic, nearly pulling me down into the muck as he slipped and fell. He coughed and seemed about to drown in the mud. I scampered to catch up with my parents, who still trudged toward that sharp, steep-pitched roof looming on the horizon.

"Dad, why did that beggar say we are in China?" I said, tugging on the hem of his clothes. "Why would he say that? Was he crazy?"

"He said that because we…are…in China," my father said. "Inner Mongolia is China."

My mother turned halfway, grabbed my hand, nodded, and yanked me, despite my dragging heels, onward to the monastery.

"My dear boy," she said, sobbing, but still pulling. "My dear, dear boy."

I was to be a monk.

Rage built within me, foot by foot and pull by pull. We had come to the land of the enemy, and they had lied to me to get me here. They'd tricked me halfway across the world, to China. Whether they were just hateful to me, or traitors to our people and our very way of life, remained to be seen. But I could bear it no longer. I threw myself down in that mud, that disgusting putrescence they called earth in that pigsty called Inner Mongolia—in reality nothing more than a Chinese province. My mother stumbled and slipped herself but caught herself on one knee. She hurriedly hauled me up before my father noticed we were no longer walking beside him, but she was too late. My father came running back to help my mother and probably punish me, but he was going too fast. His feet stopped moving, but he did not, and he went sliding right past me, slipping backward, catching himself—and then plunging face down in the muck. I laughed, and my mother let out the hugest belly laugh I'd ever heard, or would ever hear.

It didn't last long. My father rose from the muck like a beast, the mud over his face failing to mask his rage. There was no slipping, no delays, now. He plucked me up like I was a clucking chicken and dragged my flailing spindly limbs all the rest of the way to the famed monastery at Dolonnuur. I was young then, you see—and weak. I had not learned how to fight or how to bend enemies to my will. Because I had not yet mastered myself—let alone the universe around myself.

A monk I was to be.

That process only began when I entered that hall, and a line of holy men materialized out of the shadows in front of us, just a few paces into the hallowed halls of that place. The bald monks stared with stony faces at the muddy, groveling family at their threshold. They had their hands together as if in prayer, but they were not praying. They seemed to be preparing an attack of some kind of ruthless piety, a holy wrath. My father spoke first, his busy single eyebrow bouncing to emphasize his words.

"I demand you take my son as an acolyte. He has pure Mongol blood, despite drinking Russian water for all his eight years," he said, spitting over his shoulder in disgust. "He is strong, and rarely gets sick. He responds to beatings. He is not a smart boy, but he has dreams and sees things no one else can see. Back in Russia, one wise man said he was the reincarnation of nothing less than the Diluv himself. This boy will serve you monks in any way you see fit. Take him and make something of him, I implore you."

Somehow, without turning their heads or making the slightest movement, the monks shared a glance. The middle one stepped aside, leaving a gap in their line. My mother kissed me, with tears in her eyes, and she ran her fingers ever so quickly across my cheek.

"Be," she said.

I had no time to cry out or kiss her back. Because then my father grabbed the scruff of my neck and shoved me forward, and I stumbled into the throng—and into my new life. As the huddle of monks encircled me, herding me toward the deep and dark halls of the monastery within, I was aware of one thing: the sobbing of my mother echoing along the stone walls until I no longer heard it in the distance.

CHAPTER 3
LEARNING

From those very first steps into the monastery, I was an exemplary student. The monks walked me deeper within, and we were in lockstep. Down those sweet-scented hallways, the smell of burnt essences enticing with every pace. Farther and further out of the light. In total silence. The holy men made no audible breaths. They asked me...nothing. For hours, I said nothing in return. I just complied as they removed my clothes, cut my hair until I was bald like them, and then swaddled me with simple and plain robes. I let it all happen, allowing them to move my limp limbs into certain positions for the easiest tug of a hem, the simplest stroke of a blade along my flesh.

Even though we were in China, surrounded by filth and dogs, these men and boys were Mongols like me—strong and proud and sure of each step and breath they took. These were my elders. So I stared with eyes unblinking as they moved around me, prepping me like a beast for the abattoir. I did not let my guard down fully; I was prepared to strike if and when they attempted the first blow.

But that never came. Their hands prepared me for the first day as a devotee. No ceremony marked my arrival. They put me in a tiny room at the end of a hallway on the first floor. The silence was total. Night was still, no wind or far-off wolves baying at the moon. I slept, complete and deep, until the coming of the dawn, and the first day of my new life as an acolyte.

The studies began: the encompassing of all enlightenment, the acceptance of the eternal blue sky impossibly far off above that tiled roof. Considering my past lives, all of it came quite easily. I found myself completing mantras, without ever having heard them in this short life. They were within my ears and heart from time immemorial, from some time long before my birth. Other sutras I memorized by hearing them only once or twice. We spent much time on Mahakala, the fiercest protector of faithful's righteousness, and I felt as if I was merely reacquainting myself with an old friend. By the end of the first week, I was the natural leader of the students. Jealous little sneers appeared I saw out of the corner of my eye.

On the ninth day, I was on my hands and knees, scrubbing the back hallway's stones with a stiff brush, intoning a mantra. Cleaning was a task I never minded—watching each stain and grain of dirt vanish from those stones was progress, and they shined when I was done with them.

But I turned to the bucket when a shadow reflected across the dirty water within. Someone had a broom lifted high, prepared to split my skull from behind. I tumbled to the side, striking out with my foot at the legs of the attacker, who fell to the wet stones with a cry. I leapt up and brought the stiff brush bristles down across the person's face back and forth, scouring the nose and mouth until blood started to well up, easily batting away the flailing limbs trying to fend me off.

It took me a few moments to recognize the biggest and oldest acolyte in the whole monastery, a Chinese boy everyone called Fang. Every day Fang's laughter and voice echoed off the walls. He had teased me mercilessly ever since that first night. He claimed my father sold manure at the edge of town, and thus he called me "the shitmonger's son." His teasing quietly tapered off once he saw the monks' reverence of me, and his scowls merely smoldered off to the side.

But as I stood over him, the scowl had been wiped off that disgusting face, and through the blood and grime a new wide-eyed fear had taken its place. I leapt off him, kicked his broom aside, and stooped again to my bucket and the task at hand. It was another minute or two before Fang's whimpers and sobs brought the stampeding footsteps of three monks, two of whom assisted the boy and carried him off to The Yak's chambers. The third monk looked at me curiously, his head tilted as if regarding me for the first time. I shrugged and gestured at the slippery wet stones of the floor I was cleaning. He nodded slowly in understanding, tucked his hands in his sleeves, and slowly tended to the boy's howls of pain.

After that Fang vanished from the monastery at Dolonnuur, and the jealous glances from the other boys stopped. But I never again let my guard down, even for a moment, as I continued my chants and meditations with a keen ear for the softest footfall, the catching of a breath or a fluttering heartbeat behind me. The Yak and the other monks watched me warily too, after that incident in the back hallway. But they seemed intent to believe this boy Fang had slipped and fallen on the wet stones, mashing his face in the dirty floor stones I had not yet scrubbed clean.

The Yak, so dubbed by the students, was the head monk. He was a giant blubbery man, the rolls of his neck hanging loose and limp over the collar of his pale robes. The other acolytes always mocked him, and for my part I couldn't help but look at him in disgust as he waddled down the main hallway, sweating with the sheer exertion of any movement at all. The Yak was odd. Though he had the high cheekbones of the rest of us Mongolians, he was short. Underneath his massive layers of flab there was no hint of the muscle which comes so naturally to our people from riding horses or hauling huge packs out on the steppe. His eyes were deep-set, and they appeared as dark and as impenetrable as a moonless night. It was impossible to see where those eyes were focused, yet he always seemed to watch the young acolytes with an intensity that unsettled all. But even when those onyx orbs were trained in my direction, I shrugged it off and continued with my duties.

This man was my ticket to advancement. He was one of the first to recognize my abilities for what they were, and he thought highly enough of me to dismiss Fang after the "cleaning incident," as it had come to be known through most of Dolonnuur. So Fang was out, I was in—and I kept my suspicions to myself. What's more, I informed some of The Yak's underlings, the subservient monks, about the worst of what some of the other boys said. I made sure to report exactly the words they had used, and how they had said them, and who had laughed. In this way, within just two months of arriving at the monastery, I was already a singular pupil—a favorite among the monks who were the leaders within the monastery. The other acolytes became wary of speaking freely around me, since three of my more vocal torturers had been called to The Yak's chambers, and then dismissed, since my arrival.

Still I kept on with my lessons, practicing my meditations and my focus on the Four Noble Truths and the six Mahayana Perfections, and the Three Jewels of Refuge…and, of course, my one goal in this savage land to which I'd been dragged: to bide my time until I was ready to escape to Mongolia proper.

I never saw my parents. Despite my prestige at the monastery, I was still bound by the rules for the newest acolytes, and that meant no straying outside the stone walls. Only later did I find out my parents lived just two versts down the road and were indeed permitted to visit me—yet they did not. I had assumed they themselves had left for the homeland—yet they remained close to the place where they'd dumped me, without my knowing.

Six years passed. Childhood waned, the man within stirred. As it does.

I grew to the beginnings of manhood, like a sapling near its peak height but not yet stiffened with its hardest bark. I was gradually given more privileges and responsibilities. By the time of that sixth year, I was leading many of the mantras, and I was permitted to venture out beyond the monastery walls into town to procure supplies through begging. But I found theft was quicker. So I brought back costless bags of rice and bonus loaves of bread which kept The Yak fat and happy.

These were not the true perks of the forays into the rest of the world. When first I was permitted to walk those streets of my own free will, I regularly went to the edge of the town and stared to the western horizon, knowing I was looking in the direction of Karakorum and the plunder city, back when the Mongols reigned supreme over China and the world.

Still, I could not see it with my own eyes, for the hills—and the distance.

I wondered then whether the golden city with its rings of glowing fire had been the capital of the Greatest Khan or had just been a child's fever dream amid an epic journey across the world.

Aside from daydreaming, the other perk of walking the Chinese streets was the girls. They paraded before me while I panhandled on the street. At first I just gawked at these filthy peasants with the roughly pretty faces, and in response they turned up their noses at me as if they were European princesses with the daintiest of Western Sensibilities. Quickly I learned to beat them at their own game. Instead of allowing them first to humiliate me, I remained crouching at my spot near the cleanest alleyway in all of Dolonnuur, and right as they neared, I pulled the alms basket back into the folds of my robe. They glanced at me quizzically, but I stared into their eyes and used just a few of the Chinese words I had picked up so far in that godforsaken country.

"You couldn't pay me for your salvation," I sometimes said.

"Your money is an affront," I'd say other times.

"You're not as pretty as you think," I'd also say.

Invariably, this left the prissy peasant girls visibly red in the face, despite the dirt caking their cheeks. But day after day, as they came to see my alms basket disappearing from their sight time after time, I made my admonition with a bit of a grin. And they couldn't help but smile themselves, despite their flushed cheeks. Soon they were eager to pass closer and closer and wave some money in my face—even though I still pulled my basket away. Soon they sashayed past within a foot or so of my face. Despite their lack of hygiene and washing, their young musky scent was intoxicating as it washed over me.

But the prettiest of them all was not a peasant. Her black hair was everything, total, like the night sky. It swished down at her waist, billowing without a breeze. In her delicate hand she twirled an affected European parasol. She was not amused by my teasing. She wore clean clothes and sported the most sterling self-regard. She was the daughter of the merchant who sold all the luxury items in the town, the perfume and the jewels and the dresses for the richest women, and the most illicit black-market goods to be found in Dolonnuur. As she passed, each and every day around noon, twirling that parasol daintily but with more intransigence, I didn't even give her a glance. I watched the gray sky, looking away from her colorful and stylish form. For weeks she trotted past me, pretending not to care that a dirty acolyte no longer offered her attention.

But this girl with the swishing black hair got closer and closer, and walked slower and slower, each and every day.

One day she just stopped in front of me. It allowed me to inhale all of her. I yanked my basket back and looked up. Her eyes narrowed, she smirked. Her face was utter beauty. And she reached down within my robes, reached around, and dropped a single coin that landed in my hidden basket with a tender clink upon the few others. Then she rounded the corner into the alleyway, her haunches switching back and forth like a beautiful mare's. She glanced over her shoulder, and silently mouthed one word.

Come, her lips said.

And then she vanished down the tight alley.

I glanced up and down the street, then rose to my feet and hurried after her. From out of the shadows of the alleyway her hands grabbed me, tugging me toward her, and we locked together in an embrace.

That frilly parasol covered our writhing ravenous forms for the few minutes we conjoined in that ingress. It was with that girl in that alleyway that I first realized my true power: the strength of will to compel the action of others.

I asked her to kiss me, and she did. But I spoke no words. It was as if I reached out with an unseen hand springing from my mind itself and pulled her toward my waiting mouth. It was as if she had no choice.

I recoiled from my unseen grip with a sudden panic. But she kissed me, hard and passionate, right back. The rest was her agency, all her own intentions. Her mouth could not have claimed otherwise. But I knew from that single kiss and our fierce entwining that I could force the minds of others.

That girl taught me more in that alleyway in mere minutes than The Yak ever did in my years as an acolyte.

The stories of such conquests eventually reached The Yak's very ears, however. Because one fine sunny day, as I was preparing to meet my girl with the swishing black hair, one of the subordinate monks grabbed my arm. He whispered in my ear, with hot breath, that The Yak demanded my presence. I brushed him away with my hand and straightened my deel. The monk shrugged, then grabbed a broom and swept. I took a deep breath. It was not usual for The Yak to request the presence of anyone, much less the lowly acolytes. He had not once in all those past years ever sent for me, neither through my prodigious display of innate talents, nor through the occasional mishap inevitably blamed on me by my jealous peers.

As I walked the uneven stones back into the darkest part of the monastery, I knew that something different was happening. Somehow, my life was about to change forever.

The Yak was nude, reclining, rubbing his meaty hands over the rolls of his flabby torso, as I entered the open door. He gestured with one hand for me to close the door, which latched softly.

None of the rest of the doors in the entire monastery had such a locking mechanism. No one from the outside could enter that chamber, as all the monks knew.

A creaking emerged from the other side of the room. I slowly turned, and I saw The Yak emerging upward from his cushy perch at the corner of the room. With great shuffling efforts he waddled to a stand at the opposite corner of the room. But there was an insouciance to his step which I had not seen before. Perhaps it was the erect penis which poked out from beneath the folds of his stomach, like a thin snake straining to free itself from beneath a boulder. He was eating something.

"Palden," he said, chewing. "Please sit down. Make yourself comfortable. We have much to discuss."

I sat down on the nearest mat on the floor. Suddenly he was at my shoulder with a cup. I took it from his hands and instinctively raised it to my lips, as we were wont to do at the quick meals at Dolonnuur. But a strange scent from the clear liquid stopped me from drinking. Instead, I mimed a sip, and placed the drink next to me on the ground. The Yak had circled around to face me from my front. His member bobbled, eye level, just two feet from my face. But I did not look at it—I was focused instead on his face above me, as he stuffed the food into his mouth. It was a tiny round fruit I would only later learn were grapes. The squish and gush between his rotten teeth sent shivers across my flesh. He slurped and swallowed, seeds and all.

"Students have come and gone for years through this monastery," he said, wiping his chin with the back of his hand. "At the end, they have a choice of whether to carry on with their training. And so do you."

He stepped closer, and his penis swung toward me, back and forth, like the parry and thrust of an advancing sword. I forced myself to remain still.

"You were born in Russia," he said, stopping a foot from me. "You will never be allowed to travel to Tibet with the current allowances of the laws. Even if you have Mongol blood, it has been tainted from birth by living in those lands."

Here The Yak leaned forward, until he placed a meaty paw on my shoulder. His hot breath wafted across my shorn scalp like the winds across the barren plain.

"But I have ways of getting what I want. And if you give me what I want, I can get you what you want, too," he said.

His hand softly traced my back and my neck, and then gripped the back of my head. It pulled me inexorably forward. I resisted with all my might, pulling back away from the waggling cock, which loomed closer and closer.

My hand shot out, grabbing his balls like the claw of an eagle, and twisted.

The Yak howled like a wounded animal, hand falling away from my head, as he froze in pain. I stood, still cupping his manhood. I squeezed harder—but not too hard, yet.

"I don't think I'll need your help, after all," I said, through gritted teeth. "I'm not sure whether other acolytes have taken you up on your little offer, Yak. But I am content to try and make my own way to Tibet, even if I did have the misfortune of being born in Russia."

I released him. He fell to the ground.

I walked out of that room, and directly out of the monastery, my bare feet trudging through the sucking mud of Dolonnuur. I marched to the place where my mother and father had set up their yurt, years before.

The patch of wet earth was bare; nothing else remained.

I questioned all the closest neighbors, asking them if they remembered the shabby couple who came from the Caspian Sea, who had brought their son to the famed Dolonnuur monastery to become a monk. The peasants looked my dirty robes up and down, then refocused back on my eyes. When they saw my gaze, when they felt the power of my will, they had no other choice than to tell me what I knew. Like the girl in the alleyway that one moment, their minds complied. Taken together, their little insights gave me little clues which pointed me ten versts down the valley, at the farthest reaches of Dolonnuur.

The smell of feces intensified in the air as I drew closer; with each step, it seemed, I was closer to the greatest pile of shit in all of Asia. Finally, at the farthest edges of the town dump, I came upon the last lonely yurt in the shadow of a high hill. It must be the place. As I drew closer, I noted a trio of vultures wheeling around the nearest hilltop, circling lazily in the sky.

Bya gtor. The word came to me on the wind—a term I'd only heard in hushed whispers in the hallways of the monastery. A sky burial, by birds.

My father appeared at the doorway just as I approached. We did not embrace. He merely pulled the furry flap aside and ushered me into the half-darkness within.

CHAPTER 4
MASKS

Mother died a fortnight earlier, father said, scratching at that enormous unibrow. She had suddenly fallen down on the ground, had turned blue and stopped breathing. Her eyes rolled in panic for a few moments, then froze still. There was no other explanation, he said.

Her final words were, "The Dear Boy." And that was all.

"So, she is up there on the hillside, where I buried her with the help of our friends from the sky," he said, pointing upward, toward those vultures circling the hilltop outside. "Bya gtor."

My knees shook. I sat down on the ground, in the dirt. That was all I could do to keep from falling. Bya gtor—the sky burial where your bones were picked clean by the winged scavengers and taken up into the sky. It would not take long, in my mother's case. My mother, the delicate flower who coughed at the slightest draft, should never have been forced to cross Asia all the way back to our homeland. She was too weak to make the trek. She never should have left Russia. As we sat in that yurt where my father, the new widower, had marinated in the stink of shit, the vultures continued their work on the hillside far above us. I smelled my father's guilt in the small space between us, in that warm and close air. It was a rotten whiff of decay.

"You killed her," I said.

He laughed, which startled me. I thought I had him cornered, but he sneered and spat on the dirt floor of this newly empty home of his.

"Some of us in this life can't make it on their strength alone. The world will inevitably destroy them. Your mother had her own resolve, but it was not enough for this world," he said, scratching at one filthy fingernail. "But then there are those like you and me, Palden, who are plenty strong enough to bend the world to our own wishes."

Rage built inside me. This man, this shitmonger, who had dragged me across the known world only so I may honor him through my studies had killed my mother in his mad bid for vicarious glory.

In the light of a single candle, I scrutinized the changes in his face wrought by the years. His hair was gray, and his face sagged off his jowls like putrefied meat off a cow's bone. His shifty eyes had yellowed with age, perhaps greed. His single eyebrow had gone a sickly gray. This parasite of a man had brought us to this cursed land, and we were all suffering for his stupidity. My sanctity threatened by a pervert monk—the true Mongolia far off—my mother dead. It was just too much.

"What is it you do now, strongman? Sell shit by the side of the road?" I said, spitting on the ground in the same spot. "In truth, you're just a pile of shit yourself."

My father shook his head, took one giant step forward, and struck me across my cheek with a blinding blow, sending my face into the earth. It was an incredible strike, the power in those rickety limbs had been like the kick of a horse. Before I knew what was happening, I was on my feet, rushing at him, knocking him down, on top of him, my hands throttling his throat, as I spit again and again into his face. He turned away at first, still struggling at my clenched fingers, trying to pry them loose.

But then a strange transformation came over his grimacing face, the reddening bloodshot eyes of this my progenitor. His tightened face relaxed, he nodded…and an unseen force squeezed at my jugular. It was like a vice, a godlike grip on my very existence.

His eyes narrowed, and he smiled. The power was impossibly strong. I weakened. I struggled in vain. And everything turned black.

The dark faded to silence; the moment made eternity.

Sound and light returned an everlasting instant later.

"…and you need to understand that the physical strength of a thousand men is nothing compared to the iron will of a single soul, a person as pure in intent as the searing heat of a flame."

I slowly awoke to his words, eyes coming into focus in the half-light. Seated with my legs crossed in the darkest part of the yurt, my hands were folded in my lap. As I shook myself awake, I was amazed to find my limbs all free.

But something stopped me from rising. It was as if there were unseen ropes around my wrists and ankles. I was unable to even turn my head; instead I could only catch my father's standing silhouette out of the corner of my eye as he spoke on and on.

"…as you must come to understand, there are things that govern this world which are unseen and will never be understood by men," he said. "Far beyond your mother's weak constitution. Far beyond the seasons, and the rising of the sun. Farther still beyond the teachings of those monks. There is a current underneath everything which can never be stopped or even paused. It is like a river flowing down the highest mountain, which comes, inexorable and unceasing, for all time…for as long as there is a world in which to live. Nearly every person goes through life cursing chance and fate, or praying for guidance in feeble voices to gods so far beyond our skies that their invocations go unheard, let alone unheeded. They are fools.

"The true secret of everything is…the flow of this river right here on this Earth, on this plane, can be harnessed. It pushes along the strongest swimmers, and it can be altered. Dams can be constructed, trenches to siphon off essences. If you follow me."

I had had enough of this rambling.

"What are you trying to sell me, shitmonger?" I said, shaking my head groggily.

He motioned at me, and I felt my throat tighten again, strangling me. I could neither speak nor raise my hands to protect myself. He stepped toward me, and it relented.

"Dear son," he said in a soft, deadly voice. "I am trying to sell you the secrets of life and death, the spaces in between the dark and the light. And you will listen. You have no choice."

I did not have a choice. I did listen. And I did learn.

First lesson: to cease struggling against my invisible bonds. It was not for fear of punishment. When he stopped speaking, the unseen force immobilizing me loosened completely. Surely, I could walk out of the yurt and away forever. But as I rubbed my wrists and cleared my head and stood, looking at the flap billowing in the strong breeze from over the hill, I knew I could not leave. I had to know the secrets of which he spoke.

What of this current running among us, around us, through us?

But most of all, I needed to know about the vigor of his will, which had so easily overcome my own. I wanted that power. I needed that power.

I sat and I listened. He spoke, and he paced. For three days, we drank only water, and we ate only crumbs of stale bread. But there was no hunger, and there was no thirst. Because in that lesson, the body was left far behind the odyssey of mind and spirit, so far beyond and yet so integral to this planet's workings.

This man, this tiger in the tent, was a man I had never known as my father. Gone was the shitmonger. He was bigger and smaller at the same time; he throbbed in the enclosed air of that small space. His face changed its shape and form like the clouds, from dark storm clouds to feathery white wisps high in the stratosphere. Passionate fury and beautiful softness fueled his words as he recounted what he had seen, and what he had heard, and what he had come to know just through listening to the wind and watching the turn of the seasons across Asia.

I cannot tell you exactly what he told me. Even if I could repeat his precise words, it would never convey the secrets I will continue to hold most dear, even after I pass from this mortal plane. I can tell you his words were like cornerstones in an enormous castle erected in my heart. I won't attempt to tell you of each rock; it will suffice to show you the final ramparts and walls.

Instead, I will tell you of some demonstrations of his power.

At the end of the first day, he casually flicked his hand—and across the tent, three jars toppled and cracked on the hard soil. But after I blinked, the jars were all intact in their same spots, still upright.

In the small hours of the night, during a thoughtful pause, he ran his hand up over his scalp, and it left a trail of fire burning along his flesh, all the way back to his neck. The flames shot up three feet off the crown of his head, wafting plumes of smoke toward the top of the yurt. Reversing the motion over his skull snuffed the fire just as quickly. He smiled at me, his eyes rolled back in his skull all the while.

On the second day, the wind gusted through the tent, and suddenly the flaps all blew inward, flooding the inside of the yurt with brilliant sunshine. And off in the distance all around were a group of riders galloping, closing in on us. Their war cries and volleys of rifle shots ripped through the tent, whizzing past my face. I fell to the ground. From my prone position I saw my father's head again on fire, and he had not moved a muscle. But this time a blue flame erupted from his eyes and ears. And just as the horsemen closed within yards of the yurt, the tent flaps fell like curtains. Then, silence. I saw between the cracks in the tent the invaders had disappeared as quickly as they'd come, in the gray day out at the town dump, the vultures still circling in the sky.

"You see," my father said in a soft voice, again extinguishing the flames with a smooth hand, "not all is as it appears to be, in this tent, or anywhere."

My spirit took flight with his in these days. I breathed a whole new air which I had never known existed in my entire life up until that point. I was intoxicated for the first time, a level of ecstasy and need I had not come close to attaining—even from the musk and sweat of the girl with the swishing black hair.

But as much as my will was willing, my flesh cried out in weakness on the third day. Hunger and thirst finally took hold of my bones. The only sleep I had was stolen between my father's sentences, the breaths he took between eternal truths. And even then, it was the rumbling of my own stomach which shook me awake. At the advent of the third day, the old man saw with narrowed eyes I was weak.

His single brow clamped down hard over his blue eyes as he sharpened his focus on me. His yellow teeth gritted. And his unseen power lifted my drooping head by the collar of my now-filthy monk's robes. His voice, when he spoke, was soft with curiosity. There was no trace of anger in his words.

"Don't you feel the compulsion to know everything there is in the universe?" he asked. "Don't you wish to conquer the world of men and everything that surrounds it?"

At that moment, I thought only of two things. One was my hunger. The other was Mongolia.

"Mongolia," I mumbled, my eyes closed.

"Fool," said father.

I next awoke with the wind tugging at my robes, and the sun nearly set again on the western horizon. The yurt had vanished; I was on the ground, under the open sky. The firmament had turned from a deep blue to a purple and black, rolling away for the stars above. Some small embers of the fire smoldered. I stoked them, tossing on an extra log. I noticed the jars were still there. In one I found more kindling to keep the fire going. Soon the flames again crackled.

Searching the two remaining jars, I found a note in one—and a jumble of reins and harnesses in the other. At that moment, I heard the familiar whinny, and I sprinted around the hill.

And there stood Chingis, the noble beast who had pulled my family halfway across Asia. I called out to him, and he trotted over, neat as you please. I stroked him and brought him back to the fire, where I tied him to a sturdy root in the ground. I sat next to the heat and opened the note on the thick parchment. It was no easier to read by the flickering light, but I eventually deciphered the message.

"If you cannot swim the river," it read, "dam it and send the current another way."

CHAPTER 5
FALSEHOODS

The current was against me, there was no doubt of that. But I set off on Chingis without fear, still riding the strange high of my father's lessons.

The Yak back in the monastery had not been lying, even as the disgusting slob had tried to violate me. Even if I was a full-blooded Mongolian, and an acolyte in good standing, as a Russian-born man, I would never survive the trek. The sentries at virtually every warlord's border would stop me and turn me back at best, summarily execute me most likely—or enslave me for life at worst. The Yak's invitation, as repulsive as it was, had its merits. I had to get to Tibet—faith had to be my path to lifting Mongolia from its yoke.

As I rode Chingis out of town and to the west, aimless that one Wednesday morning, I was unsure exactly where I could go. I was on the cusp of being my own man—I felt this newfound agency surging in my veins and my muscles and heart. But I could do nothing for Mongolia until I forged my own way.

That meant Tibet and its immortal teachings.

But as Chingis trotted us west in the bright morning, the slow gallop cleared my head. Even if I traversed the borders, I couldn't just barge my way into the holiest places. Guards there made their livelihoods on rooting out hapless students like me, by stealing their only worldly belongings and then condemning them to a nameless dungeon from which they would never escape.

For some reason, the galloping of Chingis amid the breeze turned my thoughts to the girl with the swishing black hair. I thought of her skin and her scent and her kiss. And we turned abruptly back east before we had gone more than an hour. I only vaguely knew that I needed to see her.

Somehow, I knew if I saw her, I would know what to do next.

I found her walking away from me, near a street corner where I had begged for so many mornings. I watched her hindquarters swaying unhurriedly down the street as she twirled that frilly parasol. I felt a stirring that was not from the jostling of the horse.

I dismounted. I lashed Chingis up to the nearest post, and hurried after her, catching her just a few paces farther on. We were in another alleyway moments later. Her smooth face turned to me. Her parasol lifted high in the air naturally, as if she was floating upward. Her surprise gave way to a mischievous smirk as she molded into me. We drifted back farther into the shadows of the passageway to reacquaint ourselves, in the corner behind an abandoned old cart. As before, our clothes stayed on. Mostly.

As we lay in the shadows, breathless, safe from prying eyes, she told me her name. I forgot it even as her whispers passed over my face. I told her of my mother's death, the sky burial, bya gtor, the vultures, and my vanished father. She was not impressed with my plight and urged me to seize my fate as a newly orphaned young man.

"That is sad to hear about your mother," she said. "But your father sounds like a madman. Perhaps you're better off without him."

Her head drooped upon my chest.

"Perhaps you're better off being alone," she said, tracing a long fingernail across my stomach.

She stretched her neck out and kissed me.

"But then again…maybe you'd be better off with me," she said.

"What do you have in mind?" I asked, stroking those fantastic black tresses.

"I could take you to meet my father," she said, in a fluttering voice. "You could tell him how you're madly in love with me, and how you intend to marry me. You leave the monastery to be my husband, dowry and all. Passion, and everything after."

The half-formed idea that had reversed my course out on the plain and brought me back to that Chinese town came into focus. I had a plan. It had been there since I had rode toward this girl; I had just needed to realize what it was.

I leaned down and kissed her brow, then picked up the frilly parasol and twirled it slowly in my fingers.

"Nothing would make me so happy as to meet your father," I said. "Let's go. Right now."

Her head lifted and turned to me. Her eyes were filled with so much love I thought they would set me on fire. I helped her up and rearranged our clothing. I handed her the parasol, and we strolled back to the street arm in arm. We headed toward her palatial family home at the other end of town.

"I wonder what your father will say," I said at one point, nibbling her earlobe. She smiled.

"What?!?!" her father said, minutes later.

He was a skinny man, all spindly limbs and bones. Disease exuded from what little flesh he did have. But he wore finery over those slight shoulders. When his daughter informed him I would soon be his son-in-law, his mouth hung open, like a genuine skeleton's. What he saw before him was a penniless and shabby monk on a single horse; from behind those fancy European eyeglasses, he saw no return on investment in the union. This man would scoff at true love.

And this is exactly what I was counting on.

"You cannot marry so young," he told his daughter, shaking his head.

He paced back toward his desk, under which squatted a big heavy safe. He shuffled some papers nervously, trying to gather his thoughts. It was clear he had no problem with marrying her away to someone acceptable, but I did not fit his particular bill of lading. My plan was coming together.

"I love your daughter, sir," I told him, stepping forward, with hands outstretched. "There is nothing that can quell our passion. We are like two halves of a single whole. There is nothing that can keep us apart."

His stare lengthened. He didn't blink. But his tremoring hand turned pale, bloodless, as it clenched the chair next to him.

"I hope that it doesn't upset you, sir, but I would like to proceed with our marriage as soon as possible. I have given up my pursuit of enlightenment, because when I am in her conjugal embrace, there is nothing so heavenly as her nubile body."

At this he turned an unnatural color—what caring father could ignore that hellish bait?—but his daughter suddenly swooped in and embraced him.

"I love you, daddy, I knew you wouldn't have a problem with my dear Palden!" (I don't know why I told her my real name; I learned to discontinue this practice in all my business dealings soon after this, I assure you.)

The man's limbs were tightening, flexing against the constraints of his little girl's hug. But no man could resist that tender vise. He slackened, though fire still smoldered in his eyes. He was planning something—and I had bet everything I could bend it to my advantage.

"Bunny," he said, patting her arm, "why don't you go and see if mama needs some help preparing dinner? We should make everything ready for our new guest."

"I would love to meet my mother-in-law as soon as possible," I said, setting my hook further into the fish, watching him squirm.

"Let them set the table for us first," he said, holding his hand up at my chest.

The girl with black hair squeezed him tighter, then released him, and then came over and tackled me with a loving embrace. After that, she ran from the room with a little squeal, and the father and I were left alone. I didn't waste any time— every moment was crucial to my plan.

"Listen, friend," I said to him, dropping the dreamy inflexion from my voice. "Your daughter loves me, and I need something. You want something, too—to get me out of here as soon as possible. Can we make a deal?"

The man's brows arched far up his bald head, and then his eyes narrowed. Curiosity—and maybe a twinge of fascination—lurked somewhere there. His barter face, eyebrows wrinkled, assumed its carnivorous shape.

"I don't know what you mean," the old trader murmured. "My daughter's happiness is the most important thing to me."

I nodded and sat in his chair at the desk. He lowered himself into a smaller chair.

"Let's cut to the chase. What I propose is this," I said, tapping my finger on the desk with each point I made. "You give me a horse and identity papers and three sacks of provisions, and you will never see me again in this town. You will never again have me near your daughter."

The vendor's face screwed up in a genuinely sad expression.

"A horse and three sacks of goods? Why shouldn't I save that for a dowry for a true man for my daughter?" he said. "The identity papers alone are worth much more than your sorry hide."

Just at that moment, as we huddled close in conspiracy, the girl with the swishing black hair walked in, bearing two cups of tea.

"A celebration dinner will be ready in an hour," she said. "I hope you two are getting to know one another better. You will be best of friends for a long time, I just know it!"

She kissed first her father on the brow, and then me on the lips. She sashayed out of the room, blowing me a kiss over her shoulder before she disappeared.

"You couldn't get rid of me. She adores me," I said. "Besides, my offer is cheaper than a dowry that would lure a 'true man' in."

The merchant nodded his head in appreciation at this good sense, even as I watched his mind running calculations into the future, annual subsidies and interest and debits, with a son-in-law like me in his accruing old age. After a few moments, his face brightened, and he clapped his hands once, rising from the chair.

"We will have to hurry," he said. "Let's go out the back door. I'll give you one of my steeds, and my assistants will outfit you from the alternate pantry. I will grab the papers you need. We have to hurry—you must be long gone before that dinner is ready."

We rushed like mad, the merchant and his lackeys quickly filling sacks while I fit the newest saddle on top of the horse I'd selected, a beautiful black mare.

"Believe me," he said, grunting, as he poured some corn meal into one of the sacks, "if I catch you around my daughter ever again after this deal, there will be hell to pay. I know mercenaries, men for hire…"

"Good sir, no reason to worry about that," I said, sliding my new identity papers inside my new jacket. "I'd rather be anywhere other than China. I will be so far west, we won't even be looking at the same stars in the sky. By the way—do you have any sensible Western clothes? I may need them for my journeys."

This answer seemed to please him, and I'm pretty sure the fourth sack he half-filled with some European-looking uniforms was just for good measure, to sweeten our hasty deal.

I mounted the mare, trotted out the gate with my gains, and immediately went around the corner to the main thoroughfare. There I sold the mare right back to the merchant's own store. The cashier looked at the horse strangely, like it seemed familiar, but I patiently waited for him to remunerate me with the coins I demanded. Then I hoisted my sacks, laid them across Chingis' back on the main street, mounted him, and trotted off to the western edge of town.

"We are on a great journey," I said, whispering into my steed's ears. "We'll only get to the top of the world by playing some of the angles, no?"

The screech nearly knocked me out of my saddle—a banshee wail coming from behind me and to the left. I turned just in time to see the girl's beautiful black hair swooshing in all directions as she ran at me. She brandished something metal in her hand. Fearing a sword, I was relieved it was only a huge spoon. But before I could dig my heels into Chingis and gallop away, she brought the utensil down in a quick arc—right onto my ankle bone.

"Yow!" I howled, reaching back, trying to fend her off.

But I slid backward on the saddle and hung there defenseless. She reared back with the deadly spoon once more, and it was at that moment that Chingis, spooked by her raptor cries, started to run.

It was just in time—the heavy implement came down right where my skull had been just a blink of an eye before. Instead, the flat side of the spoon smacked the flank of my steadfast steed, who took off west toward the edge of town, unreachable even by the screamed curses of the girl. I dangled like a flag in the wind as we sped off.

"We'll meet again, Lama!" she hollered after me. "You son of a whore!"

CHAPTER 6
TIBET

The ankle wasn't broken, but it was bruised deeply and every gallop of Chingis brought a quiver of pain. It took two whole weeks to truly heal. In that time, I made seven-hundred versts, traveling from Inner Mongolia across China proper, their backward and peasant-dominated inland areas where nothing grew but ignorance and cruel local despotism.

The extra funds from selling the horse back to the merchant were crucial. I stockpiled food and water, always prepared to make another hundred versts in case I reached a deserted stretch in this depraved land—or if I encountered robbers and needed to barter for my life. In my condition, there was no chance for me to fight off more than four or five bandits, at most. I traveled, and I made camp at night with a small fire, stroking Chingis' mane, finally settling down to sleep when the cold night finally numbed my throbbing ankle to the point my eyes could shut. We awoke with the sun, and then we were off, heading to the west and south as quickly as we could. We were never off track. We had purpose. We stayed the course. Destiny hummed over the horizon.

Chingis did not let me down. He was an aging horse, and after the first few hundred versts, I sensed he'd lost the spring in his trot forever, and he breathed hard. But he kept on. He did not give up or stop of his own accord. I swelled with pride at how well my beloved horse muscled his way across that hateful land, as if his four legs were extensions of my own body, bringing us toward salvation, clop by clop.

Three months of careful travel took us across China in that arc, making verst by dusty verst upward, toward the sky and the clouds. Soaked by rains, we were dried by winds. Day by day the air became thinner, crisper, cooler. The mountains closed in on all sides and seemed to arch above our small scampering forms, like trees towering over ants.

But then Chingis and I broke through to the other side, and the heavens opened. The mountain pass seemed a gateway to another world: the path wound around one peak, with a rock wall jutting straight up to the top on one side, a precipitous fall on the other. This passage through the mounds of rock was the sole entry point to not only Tibet, but everything beyond: the greatest places of enlightenment—and my future in this life.

We stopped short.

A small guard station, a white box with a thin red pole laid horizontal, blocked the narrow way. The sentry, clad in black, stood next to it. The figure was stout, nearly as wide as he was tall in a thick coat, and a muffler wrapped tightly around his head, leaving only the blue eyes exposed. His arms were folded impatiently, as if he had been waiting for my arrival.

"*Papers?*" he asked, reaching out with an enormous hand for Chingis' reins.

As he held the horse I dismounted and searched for my identity papers. In those few seconds, I recalled my father's words about that unseen current of life running through everything, and how I may tap into it, if I was brave and focused. So I trained my mind and my will until it was pointed sharp, like a sword. And as I handed over my papers to the sentry, I thrust this invisible blade forward with all my might.

Without flinching, the sentry took the papers, and those blue eyes narrowed in a smile. A knowing smile. He barely glanced at the documents before thrusting them back at me.

"*Enjoy your stay in Tibet,*" he said, the high-pitched gravelly voice sending shivers through my flesh. "*But you will need more practice at harnessing the unseen flow if you hope to make it long in this land of so many strong souls, traveler.*"

Like a fencer, he had knocked away my thrust, and had parried and come right back at me with his own force of will. I was clearly overmatched. I detected the searing power of his being, and as I physically fell back from under its strength, the fabric fell from around his head.

The man had a bushy single uninterrupted brow punctuating the power of his blue eyes. And he had a yellow grin, a row of even and sharp teeth larger than any I'd seen before. My mind clouded, and I blacked out.

I awoke what seemed like moments later. But the sun had reached the opposite side of the sky. The sentry had vanished, along with the tiny guard house and the barrier across the path. All that remained was the empty road and Chingis, lashed with one of the reins to a root in the ground. Cursing, I sprung up from the ground, dusted myself off, and mounted my reliable steed. I cupped my hands around my mouth and called out to the valley:

"You bastard! I know you're out there! You'll see what happens when I get to the monastery! You'll rue the day you trifled with me, shitmonger!"

But the echoes of my own words—fading out in the expanse of the void—went unanswered.

The sun was just sinking on the horizon when I reached the true guard post at the outskirts of Lhasa. It was two armed men at a pinch point along the path, this time a passage between two sheer cliffs on either side. These two buffoons were just lanky youths swaddled in huge furs. I stepped down confidently and repeated my tactic of staring the leader in the eye while searching for my papers.

When I handed over the documents, I targeted his mind with my own, focusing my will sharper and harder than ever before. It was easy, and effective; these goons were not so strong as my father masquerading as a guard. This one didn't inspect my permits, or even glance at them—he just dropped them on the ground from a limp hand and walked away. It was as if he had forgotten about me. I picked them up and stared at both guards. They had turned away, and both angled toothpicks into their rotted mouths. I called out. But they did not hear me for the mountain winds. I mounted Chingis. And with a holler from deep within me, my voice echoing all the way down the valley, I sang on the final trot into the city, as twilight blotted the sky.

For three thousand versts I had not felt privation or acute need. But when Chingis and I arrived in the outskirts of Lhasa, we drew stares even in the gathering darkness. I sensed how ragged an apparition we made. The clothing and gear lay in tatters on our thin forms, and my durable steed limped from a crack in his back-right hoof I only now noticed. It was as if I had been traveling in a haze, content to drive both beast and man nearer to our graves for the sake of a few more versts, rushing toward our destiny in Tibet.

But now that I was here, I had to keep my head. For years before I had left Dolonnuur, I had eavesdropped on the other boys, listening to the stories of this holy land, this place of holy men and deities. The stories changed, tall tales told by each and every acolyte. But there was one thing that everyone agreed upon.

Upon arrival any hopeful student must immediately reach a monastery, lest one become known locally as a beggar. Because invariably the first test was the commitment to the cause, and an unwavering dive into the ascetic life. After the huge trek, the indolent may be content to rest for what they promised themselves was just a few days, just to get a good meal and some full nights of sleep before crossing the threshold at the Drepung Monastery. But the truth is these unfortunates had come so far only to fail to take the ultimate leap into the faith. So even as Chingis limped along the route toward the monastery, from among the hordes of filthy beggars surrounding us in the twilight, I picked out the young but weathered faces of these unfortunates in dirty monks' robes who had failed before they had even begun their studies. I nodded at them. By this end of my journey across China I was destitute, nearly naked and barefoot except for the rags hanging loose off me. Despite this, these lost souls looked even worse. Ending up as one of them was tantamount to a living death.

I rode Chingis around the outskirts of town, up the rocky slope to the front entrance of Drepung. I kissed his hairy brow, and whispered thanks into his ear, tears tumbling down my face onto his coat. I handed the reins to the outstretched hands of a monk sitting like the Buddha on the steps. Then I walked inside.

No one greeted me. Hundreds of monks lived inside those hallowed walls, it was still early in the evening…and yet not a person was to be seen. I stopped, closed my eyes, listened. From far off, there was a toll of a bell. Over the beat of my heart, I listened.

The ringing reverberated on and on through the monastery: like it would never end, like it had never started, like it had been there since before everything. I followed it down the first hallway, up two flights of stairs, and back down another passageway. The tolling grew louder but stayed the same pitch as I traveled toward it, in a haze, through the darkness. I passed vague stone nooks in shadow, closed doors on either side, and occasionally a window lit with the faint glow of the moon in the sky. The humming grew louder with each step. Though I could see nothing, somehow I knew the way.

I rounded a corner and found the source of this heavenly sound: the shadow of a monk with a singing bowl against the moonlight from a small window. He held the metal vessel in one hand, and circled its edge with a wooden mallet, as if he was stirring a delicious broth over a fire. My stomach rumbled at this thought. The tone continued on and on as I approached, singing with that mournful wail of patience and knowledge I scarcely understood in this lifetime, but which I certainly sensed from my past incarnations. That's why I had been drawn halfway across Asia—to this bowl and its singing. Its teachings.

The door to the monk's left was open, unlike any of the others. He stepped inside, and I followed. He walked into the complete black, and the bowl's music doubled back, passing my shoulder with a whispered breeze. Without the sound pausing for even a heartbeat, the door creaked shut behind me. The singing dwindled as it traveled down the hallway, far off in the distance, in moments. And then I could not be sure that I heard it at all, or if it was just echoing in my ears—a tintinnabulation that would never again fully leave my ears, or my heart.

A rumbling breath quaked in the darkness. It was like the growl of a feral creature. From in front of me, and below. Just the right height to be a crouching animal, waiting to attack. I tripped backward onto something soft—a cot. And then I realized with a start—the breathing across from me was just snoring.

This space was to be my cell, that figure in the dark my roommate. I lay back on the cot and rested, falling asleep in mere moments. I dreamt nothing; there was only the abyss of unconsciousness.

My eyes opened to brightness…and wind.

A big, ugly, familiar face hovered over my own.

It was Fang. The exiled acolyte who had attacked me with the broom back in China.

His grin was just inches away. His hot foul breath billowed over my face. His hands were on my shoulders, and he pinned me down with all of his considerable weight. I focused all of my will on the space between his eyes, his brain, but something there blocked my power.

"Fancy meeting you here," he said, grunting.

I scoffed at him.

"You'd better hope you find a way to keep me pinned like this," I said. "Otherwise, this isn't going to turn out well for you. Just think—you might get beaten and humiliated by someone half your size."

His face showed a moment of hesitation. I thrust upward with every ounce of strength I had left from after my cross-continental journey. It was more than enough power. Fang flew through the air and landed back on his own cot along the opposite wall. I jumped up to pound him into submission quickly and without apology, but my bones ached, and my joints crackled as I got to my feet. I stumbled forward, and Fang tumbled to the side, until we steadied ourselves just as we met in the middle of our room. His hands went for my throat, but mine reflexively slapped them away. We gripped wrists, trying to hurt each other as much as we could.

Again I focused on his mind behind those dim eyes—but I could not break through into the center of him. It was the first time since the struggles with my father that I found my new power of will stymied.

"I know you, prodigy," he said to me. "I remember you from China. You and your scrub brush."

"And I know you, coward," I said. "You remember what happened at Dolonnuur. And you know what will happen if you test me."

In the years since we had last met, I had grown. We now stood eye to eye. And we were an equal match in most other ways. But he was hugely fat; he outweighed me easily by fifty pounds, perhaps even a hundred. He lunged. We struggled back and forth, pushing and pulling and tugging and kicking at one another. But neither of us had a clear advantage.

Eventually we pushed each other away, retreating to our separate cots, tacitly agreeing we would continue our attempts to destroy one another later.

But the struggle unto death would be delayed for a long, long time. Instead, we became friends for a time, sharing the same space and air and experiences. I'll tell you how that happened—and let it be a lesson to you who seek companionship among your fellow man.

The first thaw started in the dining area on that, my first day at Drepung. A handful of the monks sat at the tables, discussing something in hushed whispers as they shoveled something from steaming bowls into their impassive faces. One of the monks saw me standing listlessly at the door and ushered me inside to the line leading to the steaming cauldron. The odor was terrible—like a mélange of sweat and fermented roots of the earth. After five minutes of waiting, I was handed a bowl and a wraithlike cook ladled some of the slop right into my vessel. I paused for a moment, and then turned on my heel toward the tables. I found one entirely empty and set down my bowl. The small clutch of monks two tables over glanced in my direction but kept talking and otherwise ignored me. I sat and started to eat, holding my breath so I would not gag.

"Not having an easy time of it, prodigy?"

I looked up at the voice. It was Fang, staring down at me. Without another word he sat down across from me.

"I didn't invite you to join me," I said.

"No, I invited myself. Because you need my help," he said.

His hand moved up over the edge of the table and rolled something across at me. I caught it without thinking. It was an apple. It was black—not rotten, but black.

"Trust me, prodigy," he said. "Eat fruit. Avoid the other garbage."

And without another word, he stood and walked away, shaking hands with a young monk at one of the other tables. I watched him saunter out of the dining area altogether. I slid the apple into a makeshift sling pocket I'd made within my robes out of some rags. Into that same secret fold, I also slid the knife I had found on the table. I soldiered on through the lumpy barley porridge with the hint of tea which the monks kept referring to as tsampa. It sucked the saliva right out of my mouth. I finished barely half the bowl (little did I know that I would eat at least some of it every day, for virtually every meal, for the next two years).

I left the dining area with a rumble still in my belly, unsure of how I would subsist another hour, let alone half of a day in my new place of learning. Only once I was back in my chamber at the end of the day did I bite into that black apple. I devoured it utterly, seeds and all, within a minute. It was juicy and delicious. The knife I carefully tucked underneath my cot. The stem I used to pick my teeth, as I stared, daydreaming, up at the ceiling.

Fang came in just as I was drifting off to sleep. He sat down at the edge of my cot and put a hand on my knee. He smiled at me.

"I told you about the tsampa," he said. "Listen to me, and you'll get along just fine here, prodigy."

I nodded and smiled at him. But my eyes swelled shut, even as he kept staring at me. I plunged into a deep sleep.

I woke up strangely sore of body and groggy the second day. My studies began early, and it was challenging beyond anything I had experienced back in China. These monks clearly meant no goodwill toward us acolytes. They were like selective chefs searching for the best ingredients for the nirvana stew. We were raw stuff, chaff and wheat alike mounded together, meant simply to be thrown into the cauldron. The end product was all that mattered, they indicated with each and every uttered word, corrected prayer, and ample punishment exacted. My hand was slapped when I attempted to rise from the floor in the inappropriate fashion that first day. Hours later I was pelted with insults by one of the younger monks.

Success at this new place was far from assured. For the first time in my life, self-doubts nested like vipers in the back of my mind. What if I could not make it work at this new place—what if I was an imposter only playing at a monk's life? What if this holy place, in the most sacred of lands, was too much for my meager faith? I thought of Chingis and wondered if we would ever travel across Asia again.

From the moment of my arrival at the monastery, the world had taken on a chill that drilled straight into the marrow of my bones. My father had always counseled me to eat as much as I could when I was cold—since that was how people froze to death, because their resources iced over from within, he said. You needed to keep feeding that internal fire, he had always told me. So I ate the tsampa, I listened, I focused, I did what I was told—just like any young person should. That third night at Drepung Monastery, I meditated on my lessons from the hours before until my stomach rumbled, jostling me awake from my half-sleep. In the darkness, I heard my roommate slip into the room with the gentle rustling of the robe around his legs, the tap of his soles on the stones. That third night, I felt him move closer to me in the blind dark, and then I felt something round and plump drop into my upturned hand.

It was another apple. Black, even amid the darkness.

I could not resist. I ate it quietly, biting it tenderly, sucking all its juice out, every drop. His breathing was slow and deep and steady. The apple was so delicious, I swallowed the seeds again.

I awoke groggy, with something poking me in the ear. I reached up and found it was the fruit's stem. But my elbow hit something. It was a body. I felt dreamily behind myself, and it slowly became clear it was the bulky form of Fang. He was sleeping next to me. I felt my heart leap, and I started to try to rise from the cot. But a soft arm encircled me, and I felt him pressing his chest against my back, his quivering loins pinned to my backside.

"Shhh," he said, from what I remembered in my fuzzy brain. "Let's just huddle together for warmth, just for tonight. I'm too tired to reach my cot."

In truth, all I remember is that his closeness and warmth in that place—that unfamiliar place which was no home to me, that tomblike cold surrounding our beating hearts—was salubrious in that moment. Never mind that he was a man. My drowsy mind wandered, my body fell limp, and I drifted to sleep once again.

I awoke and a streak of light came from the opening in the door. My head had cleared, but my body felt sorer than ever. My legs and my backside throbbed with an odd, dull ache. I looked over to Fang's side of the room, and I saw his cot empty. I stood and dressed, groaning when I moved too fast in one direction. First thing was first, I needed to find my roommate and find out if he had beaten me with a stick or something while I had been sleeping.

I found him talking with two of his closest confidantes. When the three of them saw me coming, the other two backed away, and Fang smiled. He put his arm around me.

"Hey, prodigy, how did you sleep?" he said. "I hope I didn't wake you when I came."

"I only remember that you gave me an apple, and crawled into bed next to me…"

He held a finger up to my lips, and walked me away from the other two, toward the emptiest part of the hallway. As we walked, the tall friend of Fang's, with a perpetual grin on his face, winked at me. I knew him somehow, even if only in a prior lifetime. But even as I tried to place him, Fang turned my chin with his hand.

"That is something every acolyte does here at Drepung, though no one talks about it," he said, smiling. "Feel how cold it is, even here in the morning? The drafts whisk right through the passages, in every direction. Every night up this high in the mountains gets dangerously cold. Without fires in each of our room, we must survive in any way possible."

Looking at him, I sensed his lies. But before I could focus my will on him, he pulled me back toward a door at the end of the hallway. He produced a big brass key from around his neck and jammed it into the lock. The door swung open and he pulled me inside. Before I could open my mouth, he shoved something sugary and delicious between my lips, something which melted on my tongue ever so sweetly. A morsel of chocolate.

"This is just our secret, prodigy," he said, grinning.

The wan light from the window showed the room to be a pantry of some kind. Shelves were filled with sacks and foodstuffs. The aroma of sweet, savory, and musky sustenance hit my nose. And I realized this was the most valuable spot in all of the monastery.

"Here, have a date," he said, flipping me a dark wrinkly oblong thing. I sniffed it, and then bit it. Sweetness flooded my mouth and my eyes flooded. I scarcely believed at that moment something like that existed on this Earth for people to eat. I wolfed it all down, coughing the pit onto the floor, and he laughed. He threw me another one, and then stuffed a handful more into a sack he pulled out from under his robes. He grabbed a brimming drinking vessel, which he pushed at me.

"Take these back to our room," he said, grabbing my shoulder, looking me dead in the eye as he held the corroded key up in front of my face. "And don't tell anyone about this room, and this key, and these treats. This is the way we survive the cold nights in this monastery, and how we get enough to eat. Without these, we would never make it through the winter. Without us using each other, we would not survive."

I nodded. But he squeezed my shoulder tighter, pulling his face closer to mine.

"You swear it, prodigy?" he asked.

"You're giving me second thoughts now," I said, pulling away, grabbing the sack out of his other hand.

"Come with me here," he said, walking toward the single bright window in the pantry.

I accompanied him, and he pointed down toward a crowd far below, at the bottom of the slope leading back toward the town. Even from a far distance, the failed acolytes in rags, huddled together on the ground, exuded abject misery in their poverty.

"You see those beggars down there?" Fang asked. "Those are the ones who didn't make the cut. They relied on tsampa and slept with only a single coarse blanket to keep them warm at night. And that is why they now live on the streets using rocks for chairs and dirt for beds. They did not make it within these walls."

He slid an arm around me and rubbed my shoulder. Trusting his touch, I nodded and walked away, back toward our room. I glanced back at him, and he was watching my backside, his arms crossed over his chest, like he was the conqueror of all Asia. He smiled, and I nodded at him. Inside the room I slid the bag of provisions under his pillow, and then I rushed back out to meet the head monks, and to pray harder than ever before.

Weeks, then months, passed. During that first winter I grew accustomed to those juicy black apples, those sweet dates, those nights of deep dreamless sleep. Fang seemed to have an endless supply stashed away. I came to need the calming stupor that came every night with the forbidden fruit, seeds and all. I also grew accustomed to having Fang sleeping beside me. On the rare nights when he wasn't in my cot, I felt cold under my single blanket, and I'd wish I had an arm draped over me. He knew this, and it was only when we were having a disagreement that he stayed on his own side of the room. Occasionally I realized we were acting like how my mother and father had interacted all those years ago back in Russia, back when I was a boy.

I was more concerned with trying to keep up with my studies, under the harsh scrutiny of the mercurial monks in charge at Drepung. I was always sore of body and groggy in the mornings. I chanted too loud and too quietly. I moved too fast and too slow for their tastes. My eyes were always focused in the wrong direction. All these earned sharp words of rebuke—and even occasionally a slap across the face. It wasn't just me—other acolytes had difficulties same as my own. But in my young life until that point, I had never encountered a situation unwinnable, a set of odds insurmountable, in quite this way. The monastic hierarchy was built as much on the vagaries of an eyebrow raised, the shadows shielding a face, the depths of a sigh, and the digestibility of the tsampa as it was upon the skill and purity of the candidates who had come from across Asia to improve themselves. I knew the answer to almost every question. But they only ever called on me to answer the most impossible riddles, the enigmas without solution. The ones utterly without answer or recourse. And for not knowing, I was punished.

Dreams eluded me. The rare nights when I had visions after my nightly snack, I found myself transplanted down, into the rabble below the monastery, shivering and starving without shelter in the Tibetan night. It was a dream unlike any other. I smelled the musky flesh of the mob around me, the swirl of humanity and gasping breaths, as we strained to get the closest to the passing horses and carriages and pedestrians. They went by, and occasionally the plink of a flicked golden coin sounded out in the dark like a bell tolling the next iniquity, the people clawing at the Earth and at each other like rats in their mad scramble for the shining nuggets. Blood and skin and tendons flew with each separate donation that came our way. I found myself under the crowd, as the air and life were slowly smothered out of me, as the crowd pressed in.

During these nightmares of the all-consuming mob, I awoke with great heaving breaths, swearing to myself that would never happen. And then I would feel the arm of Fang draped over me, and I would pull it in tighter around me. Even in the summer, the air seemed to chill within those stone walls as the nights reached their nadir, and I needed the added warmth of the body next to me.

I needed reassurance in those days of youth, I must admit.

Out in the hallways, amid the other acolytes and monks, Fang gave me barely a nod. Unlike his lowly status in Dolonnuur, he had come to be considered one of the star pupils at Drepung. Something had changed in him—from the days of directionless attacks like the day he ambushed me, he now knew how to turn situations in his favor. He was smarter. He could also influence minds in the same way my father had taught me. I sensed his grown power as he lay in my bed, even if his will was still not as strong as mine. But I never tested it again—he was my protector, of sorts, and there were also those black apples to consider. That fruit was my salvation.

One person whose eyes were always upon me was Fang's tall friend, with the grin and the hard jawline. He looked vaguely European, somehow. I did not know his name. But from afar, I sensed his power, which may have been as strong as mine. Whenever I saw him walking my way with a slow saunter, I walked in the other direction. I never did discover his name in Drepung.

Thus, my willpower went totally unused within those monastery walls. For some reason, my budding influence had no true effect on the senior monks. The eldest and most advanced disciples seemed to just shrug off any attempts at my reaching into their minds, their souls. It is hard to describe—they were unconcerned about my presence, like they were monolithic stones standing free in the earth, and I was the buzzing of a hapless fly. It was very disconcerting. Considering my growing powers—and my youth, don't forget my inexperience at this time—I thought all of life was mine for the taking. Remember, along my travels I had passed through tight borders using bogus documents, I had procured extra food and supplies at marketplaces from China to Innermost Asia to the holiest highest place in the world, and I had negotiated that fictional dowry for a girl I did not love. But my resourcefulness was of no use within those walls.

I felt more alone than I had ever been on the roads across Asia with Chingis. I again wondered about my trusty companion, and whether the monks had sold him to a worthy owner somewhere in the town. My mind drifted during prayers, thinking of a scenario in which I would steal my dependable steed back from a stable, and take off straight northward, back toward the eternal blue skies of Mongolia, where I might set myself back on the true path to my destiny. Truly, what is the point of learning, but not improving?

Such daydreams were broken by sharp slaps on my skull from the elder monks.

Indeed, these drifting thoughts, as part of my perpetual mediations, never failed to bring a barbed word of rebuke from the monks, who sensed my spirit drifting up and away from that place of stone and concealment. My mind perpetually wheeled from place to place, thwarting me access to my full capabilities.

The black apples, their sweet taste, had grown loathsome to me. And finally, I had one fruit which finally, utterly shattered my pursuit of nirvana forever.

Fang brought me this singular apple late on a day wracked by thunderstorms whisking between the mountains. This apple was blacker than all the rest. He gave me the fruit and left the room as he usually did, to confer with his friends. I bit into the fruit, and within that first hunk of pulp, I felt something tiny wriggling around in my mouth. I spit out the soft flesh, and from where it landed on the ground within the glow of the single candle, something moved within the putrid remains. I peered closer.

Worms. The core and its seeds within my hand were woven through, teeming with them. I threw it with disgust at Fang's side of the room, where it smashed against the wall with a splat. The worms scattered across Fang's bed were all dead. All but one of the critters had been dead by the time I had bitten into the fruit, as if its flesh was poisoned.

Puzzled, I lay my head back down on the pillow and waited for sleep to overtake me. It did not come immediately, as it usually did so easily in that cot.

For the first time since that first night entering into the darkness of Drepung, I heard Fang come in. His footsteps were not stealthy, his breathing was husky. He did not head for his own cot. Instead, he came within a step of my head. I felt the heat from his body. Something rustled. And then his hand was on the back of my head, pulling me closer. The other hand pinched my nose. My mouth opened for air.

And then I felt it on my lips.

Warm, and hard, and throbbing. The hand pulled my head in tighter. It breached my mouth and started to push down my throat.

I didn't even know what was happening before my hand chopped at the hardening member, and there was a howl of pain. I jumped up from the cot and held my fists out in front of me in the darkness.

"Why did you do that?" Fang groaned, in fury. "Why would you do that, prodigy?"

"What were you trying to do to me?" I spat.

I circled to my left two steps in preparation for my next attack. Because I knew there was no good answer, and I knew within my sinking stomach at that moment why I had been sleeping so deeply in those months, and why I had found my mind unable to grasp the harsh lessons of the senior monks. The stiffened member in Fang's hand at that moment told me all.

Fang had been drugging me, and then disgustingly attacking my unconscious body every night since I had arrived at the monastery. The aches and pains hadn't been from the cold air within those stone walls or the privations of eating the tsampa. It had been the drugged black apples, and the resulting sodomy, which had been destroying me from within. There had been no companionship and warmth in those huddles together in the same cot.

It was rape, nothing less. For the first time in my life, I had been a victim. And I had allowed it to happen—I had been unable to defend myself, through my cloud of naivete. I clenched my fists.

Well, no more. I slid my hand underneath the cot, hissing when the sharp blade sliced the end of my finger there, spurting a bit of blood.

Fang laughed out in the darkness, hearing my distress. His voice echoed loudly; his cackling seemed to pierce my fluttering heart.

"Prodigy, I just saw how sweet those lips were," he said, his voice husky and unearthly. "And that ass of yours... If you hadn't fought me off with that brush back at Dolonnuur, I would have taken it for myself all the way back then."

He laughed.

"But I ended up getting it anyway," he said. A sucking sound of his smacking lips echoed somehow in the small room, so I heard it twice. "You're my little whore now."

The knife handle leapt right into my palm with those words. And before I could even understand, or he could react, rage thrust me forward. The knife easily impaled his chest and pierced his heart. The whites of his terrified eyes shone alone in the black. I yanked the blade out and plunged it in again and again, penetrating deep into the very core of his being.

My arm continued its murderous work long after his hands had ceased defending weakly against my death blows. The blade flung blood on me and around the darkened room with each and every pull-out and penetration. It took me another minute of frenzy before I grew aware of the sound of the chopped meat beneath me crumbling wet with the same sucking noises of Fang's smacked lips.

Tears streamed down my face. Because I knew, as I caught my breath in those moments of my heart hammering and my mind racing, that life was forever changed by this moment of vengeance. I was a killer—I was a new man.

Gone were the directionless days at Drepung Monastery, prestigious though it may be. My previous cycles on this mortal plane had already prepared me far beyond what these middling monks had been able to. Even my father's insane lessons over a few hours in a shitmongering tent in China had done more for my development than the months in this fabled place where I'd ended up having to slaughter a disgusting rapist.

Opening the door and peering out into the hallway, the darkness was cut only by the dull shine of moonlight from a window down the hallway. All was quiet. It was inconceivable that Fang's mortal cry had not been heard by the other monks. But I had to try and make my escape.

I stooped over the body. Reaching through the blood-sopped robes, I fumbled around until I found the corroded brass key around his neck. I quickly switched clothes and wiped my face and hands clean from the rapist coward's blood. Out to the hallway, I crept to the pantry, which I unlocked. I took three of the largest sacks and filled them with the most valuable foodstuffs, and several skins of water. (I left the tsampa behind.) I tied the sacks together, hauling them over my shoulder.

I walked those dark halls in perfect silence, retracing my route backward from that strange night of my arrival at Drepung. Sure enough, there was the mournful tone of the same singing bowl somewhere far-off. At that moment it sounded hollow. I walked slowly but steadily in that direction. Before I knew it, I was in the monastery's main hallway, with the door to my escape glowing with moonlight, wide open. The sacks weighed heavy on my shoulder, but I quickened my pace, without any further attempt at stealth. The cold night air hit my face, and I shivered. But I kept moving.

The singing bowl was louder. Its tone echoed from somewhere off to my right. I walked along the whitewashed brick wall of the monastery, my numb arms now dragging the bags across the ground. The singing bowl abruptly stopped its whining circumlocutions. As I rounded the corner, I shielded my eyes from the radiance of a dozen torches.

A stable stood there in a tiny alcove alongside the monastery. The torch fires blazed the way as if heralding my departure from that place. Horses stood in a singular line, tails swishing, with no one guarding them. But my surprise at this most welcome development was secondary to a shock of recognition.

Because there stood my Chingis, my trusty boyhood steed. I dropped the sacks, rushed over, and embraced him.

The tears welled up once more, and my relief at seeing a friendly face— even an equine one—was total.

"Chingis, my brother," I said, sniffling. "Let's go back home. Back to the eternal blue sky."

He nuzzled my neck, and he shook his mane all over my face. The smell of this beast, my brother of another species, brought me back to the happy times of

41

my childhood before I had been sent across Asia along the one-way path of my fate. In that moment, I wanted nothing but to be a boy again, to never have met monks, or Fang or The Yak, or even the girl with the swishing black hair. To never have acquired the sad knowledge of trickery and willpower to survive a malevolent world.

But there is no going back in this life, or even in the next. This was something I knew in my bones from all the lives I had lived over the eons. We are all condemned to march forward as inevitably as the sun is forced in its path along the sky. With backbreaking effort, I slung the sacks across Chingis' back, which was just as solid as ever. His trot was strong, like he was young once more. His hoof had healed. I stroked his mane, and I cooed in his ear, and I pointed him toward the center of Lhasa. We wouldn't make the next thousand versts with those huge sacks weighing us down. But selling them would get us enough gold and essentials to take us anywhere on Earth.

The wind whistled in my ears, but on it I heard also the soft whine of the singing bowl once again. It echoed from behind. I turned around in the saddle, and there, in the flicker of the torches, I saw a figure emerge from behind the corrals. I discerned the tall figure from his wide grin, and his hard jawline, even as he continued circling the singing bowl with that mallet. It was Fang's eerily familiar friend. Shivers shook through me. I tugged at the reins, sending Chingis ahead faster, farther, and further away from the scene of my crime, and my past.

CHAPTER 7
ON THE ROAD AGAIN

My stay in Lhasa was not for long. I sold all the things I'd stolen from Drepung for the bare essentials I'd need over the next thousand versts, and for a pretty penny besides. The idiot merchant, with a long white beard, looked hungrily at my exotic items, the fruits and other delectables. I smiled and focused on his mind. Each time I attuned my sightless gaze in on a person, it honed to a sharper, deeper incisiveness. I stopped short of robbing the poor fool blind, but I took everything I felt was due myself after my reckoning with Fang. I ensured he gave me a good share of the gold coins he had stockpiled in a safe behind his wall of wares. The shine in those coins, no matter the denomination, currency, or language written upon them, meant they would come in handy wherever I may roam.

Chingis and I trotted northward out of the city, in the direction of glorious Mongolia. But we did not make it far. A wind so fierce it stopped us in our tracks blew in our faces every time we turned in that way. Each effort we made to muscle through, the wind strengthened, like a vengeful god blowing an insect backward from its nest. Each time we made it one step forward, and stumbled backward, nearly toppling to the rocky ground. So instead of continuing, I steered my companion behind a sheltered rock outcropping. The wind died down. When we emerged from the stone's shadow, the gale again picked up, now threefold in power. We again sought shelter.

The rage of that wind shoving us backward nearly stopped my heart.

Sometimes the universe points you in the direction you must go. The unseen currents shove you along, no matter your struggle. This, at least, I have learned in this go-round.

When I turned us around and instead headed west, the fierce gusts calmed, and became a gentle nudge at our backs. Chingis trotted merrily in that direction, and I stared off at the horizon, where we could be heading. But I knew the choice had already been made for us.

Days and then weeks passed. We kept going on that same path. You may laugh and ask why we obeyed the wind—but I would ask you—why do any of us take the directions in life we take? Do any of us actually control our own fate?

Does this current around us all not move you, too?

Are you sure?

I was a young man just out of adolescence escaping from a murder scene, with a death warrant pending. The blood still stained my hands, which trembled weeks later from killing my violator. I had known something was amiss in my dealings with him, but only too late. I cursed my naivete. I had believed then I had found a friend who was only trying to comfort himself as he had comforted me. I had no idea he was so depraved and had thought so little of me. I was not yet the man of stone I would later become.

Black apples, indeed.

Rapists must die. There was no other way. They did not respect other bodies—so theirs had to be violated in their turn. If they were violent, so much the better—they would meet violence, as well.

Even with my breath heavy, my heart pounding as I made my westward escape, optimism slowly returned. A kind of exhilaration filled my heart. I had seized back my agency—I had my unfaltering mount beneath me once again, and we were on the road again. No matter whether I had been the victim of Fang or the harsh discipline of the Drepung monks, I had survived with my will intact, my power greater than ever before.

Just one thing continued to bother me. This power within me, this essence which developed through all my previous turns on the Earth, had been worthless within the walls of Drepung Monastery. Even the simpleton rapist Fang had been resistant to my abilities. Even if my powers had increased and grew every day and with each and every uttered word and expended breath, I was still not in the same class as the rest of the truly faithful.

There was also Fang's friend, the nameless tall one with the limitless grin and the singing bowl. He had to have known what I had done. Would I ever again encounter him on my travels ahead? I shuddered to think so.

My mind wandered through space and time as the wind at our backs gently pushed us along. We passed wild horses, villages and fields of stone, and an empty guardhouse. Chingis headed westward, then meandered southward. The wind led us. We traveled through the clouds themselves, the pathway through the mountains grew indistinct and faint for versts at a time. My breath grew labored, and my head was light as Chingis trudged on. The path presented us with no choice. We passed the last few huts, and then were in the open terrain, still heading ever upward to the barren heights of the heavens. I watched the sky, and for some minutes at a time I believe I lost consciousness. When I opened my eyes it was dark, Chingis carrying me ever onward. I closed my eyes once again. When they opened again, it was daytime.

We were on a ledge, with the cliff's edge just an arm span from Chingis' steady hoofbeats. My horse stumbled just for a moment as we rounded a corner, and we found ourselves facing four guards with rifles. Their stern stares aimed down the barrels pointed straight at us.

This was Lipulekh Pass, though I wouldn't know that name for years to come. I didn't know then it was the uneasy truce zone where Tibet collided into both Nepal and India. All I knew was those approaching rifles, and those scorched dark faces squinting hard down their iron sights. They said nothing, they just advanced.

I held up my hand, and they stopped. Their hatred of everything beyond their border coursed through the space between us. But I could hold it at bay for the few moments I needed to activate my plan.

Even though I was stronger by far than any of these sentries, in both limb and will, I knew four of them at once were too many. So I just held them there. I reached back with a slow hand into my nearest pack. I pulled out a handful of gold coins I had kept for such occasions. I gestured with the money in the direction of the Pass, letting them know I would pay them to go through. The big guard on the far right approached, grabbed the coins, and turned back as he jangled them in his hands.

"You can pass," he grumbled in Chinese to me, "but you must dismount and swear a loyalty oath to the Raj."

"I would prefer not to dismount," I said. "My horse is strong, but advanced in years. I need to get him some water and rest before the sun sets."

The big guard nodded, then gestured to my left. One of the other guards yanked the reins from my hands and pulled me from the saddle. I fought, but I was caught off balance, and two more guards on my right pushed me. I toppled over the side of Chingis. I rolled clear of them, sprang up to my feet—just in time to see the big guard approach my horse, draw his revolver, and shoot my four-legged companion right through the head. Chingis collapsed.

"You will not need to be in such a hurry now," the big guard said, laughing uproariously as the others joined in.

My heart drained to nothingness watching my Chingis twitch the last of his life away on that cursed ground. But rage quickly cauterized the void in my heart. I reached out and focused my mind on the nearest guard, the one who had grabbed the reins, and I clouded his judgment for just a moment—just long enough for me to rush up, grab the revolver out of his hand, and shoot him in the back. The shattered bullet fragments blasted through his chest, outward toward the other three. One was hit in the ankle by the ricochet and fell—the other two hit the ground. Still holding my guard by the shoulder in front of me as a shield, I shuffled forward. They took two shots at me, but the guard's quivering form blocked both.

"Stop him! He's only one man," shouted one of them.

I advanced until I stood over the wounded one on the ground, and I executed him with a single shot to the skull. I dropped the body and focused my will on these other two. They were feeble-minded stooges at a desolate guard post without much in the way of brains or soul, so I found it quite easy to maneuver them. I had the subordinate hog-tie the big guard—the leader—with the whips they carried on their belts. Just as he finished the last knot, I killed him with another shot. The shot's echo down the valley wrested the big guard from my control, though he was already in bonds.

"You don't know what you're doing," he said, spitting at me. "This is an act of war against the British Empire. You can't hope to take on the British."

I bent over, and I tightened the whip around his wrist, and the one around his ankles. I cupped his face, gently smacking it.

"I'm going to head on down that path, and I'll take on whoever is in my way," I said. "If it's Europeans who need to die, so be it. All are equally worthy of my wrath."

He sneered, and then spit in my face. I could not help but smile. I wiped his saliva off my cheeks and nose, then flung the disgusting glop into his eyes and smeared it deep into his eyeballs with my fingers. For good measure, I spit into his face, too. He howled in anger.

"You dirty Mongol bastard," he said. "You won't even make it down to India. You won't make it past the village of fakirs. They'll eat you alive, before you know what hits you."

"Fakirs?" I said, taken aback.

He just laughed.

"You shall see. Oh, you shall see. In the Land of the Gods," he said, his shoulders quaking with evil mirth.

I did not like his tone. I grabbed him by the head and dragged him to the edge of the nearest cliff, a thousand-foot sheer drop right below his face, and him, unable to squirm away because of his bound limbs. His mood turned. He pleaded with me to set him free, that he would show me where he and other robber-guards had buried the spoils from the other, more unlucky travelers than I. But instead, I went over to the first guard I had shot, who miraculously was still groaning and moving. I threatened to blast his gonads off if he didn't tell me where the riches were.

Even through his suffering, he managed to raise a quivering finger at a rock outcropping some fifty feet back along the path. There I found some tussled dirt and dug with my hands for a minute or two before hitting upon three sacks. They were filled with shiny and wondrous things—a king's ransom, if only a minor king. Their ill-gotten thievery from pilgrims and passersby they victimized, I figured. I let the first guard continue his process of bleeding to death on the ground in peace—I owed him at least that for his cooperation. I stripped the clothes off the two human corpses and draped the fabrics over the body of my trusty, venerable Chingis. I laid my head on his still chest, my ear pressed deep into the barrel-sized horseflesh without hearing the heartbeat I had always depended on. I prayed and I cried, swearing through my tears these would be the last I would ever shed in this particular existence.

Truly, it's a promise I kept all the way to my last mortal breath. What were the use of tears in this vale of erosion and decline? No one would ever force despair on me ever again.

But my rage and sorrow were totally unhinged at that point, at that mountain pass, at the threshold of making my escape from the murders in my wake. I went over to the big guard and nudged him with my foot, so his throat was fully over the edge, and he had to struggle to keep his head aloft from the pull of gravity so far downward to the Earth. The rush of blood swelled the veins encircling his skull, as he strained to keep himself alive.

"Guess I'll be seeing you, friend," I said. "Anything you want me to tell these fakirs?"

"Go to hell!" he screamed, in terror, as dizziness pulled him closer toward a disastrous plunge.

"I'm not sure that would make a good first impression. But I'll give them your regards," I said.

I kept walking, humming my closest approximation of that tuneless little song of the singing bowl, a sound going round and round as the breeze blew me down the mountain.

CHAPTER 8
THE LAND OF THE GODS

Chingis was vital to me for more than just his steadfast companionship. After the first twenty versts, my feet grew blister-sore and tired. That first night I slept in a cave a few thousand feet lower than Lipulekh Pass. But I was not truly sure of the altitude. My going on foot seemed unreal, like I had entered a different world entirely. I started a fire on the dirt floor of the cave fueled with what previous travelers had left behind, hunks of wood and the rotted remains of a pack.

Soon I had the small fire crackling bright amid the utter darkness closing in all around. But although the cave was well ventilated enough, the smoke just sat and hovered, thickening like an angry fog all around me. It grew and grew. My head swooned, and the room spun as the flames flickered on.

But I was paralyzed; I couldn't rise to do anything about it. The room grew smokier and smokier until a golden ring of fire pulsated and grew even beyond my shut eyes. I believed each breath to be my last. Just as consciousness slipped away, a shadow slinked through the smoke, but my brain processed it as a far-off vision.

I awoke just an exhale later. But the fire was extinguished, with just tiny specks of orange coals left in the blackened soot. I felt around my person, checking for any burns or injuries or damage. But there was none—I was whole, and intact. I took a deep breath. There was nothing wrong with me. My fatigue was gone, and even the blisters on my feet had vanished. I lit a torch, and I checked the dark corners of the cave, and I investigated the dirt for footprints. Nothing. The figure in the smoke must have been a hallucination. I wasn't waiting around another hour to find out. I loaded my packs and my sacks, and I set off again through a thick fog.

Down, down, down. Hours passed, I descended, the fog lifted, and a brilliant sun emerged from the clouds, the first arrows of light slanting on the far-off mountain slopes behind. The Earth was unearthly. I rounded a bend, rubbing my watery eyes, and then there was a village another thousand feet below. The cluster of homes shone faintly yellow, and the path that meandered downward to it glowed a bit, too. It was a vision echoing the fever dream I had as a child traveling through Mongolia. I had lived this particular life before, I knew.

Marching on and on, a faint yellowish glow between my feet, like a line pointing me toward where I needed to go, as sure as the wind at one's back.

Or the inexorable push of a river's current.

The village appeared up close, in the blink of an eye—like an apparition conjured out of nothing. Three rows of perhaps forty shacks in all, smooth and illuminated in the sun, which washed them in yellow. Though there were chairs in front of the open doors of the dwellings, all were empty. Everything was still. Nobody in sight—no children playing or women singing or men shouting. No birds. I readjusted the sacks over my shoulder, walked into the center of the tiny village. I dropped my load and cupped my hands to my mouth.

"Is anyone out there?" I hollered. "Foreigner here with many valuable goods to trade!"

Tucked in my sleeve was the knife, the handle still stained dark with the tinges of Fang's blood.

I waited for a minute or more. Nothing. No one came out of the hovels, and no dogs wandered in the streets. The wind blew some debris across the center of the village. I scoffed and threw the packs over my shoulder again. I climbed to a small outcropping on the western side of the settlement. Scanning the horizon to the south and west, the land was flat, and it would be a relatively easy hike.

But this was an alien topography. A foreign place entirely—perhaps the land of India that I had heard so much about. Perhaps that idiotic border guard was right: it may even be Uttarakhand, the Land of the Gods spoken of in hushed whispers by all, even the haughty Tibetans.

I tried not to think of the guard's warning about the fakirs. But then, how was I to know what would happen next? We can only see with the eyes in our head and the heart in our chest and our all-enveloping soul—and we cannot know more than that, despite how many lives we spend trying to know everything before it happens. Life itself happens. It happens to us, and we continue to live...or we die. There is nothing more.

Which I say by way of explaining that, as I walked into one of the darkened middle shacks, searching for a place to set up camp for the night, something lassoed my feet and toppled me forward, the sacks crashing heavily atop me before I could defend myself.

I thrashed to free myself from under the weight, but suddenly something lashed around my wrists, something pressed me down hard in the small of my back. I cried out, but it was merely a whimper.

"*Don't make a move, sonny,*" said a creaky old voice, high-pitched, but somehow deep, and clearly dangerous. "*Just let me do my thing, and this won't hurt too bad.*"

Something in that quaking voice compelled me to comply, conveying this person's seriousness of purpose. I relented for a single moment, and they hurriedly finished tying me up, and stood. I tried to rise, but I couldn't even roll over. I cursed my stupidity. My assailant laughed. I was dragged across the dirt to the corner nearest an opening in the wood walls.

It was only then from the shaft of light piercing the darkness that I got a fleeting glimpse of this new enemy. The dark-skinned person was wearing nothing but some filthy rags around their groin. Their spindly limbs were the width of twigs. They moved awkwardly on their feet, like a dainty lady, like the girls back in Dolonnuur. I had no time for this. I had a journey to make, a destiny to fulfill—and another imprisonment would just not do.

I pulled mightily at my bonds, intending to break the knots this weak old figure had tied. But strain as I might, they held fast. I struggled until I was out of breath and the sweat stung my eyes. I shook my head free of the droplets, and I looked up.

The person crossed their arms and shook their head sadly at me, then slowly lowered to the ground. But they weren't sitting on the ground at all. Once my head and my eyes began to clear, I noticed this person was sitting on hundreds of spikes pressing into their rear end and legs—what I would later learn was a bed of nails. This person must have been terrible indeed to bear such self-inflicted pain and torture; the big guard's ominous threats of the village of fearful fakirs echoed in my ears.

"Are you a fakir?" I said. "Is this the village of the fakirs?"

He or she—better to call them they—pulled out a huge pipe. A tiny blue flame popped out of their fingertip, which they lowered to the dark leaves therein. As the dried shag glowed red hot in the dark, I glimpsed the face: a big swollen nose, few teeth in the jaw, and straggly bits of beard lining their sallow cheeks. Strange small breasts sagged down from the sharp collarbones. A single brow overhung the eyes. The smoke carried a strange odor.

"*The village of fakirs. That is what some call it,*" the person said. "*Others of us, we simply know it is the gateway to Agharti. The outpost where the unworthy are abused for their foolish presumption in striving to reach perfection.*"

"But what is Agharti?" I asked. "Where am I? Is this India?"

The fakir held their hands up in prayer, and twisted their hips, mashing their full weight down on the spikes underneath them. I cringed at the sight of this, and they snickered.

"*If you do not know of Agharti, then you do not know of much in this world or the next, monk,*" the person said. "*If you are truly an old soul who's been through this thresher of a world time and time again, and you wish to reach enlightenment, then you can't have overlooked Agharti, the place of perfection, the city where the gold does flow.*"

I spit on the ground and laughed in defiance, despite my bonds.

"If I'm supposed to be cowed by some freak in a ghost village who ambushed me and now plans to torture me with his or her senseless ramblings, then I am ignorant of such wisdom," I said. "But I have certainly glimpsed a city of gold. It must be the Agharti you speak of."

The fakir slowly stood. The person strengthened upon rising to full height, the limbs pulsing with a power barely visible in this plane. But the face was contorted in the most disgusting smile I have ever seen in all of Asia, with yellow teeth protruding from cracked lips and jaundiced—but blue—eyes bulging from their sockets. They strode with their long loping legs around the space and crouched behind me. The fakir's breath tickled my ear.

"*Perhaps this ignorance will see you through everything that is to come,*" they said. "*Knowing too much has driven many men insane.*"

The fakir traced their fingers over the top of my head, then rubbed a trace of my sweat between dirty fingers. They tasted it and smacked their lips.

"*Maybe you don't have to worry about losing everything, because you have nothing at all.*"

A tide of something crashed over me, inundating me, as the fakir talked on. It was...happiness. It was the strangest feeling, the joy that I'd not felt since I was a boy back in Russia, spending whole days throwing sticks into the Volga, rolling around with the mangy village dogs in the ripening fields of summer. Those long-ago memories flooded my heart. I felt those memories imbue my soul with meaning and purpose, the intimations of immortality and permanence, a never-vanishing. The neverendingness, the everlasting.

Because that was not all. The echoes of previous lives vibrated through me. The war cry of a thousand countrymen; a deep bow in prayer before a stone statue of the Buddha; holding a tiny child of my own making in my arms; the trip along a river current of gold floating down deep into the Earth, far below and beyond what any mere mortal had ever experienced and then lived to tell the tale. All of it came in a rush of the soul I had never felt before.

"*Do you feel that?*" said the spindly fakir, the voice grating through these visions, bypassing the very air in between us. "*Do you feel that overwhelming knowledge of all that is right and correct? Your place in the universe, your tattered tapestry of existence? That feeling that you have finally found where you belong?*"

But then everything changed in the blink of an eye. The abyss enveloped me, everything, and all. And the visions again whirled around me, this time in a dizzying array of horror. A beheaded man I recognized as my father on his knees before our enemies. My mother's tears fell and froze into cracks in the barren dirt. The splinters of stiff wood from a spear impaled my bloody hand as I charged on horseback at a massive line of opposing cavalry. Burning yurts splattered with blood. A strange woman's face contorted in tears and kissed my cold cheek, and the beaks of vultures pecked and stripped my flesh to the clattering bones, bya gtor, forever and ever.

"*I see you begin to understand,*" said the fakir. "*You see there are worlds beyond this one—and yet they are all one. And no beauty or atrocity, neither a perfect childhood summer afternoon nor brutal execution at dawn, is the ultimate experience in this world. Because there is always something farther beyond.*"

Their words barely made it through my clenching against the pain of those buzzards ripping me apart, piece by piece. I ached for the end, the complete dismemberment and the anesthesia of non-existence, of sky burial, of bya gtor.

"*But you have much yet to learn,*" my torturer said. "*You must know the paradise beyond, and what you are missing from the universe.*"

With a snap of the fingers, the fakir's words ceased. And the pain stopped. I opened my eyes, and I sat in the middle of that tiny shack. My limbs were freed. A single candle in front of me transfixed the night's darkness. The tiny light threw my shadow; I was not touching the ground.

All fear had melted away from within me, as I hovered in the air.

For the first time in my entire life, floating, I was calm.

"*You are now ready for the most important lessons of all, false acolyte,*" came the fakir's voice from somewhere behind. I turned, but there were only empty shadows there.

"I don't know what you're driving at," I said, mind muddled. "I am simply a wanderer striving toward the destiny of his homeland. To bring my people back to their former glory."

The laughter came from all corners of the room, the sound surrounding. I turned every which way, but I saw nothing except emptiness.

"*If that be your true purpose, you have picked quite a time,*" said the fakir. "*For while you seek to raise your little dust cloud in the heart of Asia, there are storms brewing which will consume the whole world far beyond Mongolia.*"

I assumed my prayer position. But nothing I did could block my torturer's presence out of my consciousness. I attempted to focus my will on achieving the higher plane, the river current. Yet the voice grew more insistent within my head. I slowly descended back to earth—onto the bed of nails. There was no pain.

"*This cannot be ignored with prayers or meditation beyond this realm,*" the fakir said. "*The tempests of mankind will soon sweep the earth, and no human heart, not one beast, and not one blade of grass or singular god will be safe. All will be consumed.*"

"Your prophecies do not scare me," I spat.

"*Oh, but they should terrify you utterly,*" they said, their invisible smile audible. "*Because as strong as your body is, and as focused as your will is, and as accurate as your rifle may be, you will nonetheless be part of the reckoning.*

"*Gone will be the kingdoms ruling the Earth for centuries,*" the fakir continued. "*The common man now believes he can do better. But he will do much, much worse. The emperors and dynastic families will set their armies against one another in nothing more than a blood feud. And millions will die in the mud-logged ditches of Europe, the plains of Asia and Africa. Even after the world destroys itself, it will be less than a generation until they do it all over again.*

"*The passions of the common man will unleash humanity in its utterly naked form,*" they continued. "*He believes he can make all men equal—but only under his jackboot, working at a long line of machines. He will be convinced his race is master of all others. He will kill millions with bullets, blades, fire, and gas.*"

"Gas?" I said, not understanding.

"*You do not realize the horror coming in the next hundred years,*" the fakir said, ignoring me. "*The people of Agharti will be lucky to escape unscathed, even so far underground.*"

"What is Agharti?" I asked. "Where? I have seen it only in glimpses. Is it a place in India? Is it a city? A temple? A holy place?"

The figure laughed.

"*It is not,*" they said. "*It is everywhere and nowhere. It is everything and nothing. It is of the earthly plane, and the unearthly, too. It is the center of all that might have been, and yet might still be. It is that which lies beneath all else.*"

"I wish," I said, rising gingerly from the bed of nails, "you would stop speaking in these ridiculous paradoxes. How foolish it makes you sound."

The fakir laughed yet again.

"*There is no other way to speak of the place. Especially because we are so close to it,*" they said, snickering. "*And yet so far!*"

I walked toward the door. I had enough of the androgynous maniac and their strange words, their little games. But just as I reached the threshold leading to the pitch-black darkness outside, I ran into something like a spider's web, paralyzing me.

"*You cannot leave,*" said the fakir. "*Once you reach this place, you cannot go without giving something of yourself to it.*"

I stepped back from the threshold. I raised my arms to the shadows.

"You want to take something from me?" I said, pounding on my chest in challenge. "What could you possibly take other than my life? I can give you what is in my pack, but I assure you it will disappoint."

"*We shall yet see what you have to give,*" the fakir said.

The flame of a bigger candle flared in the opposite corner of the room, brightening the room a bit. I took a few slow steps forward, my feet dragging in the dirt, before I noticed that the candle was in the fakir's hands. The holy figure turned and walked back into the corner, and I followed out into a hallway, leading to yet more rooms.

It was impossible. The shack had been tiny, a single room from the outside, but suddenly it opened up into a labyrinth of passages and space and windows looking out onto the same impenetrable darkness. With each step we descended, and the air warmed by degrees. A carpet appeared underfoot, and the wood of the walls shined a bit in the candlelight. My guide hummed a bit as we went, their back in shadow to me.

"How is this even possible?" I asked. "The shack was barely a single room, and now we're in a palace?"

The fakir clucked their tongue, gesturing at the voluminous darkness all around.

"*You need to listen, and not ask stupid questions,*" they said, in a sing-song voice, tune inscrutable. "*You would not comprehend the answers. Here we are. Sit.*"

We were in a new room, a circle softly lit from candles unseen. We had entered through one of six doorways, and the others were arranged around the circumference of the wall. In the center were two cushions. Unibrow furrowed, the fakir sat at one and offered the other one to me with an open palm. I sat, and they set the candle between us.

"Are you not my father?" I blurted out.

"*Meditate on the flame, and tell me what you see,*" the person said, ignoring me.

"What do you want from me?" I said. "What is this place? Why am I here?"

The fakir's sigh filled the room, and it stirred a draft throughout the cavernous space. It whisked along my skin, giving me shivers.

"*There is nothing you can provide,*" they said, and the flame flickered and split in two, forked like a burning snake's tongue. "*But there is a destiny which you must fulfill. You were always going to come here. You had to come to this threshold, sitting at the cusp of Agharti, the perfect place down below, the fulcrum upon which the world turns.*"

I laughed. My expended breath flickered the candle flame—and it again split, making four flames.

"Focus your mind and your spirit on these flames, young acolyte, and you will possess wisdom beyond any man in all of Asia," the fakir said. *"Through my voice I will help you tend to it in your journeys to come, unto death."*

Truth flickered in their words. I softened my eyes, until the flames were mere hints of far-off sparks in the deepest dark. From even farther off a shape like a giant bird rose in the light. It was the fakir's hand ascending to the ceiling. As they lifted their palm, the fires rose too, until they consumed the room in a brightness blinding me totally.

I awoke to a bright sky.

I had a shovel in my hands.

I stood just a few paces outside the shack.

My hands moved of their own accord, scraping the blade along the dirt. I blinked, and I was unable to remember exactly how I was working outside in the daytime when I had last been in a trance in the cavernous empty dark space inside the impossible palace. Now nude, the cool wind whistled over my body, but the golden sunlight warmed my bare skin.

My limbs throbbed. Although I could not remember the ensuing time period, I knew I had agreed to whatever the fakir's terms were.

Somehow, I knew I must dig.

I gripped that shovel, and I wiped my brow, and I started to scrape out parts of the earth. Flinging the clumps over my shoulder, I set to work.

After years in a monastery, performing light domestic chores like scrubbing floors, my muscles were completely unaccustomed to long, hard labor. By the time I was standing in a mere divot, my arms were on fire, and my back stung. But I kept at it. I did not know why. I felt this overpowering urge to plunge deeper into the earth. And slowly, as I reached two feet and three feet down, my limbs became numb and weak. Soon I was only prying out the merest clods I could toss aside, most tumbling into the bottom of the very hole in which I dug. I was getting nowhere.

"Not getting too far?"

Shielding my eyes from the hazy sun, I looked up. The fakir stood above me, eating a piece of strange golden fruit I had never seen before, or since. They smiled, as the glistening juice ran down and dripped off the chin, down into the hole with me.

"Hard work to reach Agharti, the subterranean kingdom of perfection, is it not?" the figure said, taking another moist bite of the sweet flesh.

Out of breath, I grunted. I hunched over and took another large shovelful, and I spun and flung it where the fakir had been standing—and it cascaded right back down into my hole. Because the holy man had vanished.

I continued digging. I had to. My hands would not let me stop.

Anger coursed through my aching body. But though my mind rebelled, my body would not. How dare this charlatan fakir, this holy faker, inhabitant of this forsaken ghost town, subject me to hard labor? But my mind refused to reason. Instead of simply dropping my shovel and climbing out of that trench, something urged me ever downward. My hands, arms, and lungs burned steadily with a cool fire defying rational sense.

I just had to dig. That's all I knew. It was not within my power to stop.

As the hole swallowed me down to neck-level, it was getting dark. But the moonlight cast a glow like the day, and I kept going.

I hummed the tuneless wavering song of the bowl back at the monastery, and even though my joints burned even more, I kept going right through the dawn. At that point I was in the hole over my head.

At that point, with the greatest effort imaginable, I dropped the shovel. I forced my hands to reach out to the dew on the morning grass, scooping it up and sucking the trickles off my palm. It tasted cool and sweet. Parts of the bizarre fog over my brain lifted a bit, and as I greedily harvested more of the morning moisture off the leaves of grass, I began to remember my purpose in that hole.

"Agharti," I said out loud to nothing and everything, "is the place of perfection."

Like a spell had been recast, my hands again grasped the shovel of their own accord. I stabbed deep into the earth, flinging dirt everywhere.

"The place I had seen on my passage through Mongolia. That is what the fakir made clear to me," I rambled, growling as I pushed my body once more to its limit. "The perfect kingdom. Only the purest gain entry. But I intend to storm the gates at an entryway they will never expect."

Rambling, rambling. I knew not what I was saying. The words were someone else's.

I worked all that day, as the sun angled over the edge of my hole and then beat down on my back. My flesh seared. Time passed, endless and finite at the same time, as I dug deeper. My thirst became all-consuming, my palate throbbed. My arms could no longer rise above my shoulder. The sun descended. The dirt fell all around me, as I buried myself alive. My heartbeat slowed and my breath came slower, despite my labors.

Just as I felt I was about to collapse, ten feet deep in the dirt, forever embedded in that Indian muck, my toes were suddenly damp. I looked down to see if I was hallucinating. Water bubbled up in the hole. I'd struck an underground spring. The fog around my mind dissolved. I fell to the mud and desperately splashed slop—as much wet dirt as water—into my bone-dry mouth, over my scorched tongue. The coming night had cooled everything, and I settled into the sludge, my heart thumping hard and constant into the sopping earth.

As the filthy water brought some life back to my worn body, my mind totally cleared. My hands no longer clutched the hellish tool. Whatever spell the fakir had placed upon my soul dissipated, as the filthy water slaked my thirst. I knew then it was a fool's errand on which they'd sent me—only through hypnotism and sheer willpower could you convince an otherwise rational being to take a single measly shovel and dig straight down into the center of the earth, toward the paradise no mere mortal had ever claimed to have seen with their own eyes, Agharti. This fakir, this false holiness, had instead struck me unawares with their considerable powers— and then set me to work. It was intended to be a labor unto death. Their purpose had clearly been to allow me to dig my own grave, wait for my heart to give out, and then simply kick some dirt over my pit, without ever having to mention it to another soul. It would have been clean, and neat, for the fakir.

"You son of a whore dog!" I rasped, my throat still dry and sore from my heavy exertions and the searing day. "I will find you! I will emerge from this hole, and I will find you, even if I have to scour the earth for the rest of my years to find the true entrance to Agharti!"

I climbed. But the side of the hole was too high. I slid back down.

The wind howled over the top of the ditch, a sound like far-off laughter.

I stood up. I picked up the shovel, and I dug. But this time my hands moved by my own agency. I went sideways, attacking the dirt walls with the blade of my shovel. Now rage powered my movements, in the dark. I felt I was battling something bigger than I could name or even understand, as the hole collapsed at my feet, but I gradually rose, foot by foot and yard by yard. This time, I was in control.

The sun had still not risen, but the sky contused with light, as I stumbled, naked and dirty, the last steps up and out on the steep ramp I'd dug over a hatred-filled night. Although my body ached and I yearned to collapse and sleep on the ground right there, I fought down the urge. Instead, I stumbled toward the hut, going around the back to the sole window to peer inside.

But when I rounded the corner, there was no window. There was no door. Instead, a little well squatted at the foot of the hill behind the hut. My thirst, now exacerbated by the silt coating my throat from the dirty puddles I had greedily slurped up, overcame my hunger for revenge. I stumbled to its stone edge, and I wrestled at the crank, turning it as fast as I could. It was exceedingly light, and the bucket came up in mere moments. I reached out for it, and as I leaned over...I was blinded.

A shining light beamed up into my eyes from the depths of the well. Warmth bathed my cheeks, too. I drew back and rubbed my eyes. As my sight returned, I shielded my face with both hands, leaving only small cracks between the fingers through which to see. I crept forward and peered over the side.

And my soul leapt up.

Impossibly far beneath me lay the cityscape I had glimpsed as a sick boy in a delirious fever, in an alien land. The fantastic golden metropolis. But this time I was closer still. I saw the aureate rivers, the tiny people paddling once again. But now I saw more: the faces as they laughed and enjoyed their paradise, and the bustle of the streets. The ziggurats and minarets, the brilliant buildings that lined the flaxen thoroughfares this time were in clear detail. They were magnificent. They were perfect, in a rising and falling more graceful and awful than the Himalayas themselves, lined up in an order that sang to my soul—the very encapsulation of the concentric beauty of this universe. Together the city stood hard, in sharp relief against the deep abyss—the blackness that underlay everything. And that was beautiful too, that contrast between everything and nothing at all.

This was the true entrance to Agharti, not through some hand-dug hole in the middle of the Indian earth, or through some overlooked mountain pass. This was a portal as unassuming as it was hidden, and only visible to those who could see. If only I could make it down to the bottom of that chasm…and reach it…at that moment when I was nearer than ever before!

I had a plan. I'd grab that bucket and ride the rope down. I would have to pray for a soft landing, somewhere down below, especially if the line stopped short of the bottom. But I would deal with that when I reached paradise. I'd aim to fall into one of the shining rivers. Surely they would cushion a fall, and no one could drown.

I reached out for the bucket. I tipped it over—and something scuttled out. I saw only a flash, frozen in the moment: a single red scorpion flying at me, tiny claws wide, before it landed on my face.

Before I screamed, it struck me again and again, right between the eyes. I only had the flutter of a poisoned heartbeat to panic before I howled and tumbled backward, and then I was falling backward, until my skull crashed into the hard ground. The venom worked instantly, paralyzing me. The sun blinded me, and tears streamed down my face. The red scorpion vanished somewhere during my fall.

A shadow over me eclipsed the sun. A human figure stood there. The glare from the sun had to melt away from my eyes before I saw the details of the dark visage.

And at that moment of chaos in this insane universe, when everything stopped making sense, my heart ceased to beat.

It was that beautiful face of the girl with the swishing raven hair. Her lips were pulled back from her teeth, which lengthened and sharpened to fangs like Scythian daggers as she leered down at me. My heart thundered in terror at the impossible sight. She said something muffled through those horrible tusks, and she leaned in closer. But I blinked, and she turned away.

When she turned back, her face had changed. Now it was Fang, that dead rapist, peering with black skull sockets deep into my eyes. There was no smile or any expression at all—it was just the cold detached judgment of the dead, boring into me. I hardened my eyes, daring him to make the same error I had made, to condemn himself in this life the same way I had. To kill, to condemn two souls forever and ever. To my surprise, he did not—he simply covered his face in his hands. When he pulled back his fingers, there was an even bigger shock.

It was my father there, sneering, brow scrunched hard over eyes the color of a searing blue flame. He reached out to touch me with impossibly long fingers, claws that stretched like vines outward toward me, and sharp fangs growing longer still in his horribly widening maw.

I screamed again. But my throat made no sound. I shut my eyes tighter, ever tighter.

After another eternity, the sun spinning around the entire world, I opened my eyes again to darkness.

Darkness. Gone was the sun, gone was the looming form of my father. And gone too was my paralysis—I rose and scrambled around in the thick blackness, thinking I must have reached a divine punishment in my evident death.

I smelled smoke.

But my hand scraped across a dirt floor, the hard earth and pebbles of this world—and then my hand struck something familiar. It was one of my sacks.

I reached in, and pulled out a piece of bread, I greedily took a bite. It was a little stale and splintered between my teeth. But it was not moldy. As I chewed in the utter dark, I breathed in strange, burnt, familiar air.

And then I noticed two red dots off to my right. They looked like eyes. I heard a whistling far off in the direction behind me. I clambered to my feet and stumbled blindly toward the sound, rushing away from the glowing orbs in the silent darkness. Fresh air hit me, a slight breeze.

I was in the cave.

I had never left the cave—or the smoky hallucinatory sleep. I had never entered the Land of the Gods at all.

I felt along my jaw. My chin was smooth—as smooth as if I had shaved that very morning. And suddenly I knew that to be the truth of the matter. Less than a night had passed. My ordeal in the torture of searching for Agharti had been perhaps an hour, perhaps less. Just enough time to dream of an adventure and an excruciating torture session. I'd never reached the land of the fakirs at all. I nursed the two red glowing coals to a small blaze again. I devoured the remainder of the breadcrumbs and talked to myself; back and forth, two sides of the same conversation.

But my disoriented brain quickly righted itself. Rage replaced my daze, as I considered the affronts and ill fortune plaguing me ever since my accursed escape from Russia. Especially when I thought of my father and his ambushes and torments. I half suspected the fakir himself may have been my own progenitor— but the thought itself was dizzying, and I could never be certain.

The fakir had been fake, I decided. Nothing more.

I pissed on the embers of the fire, which sizzled with finality.

"Enough of these portents!" I hollered, my voice echoing off the ancient stone. "No more trickery. Now is the time to move through space. Now is a time for action."

The odor of burnt urine filled the cave, and I rushed out.

CHAPTER 9
AN EXPEDITION

Moments later I was on my way north, headed back the way I'd come. The odyssey of the mind, or whatever the fakir's fakery was, I left behind. My focus was on the road ahead—and how to reverse the current within and without myself. To bend the universe's river to my whims.

Years pass, and none of us can riddle why. A lifetime vanishes in a succession of breaths. Struggle for survival has a way of making time whisk by, like clouds on a bitter wind. But this time, the wind was at my back.

Tibet was my waypoint. But I needed to avoid the monastery, obviously. Not that I would ever stoop so low again as to join up with rapists who styled themselves as holy men. For just as long as was necessary, I'd use Lhasa as my base of operations until my return to Mongolia, my people, and my rightful place.

First, the trek through the Himalayan highlands. And of course, the never-ending search for Agharti along the way.

Because that view of the mystical underground kingdom had been intoxicating, like the sweetest draught of wine, or the stiffest pull off a tobacco pipe. Accessing the resplendent kingdom, that paradise, was a perfection that the rest of the human race could only dream of. But I had seen it with my own eyes, and I was one of the few who had made it within touching distance. I would be the first man to get there, alone among monk, or king, or commoner. And then I'd have something that no one else would ever have.

But as I ascended slowly into the highest mountains on Earth once again, keeping my eyes wide open, I knew Agharti was still years away. Another portal wouldn't just appear for me, at the bottom of a hole or a well, or in my hallucinations, or anywhere else. Most pressingly, there was the business of Mongolia to attend to. I needed to fulfill my prophecy and promise. I needed to prove my father wrong. I needed to save our ancestral land. It was my destiny, as the return of Amursanaa himself. Only by setting the world to rights, could I attain the otherworldly.

These thoughts swirled in my head as the oxygen lightened, and the clouds grew ever closer in the sky. It was springtime again, and my blood warmed in the beams of the sun. At night I made an encampment and huddled near a smoldering fire, sleeping lightly as I listened for highwaymen to approach.

The highwaymen never came. Instead, I became the robber just a few days later when I ran out of water.

They were light skinned, with pale and puffy faces. They resembled the Russians who extracted the taxes and the tributes when I was a child. If they were soft explorers unacquainted with the highlands, I could take advantage of their ignorance. I crept closer. I honed my mind and drew my blade.

Three men: a smaller one who must have been a teenager, and two bigger ones. The smallest one was tending to the horses, while the other two were seated, looking down intently as they polished rocks, for some reason. When I was within ten feet, I cleared my throat. The two men jumped up, reaching for knives at their side. But I was already overpowering them with sheer will, prying their fingers from the sheaths, pushing their minds straight down into the pits of their stomachs, where they could do no harm. They collapsed to the ground, still alive but jaws slack, their minds mere stupefied mush in my grip.

I heard a tinkling behind me, a rush of footsteps shook the soil at my feet. At the crucial moment, I held my hand up.

Silence. But I felt a breath on my neck. I slowly turned.

There stood the youngest of the three travelers, trembling, his hand frozen aloft with a small sharp shovel stopped, mid-swing, just short of the hairs on my neck. His eyes blinked, his hands tremored, and a drop of sweat beaded on his brow that glistened in the sun.

I nodded at him, then I turned and stooped and rifled through the pockets of the two on the ground at my feet. Some pouches of tobacco and nuts, a desiccated human ear on a string, and two clusters of keys were all they had. I stood and turned and put the ear gently between the lips of the younger one, who whimpered for a breath. But I silenced him, and I surveyed the rest of their campsite.

I started with their wagon. My search turned up sacks and trunks with a wealth of knick-knacks and bric-a-brac. Useless things, like flimsy bracelets and ornaments made of worthless wood and dull stones. Container after container held disappointments. One thick rucksack even contained a mound of heavy rocks—and nothing else. I moved onto the two horses, and their saddle packs. Their provisions of hardtack and rice and a few skins of water I seized.

In another side pocket I recoiled: within a pouch were a line of women's severed fingers, with nails all painted a sickly green color.

Beneath these ghoulish trinkets I found the best prize of all: a mound of gold coins, from the far-off kingdoms of Europe. The Sensibly Western writing on their worldly riches confused me, but I knew they were valuable. During my search, my grip had slipped on the three travelers, who struggled to free their bodies from my will. I reasserted my mental grip and walked back to them. Their eyes told me their terror had tripled, especially when I slid the shovel slowly out of the hand of the youngest one, whose blue eyes trickled slow tears. I tapped him on the shoulder with the blade of his tool. I clucked my tongue and shook my head.

"It wasn't you taking fingers and ears from some nice ladies along your travels, was it?" I asked.

I brandished the handful of fingers in front of his face, then let them drop onto the two other paralyzed men. One of the digits fell into the open maw of one of them, obstructing part of the airway deep in his throat. He choked. I laughed.

"I wonder what you fellows could want with severed body parts of women on your travels? And just who these delicate appendages may have belonged to?" I asked.

His young pale skin was nearly translucent, as if made of bloodless wax. I stooped and plucked the severed finger out of the throat of his choking comrade, and then I scratched its long green nail across the young one's pale cheek. A trickle of crimson ran down his skin, right to his shoulder, joining with the clear tears. He struggled against my willpower—and unlike his compatriots, it was hard to keep control of him. Though he appeared to have no training or spiritual discipline in his past, he had a natural resolve that cannot be developed in a monastery or through contemplation on ethereal planes. I strengthened my grip on him, but even as I regained control, he broke free for just a second—just enough to blurt out two words.

"...you...deserve..." he groaned.

But then I forced him with my hand down to the ground, and bent him forward, exposing his neck. I brandished my knife, holding its serrated edge to the base of his skull.

"It's time for me to move through space," I said softly. "I will leave you and your two companions with enough water to make it to the nearest village at the end of the valley. You may also keep your grotesque little trophies. But I am taking everything else."

I took the least diseased of their three horses. It was a lackluster beast, but would have to serve as my mount, considering the situation. I named her Börte. The other two I untied and released to the wilds of Asia.

I prepared my new cargo for the trek back to Tibet. I emptied the rucksack of its rocks but kept the bag. I stuffed the other two sacks into a pack, which I slung on my back. I stared at the trio of murderers still prone at my feet.

"Do not try to follow me," I said. "If you ever try to track me, I will destroy you with such vengeance your ancestors will feel it in their graves. Consider my taking of these items as a toll for your travels. And for your crimes."

Trotting to the east, I pulled up short on the reins and turned on the horse's back. "Welcome to Innermost Asia," I said. "Tread lightly."

Indeed, I had lied. I left no water at all for those murderers. After my hold on them slipped when I was a few versts away, their end would be an agonizing and thirsty one. Hopefully, the spirits of all those dead women would come to pay their disrespects to their desiccated forms there in the barren wastes. Nature would mete out justice.

My laughter echoed across the Himalayas for hundreds of versts in every direction outward into the world, on the way back into Tibet. Setting things to rights not only brought me great satisfaction; it was also deeply funny in a way that defied description. Essential truth, things laid bare, always seemed hilarious. I only regained my composure as I neared the outskirts of Lhasa.

I took a deep breath of the thin air, and I separated my pack into three. I kept the essential provisions in the knapsack. Into one of the sacks, I stuffed all the worthless metal trinkets I had robbed from the Russians, and on top I placed a pouch with the few gold pieces and true valuables I had. In the second sack I tossed about fifty pounds worth of rocks, around which I tossed a handful of the metal knick-knacks. I tied each sack off with a knot my father had taught me back in Russia—the quintuple underhand constrictor hitch. It was a knot made of thirty-seven different turns, impossible to undo without the secret knowledge of its making. It was even harder to re-tie. I hoisted it all onto my back—and went clanking into town, grunting under the weight.

This time I avoided Drepung entirely, of course. Instead, I went to the slums on the other side of Lhasa, which the monks had barely spoken about in whispers—but which Fang and I had visited for illicit adventures several times during midday errands.

The pawnshop was still open for the day, as I slid in the door just as the sun arced over the mountains. The sacks had become heavy, and I was slick with sweat as they slid off of my shoulders inside the threshold of the pawnshop. I carefully laid them on the floor. The inside was darker still than the dying light of the day outside. It took my eyes a minute to adjust. Finally, I discerned the outline of chaos.

The place was cluttered with every manner of item, piled and leaning and hanging and thrown aside in the corners and dusty crevices: statues, robes and keepsakes, weapons, masks and paintings and chimes lining the walls. I walked farther inside, leaving the bags, smelling the must. It was only when I was a bare five feet from the counter that I noticed the elfin little proprietor of the pawnshop standing there totally still, staring at me, and I jumped back. I had taken him for a gigantic marionette and had only noticed him because the whites of his eyes flickered over my tattered clothes when I scratched my crotch.

"Good day, sir. I would like to propose a business transaction," I said, bowing.

The pawnbroker pulled out a pipe and lit it. The languid movements of his hands and eyes half-closed told me he did not care for my business; apparently I had roused him from his slumber with the noise of my arrival. I smiled and stepped right up to the counter, slapping my hands down on it. I leaned forward, so I was inches away from him. The acrid odor of the tobacco stung my eyes, but I stared into him without blinking.

"You want to make a deal," he said, his tiny mouth snapping shut tight after each syllable. "What are you offering? I am a rich man, and there is not much that can entice me anymore, young one."

"I would like you to hold onto some things for me while I conduct business in Lhasa," I said. "I am a lama, duly trained, and I simply need to rest my worldly bones before I carry onward back home to Mongolia."

The merchant churned the air with his hand impatiently.

"Yes, yes, yes. What collateral are you offering to ensure any kind of loan I give you?" he said, exhaling a huge cloud of smoke at me.

"Let me show you," I said, hauling the sacks up on the counter.

The mix of metal, stones, and a few valuables landed with the most perfect thud, clank, and tinkle. It was the sound of heavy treasure, of weighty gold and untold riches secreted away in sacks. The three sacks sounded, even smelled, like a fortune. The pawnbroker's eyes widened.

He was asleep no more. Greed, the great awakener, had roused him.

But I pretended to take no notice. I was working on the quintuple underhand constrictor hitch, focusing on reversing the thirty-seven movements in just the right order so that this hardest of all knots would come undone. It was exacting work, and I strained my mind to remember each twist and turn. Once I reached the crucial half-hitch midway through the process, I knew I had it. The gnarled maelstrom unraveled in my assured fingers, as the merchant watched with awe as the tough rope swung apart like a dissipating storm in my grasp. Without hesitation, I plunged into the sack with the gold. I breathed it in, and I grasped the few gold coins so there was a heavenly clatter of riches that sounded like a downpour in the richest treasury in all the world. I jangled a few more, letting them fall upon the worthless trinkets, the sound absolutely kingly. I pulled out a handful, making sure to let a few roll out from my fingers and across the countertop. The merchant slapped the rolling currency down with both hands, pinning the coins down like a cat would a mouse. I felt his predatory leer at the gold in my hands, but I suppressed my smile. I had to keep my composure to make it all work.

I carefully stowed away the gold in a pocket of my robes, and then I rethreaded the knot. My hands moved in a virtual blur of their own volition, even as the pawnbroker's eyes darted back and forth, trying to catch each individual twist. But my fingers were too fast by far. The only way this man would ever get into these sacks would be by slicing them open and outright stealing from them. That would be a hanging offense even surer than a murder charge, considering the laws of Tibet. I pulled the knot as taut as I possibly could, I wiped my brow, and I smiled at my new business partner.

"I would like to leave these bags in your care," I said. "Can you take them, in exchange for a small loan, until I get back on my feet?"

His lips widened around his sharp teeth, his eyes slanting to predatory slits. I smiled innocently.

"An interesting proposition you present," he said, folding his hands in front of his chest. "What is your offer, young man?"

"Cash, of course," I said. "And a bit of collateral, besides."

I turned my head, and the only thing with any color in that drab dark room caught my eye.

A Mongolian yellow deel, bright and unwrinkled, hung from a peg in the corner of the room. I walked over to it slowly, saying nothing, and I ran my fingers over its hem. It was smooth and tickled my fingertip, like its playful rustling had a life of its own. It was magnificent, something clearly from my homeland's past— but also something that displayed the splendor and the possibilities of the future. I ran my knuckles along the smooth fabric over the chest.

"I will take this," I said.

"It's a deal," he said, clapping his hands.

I turned, and something else in the darkness caught my eye. It was a military uniform, European-style, and it came with lapels and medals and a few pieces of dull brass scattered across its front and shoulders. I patted its rough material, and I smirked.

"And I will take this sensibly Western getup, too," I said. "And that blade in the bright green scabbard. I think those might suit me, as well."

"I agree, I agree," he said, eagerly. "Take it all. And come—let's arrive at a price. Come sign and finalize our little arrangement."

I also grabbed a tiny jar of chloroform he had on the counter. He threw it in, with a wink, as a little bonus in our deal.

Lama With A Gun

A short while later I walked out of that place into the starry night with my two new layers on, the European military uniform covered completely by the stately Mongolian deel. I had left a false name with the pawnbroker. Truly, I felt like an entirely new person. Several new people, in a way.

I only returned to the pawnshop at the end of the next day, after a long day of amassing more worldly goods. My plan worked perfectly. I walked to an alleyway about half a verst from the monastery. It was a narrow passage between a hotel and the only brothel in Lhasa. It was, of course, a path the Drepung monks knew well and frequented. Even the morally upright ones used it as a shortcut to the markets.

At the first light of dawn, I tucked myself into a recessed doorway halfway down the passage. I masked myself, and I waited. I heard the first footsteps a few minutes later. I waited, and right as the figure hurriedly passed through the shadows, I sprang up and walloped the person on the back of the neck, knocking them out cold.

Sure enough, it was a monk—one of the younger ones just starting out as an acolyte. I dragged his unconscious body back into the shadows, and I stripped him of all his belongings. The older monks had clearly sent him to procure some expensive items for the monastery; I took two bags of coins, and some other precious stones they had sent with him. I blessed my good fortune, dragged the body back to the farthest nook of the alcove, and waited again. An hour passed, and then another set of footsteps…and a woman met the same fate. She was a common street walker; by the looks of her she was one of the denizens of the house of ill repute around the corner. For whatever reason she had very little money on her— just a Russian ruble or two. I gently stowed her body atop that of the young monk from earlier, who was by then snoring softly, almost peacefully.

It went like that. By noon, as the sun reached its apex, I had collected four total bodies in my little alcove—another monk, and a fat little Chinese merchant who had evidently been waddling his way to the local bank when he encountered me. (I had to knock out the monk and the woman once more apiece with the chloroform on a handkerchief.)

I was a richer man for all my enterprise—but I was an exhausted one, too. Robbery takes focus—and timing. Striking at the perfect moment is paramount. But even with my power of will, it was draining. So just as the first young monk was starting to stir once more, I slinked out of the alleyway, and back to the pawnshop.

The proprietor practically jumped out of his seat when I pushed through the door. (He had been tugging at the quintuple underhand constrictor hitch and sweat beaded his brow. I pretended not to notice.) We exchanged pleasantries, and he produced my two sacks. I meticulously untied and unlashed the knot on one with the riches, and I stowed away the bags of coins, making sure to jangle them tantalizingly as the pawnbroker watched with bated breath, trying to memorize every flourish of my fingers. I tied it back up tight with another knot using the thirty-seven twists and turns, and then I gave both sacks back to the merchant.

I noted a new golden vajra, a shining and magnificent piece the length of my hand, hanging on a hook behind his head. It was the symbol of power, of diamond and thunderbolt, a quadruple Tibetan club, and just looking at it made my blood rush. But I quickly averted my eyes, keeping myself from showing too much interest in it. I told him I'd see him the next day, and then I walked out.

I spent the rest of the day with one of the women at the brothel, lavishing her with flowers and some other gifts besides. We fed each other market fruits, which I could easily afford after my gains. She was most grateful to me. As I left the next morning, I ran headlong into the prostitute I'd robbed, whose head was wrapped in a bandage. Yet she still carried her head high back through the threshold of the brothel. I bowed to her and kept on my way.

This time I set up in a different alleyway, a few hundred yards closer to the monastery. But it was still along the same path the monks took to the market. I was planning to rob at least a few passersby over the next few hours, to ensure I'd have enough money for my Mongolia plans. I donned my mask, and stretched my limbs, and waited. But my plan was cut short, because the first footsteps proved quite good enough for my purposes.

Two of them were there, holding hands. One was a man in monk's robes—and the other was a woman. As I leapt out, I knocked out the man with a quick blow to the neck. The woman whirled around in terror, and there was no doubt from her painted face and shiny adornments that she too was a prostitute. She recoiled in terror, holding her hands up in front of her, cringing. But I held my finger up to my lips to silence her, and I crouched over the unconscious monk. Once my theft was complete, I noticed she was still standing there. I shooed her away with a wave of my hands. She shuffled awkwardly away in her fancy sandals, slipping twice—a sight that made me laugh yet again as I set to my work.

Once I rolled the limp body over, the face made me recoil. It was Fang's friend, the one who had spoken conspiratorially to my roommate whenever I was out of earshot. The one with the grin, the hard jawline, and the impressive stature. The one with the singing bowl as I had made my escape. I reared back and kicked him once in the ribs, but the body simply jostled to the side. He was out cold. I skipped the thrashing, and I simply rooted through his robes and a bag he was carrying. He must have been carrying the monthly budget of Drepung. Dozens of golden and silver coins from places as far afield as Japan and Korea, and even those of Germany and France, were in that sack. I laughed, and then I dragged his body into the darkest shadows I could find in the narrow passageway, and I emerged back out into the streets of Lhasa.

Something bothered me about that grin, even when he was unconscious. I saw the sharp teeth better up close, the tense sneer despite the unconscious state. He looked almost European, like he was a Russian from somewhere on the Siberian steppe. I had reason to fear him. I walked a double-quick pace away.

I visited a horse trader who was on one of the main streets. I traded in shoddy Börte, and I bought a black horse and two white camels. I prayed and named the horse Kublai and fed and watered the camels. I was ready to continue my quest.

But there was just one more loose end to tie off forever. Together we all trotted back to the pawnbroker's establishment.

He watched me with ever-increasing ardor as I untied both bags this time. I made a show of putting a fraction of the gold coins in the first sack. I glanced quickly to make sure the vajra was still hanging on that hook on the wall. Into the second one, containing merely stones, I mimed putting the sack of coins I had taken from the monk. Then I lashed both tightly with the quintuple underhand constrictor hitch. But I only slung the first bag over my shoulder. The second I left on the counter, gently patting it with my hand.

"My good man, I need to keep this for an extended period in your capable hands," I said. "It contains some of my most prized possessions, and I want you to hold onto them, while I conduct business elsewhere. It may be dangerous, and I may not return for a number of years. Can you offer me an extension to our loan?"

The elfin merchant looked at me, puffing his pipe, the inscrutable look again crossing his face. But I adjusted the second bag, which clinked with the sound of fake riches, and the dreaminess of greed again conquered his face.

"Something to sweeten the pot," I said, reaching out and pulling down the golden vajra off the hook.

A smile crept across both our faces, each of us assured we had made an incredible deal.

But only one of us truly understood the full terms.

I walked out of that place with two years' worth of gold, the golden vajra pinned to my deel—and the assurance I would eventually return to buy back my bag full of worthless stones. He stowed it with some difficulty on a shelf in the back corner of his shop, as dusty and dark a spot as he had. We had bowed to one another, and then I went outside. As I walked away, I knew he would spend untold hours on the unconquerable knot.

Laughing, I mounted Kublai, grabbed the reins of my two white camels, and jangled the coins. Even with the darkness gathering, my future was limitless, the promise as never-ending as the horizon. My caravan of one headed to the north and east, without so much as a glance back at the holy city which had taught me so much.

That holy city had failed to tame my spirit.

I was ready for the land of the eternal blue sky, at last.

CHAPTER 10
THE HOMELAND

These long-lost countrymen of mine needed a savior. They needed me—a man I had decided to call by a new name.

Ja Lama is how I would henceforth be known.

These countrymen, these strangers I came upon in the west of the country lived in poverty, with few possessions aside from their meager flocks. Their steps were bowlegged as they crushed the sparse grass of the plain beneath their feet. Seven centuries had passed since the Greatest Khan had driven them on horseback on an irresistible tempest of conquest and fear across the entire world, from ocean to ocean—and they were still recovering.

But they were my people. Even if they did not know it yet. I had come from the top of the world all the way to the homeland I barely knew…and I had already pledged my soul and my destiny to them.

The first settlement I came upon in Mongolia was a bare dozen tents, with children and goats kicking around in the mud, braying at the eternal blue sky and the impossible sun. The women circled around a massive cauldron, endlessly simmering. The men crowded around small games of chance, mostly the anklebone flippings of Shagai, spitting on the ground and murmuring curses at fate. One of the children kicked a ball in the opposite direction, right at us, and it hit Kublai in the face. My takhi bucked and screamed with a shrill note.

All activity ceased—the goats stopped chewing their cud, the children dropped their throwing rocks, the women looked up with a strange mix of fear and boredom, and the men stood and reached for the blades at their belts.

But I calmed Kublai and kept him trotting forward, and I showed them no fear. I focused all my willpower on these simple people of the land. And what's more—for the first time—I opened my entire self to them. Using my willpower, I opened myself to their gaze, their scrutiny. These people would see into me, as much as I saw into them.

These simple people of the land were the first to see clearly into my heart.

The glares softened. The hands drifted away from the knife scabbards. Smiles appeared.

Kublai stopped within a muzzle's distance of the first group of men, who paused their throws of the bone dice on the calfskin in the middle of their circle. The men looked morose until they saw the vajra pinned to my deel. The vajra—the golden four-pronged club that represented ultimate unconquerable power in the universe—was polished to a perfect brilliance with a clean rag and some spit. Grins rippled across their faces, many revealing blackened gums with no teeth. I smiled back and dismounted.

"My friends," I said, now on the same level ground, "I have come to liberate Mongolia."

Their jaundiced stares were unblinking. Then one at the back of the crowd, a lighter-skinned looking fellow who was so rippled with muscle his face flexed, spat on the ground.

"Another self-important holy bastard arrives to save us from ourselves," he mumbled, waving a hand at my clean yellow deel, which stood out even starker from their worn furs and skins.

The laughter started, one and then three and then seven of them, doubling over, laughing at the newcomer. It carried over to the kids and women through the rest of the settlement, who had no idea why they were laughing at all. But they joined in the hilarity, as well.

"Holy bastard—that's a good one, Jimbe," hollered one.

"Can you believe this?" called out another.

"This stupid monk thinks he'll kill off the Russians and Chinese!" screeched yet another.

The only person not hysterical with laughter was the muscled fellow at the back, who just smirked at me.

I was ready for this. Even as the uproarious laughter continued, I pushed through the crowd. And as I did so, I pulled my deel over my head and over my shoulders.

Gasps silenced all as they saw the drab green of fatigues—a pressed and crisp military uniform. All dull and deadened to the eye—except for the bright green scabbard at my belt. A soldier had suddenly appeared, from within a laughable holy man.

I did not pause. I walked straight at the man, even as I tossed the deel behind me, grabbed the knife handle, and drew the blade.

The man's face suddenly went pale—paler even than his light flesh had been while he was wisecracking from the back of his crowd. He backpedaled, his big muscles quivering on his bones.

I came within fifteen feet. He fumbled at his own belt, where his shaking hands grasped at his holster. But I reached out with all my willpower and rushed him at the last moment, as he drew his gun and fired.

The bullet sailed over my shoulder, and I crashed straight into his sternum, knocking him back a few feet. Then I was upon him, knocking the old revolver clattering out of his hands, and pinning down both his arms with my knees. I raised my knife high with both hands, ready to plunge downward for the fatal stroke.

Everything was still. Even the goats stopped chewing their cud, watching intently. The closest child to me, holding a ball not ten feet away, blinked. I winked at him.

"I have not properly introduced myself," I said. "I am Ja Lama, and I have returned to my homeland after too many lifetimes of exile.

"You see, I am your kin. My blood ancestors were on the wrong side of the mountains, exiled by the Chinese to farthest Russia."

I heard a groan in the crowd—the unburdening of the pain and loss of centuries inflicted by those hated sons of Han.

"My bloodline attempted to carve out a new life in the Czar's lands. They tried to leave Mongolia back in the past, back in the east," I continued. "But Mongolia only grew in our hearts and minds the harder they pulled us away."

The crowd nodded. These people had not been exiled, these people of the land who had stayed in meek defiance of the Chinese. They knew all too well the love of our common home—and the agony, grief and desolation that came with tending that homebound hearth.

At that moment, I took a deep breath. I sheathed my knife, and I stood. Yanking my strong, light-skinned antagonist to his feet with a single tug of his arm, I embraced him and then spun him free, back into the crowd, where he was absorbed back into the throng.

I pulled a sack out from a deep pocket. Holding it aloft, I used the prayer voice I had honed over so many hours of studies and faith in China and Tibet. That faith now amounted to convincing my countrymen of their shared destiny with me. If ever a faith more pure was attained in Lhasa or in the paths of the Buddha himself as he had walked the roads of Asia, I know not where. And they needed to feel that in the very marrow of their bones.

"We need not live in fear anymore," I said, my voice echoing out into the muddy and barren valley. "We are strong, and we are together. The last time our people came together and decided we would fight the bastards in a single direction, it carried us all the way to the halls of Europe. We made kings scream like little girls. Queens wept."

At this the older ones in the crowd laughed. They were clearly pleased with the collective memory of being world conquerors—even though such an achievement was centuries before their own births. The glory still echoed in the roar of blood in their ears. The younger ones stared up at me with glassy eyes, imagining the glories I promised.

"You need know: the dominion of the Greatest Khan can be ours again. We have a destiny," I said. "We stand alone in Asia. We can again exploit our enemies' weaknesses. The Han bastards are too busy trying to eke their independence from the white devils. The Russian maniacs have never been in so much disarray—the Czar's orders would barely reach Siberia much less be carried out."

"Why would we follow you when we have the promises of the Khenbish Khan?" said one.

"Khenbish Khan?" I asked, befuddled. "Who is the Khenbish Khan?"

"Pay no attention, Lama—the Khenbish Khan is a mere legend," croaked one old woman's voice. "A figment of some imaginations."

"Please continue, Lama!" called out a man's booming voice.

I had their attention, I saw. But they were looking at me with more curiosity for the sack I had pulled out than of actual connection with the words which I spoke.

I was about to ensnare them.

"I stand before you as the reincarnation of Amursanaa," I said. "And I ask for the allegiance you pledged to me two centuries ago, when I led us to independence."

And with that, I shook my bag and out fell some shining golden coins. The peasant eyes widened to comical dimensions, and the mob seemed fit to burst with sheer excitement. I walked through them, taking the slow and deliberate steps of the monks of Drepung but in the European military uniform, creating a visual dissonance that confused and dazzled them. It was nothing they—or anyone—had seen before.

"What has this Khenbish Khan you speak of ever done for you, truly?" I asked.

As I went among them, I pressed coins into the outstretched palms. The hands reached out for them, and occasionally clutching the hem of my uniform. As I went, there were little whoops and cheers. This was more wealth than these people had ever seen in their entire lives in that desolate valley; this otherworldly glitter had never before tickled their eyes. At last, I reached the opposite end of the crowd, and I held the empty bag up. I had just enough gold pieces to satisfy the village. I heard a sound—it was laughter.

I turned and I saw it was the light-skinned muscular man—my original antagonist in this place. He snickered, and the crowd hushed. It was clear this opponent of mine had some kind of sway in this place, among his people.

"But Amursanaa, as you must know," he called out, "won independence just for a short time, before he was himself killed. You must have particularly painful memories of being beheaded, do you not?"

He laughed, and some of the men closest to him, those who had been playing games of chance with him before my arrival, chuckled too. But all sounds ceased when I walked at him. He flinched ever so slightly as I reached out, quick as a cobra, and clutched the back of his neck.

I squeezed with my hand—and with my mind, too. His brain struggled against my willful grip.

"I can assure you, whatever lingering impressions I have of that existence only strengthen my resolve to ensure it doesn't happen again. No matter how many others will have to lose their heads so I can keep mine."

I gazed deep into his straining eyes, already becoming bloodshot with the strain against me.

"It won't happen again," I repeated. "The enemies of the Mongols will be the ones paying the ultimate price, this time."

As I released him, a delirious cheer went up through the crowd. The men who had heretofore been terrified of me rushed in and slapped me on the back. A few of the women kissed me, and the children hugged me around the knees.

They celebrated me. Even the pale-skinned man who was my antagonist reluctantly bowed to me and offered me his greetings as the local leader—though insincerity tainted his words. His name was Jimbe. (His mind was strangely elusive; although I could grab it, it was like a strong fish that flopped from my grasp. But more on this later.) These villagers welcomed me as a hero, now that they had seen my powers of persuasion. The elders, a group of white-bearded men, walked with me into the easternmost limit of their encampment. They pointed up at a stockade on a hill not more than two versts off.

"That is one of the Qing garrisons," said the eldest with a quaking voice, standing behind me, watching the far-off enemy. "The sons of Han have set up nine such fortresses on our lands, and we have been unable to oppose them."

The men surrounding me nodded in unison, their arms folded. But their faces were not resolute or angry, let alone rebellious. Sniveling, their eyes darted from the fortress to the sky, and then made surreptitious glances at my uniform.

I glanced into their eyes, each and every one. And one by one, they all looked down at the ground and shuffled their feet, fiddling with the furs and skins draped around their bodies. The Chinese, the sky, even just my strange uniform had struck fear in their hearts.

"I am not one of them, I can assure you," I said. "The uniform is merely to let them know I mean business."

They nodded and then led me three versts farther down the valley. The entire village was in tow, with the women carrying the infants and the children kicking the rocks at one another and even the goats trotting along, clanking their dull bells. The eldest men stopped and pointed up toward a silhouette dark and high against the bright sky.

"That is the garrison that is the least well-defended," said Jimbe, crossing his arms in front of his chest. "We could take it in a rush any time. We could do it now. If you're so committed to driving these Han bastards out of here, why don't you make good on your boasts, right here and now?"

As if in reply, there was a shriek at the back of the crowd behind us. I turned, and the crowd parted. A screaming child scrambled through the dirt, at the back of the mob. A ram was aggressively butting the boy with huge hard horns twisted by years of dominance. No one from the crowd moved. The horned beast was practically on top of the boy, about twenty yards distant. None of the men made a move to help.

I drew my Colt and fired without aiming. The animal recoiled, stumbled backward, shuddered, and fell. The boy stood there, dazed.

As one, every face turned toward me, wide-eyed with wonder.

By the time the ram was slaughtered and roasting on a spit, the boy was bouncing on my lap, the other children clustered around the rock on which I sat. The adults huddled all around, staring at me. The fire flickered in my eyes, casting a glow of home into the rapidly gathering blackness. I told them stories: of my travels across Asia, of the monasteries in China and Tibet, my fights with robbers, the storms raining continually on my head and the winds gusting in my face along the many roads I'd traveled. I didn't tell them everything. But this Jimbe, as I now knew him, looked at me suspiciously as he turned the meat slowly, with a steady strong hand on the spit.

"Why did you leave Tibet?" he said. "A monk's life is pretty cushy."

I glanced down at the ram-battered boy in my lap and gave his shoulder a reassuring pat. But he was already falling asleep, because of the toll the many bruises and the terror had wrought on his body. I stroked his head.

"The strict life of the spirit is not for me," I said. "I am a warrior and avenger, not a monk. It took me years to discover this, as I searched for my true calling from within those monastery walls."

"What monastery was it again?" Jimbe said, cranking the dead animal over the flames.

"Jokhang. But I moved around to two smaller ones, too," I lied.

Jimbe nodded. He stopped turning the spit, grabbed a knife, and sliced off hunks of the meat, which were passed around the crowd. The sounds of gnashing and masticating mingled with the crackle of the fire. The boy was asleep in my arms. His mother wolfed down her morsels and licked off her fingers, and then reached out for him. But I only shook my head.

"He can stay here a little while," I said. "I am quite content. Take your time."

The next day Jimbe and the men vaulted atop their horses and led me on a hundred-verst trek to the ends of the valley. The Chinese strongholds were found every other ridge or so. They were not big, but it was clear they were built with thick stone. On most I saw the tiny figures of sentries watching.

At first my companions seemed to shrink onto the horses' backs and took circuitous routes through the shadows on the edges of the valley. But I rode purposefully straight, right in a line past these fortresses above. I heard their scoffs after the first few passes, but they dropped into silence when I was not gunned down. And then they mimicked my riding style, getting ever closer and more daring in sight of the hated Han frontier soldiers. By the afternoon, their voices buzzed with their newfound bravery.

"We should ride up on each of the fortresses and seize them!" shouted one of my riders.

"They are weak, and we are strong!" hollered another.

"Let's kill them and scatter their entrails to the birds!" cried a third.

Furor, frenzy rippled through our little throng. Some bloodlusty roars echoed off the nearby ridges, and I saw some movement in the nearest outpost high up. It was the glint of a spyglass, perhaps a rifle scope. Things threatened to spin out of control before my plan had even materialized.

Before I could open my mouth, Jimbe held up his hand. The clamor immediately settled. All watched him expectantly, but he just held his hand aloft like that, not saying anything or even blinking, for a minute or longer. All that could be heard was the whistle of the wind down the valley, and the soft whinnying of the horses. Finally, he lowered his hand.

"We have come this far with our new friend," he said, gesturing at me with an open palm. "Let's hear what his plans are. Any man who is the reincarnation of the great Amursanaa must have something up his sleeve to defeat these Chinese bastards."

He stopped speaking. All eyes turned to me.

I smiled. Now I had them.

"Now is not the time," I said. "We must be patient. The heavens have not yet decreed the right time to strike. From my meditations, I have determined that the Year of the Dragon is the most auspicious time for our struggle against the Qing yoke."

Their stern faces bobbed up and down, nodding earnestly. The wind whistled through our caps, whispering truths in the ears of all.

"Let it be so," Jimbe said, eyes closed, face upward.

He motioned for the rest of the crew to lead us to the next lookout point. They carried on. But Jimbe delayed, and as we brought up the rear, he edged his white horse next to the black flanks of my Kublai.

"I trust you are not saying specifically what Year of the Dragon for a reason," he murmured. "You have my allegiance, but just know: our people expect change. And they deserve change. Deprive Dzungaria of that, and you will find no fiercer enemy than me. Take your time, take your years, holy man—but know that you cannot put off the fight forever. I will force it upon you."

With that, he whipped the reins, and he sped ahead. I glanced at the shadow atop the fortress on the ridge, and I waved. The figure ducked lower, still observing me in the glinting spyglass. Kublai and I then trotted into the dust cloud my nascent army had kicked up on the trail.

I stayed with this village through the end of the day. That final night there was much eating and merriment, and the children loved to hear my riddles and watch the illusions I conjured in their minds before the nighttime fire, demons, and ancient warriors and the like. The men looked at me with hopeful gazes, and the women stared at me with longing.

One of the nubile females, face covered, brazenly crept into my darkened tent at the nadir of the night. She kept her face obscured even as her magnificent body emerged from her clothes. She tugged off my deel, and climbed onto me. As our breathing deepened, she slid some ropes around my wrists, binding me fast to the tentpole.

It was only then that she slid off her shawl, spilling a cascade of swishing black hair across my face.

It was my fiancé—the girl from Dolonnuur.

She smiled down at me, squeezing my cock within her. I yelped out to Jimbe for help, but she gagged me with my deel.

"You thought you could just walk out on me," she said, bending down, softly kissing my cheek. "For this you will pay."

Over several hours, the waves of lust and terror ebbed and flowed through my body. She would nibble my earlobe and bring me to the height of ecstasy—and then suddenly raise a sharp knife to my throat. She nicked my chest with the blade several times and sucked the blood from the wounds.

I tried again and again to crush her will, but my powers were worthless. Her rage and desire were too much for whatever innate strength I had.

I was at her mercy. And though I hated those who would force themselves upon another, I admit this…was different. She knew it. She laughed and licked my face like a hungry beast.

"Lover, I just want…you to…know that…this passion is…all…on my…terms," she said.

She was perfect. My heart leapt up. My ardor surged through my body and into her. Lust and adoration melted my icy fear.

"What is your name? I must know your name!"

She smacked me across the face and sucked some more of my blood from a vein in my arm.

"I told you my name when you asked for my hand," she said. "If you can't remember, you will never know."

The next morning, my bones aching from the nocturnal tussles, I awoke to find the girl with the swishing raven hair gone. A note was stuck to my nose. My wrists were free. I reached up and read.

"See you down the trail," it read in Chinese, "in your dreams."

I shook my head, woozy from a sleepless night and a little lost blood. But I couldn't help but smile.

Body throbbing, nerves ablaze, my groin sore as a beaten dog, I slung my packs atop the two white camels. I mounted Kublai and started trotting eastward. Before I made it a dozen paces, however, the mounted form of Jimbe raced along at speed, and came to a clattering stop right in front of my steed, blocking my path.

"Where do you think you're going, holy man?" he said.

"I am heading through the mountains to Ürümqi," I said. "If we hope to be ready for the Year of the Dragon, I will need to muster the troops from among our people. There are millions of Chinese, and each pair of hands must take the lives of at least a hundred of the Han bastards."

Jimbe held up his hands. In each was a revolver.

"I will give you a thousand heads myself," he said. "I am coming with you. Better you than this phantom they call the Khenbish Khan."

I said nothing but turned Kublai, so we trotted around him. Jimbe and his horse fell into step alongside. Only after an hour did he holster his sidearms.

For a hundred versts or more, we did not speak. We did not have to. Our silence, and the feel of our horses traversing the Tian Shan ridges, were all we needed to link us irrevocably in that moment. Only once did we glance at one another, nod, and then continue to listen to the vibrations of the universe around, the future echoing ahead.

It was strange to have a two-legged companion on my travels.

When the next village appeared out of the horizon mists some hours into our journey, Jimbe raced ahead toward it. Without an explicit conversation, he became my advance messenger. And indeed, when I arrived at the settlement, the peoples' eyes bulged at me.

It must have been quite a sight: the whiteness of my two camels, the black of my steed, and the shine of the pale sun off my yellow deel. Kublai carried me at a saunter into the center of the circle of tents, and I dismounted with a huge swing of my legs, landing on the firm Dzungarian earth.

"My friends, it is time to seize back our destiny," I said. "I am here to join you in driving out the Han bastards, after so many centuries of slavery."

Mostly silence in this new crowd…but one cheer. I cleared my throat and began to tell them a story. And that was all they needed.

CHAPTER 11
ÜRÜMQI NIGHTS

It went like that.

From those first two Mongol villages, we encountered at least a dozen more along the serrated twists of the Tian Shan. At each village, Jimbe heralded my arrival, and I rode up afterward and gave my speech. I rationed my gold pieces, so there were always little gifts for even the poorest of the nomad children who gazed up at me in wonder. But wonder wasn't all. Desperation was there, too: from the smallest children to the most ancient elders. These people lived like sad ghosts in the shadow of the slaughter that had robbed them hundreds of years before they were born. No one knew whether this burden survived through their oral traditions; or if they felt it in the chill of their bones out on the frozen steppe; or sensed it within their blood itself, the current flowing atavistically in their very veins. These Mongols in the Tian Shan were the hardiest of all our peoples: the few survivors of the massacres perpetrated by the Kazakhs and Chinese and Russians, and a small minority in Chinese lands.

While my ancestors had been driven thousands of versts away to southern Russia, these hardy souls had evaded their persecutors and eked out survival. So even if they were living that twilight half-life, I had to have respect for what they had done: they had held out in the homeland. They had represented the lineage of the Greatest Khan so that the universe may always remember the Mongols had never been fully driven out of their lands.

Thus, I told them what they wanted to hear, and through the cloudy despair of centuries crusting in their eyes like so much dust, a twinge of hope sparkled in each and every gaze.

Looking at the quiver of excitement in their limbs as they listened to my words and nodded and whispered excitedly to one another, I realized my path from Drepung Monastery to this desolate horizon had always been directed true. All the hours of meditation and the fulfillment were a pittance, a middling experience. That life had been a slow suicide of stagnation. Not so with this: moving through space, putting a plan together for this lifetime and among these my people. This was truly my destiny, connecting with these lost brethren of mine.

I was changing the world, with each salutation, and each word I uttered. All was action. When they asked me how soon it would be until we could start the fight, I told them to wait for the Year of the Dragon. They were so swept up in the moment—and so few of them knew of calendars of years—that they put their everlasting faith this goal would not be long, that it would be a mere matter of days and nights before the Chinese would be driven out in an epochal wave propelling history forward. I did not disabuse them of this, of course.

Strangely, the specter of the Khenbish Khan again and again reared its head, in whispers and rumors. But no one knew anything beyond the name, it seemed. No description of this apparition, this would-be leader, was available. We continued our ministries and became considerably less concerned about this competitor who seemed to exist only in legend.

But still I wondered…

The black-haired girl had vanished. At each village no one seemed to know of those swishing raven tresses, that untamed beauty. I sighed, and we rode on.

This travel was slow, not only from the pace of the camels, but also from the well-wishes we accumulated at each and every stop. These people fed us, the men embraced us, and the women tended to our every need, both day…and night. The children in particular wanted to play with their "Uncle Lama," as I was invariably called. I lay on the ground, and they crawled all over me, laughing and wrestling each other. I didn't mind this. There is nothing so pure as a new soul, trying again in a new existence with eyes wide and bright before the ugliness of the world corrupts all to blindness.

"Hey—what's that?" one boy said at one of the villages halfway along our journey, as he pointed down at me.

He was pointing at my bare belly; I have never had a belly button. The boy exposed his own navel, where there was the scarred-over vestige of the umbilical cord that had sustained him in his mother's womb. I smiled at him, and I shrugged. It was Jimbe who spoke up.

"Uncle Lama was not born of this world," he said, flexing his arm muscles. "He was dropped into our world from his previous existence as the great Amursanaa who once led us to greatness. This time he has come back to finish the job and drive the Chinese out from our rightful lands, once and for all."

The confused boy's brow furrowed as he considered this. But then, quick as a storm whisking through the Turpan Depression, he whooped—and landed with surprising force on my solar plexus, driving all the air from my body. I recovered just in time for the dogpile of the rest of the children, laughing and screaming with delight. Through the chaos of limbs and joyful roughhousing, Jimbe's impassive face watched it all.

It went like that along our entire journey, slow moving as it was through the Tian Shan. The joy, the elation, the premature celebrations—and the watchful eye of my companion alongside me for every step.

Finally, we reached that farthest-flung outpost of the Han's reach into the untamed heart of Innermost Asia: Ürümqi. My memories of the city from the time passing through as a child were indistinct. Even though I had some recognition of the dusty bustling streets from traveling this part of the Silk Road with my father and mother and Chingis and Gerel—around the time of my illness and delirium and my first vision of Agharti—I was stupefied by its sheer size. It had grown to become a metropolis in its own right, in just those few short years. The hustle of these enterprising Chinese, these short shopkeepers and manic women carrying on with their three and four and five children from streetcorner to streetcorner, stood in polar contrast to the tall and proud Mongols who lived life true to their land, feet flat on the ground.

Pigs and cattle sauntered through the city, getting in the way of the horses and carts that were stopped in lines in every direction. Chaotic shouting, curses, the stink of rot. Jimbe looked at it with terror in his widened eyes. The simple life of the steppe had not prepared him for such a hellish vision of pandemonium. I laid a hand on his wrist, telling him we needed to keep calm, to continue our mission for the good of the people. He clenched his jaw, and we trotted through the traffic, double-time, as I shouted in every language I knew to clear the way.

After a few hours of questions, confusion, and bribes, we made our way to the far edge of the city. It was near the garbage dump, where the local Mongols were stuffed into hovels that swayed in the wind off the mountains. If the other parts of this forsaken pit were dirty and filled with frantic mayhem, this was quiet, slow-moving, and languid. Old men smoked pipes in doorways, watching us as we trotted past. We rode to the end of the row, then tied up our mounts and set foot in this last sad refuge of the Mongols in what was once proudly called Dzungaria.

Beware, said a voice in my head.

I wheeled around, but no one was speaking.

Beware the grinning face, said the voice again.

It was the fakir's voice. It took my breath away. I tried to pay it no mind.

Beware.

"Shut up!" I hissed. Jimbe glanced at me, clearly worried at the argument I was having with myself.

I set my two feet on the streetcorner in the center of this slum, I held my hands to the sky, and I shouted. I envisioned inveighing against my father, pleading with him for the fate of these my people. Then I directed my words to the universe itself, asking whether it was fate or just the rotten luck of the Mongols. I balled my fists and shouted at the clouds, then I turned to Jimbe, on my right, and I asked him, rhetorically:

"Is this what we have come to?" I asked him. "Have our people been stamped into the dirt of our forefathers until we live like dumb beasts? Penned in like impoverished cattle at the end of the Chinese Empire's rod?"

I raved on and on, and a crowd gathered around. The old men smoked, approaching, puzzlement narrowing their eyes. Some of the women looked fearful. The children stayed back, but the men…they walked up with faces twisted in anger. All gazed at the golden vajra pinned to my lapel. Jimbe was stupefied, like he suddenly realized he'd thrown his fate in with the fortunes of a madman. He turned to walk away, but I grabbed his collar and grasped him with all my powers, of both mind and body.

"Is there nothing we can do?" I raved at the heavens. "Is there anything that can be done?"

Jimbe squirmed with all his might against my grasp, but my hand held him like an iron vice. I pointed at the crowd of dozens who had gathered, my finger like a talisman forcing them to shrink back from us.

"Because I will tell you, lowly Mongols," I said. "If we only stick together, we cannot be beaten. We cannot ever truly be defeated. I am the living proof, I am the reincarnation of Amursanaa, the leader who brought us glory once. That glory will be ours once again!

"The heavens have decreed these lands as ours, and we must realize in our hearts, and blood, and bones that we are one. If we pledge our lives and our destiny to one another, we will again rule Asia. From the top of the world to these lowly hovels, and across the wide swath of the Silk Road and beyond, from China to Russia, to the gates of Europe!"

I paused at this moment. Jimbe had stopped fighting to free himself, and I let him go. Starting with the women, a cheer rose from the crowd: from the creaking old voices of the pipe smokers to the screeching children and the hearty war cries of the men, so many centuries unheard. I smiled, and I moved into the crowd, where hands and hearts welcomed me with utter love, Jimbe at my heels. Hands slapped us on the back, and lips pressed against our cheeks in greeting. We were making a difference. The ancient tide was turning, the currents of history advancing within our very hearts. I gazed out along the adoring crowd.

Amid the beaming faces, one at the back caught my eye. The typical Mongolian headwear did nothing to hide this European-looking one that stuck out—the head that was shoulders above the others. The hard jawline, that grinning face. The angry blackened eyes. There was something terrifying in that juxtaposition. That visage seemed to be frozen amid the chaotic revelry of dozens shouting their allegiance to my new cause.

Beware the grinning face, the fakir's voice barked inside my skull.

I pushed through the crowd, past the handshakes and kisses, forcing my way forward to the furious form. Several men embraced me, and two women bowed before me and kissed my hands. I graciously thanked them, and then plunged the rest of the way through the adoring mob—only to find nothing. The grinning figure was gone.

Hands grasped me. Even as the crowd hooted and raised us up over their heads and took us to the village square, I could not shake the vision of those eyes boring into me.

"Who do you think it was?" I asked Jimbe, in between bites of goat, in our room some hours later.

Jimbe ran his hand over the arm of his woman for the night, a skinny widow who had fallen asleep right underneath him an hour before. Mine was on the other side of the room nearest the window, snoring softly.

"I saw no such person," Jimbe said. "What does it matter, anyway? The Mongols in this town know we are here to liberate them. At this rate, we'll have the length of the Silk Road rising against the stupid Han long before your Year of the Dragon!"

He grabbed the woman's ass and growled triumphantly. I tore another strip of meat off the drumstick with my incisors, and I shook my head. I was not so sure as my steadfast companion. But he was still in post-coital bliss. My experience that evening had paled in comparison to the girl with the long black tresses in Dolonnuur. And that face of the grinning nameless figure unsettled my stomach; that face too would not leave my mind's eye.

"We shall move again through space, and through time," I said, rising. "I think maybe the Romanovs have their spies deployed here in Dzungaria."

"What—are you crazy?" Jimbe said, dipping his head down to kiss the swarthy flesh of the widow. "Why would we leave such a place when we've been welcomed with such open arms. Such sweet open arms." His mouth wandered across a breast, ending up at a dark nipple.

I strode over and grabbed his ear, yanking him up with as much force as I could muster. He howled. The woman shrieked, and ran naked from the room, her taut body disappearing into shadow and memory. Mine snored on.

Two hours later, we trotted east under the milky swath of stars. Jimbe and his horse grumbled, while Kublai stumbled, half asleep at that strange hour. The camels were wide awake, somehow.

"Why did we have to leave in the middle of the night?" Jimbe whined. "We could have stayed at least a few days. I enjoyed that woman's company. There is no delicacy we would have been denied. You are a fool for panicking over some smiling phantom who doesn't even exist."

"And you are a fool for thinking that we are on some victory tour!" I hissed. "Our road promises to be long, and we are just at the beginning. We must tread carefully with each and every step."

Three explosions of dirt erupted on the moonlit ground before us, gunshots echoing all around. Our horses reared back, and then we were off breakneck toward the south, headlong toward a ridge that protruded straight up from the Earth. A rifle flashed from the top, high above. The rounds whistled by over our heads. I let go of the reins of the snow-white camels, which trotted off stupidly into the night.

I drove down hard on my steed and toward the base of the ridge. As we pulled within a few paces, I pulled up hard on the reins, and then I leapt off.

I pulled off my deel and drew my Colt from its holster. Jimbe came galloping up, too, and he too drew his sidearm. I motioned for him to head west, making clear I would circle around to the other side to find a scalable slope to the top. But he just looked at me, mouth agape, uncomprehending. I cursed under my breath in every language and searched for a way up to the shooter.

Twice I reached gaps where I could see upward—and the sniper took a shot at me each time. The second time his bullet grazed my shoulder. The sting was hot with my blood. I cursed again and carried on behind the rocks.

A few minutes more, and I found the slope. Only still shadows loomed above. Step after careful step, I crept upward. Finally, I reached the boulder outcropping shielding the overlook.

The pale moonlight bathed the entire scene in a surreal glow. I pressed my back against the rock. I breathed twice, calming my mind to a meditative state. I cocked the Colt softly, and then sprung into the clearing.

Nothing. I waved my revolver in all directions, but there was nothing.

The smoldering embers of a fire were there, and spent casings clinked under my feet. I listened. Rustling off to the south.

I rushed in the other direction, to another overlook. From my vantage point, I saw a shade scrambling down toward a horse, some hundred yards off.

I squared myself, took aim, and fired. The blast dropped the figure. I started running to collect my quarry. But just as soon as the silhouette hit the ground, it leapt up and staggered to the horse, which it awkwardly mounted. I squared myself again. The horse and rider galloped. I fired—and missed. The assassin was out of range before I could line up another shot. I spat in disgust on the ground.

"Hands in the air!" came Jimbe's voice from behind.

I raised my hands, scoffing.

"It's me, you knucklehead. He got away," I hollered. When he lowered his sidearm, I slapped him atop his skull.

I raised my fist at the sky.

"How did you know?" I asked the voice, my father, or the fakir or whatever or whoever it was that had been speaking to me.

But there came no reply. Jimbe looked at me like I was insane, perhaps contagious.

We used the same campsite our failed assassin used, stoking the fire up to crackling flames. We hitched our horses to a dead bush near the edge of the clearing and hacked some of the extra branches off for more kindling. I tracked down the camels, whose glowing white flanks were easy to spot in the moonlight from only half a verst away. We ate a few morsels we had taken from Ürümqi and then lay back. Jimbe had first watch, and I turned on my side to sleep a few hours. But my companion kept rustling around, his restless feet crunching into the dirt and stones, back and forth, for an hour or more. It set my teeth on edge, and I waited in vain for the peace of sleep to carry me away. Finally, I rolled over to face him.

"What is it?" I said.

Jimbe snapped a stick, and tossed it on the fire, shooting riotous sparks that vanished into the night air. His voice was so quiet I barely heard it.

"Do you really believe all you say?" he said.

I propped myself up on an elbow.

"I don't know what you mean, friend Jimbe."

"I mean," he said, picking up another stick, "when you talk about the greater destiny of our people and our destiny to again sweep across Asia and all that. Is that true?"

He snapped the twig in his hands and threw it too on the fire. But this one was wet, and it hissed harshly.

"Or is it all bullshit?" he said. "Why the camels and the gold and the big speeches? Why not action? Why not start the rebellion now?"

I rolled onto my back.

"I can understand why you would think that we should immediately attack," I said.

I stood, dusted myself off, and grabbed my Colt. I sat on a rock at the edge of the circle, across the fire from him.

"But my years of silence and meditation in Tibet and China taught me that though this lifetime is fleeting, it is also all about timing—and patience," I said. "The Mongols, from the Tian Shan to the base of the Chinese Wall, are not yet ready in their hearts to rise together. They are like a green fruit still hanging on a tree, and not yet ripened for the picking."

His head turned, and the fire glinted in his eyes for a moment.

"And are you the one to harvest this fruit?" he said. "Are you really the one destined by your birth, in this lifetime, to be the leader of us all?"

Laughter erupted from my throat and echoed out in the night.

"Yes, my good man, I'm pretty sure I am the best reincarnation of Amursanaa that we have at this moment."

Jimbe pointed across at me with a knife he suddenly had in his hand. The blade, and his eyes, shone in the light.

"I'm not fucking around, Lama," he said. "I need to know what the plan is."

I set aside my Colt, crawled toward my blanket, and laid down, with my back to him.

"You will know in good time, Jimbe, when it suits me for you to know," I said. "Now get back to keeping watch so we aren't murdered in our sleep."

I heard him rise. His footsteps crept toward me. His breath quickened.

I was already focusing my entire will upon his being, his essence. I never wanted to use my intuition and powers on my own people, unless absolutely necessary. And he was also somewhat resistant to my wiles, as I have mentioned.

But he was not totally immune to my powers—and this wayward sheep needed to be punished by the shepherd.

I sensed his intent to test me yet again. He would start by attacking me, and depending on the outcome, would either kill me outright, or leave me to be eaten alive by highwaymen and vultures. I saw it all so clearly in a thought as brief as a blink.

So even before he had taken three steps toward me, I plunged deep into his being. And despite that strange flopping fish resistance of his, I clamped down as hard as I ever have onto another soul. I felt his heart miss a beat, and I sensed the impact as he dropped to his knees. Only then did I turn on my side to face him, with a smile. I had him.

"I know you doubt my commitment, and my power, to make this happen for our people," I said. "I see you would even put my life on the line, right here and right now, around this camp we share as friends and allies. So...allow me to pose the same riddle to you."

I crawled in his direction, about six feet away from where he had fallen like in prayer. His face strained against the metaphysical bonds in which I had trapped him, the veins in his neck bulging. His eyes were wide, terrorized. His hands trembled as they rose with his own blade, the knife handle above his head. And then, together, they started the slow arc down toward his chest.

He could not scream. I would not permit him.

His unbelieving eyes watched his own hand sink the knife through his rib cage, and saw, back and forth, with the blade. The crack of bone and the rip of meat came to my ears, but scarcely louder than his labored breaths, which grew ragged as he punctured his own lungs.

I stood and I dusted myself off, even as the self-mutilation continued and the blood gurgled in his airways, rippling his breath. I walked the few paces to my struggling, mutilated compatriot. I crouched down on my heels so we were face-to-face. I winked at his disbelieving face.

Then I reached inside his chest cavity. It gave little resistance; he had made superbly clean cuts through his own anatomy.

I pulled out his heart, which I wrested free of an artery with a little extra tug. It convulsed one last sad throb into my palm.

"So, what's your verdict: do you think I'm the right hand to pick the fruit?" I said, holding his heart, which convulsed thick red streams down my wrist as I held it to his horrified face. "I still do not think it ripened to my taste."

He fell to the ground, lifeless. I tossed the heart on the dying embers of the fire, which sizzled and hissed. I wiped my blood-soaked hands on the nearest rock and went back to my blanket and settled back down for a peaceful night's sleep, confident both my would-be assassins would not try again amid the utter black and the silence.

I awoke with the dawn. I went over and re-started the fire. Then I stooped down and grabbed Jimbe's shoulder. I shook him, and his eyes opened, and he sprung up with a gasp.

"How did you sleep?" I said. "I hope you're rested. We have much distance ahead of us today."

He didn't hear me, he was panicking, reaching under his clothes, which were all intact. There was no blood at all on him. His chest was whole; he was complete. He felt at his jugular for a pulse, and finding it, he sobbed deeply.

"Lama, I had the strangest dream," he said. "We had a fight, and you…killed me."

I put my finger to my lips and shushed him.

"There was no fight," I said. "We just had a long debate about the nature of our journey. I trust I have convinced you that we are better working together than at cross purposes."

He nodded, rubbing his hands over his delirious head. I patted his shoulder and raised myself. I slung my bag over the back of Kublai. I lashed it down, and stretched my arms high overhead, and yawned.

"Say, friend—could you bring me water?" I said.

Jimbe stood and stumbled to our supplies atop one of the camels. I waited for him to return with one of the skins of water. He rubbed his eyes and watched me, trying to rouse himself.

But when I dumped the water over my blood-coated hands, washing them of so much coagulated thick red stuff which had blackened and encrusted overnight, he recoiled. He gasped and his eyes rolled back in his head. He fainted in a heap to the ground. I chuckled and ate a little breakfast while I waited for him to awaken the second time.

When he finally did open his eyes and rise, Jimbe asked me no questions. But he now looked at me with a mix of fear and reverence that I appreciated. I knew I had my adjutant in place, and now our work could begin in earnest.

CHAPTER 12
ULIASTAI AND BEYOND

The oppressive heat, the hysterical swelter, ushered us into the Turpan Depression. In our hasty exit from Ürümqi, and after the ambush, we found ourselves within the desolate undulations of the desert. I navigated us north, to keep from crossing into the deepest stretches of the sands and winds.

As we trudged through that inhospitable landscape, I knew I must break the silence between me and Jimbe, as humbled as he had been. I spoke to Kublai, the horse underneath me, and not the man riding alongside, as I described my Agharti vision. As our horses trotted upward and to the northeast along the winding road, I talked for hours about what I had seen, with the rivers of gold and the absolute perfection which I alone had glimpsed from this human existence topside on the Earth. The subterranean depths were our ultimate goal, I said—to make an independent and strong Mongolia an earthly outpost of the golden dream paradise where people sailed on rivers of gold in golden boats, eating and breathing gold, without war or suffering of any kind.

"...and I know that we can find this place yet again, if we only leave ourselves open to the possibility that the universe will show us the way," I told the horse.

Without thinking, Jimbe made the first noise he had made since his near-death experience: he scoffed at my words. I shook my head and smacked him upside the skull, knocking off his hat. But he caught the cap before it fell. He glanced sideways at me apprehensively, and I pointed at my right temple.

"Remember, friend, I don't need to raise my hand to lay you low," I said. "I can just pluck your heart like a delicate flower whenever I so choose. But you must know that I don't want to abuse you. I only want you to work with me. If you trust me as you did when you first joined me on the journey these few weeks ago, you will have your faith back. I just ask you to keep that faith alive, like a bird in a cage. Give your heart to me willingly."

He did not scoff this time. He nodded. And we rode on.

We climbed out of the sands, farther to the north and east. A thousand versts we traveled, stopping occasionally to meet with the Mongols along our paths who listened to what we had to say. Jimbe was the perfect partner, again and again he rode ahead and warned villages of my coming. He primed the crowd during my speeches with little yips and hollers of approval.

But he had no agency—he had become my lackey. I cannot say it troubled me during that stretch of my long journey. I needed support, and not criticism, from my right-hand man. And Jimbe was the perfect tool when he was compliant.

These villages welcomed us with open arms. My words, the sight of my immaculate white camels, and the sparkle of my gold coins flipping into their palms lit their faces. I made them pledge never to forget me, and I led them in various chants about the Year of the Dragon—whatever came into my mind. I improvised. I discerned the vibrations of these my kinfolk, and I played to whatever they needed to hear.

Invariably we left each settlement with provisions and cheers—but not until being cared for and comforted through the night by a maiden or two (or three). Jimbe's spirits improved immeasurably with each stop we made, with each hot meal and stint of carnal delight, the caresses of the welcoming local women. He grew despondent when we had to make camp under the stars alone. But I told him stories about Dzungaria and our peoples' exploits when we had not only the Kazakhs, but also the Russians and the Chinese, under our yoke. And it would placate him for another day's journey into the heartland of our peoples.

We came upon a solitary mountain hut in the third week. Rounding a ridge, we came abruptly upon the mud dwelling, small but sturdy and well-built. As we approached, a tiny figure appeared in the doorway—a young boy, no more than six. I bowed. The boy nodded. Jimbe rode a bit ahead and was already speaking to the child when I pulled the reins taut in front of the shack.

"...and we have been a week's journey and the dear Uncle Lama could sincerely use room and board for a day," Jimbe was saying.

I held up my hand for silence, and then I vaulted off Kublai and strode up to the boy. I patted him on the head.

"A fine boy, a remarkable boy," I said. "Where are your parents?"

He pointed to the south.

"They left four days ago," his voice barely a whisper. "My mother was sick, and my father took her to a doctor at the village in the next valley."

"We would be honored to stay with you for one night during your vigil," I said. "Will you do us the honor of hosting us?"

The boy shrugged and pushed in through the door. Jimbe rubbed his palms together and followed him. I entered last.

The cabin was tiny, with barely enough room for all three of us to move around at once. But as is always the case on my journeys, the unexpected wonders of this world never cease to amaze.

The interior of this small house was covered with riches: glinting jewel necklaces, shelves stocked with heavy gold which rattled a bit with each gust of the mountain wind on the flimsy dry mud walls, and rich tapestries the likes of which put the adornments of Drepung Monastery to shame. Jimbe's jaw dropped, and he clutched at my arm as his knees wobbled. I straightened him up and set him against the one wall. Then the boy and I sat down at adjoining parts of the two beds in the small space.

"When do you expect your parents to return?" I said.

He shrugged. He pulled a drinking pitcher out from near his feet and offered us each a sip of the contents. The water was stale and musty, like it had been sitting there for some time.

"I will just wait until they come back," he said. "It may be just a few days, after my mother recovers. Or if she does not get the medicine she needs, it could be weeks until the funeral is complete and she is buried, bya gtor."

I nodded solemnly.

"You are a wise boy, for just your few years on Earth," I said.

"It's not the years in this existence," he said. "It's the last few lifetimes which have shown me truly the patterns of mortal existence. You see, I am the reincarnation of the Diluv."

I ran my hand over the scabbard of a long ceremonial sword hanging behind my head.

"Who made such a bold proclamation at your young age?" I asked.

"It was the Bogd Khan himself, sitting in Urga," the boy said.

I kept my face impassive, unflinching. The Bogd Khan's immense power was only as notable as his notorious poisonings of his enemies, and the strange zoo he kept in Urga. (You will hear more of the Bogd's pernicious influence later in my journeys, mark me well). I did not betray my shock at the Bogd's evident connection to this tiny boy. But I saw Jimbe's jaw drop. He mumbled something and was about to fall to his knees and worship this child, but I tackled him back upright before he could stoop at the feet of the precocious little pipsqueak.

"That is impressive," I said, my arm around the shoulders of my companion to keep him from collapsing in an obsequious heap on the dirt floor. "I am a reincarnated soul, myself. I am the return of Amursanaa, our leader from two centuries hence."

The boy scratched his nose.

"I guess then we are both destined for greatness," he said, in a tiny, flat voice.

"I believe we are," I said, in an equally barren tone.

In truth, I sensed the power of this boy. He would be a great leader, if given half a chance to lead our people. By the time he came of age, he could be a true ally. So even as the glinting of the gold and the treasures in that hut winked at me with a promise of pushing my journey ahead that much farther, I knew we must leave him and his strange vault of riches alone.

"I think we will pitch our tent outside," I said, bowing with Jimbe in a half-headlock in the crook of my arm, then jerking him back upright. "We will keep vigil with you for at least this night, so your wait is not lonely."

"If staying one night would rest your conscience, I gladly welcome your presence," the boy said, picking up a piece of stale bread, cracking it in his tiny hands. "Either way, I am fine."

We walked outside, and the boy followed. The night fell fast on the horizon. Jimbe and I pitched our light tent and unloaded our gear inside it. Then we built a new campfire at the unused hearth. Jimbe noticed a wild ass at the edge of the firelight. He grabbed his firearm, aimed from one knee—and squeezed off two perfect shots, in the blink of an eye, neat as you please. The ass dropped. As we butchered and then roasted the carcass on sharp sticks over the flames, the horses and camels wandered off down the valley, into the shadows.

"Aren't you concerned about your horses? Your camels?" the boy asked with some concern for the first time in his voice.

"Don't worry about that," I said. "These beasts will come when I call, no matter how far they may stray across this Earth."

The boy raised one eyebrow. But then I handed him part of the cooked beast, and he devoured it in a frenzy, like he was an animal himself. I wondered about this child. Although he may have appeared to be a wise old soul, capable of taking on the world, he was nonetheless still a boy, with all that entailed. I offered him the rest of my portion of the roast, which he wolfed down just as greedily as the first cut. As his little teeth tore at the seared flesh, and his lips smacked and became blackened, I saw my very own self in that boy. A boy whose birthright of a life of freedom in the wide-open spaces of Mongolia would never be possible without someone to wrest it back from the past. I patted his head.

"Eat well, son," I said. "Because you will need to grow big and strong, for the sake of Mongolia—and for all of us."

We left at daybreak the next morning, without touching so much as a single valuable from that strange rickety hut with the boy, who held a spindly hand up from the doorway in the dawn light as we departed. Jimbe again complained.

"Why didn't we take any of the gold?" he said, beating the fleas from his clothes in the brightening sun's rays. "He even offered us some. It would have been so easy."

"Because that boy is one of the Mongols who might be a khan in the years to come," I said. "That boy could be the Bogd Gegeen someday, with the right schooling. You sure seemed impressed with his past lives if I recall correctly, bootlicker."

He scoffed.

"I was only showing the youngster some respect," he said. "It seemed like he needed some bucking up. But then I saw all that gold…"

I laughed and urged our horses and camels onward.

"I just hope you offer me such platitudes once our journey reaches its end," I said.

"If we do even half of what you have set out for us, then I will shine your boots for eternity," he said. "With my tongue, in the desert, at high noon."

"You better start drinking water now to prepare," I said, laughing. He laughed, too.

Hundreds of versts passed in a blur. We became a team, Jimbe and I, setting camp at defensible spots at dusk, watering and grazing the animals, as we prepared meals around a campfire. Jimbe became something of a chef in our weeks of travel, and my stomach rumbled as he roasted our daily kill. Our meat was succulent and fresh, the blood of the beasts still warm. The trail provided favorably with each successive hunt.

Twice we heard hooves at twilight, and we fortified against attacks. But none ever came, and we saw no one. Jimbe shook his head and slept soundly each night, even leaning on his rifle when I appointed him to keep watch. I only dozed, aware of the stars in their courses around the Earth and somewhere deep within the planet the continuous bustle of Agharti, keeping time with my beating heart.

We were being followed. Trouble lay ahead on the trail.

Uliastai appeared out of the wavering midday horizon not long afterward. Jimbe whooped and set off at a fast trot, to prepare our way in advance. But as I rode, I checked my Colt, greasing the action and loading an extra cartridge in the chamber even as I closed within a verst of the town. True to form, my companion had already built a crowd when I arrived.

But this time was a little bit different. Uliastai may have been founded by the Qing a century earlier, but it was a clearly a Mongol town in heart and spirit. The crowd was already whipped up into a frenzy at the sight of my two white camels. I waved and handed off the pair to the nearest men. I flashed my gold, which glinted in the sunlight.

"Ammmurrrsssssssanaa!" shouted one woman, a young pretty creature who smiled to reveal big black gaps where her teeth had once been. She fell at the feet of Kublai, who reared back. "Ssssaaavve us from the Qing yoke!"

"You must save us!" shouted a young boy.

"Chop the bastards in half with your sword," croaked an old man at the back.

The cheer was deafening. I threw a handful of gold into their adoring outstretched hands, some caught the coins, and others scrambled on the ground for the many pieces that had fallen. They were transfixed on me. I smiled.

"Where do we start, good Mongols of Uliastai?" I shouted. "Who are your leaders who can help me light this fire?"

A roar among the mob.

Ten minutes later, the crowd ushered us to the front of a squat white building with a heavy wooden door.

"The three princes will be able to make it happen," someone from the throng mumbled in my ear. "You have to convince them to support you. Even if they are focused on…other things."

We pushed through the door, the hinges squealing. Inside was thick smoke that stung our eyes. It was the smell of opium, that warm and tangy odor of burnt sin. A low light flickered at the end of the room, somewhere amid the haze. We went toward it. And there emerged a scene of debauchery. Three men dressed in resplendent robes lounged on chaises, nearly horizontal. The trio held hoses connected to an opium hookah atop a center table. Nubile teens dressed in scant silk knelt at each of their feet. But they paid no mind; they all spoke languidly at the same time, none of them hearing the other, as smoke poured from their mouths. We approached.

The one in red robes shook his hand above his head, rattling something inside his palm. The other two watched with eyes barely cracked open, still talking. I reached out and grabbed the shaking hand, pulling out the clattering Shagai shards. The brittle ankle bones of sheep scattered in fragments over the table, and into the hookah. The three of them dropped their smoking hoses and stared at me. The one who had been holding the pieces rubbed his smarting fingers in his other hand. He struggled to rise. He was bald with a thin face, with a long thin moustache which drooped down over his chin. His wide eyes were spotty green, like a growth of mold.

"How dare you!" he hollered. "We are in midst of a game!"

"You scoundrel!" hollered one of the others, plump and sweaty, in a purple robe.

"Outrageous," murmured the third, bedecked in shining blue silk.

But as they struggled to rise—red, purple, and blue princes—I leapt forward and grabbed the hookah. Gripping the hoses tightly, I swung the apparatus high over my head. Putrid water splashed everywhere. The girls quickly scattered to a darker part of the room at the far corner. The three princes finally started to rise to their soft-slippered feet, pushing up from their catatonic drug nests. I let the hookah fly, and it smashed against the wall in an explosion of glass, smoke, and water. The one in the red robe staggered to his feet in front of me. I held his shoulder with one hand, keeping the flailing little man at bay.

"Listen to me," I said. "I only smashed your contraption because I need you thinking with a clear head in the negotiations to come."

The other two had risen to their feet to examine the wreckage at the far wall. But the cloudy look in the eyes of the red-robed one in front of me suddenly melted away, like a fresh wind had blown those skies clear. His brow furrowed, as he looked up and down at my yellow deel.

"You must be the Lama everyone's talking about," he said. "Ja Lama, the bandit with Buddha at his back."

"You have heard of me," I said.

"I have heard tales of some of your journeys, from Ürümqi and across the desert," he said. "You are the monk inciting the Mongols to rise up against the Qing yoke. A boy with whom I correspond out in the mountains claims you are the reincarnation of Amursanaa."

He could only be speaking of the Diluv boy. I held back from asking how he would have spoken with the child so soon after we had left. Instead, I nodded, and I cocked my head toward the door.

"We have support everywhere we've stopped," I said. "The people are ready to rise. They know that the time has come to take back our destiny."

The one in the purple robes snickered and strode back to his couch. He chewed a wad of the now-cooled opium.

"Claptrap, claptrap," he said. "These peasants don't know how to till the land, much less how to fight the Chinese off of it. You're living in a fantasy world, you rabblerouser."

I reached out toward him in the purple robes with all my mind and squeezed. He grimaced, clutched his chest, and collapsed to the ground. The other two looked at me fearfully.

"Cross me at your peril," I said. "But more importantly, think of your legacy. Think of how you would be struggling against the winds of change, against the current of progress. The Mongolia of the future."

The other two nodded, and I motioned for them to sit down at their chaises. They rubbed their faces, these men in purple and blue, and they complied with quick steps in those little dainty feet. Their clean faces and delicate fingers trembled, and I had them where I wanted them.

"Let me start by saying, I think you have been remiss in your treatment of these peasants, as you call them," I said, holding up my hand to quell their protestations. "All you need to know is that these people think you have been selling them out to the Qing for the entirety of their natural lives, whether it's true or not."

Their silence told me all I need to know. I nodded. I snapped my fingers. And the one in the purple sat up from the floor.

"What the...?" he said, rubbing his bald head.

"Come," I said, patting the chaise next to me. "Let's have a conversation. You tell me what you have heard about me, and I'll tell you what happens next."

I pulled some of the Shagai fragments out of my sleeve, and I rattled them. And before I rolled them out between all of us, I smiled. I knew what the prognostication would be even before the bones hit the table.

An hour later, the door opened...and I gently pushed the three of them out into the midst of the mob. When we were in the center of the crowd, amid the gathering darkness, I again snapped my fingers in the face of the purple-robed one. He proved most compliant.

"We have decided," he said, in a wavering voice, "that we should send a petition to the Qing emperor in Beijing to inform them of our determination..."

The boos erupted from the crowd, resounding through the neighborhood, off the dirty walls and cracked masonry of the ghetto street. A petition was not enough action for the mob. They demanded the blade, and bullets. I held my hands up in the air.

"Mongols! Listen!" I shouted, silencing the throng. "You must know: this is a first step toward freedom. The princes have agreed to use their considerable influence to help us try to do this thing peacefully. At first."

"Fuck peace!" yelped an old man. "What those damned Chinese need are sharp spears up their asses!

"Yes, fuck them!" yelped his wife. "In their asses!"

The laughter was uproarious, and I joined them. But I tamped it down.

"Perhaps," I said. "But why don't we give ourselves some time to sharpen those spears to the finest point possible?"

The crowd murmured, and I knew I had them. Their rage waned. And their brains and souls hummed as all collectively dreamt of Mongolian glory.

Three hours later, we finished collecting the signatures by torchlight. These illiterate commoners filed up, one by one, making their primitive marks on a long scroll we had picked especially for the purpose. Most of the marks were mere slashes or simple Xs piled up on top of one another, seeming to signify nothing. But it was good enough. These were true actions, true words, and true intentions. The crowd brimmed with excitement, waiting to suddenly be lifted off the earth—or plunged straight down to Agharti, the golden paradise.

But that was not completely true—as I scanned the crowd, I saw one familiar face at the edge of the crowd. I did a double take. Underneath that grime was a grinning, pale European-looking visage. I stared hard at him, and he was staring hard back at me, with that hard jawline flexed to the utmost.

It was the face of that confederate of Fang. The assassin who had been tracking us. He had followed us all the way to Uliastai. With a grimace, he raised his hand.

In it was a revolver, pointed straight at me. No one else saw him, and it was lost in the jubilation all around.

Without a thought, I sprinted out from the throng and around the edge of the crowd as fast as I could. The killer had only time to cock his gun by the time I reached him.

As if the world had stopped spinning for everyone but me, I closed the distance—and I slammed into his body just as the crack of the revolver erupted near my head.

The bullet went wide, just over my shoulder and up into the night sky.

My momentum drove the would-be assassin hard into the dirt, and I felt something crack inside his body. Pandemonium erupted all around, a few people screamed, and feet stamped all around. A few strong hands were on my back suddenly, but I was busy subduing the attacker with a torrent of punches to his right orbital bone, which shattered, and a knee to his midsection. His body went limp.

But even as others lifted me off him, he suddenly revivified, springing up and taking off. I crouched down and grabbed the revolver, but just as I cocked it, aimed, and pulled the trigger, it jammed. I spat and threw it down. Even though some of the men chased him down the street, the assassin quickly made good his escape, despite his injuries. Hands were all over me, hugging me, and wailing about the attack on their savior who had narrowly escaped through his own ingenuity.

I didn't tell them I had used my mind to force that pistol to point up into the sky. I would have been too late, and dead, if I hadn't resorted to my special strength, my reserve of inner resources. But I was exhausted by the effort.

These people would not understand—they would only think I was some strange shaman. I let them believe I was just physically unstoppable. Thus, I had to seize that perfect moment of salvation and redemption.

"My friends and allies!" I growled, voice raspy, over the throng. "These rascals will never stop trying to kill our movement. But no matter what happens to me, remain resolute! We will start with our little petition, and if this too fails, we will shove it down their throats!"

"And up their asses!" yelped the old lady.

A roar erupted from the crowd, which had grown to include hundreds. Everyone lined up to make their mark on our parchment. Even the three princes seemed to lift from their poppy-clouded haze long enough to join in the general joy and merriment.

The petition crisscrossed Uliastai, and every Mongol signed it, including women and children. Even the meek ones, the younger boys and the squeamish girls, fairly lit up with power they had not known before as they pushed the sharp point of the quill into the parchment. The point of the writing implement impaled the skin of the parchment seven times, mimicking the sharp spears they clamored to thrust into the body politic of the Qing. Even the local Kazakhs signed it. Every stroke was genuine; not a mark was forged.

A few hours later, the crowd was still gathered as we loaded up the best horseman in the entire city, gave him the petition, and whipped his beast eastward toward Beijing, and the Qing emperor. A feast was held, with newly slaughtered goats and the best produce from far-off lands, embezzled from traders along the Silk Road.

We all stood around, laughing and eating around the bonfire, and some of the men did maneuvers on their horses, impressing the rest with their prowess, as the animals bucked and whinnied for our amusement. After hours, and in the darkest pit of the night, the party broke up, with the children and their mothers wandering away to their homes amid the shadows, and quickly thereafter the elders. The men held on longest, but the drunkest collapsed to the dirt. Their sober compatriots carried them home. The three princes set us up with nubile women who, we were assured, would please us. Indeed, they did not disappoint.

We awoke the next day and began our sabbatical, our wait on pins and needles for the next episode of our struggle. The petition would reach the Chinese, and there would be a reaction. We needed to wait—and see.

Days passed.

We played games with the children by day, mostly buzkashi—the Kazakh game where all were mounted, the objective to fling a goat carcass into a goal. We had great fun for hours. Even though it was a foreign sport and something I had never known back in Russia, I caught on quickly. I was glad to let the children run circles around me—until, every so often, I would crack Kublai's reins. Then we gusted like the wind, none could catch us, and we'd score every time.

At night we told stories, mostly boasts of feats of strength and heroic theft. Hearing one old woman's tale gave me chills then, and for the rest of my life.

It was about the greatness of the Mongolians and how it had been stolen, only temporarily, by the Chinese. Her boy, weakened by the privations inflicted by the Qing, fell ill and died. They left him on the hill for the birds, bya gtor.

But just the very next day his body was not there—and the last anyone saw of his mortal remains was his phantasmal form riding west across the horizon on a dark spectral horse.

"The Chinese cannot stop my boy," the old woman said. "Even now, my son, he is riding, riding. Every passing breath is a moment closer to the resurrection of the conquering khanate. Riding, riding. Riding, riding."

Even as she kept intoning that single word, these faces watched me. These simple faces sought out my counsel and wisdom, my vision of the future. And it filled me with wonder.

Riding, riding.

Something changed on the sixth night. Everything must have started with the comet, a fiery streak flying far off in the blackness, somewhere around the crimson puncture of Mars, visible to only those of us with the sharpest sight. But the strange thing is, this dot moved visibly, and detectably. It made an entire circumlocution of the sky, as Jimbe and I watched. The princes were the only others to take notice. The trio of them witnessed it, with mouths agape like baby birds waiting to be fed. Intermittently they huddled together and talked at each other in hushed whispers no one else heard. But I saw them nodding solemnly, pointing up at the astral phenomena—and finally agreeing upon something unanimously.

Those three drug addicts left in the middle of the night. No one had been told beforehand, certainly not me and my traveling companion. Nor did anyone aside from me seem to notice. Something was coming. Though there was a perfectly logical explanation to the portent wheeling around our heads so high above Uliastai, those princes had seen an omen in the phenomenon. The three narcotized idiots had come to the same conclusion, and they had not liked it.

So as the children danced, and the girls filled my cup, I kept my hand on the Colt under my deel. That night, too, I slept alone, though I heard Jimbe's frolics with two young women in his own bed in an adjoining room. I told him nothing of my suspicions. It would have been no good to have my adjutant jumping at every shadow and shout across the town.

"Why are you not eating your fill?" he asked me the next day through a mouthful of meat, gesturing at me with a ravaged goat leg he held in his hand. "Don't we need to build our strength to prepare for our push onto Urga?"

I nodded at him, but still I said nothing. He didn't persist. Instead, he pulled a young shapely woman down onto his lap, offering her a bite of his greasy drumstick.

That seventh day passed. That night I didn't sleep at all, listening to Jimbe's little erotic adventures. I meditated for the first time in months, bringing visions of Agharti flooding back into my mind's eye. My father was there, too, amid the swirling gold. His mouth moved like in a chant. But I could not make out what he was saying for the rush of the currents. And then it was morning.

Breakfast that day was quiet and slow. By the early hours, our crowd of admirers had thinned just to some of the help in the red-robed prince's mansion. Even the few who had stayed on with us dragged their feet to the table, eyes bloodshot, some yawning, all deliriously hungover. The week-long party had drawn near its end—but I wasn't aware how quickly it would truly be over.

"Water, sir?" said a thickly accented voice from behind me.

As I reached for my Colt, I felt something hard jab my neck—the cold steel of a gun barrel. I raised my hands.

"Drop the weapon. Stand up," the voice commanded.

I did so and slowly turned around.

There stood the grinning man, my nemesis, the would-be assassin.

This time he wore an eyepatch, over his shattered orbital bone. He grinned, showing perfectly white teeth from within his thick beard. On his newly lopsided face, his smile looked more horrendous than ever.

"You are not so tough now that you are without a weapon," he said, laughing a bit.

"Tougher than a man who draws a gun on someone unarmed," I countered.

His eyes narrowed, and his lip quivered. The rashness of action crossed his face—the ripple of impulse—and I knew he'd pull that trigger.

But warlike cries erupted, hysterical barking in Chinese, and suddenly there were armed troops with thick uniforms and bayoneted rifles spreading through the crowd. The Mongolians murmured, clearly ready to rise up and strike at the enemy. But these mathematics were easy to figure. Most of the Mongols of Uliastai would be mowed down, and the rest hunted down like dogs, if the rebellion came at that moment. Nothing was ready, and I cursed my existence even as I compelled the grinning maniac from pulling the trigger. It was all I could do—his will had grown stronger, too resistant now for anything else. This adversary of mine was now very much my match.

I stood slowly and raised my hands to the sky. And I spoke.

"People of Uliastai! Mongols! Stay your hand!" I hollered. "This will all be cleared up in a matter of moments, once these depraved sons of whores are convinced that we have no ill will toward them."

General laughter erupted from the multitude, and I nodded. But my mirth was short-lived, because a stocky son of Han strode up and knocked me right in the gut with the butt of his rifle, knocking the wind from my lungs. I crumpled to the ground. The crowd went dead silent. Pairs of hands grabbed me and dragged me into the town square. I struggled to breathe, just as the grinning man punched me square in the nose.

I had a vague notion we were then inside a building—it was the same house of the princes where we had been staying. But now everything was different, the opulence destroyed, that elegance smeared. The reclining chaises were overturned, all the other hookahs were smashed, and every other stick of furniture was splintered. The shining valuables and other treasures scattered around the house vanished in moments into the burlap sacks carried by the Qing dogs in military uniforms, with rifles slung leisurely over their shoulders. Half of them had cigarettes in their mouths and bottles in their hands, and the other half were diligently robbing everything in sight. I noticed all this just before someone pistol-whipped my skull, sending me into darkness.

An utter abyss enveloped me—an absence of sensation I had not felt since my illness on the Silk Road. But this time there was no Agharti, no glittering gold promises of a horizon yet to come. I sensed only the void, a pit which hovered out somewhere beyond my consciousness, unfathomable.

Water drowned me, splashing over my face and up my nostrils and within my ears. I gasped for breath, and I found it. I was awake. My limbs were tied. I blinked, and I was in a darkened room with stone walls. Musty dankness surrounded me. I smelled it even through the stagnant water soaking me. I was clearly no longer in the house of the princes.

"You are no longer in the house of the princes," said a voice.

Following the voice to my left, I saw my enemy. He had his eyepatch off, and he was gingerly fingering his naked eye socket. The grin flinched with each pang of pain. I forced myself to smile back at him, and I spat out the salty blood filling my mouth.

"Wherever we are, it's unfortunate your ugly face came with us," I said.

My nemesis jumped to his feet and ran toward me. Just as I reached out with all my willpower, he reached into his holster, produced his pistol, and struck me across the face with his barrel. But it was a glancing blow, as my power of will kept most of the force of his arm back. And I strained to crush him with my mind.

His body jolted. His raised hand shook, as he tried to lower it. He staggered backward three steps. His knees buckled, and he fell to the ground. And as his eyes bulged up toward the dark ceiling, his pistol slowly raised, and the barrel angled until the muzzle was pointed directly at his temple. His neck strained, and his free right hand shook as it struggled to wrench free the death grip on the weapon in his left. But his finger quivered on the trigger, ready to pull.

A door flew open behind him, sending in light throughout the dungeon. Two Mongols, lamas in shining bright deels, appeared at the door. Distracted, my focus relented on my tormentor, who collapsed to the ground with the exertion. But he promptly grabbed the gun and aimed it again at my head from his place on the ground. My two countrymen rushed forward, grabbed his hands, and yanked the gun away. They shoved him to the far end of the room away from me. Relieved, I relaxed my force, and slumped in my bonds. I was thoroughly spent.

"You will not be ready for me the next time you see me, false prophet!" shouted my enemy, as they pushed him out of the room and swung the heavy door shut, enfolding the room in darkness once again.

I laughed out loud.

"See you in the afterlife, bandit!" I shouted. I closed my eyes and breathed out hard and slow. I opened my eyes, and there were the two lamas. They stared down at me, with arms folded. One wore blue, and the other red. But they made no movements. They didn't even blink. Their faces were cragged. Both were old, triple my age, and their very flesh seemed prepped for the grave. I nodded at them and tugged at the hands behind my back.

"Brothers," I said. "I could use a little help here."

They stared down at me, then glanced at each other. Nodding, they strode forward, their deels swinging together like they were a single four-legged creature approaching.

"We have understood that you have been trying to foment revolution," said the one on the left, in blue.

"To try and force an idiotic and doomed uprising," said the red-sashed one.

I relaxed my straining limbs and shook my head. This was clearly something more than a rescue operation. I had to tread carefully—and I sensed that my powers of mind would be useless against these trained holy men.

"I only want what the people want," I said. "You have seen yourself how they struggle just to survive."

But as they drew ever closer, I identified that look of overwhelming impatience in their relaxed brows, the slow roll of their eyes over me. It was a mercenary gaze, and not holy in the slightest. These were the roughest lamas imaginable. They stopped a foot away from me, and I could see their unshaven faces tighten.

"You're with them," I said.

Both shook their heads with barely perceptible, but coordinated, movements. The one in red took a deep breath, sounding for all its worth like the wind blowing across the steppe on an overcast day.

"You must realize, son, that we have waited a long time to be able to plant the seeds of our freedom," said the one in blue.

"This fool will ruin everything we've built up over years," the other hissed.

They broke apart, pacing around me, circling the chair. My head spun as these two inscrutable Mongols went around and around.

"You're saying you had a plan for independence…?" I started to say, but they both scoffed.

"You have stumbled into a situation you know nothing about," said the blue one. "And you have jeopardized years of planning."

"This fellow is a complete moron, probably a stooge sent by Russia to bungle everything from within," said the one in red, continuing to talk as if I were not there. "Perhaps we should throw our fates in with the Khenbish Khan instead."

The two of them sat on the floor, and assumed meditation poses. Within moments, their eyes fluttered up in their sockets, and their bodies lifted a few inches off the floor of the cell. No ordinary ascetics were these. Their powers were easily stronger than my own. They had merely transported themselves elsewhere with a breath.

I meditated too, and a few minutes later I was traveling high through the stratosphere, then deep into the stone of inner Earth, in the direction of Agharti. And from somewhere off in the ether, I heard the two monks discussing something, seemingly unaware of my presence. Still sailing through the currents, I listened to their words. Finally, I glanced to my left, and there the essences of the holy men hovered on golden planks which floated along inexorably. They were unaware of me amid their in-depth talk.

"Do you truly think he is a stooge, as you said?" said the blue one.

"I think he is a mongrel dog from Russia, the Caspian basin," said the one in red. "The cowards from the other side of the river who fled the Han, rather than fight and suffer alongside us, all those years ago. For centuries they hid in exile from their true destiny."

"Perhaps," said the calmer one.

Their eyes were lit with a strange, many-colored light. I closed my eyes and reached out in the distance between us, drifting closer the better to hear them. The ether around them was golden, a flaxen island amid the vast emptiness of black on either side. One of them scoffed.

"It seems he has forced the issue," said the one in blue.

"He has, the idiot," said the red one. "And you know what that means."

"Yes."

I stirred myself from the trance, snapping back through time and space back into my corporeal body like the crack of a whip. The two of them still floated in front of me, and I struggled to free myself from my bonds. Even as they drifted back to earth and stirred to consciousness I strained vainly against the ropes.

These two had only one option, I knew…they were going to take the opportunity to eliminate a threat to their plans. With a rising sense of horror in my chest, they lowered back to the ground, and their eyes slowly opened. They rose to their feet and stared at me. My limbs fell slack, still lashed immobile. It was over.

"Do whatever you need to do, brothers," I said, pride souring every syllable. "There are things greater than us, even for this reincarnation of Amursanaa. I will do better next time around."

They stared at one another with puzzled faces. The one in red robes circled around me. I waited for a blade at my neck, or the blast at the base of my skull.

But instead, I felt a slicing around my wrists—and the bonds loosened. I shook them free, and raised my hands in front of me, rubbing the blood back into circulation. Then they fell loose around my ankles, and I kicked them free, too. I stood. The monks stood to either side. I reached into my deel, and I felt for my Colt. To my surprise, it was there.

"There won't be any need for that," said the blue monk, coolly. "You are free to go."

He nodded at me. I turned around, and the hot-headed one in red sheathed his shining blade with a tight nod of disapproval.

"You can continue your insane quest, though nothing good will come of it," he said, all the anger drained from his voice. The blade vanished under his deel—and out came a small bottle.

"You will need to organize better next time," said the calmer one in front of me. "Whichever Year of the Dragon you choose—whether it's this one, or the next, or the one after that."

"Or the one after that."

"Just realize: the eternal blue sky is all that lasts forever."

"It's all that matters."

The two of them went to the opposite side of the basement, and they again sat on the floor, facing the crude stone wall, meditating again. The one in red held the bottle out, and shook some pills into his palm, and then the hand of his compatriot. I turned away and searched the dungeon's darkness for the doorway. I found it.

I was just mounting the staircase when I heard the thundering footsteps along the floor above. I fingered my Colt, momentarily deciding, and then I melted into the shadows of an alcove at the landing before the ground floor. I sank deeper into the black, completely hidden from the approaching bootsteps. But then I bumped into something soft. I grappled with it.

"Help!" came the squeaky voice just before I clamped my hand over the person's mouth.

But even as I did so, I knew it was Jimbe, being ever the jumpy coward. I pushed him flush against the wall.

"Silence," I hissed. "We may be able to escape if we just…wait."

The steps thundered ever closer over the floorboards, closing toward the stairs.

"I was just about to come and liberate you!" whispered Jimbe.

I patted his head with my free hand for a second, then again covered his mouth—just as the troops trudged down the flimsy steps. They passed us. We watched from the shadows, breathing slowly. Russian, and not Chinese, soldiers rushed past. I heard Jimbe's breath catch in his chest, and I gently tapped his nose with the barrel of my Colt, silencing him still.

Muffled footsteps shuffled across the dirt floor of the basement below. Shouts in Russian echoed up the stairwell.

"The two silly bastards poisoned themselves!" hollered a voice. "They're dead!"

"Well then," shouted another voice, this one from up above us. "Put a bullet in each, to be sure. Then collect the bodies. We'll report back to the administrator we've achieved the objective."

I knew the voice as my would-be assassin, the monocular wonder. I gritted my teeth. Two quick shots echoed out below.

My hand tensed on the Colt, and I felt the urge to charge up the stairs and empty the entire magazine at the fool. But I held my hand, and we waited. Jimbe gasped for air.

The limp bodies of the two lamas were hauled out like leaking sacks of grain by the rough hands of the Russians. We watched as both of the corpses went by, their slackened faces with frothing poisoned mouths agape passing in a moment. The footsteps receded into the distance. More Russian talk above, this indistinguishable from the hoots and cheers and stomping feet of the apparent mob above. Jimbe trembled.

"They were going to execute the princes, if they hadn't run away first," I whispered. "They would have killed us, too. But the monks' deaths are enough to sate them. At least we can hope. They may not know we're still here."

Just then we heard a bell. It was a tiny bell, the orderly tinkling so unlike the singing bowl's wandering through space and time. It was like an awakening from an eternal dream, and at that moment, I can now admit, fear tickled at my collar and my heart was near to bursting.

"And you two hiding on the stairs," called out my nemesis. "You can come out of there and join us. We won't kill you, probably. At least I can assure you, it's not part of the official orders from Moscow."

We did not voluntarily emerge from our hiding spot, of course—despite Jimbe's idiotic attempts to give himself up. I had to pistol-whip him to prevent his running out and falling at their feet and begging for mercy. I crouched and waited for them to come and drag me out.

Their siege took the better part of an hour, and even when they took us, I managed to shoot two in the gut. They ended up tossing in a burning torch. Cursing, knowing I had been out-strategized, I dragged Jimbe's unconscious body out quickly. They bull rushed me all at once. Despite my strongest push of mental will, and the fiercest resistance I could muster, the platoon knocked me to my knees and heaved me at the feet of the one-eyed bastard.

"Our orders said not to kill you," he said, towering over me, still grinning that mad smile, scratching at the eyepatch fabric. "But they did not preclude certain...liberties."

He clapped a single time, with a sharp report. And they took me away.

The rest is not worth talking about. They took turns abusing me with fists and feet in the worst ways imaginable. Jimbe remained unconscious during the whole thing, but he suffered much the same fate.

Amid much laughter and shattered bottles of wine, we were thrown back down the same cell where the unfortunate monks had offed themselves. Indeed, the bloody stains where they had vomited up their foaming poisoned organs still glistened in the light of several wall torches. I lay face-down as I contemplated our fate, Jimbe and I.

To have come so far across Asia, in both directions and with so much promise on the horizon—but to have it end this way—was an ending I refused to accept.

Still, I seriously considered what my next existence would be. Would I come back as yet another exiled Mongol, trying to make his way back to the homeland, to begin the struggle where I had left off in this abortive life? Might I start off as a baby in Uliastai, on the steppe, being weaned on the legends and culture from the start?

Or would I slide backward—would I instead be a Chinese peasant whose ineptitude would, in an obverse way, assist my Mongol brothers' struggle against the yoke? Considering how foolishly I had steered this latest life, I could make a confident prediction it would be this final fate; I would be punished through my own incompetence, the squandering of heaven's gifts of chance. Frittering away such opportunities would never be smiled upon by the universe. I sat against the wall, knees drawn up, my head down, and I slept, without even the pretense of meditating. The darkness swallowed me.

A rough hand awoke me. It was more Russians. They dragged me out. They took Jimbe, too. I was carried with my hands clasped behind me though no handcuffs were affixed to my wrists, preparing myself for the firing squad I was sure waited ahead.

But when I saw no sign of the eye-patched enemy of mine…at that moment I realized this was another thing entirely. The powers that be had made their statement; they had laid me low. They would no more execute me and my assistant than they would crush two ants scrambling across the bricks of a palace courtyard.

Looking into the eyes of the soldiers, these professionals compared to the brigands who had torn through the princes' house, I finally understood. They had simply wanted to crush an upstart rebellion. By forcing the suicides of two respected holy men, they had cowed the local populace. Word would spread: the second coming of Amursanaa had been disgraced.

They dragged me to a jail in the middle of Uliastai. The professional Russian mercenaries threw me into a cell, where Jimbe cowered in a corner.

Immediately after they locked the door after us, and I heard their footsteps retreat back down the hallway, I sprang up from the seat and began rifling through the belongings they'd thrown in with us—all we had collected upon our trek across of half of Asia: a few blankets, my passport, a few tinkling Colt cartridges, the folded tent, a half-eaten roasted goat leg. But no firearms, or my green-sheathed blade.

"What the hell are you doing?" said Jimbe, parting his hands to reveal a wet face, still crinkled with tears of pain and rage.

"Dry your tears my friend, because we have work to do," I said, tossing him the pungent meat.

I exclaimed as my hand closed over the treasure I had sought: the golden vajra. I closed my eyes and squeezed it in my palm.

"What do you have?" he said, wiping his cheeks with his dirty sleeve. He took a big somber bite of the meat.

"This," I said, walking over to him, "is the promise we have made to our people. And we still have it. As long as you keep this, I will return. And in this sign, we will conquer. You must hide it however best you can, and once you get back to your village, wait for the signal."

I took his hand and pressed it into his wet fingers, closing them around it tightly. His mouth hung open, agape, as he slowly opened his hand to reveal the glittering gold of the vajra.

"Bullshit..." he said, rising, his face contorting with despair.

But at that moment, the Russians burst through the door and grabbed me, like thieves pillaging the last treasures from a castle. As I was dragged away, I had only a moment to impart my wisdom.

"The Year of the Dragon!" I hollered. "Never forget, Jimbe!"

With a jab in the arm, they drugged me with some concoction that made the next few days pass by in a blur. I saw only vague tints of gold behind my eyelids, and I knew that I was not exactly in the world, but I also knew that I didn't know anything else.

I felt the sting between my legs. That's all it was, at first—a sting, and nothing more.

CHAPTER 13
DOWN AND OUT IN ASTRAKHAN

The jostling and the shouts and the clanking metals. The wind whistling by. And the odors—oh, the odors, the cattle and manure and vomit all mingling in a stew of putrefaction…

The hallmarks of the long, humiliating kidnapping back to exile.

I was in a kind of stasis, unable to rouse myself for even a moment of lasting coherence, beyond a paralyzing despair over my life so far, and my short pointless years to come. I was in a compartment, and unable to move. The back of another wagon, like the one I'd been tucked into as an ill and delirious child heading east. But I was an ill and delirious man as I was spirited west—back the way I had come all those years before.

Even then, in my fog of narcotic haze, I sensed a part of me was…missing.

And I felt tragic, like a true reincarnation of one of our Mongolian martyrs. The physical pain only seeped in with the cooler nights, the darkness.

The excruciating pain wracked my lower half. Gradually, over days, sensation returned to my extremities. But I wished it had never come back at all. Only pain seared through the very core of my being every time I moved my legs. As I drifted like a leaf along the wind of my subconsciousness, it only got worse. What seemed like moments were likely days or weeks. And as I gradually roused from my stupor, I was confronted with my horrifying new reality, as my hand drifted down my sweaty chest, across my abdomen, and down to my crotch.

Nothing was there.

I had no cock.

I felt around frantically, but it only made the inflamed tissue burn like the hottest fire on Earth. The shock of the pain and the discovery together dropped me into utter darkness, removed even from the bouncing of that damned cart heading west.

The cart jarred, tipping me sideways, my head thumping hard on the window of the carriage. The shade over the window whipped me across the face. The waking relief of a nightmare's end washed over me—but ended abruptly as I shifted in my seat and felt the pain again surge. Despite my druggy haze, I had not been hallucinating. I had suffered the twin indignities: of the bloody scars that stood in place of my manhood…and the slow and painful exile back to the hateful deserts of southern Russia.

Through the window, I watched a massive dirty lake spread alongside the road for as far as the eye could see. It was the sickle-shaped monstrosity of Lake Balkhash—a name I would not yet know for many years. The overpowering smell—a pungent resin from out of nowhere—made me sick to my stomach, and I vomited for long stretches, out the side of the cart. I would later find out the odor was the disgusting asafoetida tree of Kazakhstan.

I didn't know many things at that time. Truly, I had much yet to learn. Two riders kept the carriage moving during daylight, and we mostly rested at night. They were armed buffoons, easy pickings if I was at full strength. But my will had been drained—along with most of my precious blood—in that struggle and mutilation back east. I put up no fight, along hundreds and then thousands of versts. I was less of a man than I had ever been.

We arrived in Astrakhan in the fall—not that it mattered much in that hellish place where the putrid air hangs lukewarm on the flesh, even in the winter. I was imprisoned in a dark apartment building where the filthy window shutters did not open. The warped glass allowed only the slightest peek of the outside world. It had a musty smell mingling the odors of all those convalescents who had died before. Three floors, seventeen rooms, and crooked floorboards—everything was off-kilter, and a chaos of neglect reigned. The smell of rotten food always hung between the second and third floors leading to my new apartment. The cockroaches were brazen, daring even in the daylight to confront the residents in the middle of the hallways. Occasionally, as a feeling crept along the skin, one got the sense it was the people, and not the bugs, who were the true transients in that place. The vermin belonged.

The courtyard, a bullseye of dirt naked to the sky at the heart of the hovel, was the place I wasted the next weeks and years to come.

There was no chance of departure or escape, you see. I saw the Czar's secret police in the other windows all along Pestelya Street. These shadows smoked pipes, they paced back and forth behind the glazed windowpanes. But always, they watched.

From that courtyard within, I focused on the sky. First, through the physical pain. Then, as my wounds healed, through the rage of a life derailed. And finally, it was through the boredom of days I watched passing by the angles of sunlight on the cracked dirt of the ground. Overhead the clouds were always sparse and shaped like nothing at all. I dreamt of nothing. Agharti and Mongolia were in another universe entirely.

I just was. And I remained so.

Sometimes I cursed at the guiding voice which had abandoned me to that cruel fate. How had my fakir father not warned me of the evils which had been surrounding me?

The courtyard was bare except for a table and three chairs. The other two were always empty. Dead stumps of shrubs protruded stubbornly from the ground up to a cloudless sky that never dropped rain. I always kicked one or another of these little stubs. None of them ever budged. Instead, I used them as uncomfortable foot stools, and I had relative peace.

Except for the goat.

The goat was tied to the biggest of the stumps, a dead tree that stood as tall as me. But the beast was tied with such a long rope it went anywhere it pleased inside the courtyard. It bayed all day, to the point that its hoarse alto croaking became as natural a part of the day as my breath, as the slow and indeliberate beat of my heart. It had no owner. It just belonged to the place. I never saw it eating or drinking. It sported big pendulous testicles that swayed as it walked, like soundless bells. Its baying was almost always followed by it mounting one of the chairs or one of the splintered stumps, rubbing a massive erection on its target. Occasionally it fucked these inanimate objects with enough force that, when it dismounted, left its own blood trail in the dirt. But it never seemed to mind. Once—only once, in my first week of exile—it mounted my knee. At first, I thought of swatting it away, but then I refocused my attention on the sky and waited. After a minute, the goat hopped off, snorted with disdain, bayed at the filthy brick walls, and then mounted one of the smaller stumps in the courtyard. And after completion there, he sauntered off, leaving a trail of crimson on the way to his corner, where he lay down in the dirt. My leg, it seems, was not a good sexual target. We had an understanding.

The days passed. I cannot tell you exactly how many. I can tell you seasons marched, that warm sunny days were followed by a brisk snap of the autumn wind, intermittent snows, and back into the spring. Sweat on my brow gave way to my breath icing in the air in front of my eyes within moments of one another. Nothing bloomed in that courtyard. People died and were carried out of the building by the Czar's secret police, and others arrived. No babies were born. All my fellow residents were invalids and cripples. I was the only one not at the brink of death. And yet in those days I yearned for the end more than anyone else on the whole Earth, let alone that building.

My next-door neighbor was a Russian man, a huge swarthy drunk named Boris who fell, slid, and crawled partway down the stairs every day at the crack of noon to get the mail in the lobby. The invalid would ascend the flights up on elbows and knees like a spider with only five legs, stair by excruciating stair, breath heavy, until he reached the top of the tiny mountain. Invariably, he slid letters under each door along the way, like he was the building's resident postman. I, of course, never received anything, with my illiterate parents long gone and my exile effectively having cut me off from both the place of my birth and the movement I had created. Of course, the Czar's secret police would have confiscated any letters anyway.

During Boris' epic journeys up and down the stairs, filled with agony and ecstasy in intervals lasting minutes, I bid him good afternoon on my way to fix tea, stepping carefully around his struggling form, and I'd meet him again on the way down. Sometimes I would go for two cups of tea in the time it took him to make the round trip. Occasionally he asked me for a hit of vodka to fortify him on his odyssey, and I would bring one of the bottles from his room and lower it to his distended lips like a mother would offer a breast to her baby, and he would suckle a few mouthfuls with relish. Then he'd wave me away, and I'd return the bottle to whatever dark nook of his lair from which I had retrieved it.

While I was in there, I noted the Tula revolver on the nightstand, a pale Russian imitation of my long-lost Colt. From the bullets scattered across the floor, I bent down, and picked one up, and stuffed it in the pocket of my robe. You may not always need a gun, but you never know when a bullet may come in handy. That is a fact of this life.

But despite my ministrations, Boris went slower and slower, groaning in pain and suffering, with erratic breaths, as time ground on. And I felt I must intervene—if for nothing else so I could at last have some peace in the courtyard. Stepping around his contorting body on those stairs had become a real hassle. His suffering broke me out of my reveries of nothingness, yanking me back to awareness of the air I breathed, and my thoughts, and this life in which I was still mired.

I had to do something.

One day, I sat in my usual spot in the courtyard, with the pile of the building's mail on my lap. That day Boris moved slower than ever before, each step driving a howl of pain from deep within his tortured frame. With a knife, I carefully carved Boris' name into the bullet I had taken from his room. At last, he reached the threshold where he was visible. He did not have much life left in him.

"Lama—good morning, sir—could I trouble you for—" he said.

But he squeaked as I grabbed his arms and dragged him into the courtyard. I hauled him up and set his massively pudgy body in my usual chair. I stuffed the stupid mound of mail in his mouth before he could get a word in edgewise. I held the bullet up in front of his face.

"Don't move a muscle, Boris," I said, holding up a finger. "I'll end your misery in just a moment."

The terror that lit up his eyes brought me half a thrill. But I could not bring myself to savor it. I turned and hustled out of there, striding up the steps to his room, where I grabbed his gun. Back downstairs, as I neared the threshold and emerged from the shadows into the threshold of the courtyard, I saw Boris' mouth open in utter terror, eyes boggling at the sight of his own gun in my hand. I only nodded at him, and I did not stop on my way to the front door.

And for the first time in however many weeks or years, I again emerged on the outside, onto Pestelya Street, Astrakhan, Russian Empire, continent of Asia, planet Earth, spinning and wheeling once more around the sun. To my surprise, the Czar's secret police were nowhere to be seen...but I knew they were watching from some window or alleyway. I did not care—my errand would be quick. They could arrest me afterward, for all I cared.

I had the perfect cure for Boris. I strode up to the nearest hitching post, and I saw a horse that didn't look too unlike my long-lost Chingis, though it was a different color, a red hue like an angry dawn. I swung my leg up and mounted the beast, and I leaned deep into its mane. Sitting bareback for the first time since parts of my anatomy had been removed was a strange sensation indeed.

"Let's go for a little ride, friend. It won't be too far," I said, driving my heels into its ribs.

And we were off, a little too fast at first, with my hips swaying almost off the back of the animal in the first hundred yards. But riding was something a true Mongol never forgets, once you have learned right. I'd been a horseman of the highest caliber since I was a boy, so I straightened out quickly and drove the steed on ever faster, out and down the neighborhood, along the lugubrious Volga, and then to the very outskirts of town. I rode into the wastes, the barren terrain, the dead Earth, until desolation surrounded me.

After a few versts more, I pulled up on the horse's neck, and I turned him around. The city was nearly out of sight on the horizon. I dug my heels into the horse's flank, as I made my preparations. I pulled out the revolver and the carefully inscribed 'Boris' bullet, and I loaded the weapon.

I aimed the gun past the crimson horse's head, in the direction of the town. Using the sun as guide, I aimed in the direction of Pestelya Street—in the direction of where Boris lay cringing in the courtyard, sobbing with still-smoldering terror of the crazy neighbor who'd stolen his gun.

I squinted down the iron sight, and with stillness of breath and heart, pulled the trigger.

The badly built Russian firearm roared across the river valley. The horse bucked in panic, and I clutched onto his neck as he took off to the east. Wild, swinging abandon in his gallop, terror blasted out of each breath as he sprinted at top speed. He was fast, the ground blurred. My heart beat hard, in time with his own as I clutched to his back and pressed the warm barrel of the gun against his chest, as one and then two versts passed. My heels dug into his reddened flanks, and I squeezed with my fingers into his neck. After another half a verst, he slowed to a trot. I breathed into his mane, and I whispered into his ear as we together felt the breeze of the Volga delta blow into our watery eyes.

"Easy now, boy," I said.

At last, I pulled up on his neck, and he stopped. With slow and deliberate hands, I turned him around, and we slowly made our way back toward the city. I realized I no longer had pain while riding. Even the chafing I had once felt whenever riding bareback was gone. There was less of me to feel the trail, and the wounds left in its place had healed. This was the one advantage of being half a man, I supposed.

I inhaled the wind and basked in the sky (even that drab Russian sky), and I knew I had missed the freedom of just…being. Existing on one's own terms, deciding how and where to take a breath—and even whether to take another one at all.

I tried to tell this crimson horse my exhilaration, my rediscovered joy.

"Friend, you have no idea how much I have missed the space to talk freely, and the ears that will listen to me," I said. "My destiny may not be Mongolia, but I am certain of one thing: it is to be free of chains and bars and locked rooms. To move through space."

I stroked his dark-streaked mane.

"My fate is to remake the greatest empire of the steppe, or to die trying," I said, knowing I needed only myself as the audience for such a proclamation. This horse with no name did not care like dear Chingis would have.

By this time, we had returned to the outskirts of the city. The women washing their clothes in tubs, and the dirty-faced riffraff on the street watched me saunter by on the red pony, spinning the empty revolver on my trigger finger like an American cowboy. On the streetcorner nearest the invalid home, several of the Czar's policemen approached, but I held up my hand, freezing them in their tracks. I made it the final few yards to the hitching post, and I dismounted and tied up the crimson animal. I held up my finger, and the policemen stopped.

"No need to arrest me. I return willingly. Please give this horse's owner my regards," I said. "It is a true beast and has served me well."

I turned and went into my building—and they slammed the door behind and turned the key. I had not made it more than three steps within when I was tackled by a huge form, squeezing me around my midsection. I had barely a chance to take a breath, and I was nearly knocked out by the reek of vodka and sweat and piss. It was Boris, and he was sobbing into my chest.

"Lama, I can walk!" he bellowed, hysterically crying.

I went limp in his arms and patted him on the shoulder. He lifted me, seeming to test his own strength, and when he found he could hoist me easily, he set me down and started crying more with the discovery of his returned powers, the end of his infirmities. I walked him, with my arm around his shoulder, back to the courtyard. I helped him down into one of the seats. He held his face in his hands, and I went up to my garret and made two cups of tea. When I returned, he sprung from his chair at the sound of the cups rattling in my hand, and he grabbed one in his huge hands and smiled.

"The devil it was, to be crippled," he said, his beefy fingers cradling the delicate ceramic. "You know I was a mountaineer—one of the kingdom's best explorers? The Czar personally pinned medals on me. Twice."

"I did not know that, Boris," I said. "Fascinating."

He reclined in the chair, and I sat on a nearby flat stump. The goat came by, clanking that dull bell and swinging those big balls. It came within a foot of the steaming cup of tea in front of my face, stupidly chewing its cud. It almost looked as if it was about to start talking to me. I pursed my lips and blew in his face, and the animal scowled, turned away and went to the other side of the courtyard.

For minutes, the dreamy look slackened Boris' face, and he leaned back in the chair, hands behind his head, eyes up at the sky. He looked like a man half the age of the one who had struggled each day in the quest up and down the stairs to retrieve the mail. He leaned forward, rubbing his temples. His look was very serious.

"I'm not one to ask questions, to seek out the whys and wherefores about the mysteries of life," he said, pointing up at his head. "But I have to ask—how did you do it?"

"How did I do what?"

"Cure me. Make me walk. Take the pain away. All of it."

"Oh—that," I said, setting the cup and saucer aside on the ground, where the goat promptly trotted over and slurped the dregs of the tea. "That was just a little gun magic."

"Ah, gun magic," Boris said, nodding, seeming to understand. But then his brow wrinkled. "What is gun magic?"

"Gun magic is a great tradition of the Mongolians on the steppe, as I learned it in Tibet from Chinese monks," I said. "Basically, you take a gun, and you write the intended disease target on a bullet. Then you fire the bullet at the person's illness."

Boris nodded dumbly.

"But won't that kill the person?"

I smiled.

"Not if you're a few versts away, it won't," I said. "The physical bullet only goes so far. The magic of the shot, its intent, continues on to the target—the person's disease. Do you understand?"

After a moment, the concept sunk into Boris' thick skull, and he was hooting and hollering all over again in that courtyard we shared. Truly, he was quite a physical specimen again. This mountain climber and august hero of the Russian Empire picked me up and flung me around like a rag doll in his elation.

Needless to say, the mail arrived early every day from then on. In fact, after the third day, Boris took to walking the two versts down to the post office to pick the mail up himself at dawn, instead of waiting for the postman to arrive in the afternoon. The Czar's secret police did not seem to care. He whistled and had a fair trot to his step like that of a teenager on his way out on a date with the prettiest girl from the village. Life had been renewed; happiness and energy exuded from his every movement.

It became exhausting for me. Boris was everywhere at once, with a quip and a click of his heels. One warm sunny day I opted to stay in the cool dark of my room. But Boris burst in, and over my protestations he felt at my forehead for a fever. He brought me a cup of tea and nursed me back to health, even though I only wanted to die. On rare days he went off into the city and gossiped among his old colleagues in the veterans' circles for news beyond Astrakhan, beyond the Volga. Invariably, it was old wives' tales: about the railroad stretching civilization across Siberia; crazed revolutionaries in the Russian cities who plotted the total overthrow of all world governments; and a mad monk, a sex maniac with an enormous cock, who had taken up residence in the Czarina's bed in her St. Petersburg palace. He told the tales with relish. There was something unflappable about this mountaineer Boris once his physical abilities had returned.

One day, Boris saved my life.

Two months after my gun-magic cure, Boris went out at the crack of dawn. I heard him go, and I went to the lobby and watched him make his foray out and down the street through a crack in the front door. Good, I told myself, at least I will have some peace for the next hour or so. But I did not close the door after him. And just as soon as I saw him disappear around the streetcorner, a thin hand suddenly appeared in the crack, and rapped against the door, rattling my slumber. I drew back, the door creaked open, and a person appeared.

A flamboyant merchant stood there. This diminutive man of business looked like nothing so much as a woman of pleasure, with high heels bringing him just up to my shoulder. He had a painted face, with rouged cheeks and darkened accents around the eyes. His high voice was effeminate, and he sashayed with a finger outstretched, which he pointed at me. At each silk-covered shoulder was one of the Czar's secret police.

His words sounded like gibberish. Despite growing up on the banks of the Volga, Russian has always been a slow puzzle to me, each sentence like a difficult knot in a tough rope. But after a minute, as the Czar's secret police's stern faces came closer, their voices growing in insistence, I started to understand.

The merchant was accusing me of being a horse thief—of branding his property and using it for a religious ritual. It was all very strange. I almost had to laugh, considering the elaborate details he had concocted for this story. But then I came to realize the seriousness of the allegation.

"...and this man had the nerve to just take my poor horse out on an expedition beyond the city walls. That time he returned the beast, one of my best, but he has since taken it for good from its hitching post outside..."

The cops narrowed their eyes and took another step forward. Their hands were at their belts, though not yet at their gun holsters. I stepped back, and held up my hands, showing them they had nothing to fear from me. In truth, they did not— at that moment. I was resolved never to engage in the violence that had landed me back in Astrakhan in the first place.

But they drew their sidearms as they approached. No hatred was in their eyes—just a kind of boredom, a cruel curiosity like a predator watching its prey through the leaves. And this is precisely why fear hit my heart for the first time since I was hiding on those Mongolian stairs with my hand over Jimbe's mouth. Instinctively I reached out for their minds with all the might of my willpower.

But they didn't even break stride, as they kept coming at me. I flinched; I must have completely missed my target. I bore down and focused again and reached out to just the one on the right. Even as both of them grabbed my arms and stuck their pistols into my ribcage, the realization finally hit me: I had spent so long in that courtyard staring aimlessly up at the sky, the might of my mind had atrophied as much as the muscles of my body. Even as I tried to shake off these slack-jawed provincial lackeys, their physical grip on me was like iron. I was utterly powerless, for the first time since I was a sick and delirious little boy being carted toward my destiny.

"You should beat some remunerations out of him," said the dandy merchant, tittering with a coquettish hand over his rouged mouth. "Then you can throw him in jail for all I care."

But then his eyes grew wide, and his hands dropped. He saw something behind the three of us. The two policemen noticed it too late.

Because by then Boris had grabbed both of them by the scruff of their necks. The two swung wildly, trying to point their guns. It was too late; in one gigantic heave, Boris' massive hands smashed their two skulls together, which made a sickening crack, like two thick eggs. The policemen dropped to the floor, and one convulsed in his final throes, the other stone dead. I snatched the guns out of the dead men's hands and pointed them at the merchant.

"Do you know this character, Boris?" I asked. "This man has accused me of stealing his horse. Can you tell him that I have never taken his horse?"

"I didn't mean to hurt them bad," Boris said, shaking his head sadly, looking down at his hands. "I just forgot how strong I was…I am."

"Boris, what's done is done," I said. "Do you know this man?"

"Sure, I guess," Boris said, shaking his head. "It's Vasily, the sheepskin seller, ruby cutter, and whoremaster. He is also a thief. But if we're being totally honest, you did take the horse the one time to cure me."

I grimaced at him, waving the pistols irritably.

"But yes," Boris said, seeming to take a cue, smiling. "The other times I stole the horse, to be totally honest."

"Aha!" hollered the merchant, waving his finger. "You admit your crime!"

But Boris grabbed his protruding digit in one of his huge bear paws, and twisted, sending the frail merchant down to the ground, wailing.

"I would not get so possessive of your beast, Vasily," said Boris, twisting just a bit more, eliciting a higher howl of pain from the man of business. "I was only borrowing it, and you know it."

"And you should know," I added, "that the local authorities are going to consider you as responsible for the deaths of the two policemen as we are."

Boris released his hands, and the trader pulled his throbbing fingers in close to his chest. He groaned and shook his head.

"They would never think that I would do something like that. I am the secretary of the Chamber of Commerce," said this Vasily. "The regional office knows I am a sound supporter and abhor violence."

"They will think that, until we implicate you," I said. "I can tell a convincing story of how you led the Czar's secret police to us, so we could kill and rob them. And are you really so confident that they won't just lump your degenerate self with the two of us? Are you absolutely sure that someone would intercede on your behalf?"

A look of hurt that was beyond the physical pain flickered across the wayward merchant's face. Boris picked him up by the scruff of his neck and put him on his feet. The salesman's eyes darted from my large friend to me, and back again.

"What are you suggesting?" he said.

I glanced at Boris, and he shrugged, clearly without an idea.

The fakir's voice visited me again, for the first time in years, at that moment. It vibrated through my very soul.

Take these two and head east once more, it said. *Siberia is the only way. You must escape this living death in Astrakhan. Now is your chance. The Czar's secret police are not watching right at this moment.*

"I suggest we cover these bodies in the basement with some heavy blankets," I said, without missing a beat. "Then we get on a couple of your horses, Vasily, and we go to Siberia. We take all the gold we can carry."

The merchant shivered, like he could already feel the blast of icy winds from the north freezing his wobbly spine.

"Siberia…" he said, moaning.

"A good plan!" said Boris, who clapped his hands and trotted up the stairs. "I'll grab my things. I'll be ready in a few minutes. I will ride the red one."

Vasily and I waited in silence for a few more moments. Finally, he glanced up at me.

"You know—I wouldn't tell anyone about what happened here. We could just go our separate ways," he said. "I'd keep the secret for the rest of my days."

"Those days would be few," I said. "Because while you may think I'm bluffing, the authorities would rather just hang you, to make a tidy solution of a messy situation. Especially considering your evident…persuasion. If I'm understanding you correctly."

Tears sprung to his eyes.

"But wouldn't you vouch for me, tell them I'm innocent?" he said, like a child.

I laughed in his face.

"No one cares. Everyone is guilty in this life," I said.

I said my goodbyes to the damned goat and walked out. Nothing was left behind upstairs anyway, other than years of atrophy and want.

After taking the red stallion and two more horses from the merchant's stables—we had to convince his live-in manservant Artyom this was a short trip, and he wasn't satisfied until Vasily had given him a tender kiss and assured him with the sweetest lies that he would be back by sundown—we set out. We didn't make it more than a few versts before we had to make camp. We stowed our provisions and packs and steeds on a wooded ridge. Vasily trembled. Boris and I glanced at one another; I shook my head, but Boris only shrugged.

Vasily was an excitable man, with his perfumes and adornments and silk finery. Outside of the city he was like a fish out of water, a dandy domesticated pet thrust into the wild. He had brought a thick fur coat along with him, and as the sun disappeared to the west, he threw it over his slight shoulders and sat slumped next to the fire we built nearest to him. As the stars cycled by overhead, Boris and I discussed the next steps for survival. But I let him do most of the talking—I knew it was better if I could guide this gentle but simple giant to the next correct conclusion, instead of directly willing him to my stance. At that point, I knew my powers of persuasion and will were not available to me. I needed to be crafty. So I asked him about his hopes and dreams.

"I just want to be independent, free to pursue all the things I've never gotten to try," said Boris, laying with his head on the dirt. "I don't care where it is, Georgia or in Siberia or the Ukraine, or even China. I just want to farm, and have my own land, and be able to defend myself against my enemies."

"What enemies?" I asked, tending the fire with a piece of iron we'd found on the ground.

"Oh, you know," said Boris, sighing. "Everybody."

He scrambled up and lunged at Vasily, who shrieked like a woman. But Boris' hand instead plunged into a bag next to the shopkeeper—pulling out a flimsy piece of paper in his enormous fingers. Boris laughed a great throaty laugh echoing out among the trees in the darkness. Vasily sobbed once with relief and held his head in his hands as he cowered. Boris bounded toward me, holding the paper out.

"You will read it for me, yes?" he asked. "I've never been too good at reading."

I motioned for it, and he handed it over. The letter was something official. It was hard to make out the gnarled Cyrillic typeface, and the handwriting interspersed within the characters. I squinted in the firelight, angling the letter this way and that to decipher the baffling Russian language, which, as I've said, was never my strongest tongue.

"You understand?"

I nodded, but I wasn't immediately sure. Maybe I understood, and maybe I didn't. After all, what are words but noises in certain order? Do they actually signify anything more? Don't they actually just corrode the true meaning of life, and action, love and hate?

It was such a nasty letter I reread it three times.

Dear Boris,

I realize that you cannot read this. Illiterate and crippled piece of shit that you are, I understand that your pickled-drunk body will force you to take most of the day traveling down the stairs of that convalescent prison in Astrakhan to collect this letter. You may even break what's left of the bones in your neck as you try to get up the staircase. Truly, it will not be easy for you to lay your big dumb hands on this measly piece of paper. After all that, it will be even more difficult to find someone to read it for you who will effectively convey what I mean to say.

I always had a limited amount of respect for people of your standing and stature. You may be a giant physically, but you are a midget from the neck up. If you can't understand that, hopefully your reader can tell you this: Your brain is tiny. You are stupid. You have no agency in this world. You have no control over your own life and fate, and for this I feel nothing but contempt and scorn for you. And I laugh, thinking of your cries as you fell down that well while we had tasked you with rescuing that beast of burden stuck halfway down the length of it. The beast drowned anyway, despite your best efforts. And your life was, for all intents and purposes, over. Because you yourself are a beast of burden which has outlived its usefulness. It couldn't have worked out any better for me or for the unit.

I write all this now that you are an invalid somewhere in the farthest reaches of the Empire. (Are you still on Pestelya Street—or have they finally sent you to Siberia to die, once and for all?) I really could not care less. This letter will reach you, somehow. I don't care if you are bedridden and soaking a dirty pillow with drool, tortured by festering bedsores.

No, the reason I reach out is due to…protocol. Owing to the practices of our unit, as you may remember, I am required as your last commanding officer to send you a letter detailing the expeditionary force's latest movements. Like a knife, we are plunging to the very heart of Asia, to the Earth's highest elevations, to the top of the planet. We will achieve what no European force has done before—to get into Tibet. The Czar has commanded the scientists to map out a whole new world which has thus far eluded us. It's a trip that will make history, and it will be a journey written in books for centuries to come. It is a mission to which I am obligated to invite you due to…protocol. And it is also an invitation I am only proud to extend to you, knowing how impossible it will be for you to even receive—let alone hear and understand it.

The unit is moving forward, and you are stuck in your private damnation. And for this I am grateful. Perhaps we will see each other in hell.

Sincerely,
Sgt. Nikto Pravitel

The postmarked date said 1899. Nearly a decade had passed while I was down and out in Astrakhan, I realized.

I read the letter through three times, just making sure I had not misunderstood some fundamental riddle, that there was no kind of coded message within these hateful words, or some anagrammatic sleight of hand conveying some other meaning. That name Nikto Pravitel seemed to glow out at me like some kind of warning.

I folded the paper. Boris was still watching my face intently as he reached out and took it back.

"What does it say? What does it say?" he said.

"It's...an invitation from your old expeditionary force commander, Nikto Pravitel," I said. "He writes to inform you that he is leading an expedition into Tibet with your old unit."

Boris stretched and yawned.

"Nikto, the stalwart foot soldier. He has to inform all the surviving members before each mission," he said, laying back. "Nikto always follows the rules."

He flinched, and scratched at his back, which stiffened beneath him for a fleeting moment.

"At least, he almost always followed the rules," he added. "I counted him as a friend once, before my accident. Did he have anything nice to say?"

"Not much," I replied hastily, rising. "It was all business."

I went over to the horses and fed and watered them, considering the value of having Boris at my side, and the return trip to Mongolia. I could not tell him about the duplicity of his old compatriot. Before he could know that truth, I would need to marshal some resources, chief among them the most precious commodity of all for any man: time. So much time had passed since my humiliation in Mongolia. I had withered on the vine for nine whole years.

The powers once pumping through my veins had slowed to a trickle. I muttered to myself as I forced my ire down and I set my head down to sleep. Even my horsemanship was a bit rusty, I discovered as I scrambled atop the back of my beast as we fled the city. I was a mere nub of the man I once was, in more than one sense. But I believed that, with time, I would recover some bits of myself.

All this factored into my plans, and what I must do next.

"Boris," I said the next morning as we slung our sacks on the horses' backs. "I've been thinking. Perhaps we should go on the Tibet expedition with your old unit."

He regarded me with pale blue eyes like Arctic ice. He ran his hand through his gray hair.

"Lama, I know you have given me back the gift of my legs and arms," he said. "But I don't see how I could return to a life scaling the grandest mountains on Earth. The most rugged terrain imaginable. It seems like a fantasy."

"I am no spring chicken myself," I said, my hand over my heart. "But that's why we will do it together. You will catch me if I fall off a cliff, and I will make sure that you have a hand at the top to brace yourself with. If we stick together, we cannot lose."

Some clouds lifted in those blank eyes. I still had a way with words—and it was this power alone I had retained in my years of convalescence. I was glad for it.

"Also," I added, finishing my pitch, "it is way less likely the authorities will find killers of the Czar's secret police far away in the Himalayas."

To this he nodded gravely. He fastened a strap down on the flanks of his steed, then spun around. He shook my hand, in that very formal European way. His hand was like a steel wrench. When he released my own, he kissed both my cheeks, and hugged me. But suddenly his grip slackened.

"What do we do about him?"

Boris pointed at Vasily. The merchant's thin fingers were picking some miniscule burrs off his silk sleeve, his face screwed up in revulsion. He recoiled at a bug crawling on his leg, yipping like a poodle and slapping at it.

"You think he'll make it?" Boris said. "Perhaps we should just put him out of his misery now."

He patted the holster of his revolver. But I stayed his hand.

"Boris, I feel we may have use yet of him in the trek to come. This expedition with your Sgt. Pravitel."

CHAPTER 14
TOP OF THE WORLD

This Sgt. Nikto Pravitel who had sent Boris that hateful screed, that enraged scream on paper, looked so very familiar. One of his eyes had a dead stare and there was something in his air that seemed to scream from my past. But a massive beard covered the entire bottom half of his face, and he remained silent for months at a time. His eyes narrowed when he saw Boris and greeted him with a duplicitous handshake. But this Pravitel's gaze never left mine.

I had a suspicion. But I thought better of it. It could not be. This life was not full of such coincidences, I reasoned. So I pushed the thought from my mind. We saluted and went our separate ways in the camp.

This first meeting was in the second week of July, in the foothills of the Altai Mountains, west of Kobdo. My heart ached to be at the threshold of the homeland—I smelled the odor of liberation and rebellion downwind. After years and thousands of versts of forced separation, I heard echoes: the war cry of Jimbe, the roar of the enraged mob, and the ghosts…the remonstrations of my father, the tortured lamentations of my mother. Somewhere in there were the murmurings of the spectral fakir, that ungendered voice, but I never made out the words.

These dangerous men were inscrutable behind those hard opaque stares. Some smoked, some whittled wood, some checked the stocks of their rifles, and the remainder just walked around the perimeter of the camp like restless predators waiting for prey. But all sixteen were united with a purpose: to survive and get rich. We were handy with a gun, and steadfast on a horse, killers at will. I was the only one in our group who was not strictly military in my training. (Never did I mention my time in the monastery.) We were soldiers and men of fortune brought together by the expedition's leader, the great P.K. Kozlov, the Czar's most trusted imperialist of the new century. Kozlov was tall, stiff, upright, unimaginative, plodding; a Russian soldier born a peasant, but who rose through the ranks to become one of the Czar's curiosity seekers. In so doing, he had become somewhat of a curiosity himself.

I was hired on as a backup to one of the Russian guides—a man named Agwan Dorzhiev who was supposedly friends with an emissary of the Dalai Lama. Vasily was signed on as a supplies man when we arrived in the Siberian village, because at that time of the season, they were looking to add to their number, just to hedge their bets in the years-long journey to come.

We sixteen men of action were joined by scientists and bespectacled experts who reported to Kozlov. We knew these civilized men would at least need to be able to defend themselves, in the dire moments bound to occur over the thousands of versts of bad road and unblazed trails ahead. Before leaving, we collected the empty vodka bottles, lined them up on an ancient fence, and placed firearms in their soft scientific hands. Some took to it quickly; most would never be able to hit a yak at four paces. But at least they could load the ammunition, pull the trigger, and repeat. By the end of the week of training, the fence had mostly collapsed, some of the bottles shattered—and we knew we were as ready as we would ever be. Vasily the dainty merchant too hid among these men of science...and he was just as hapless with a gun as most of the rest.

The mercenaries played games as we neared a departure. As much as I wanted to avoid scrutiny, I could not avoid a dare. I have always been a deadeye. One afternoon, I accepted their challenge. They set up the targets, and I exploded four bottles from fifty yards in less than two seconds, cocking and pulling one after the other with one of the group's revolvers. The final shot echoed out across the valley, and a few of the scientist types gasped with adulation. Some even clapped. Kozlov himself came striding up.

"Good shooting, my friend," he said, handing me a Colt handgun, pointing up at a circling vulture. He took his other sidearm out of its holster. "Now let's see who can hit that carcass feeder out of the sky first."

We had one of the scientists toss his hat in the air, and the moment it hit the ground, we drew our guns. Kozlov fired off one and then two shots, but both missed. I exhaled, sighting slow, and then gently squeezed the trigger. The bird jerked, then plummeted to the ground—splatting atop the head of Nikto Pravitel, who shrieked and frantically slapped the guts and blood off his overcoat and out of his enormous beard. There was much laughter and merriment. Kozlov nodded, with a slight smile.

"You will be useful for more than your translating abilities," he said, patting me on the shoulder. He called for one of the servants, who brought me a .44 Winchester lever-action repeater. I ran the piece over in my hands. It was well-oiled and clean.

"Take care of it—we may need you to use it much in the travels ahead," he added.

"I'm at your service, Colonel," I said, nodding.

Nikto Pravitel glared at me, still wiping off the bird blood with his hands. I stared back into his lazy shiny eye. I blinked. His eyes did not flicker, as covered with guts as he was. I could not see his face for his thick beard, but I will swear forever after he was smiling—hatefully.

When the party moved out from Altaiskaya, after singing an off-key Te Deum without any bells or accompaniment or music whatsoever, I was put on one of the advance scout teams, with a bunch of the Russians. I was the lone Mongol. I never turned my back on Pravitel, who in his turn never let up watching me.

The highwaymen, robbers, brigands, and packs of murderers of Asia were not the problem from the outset. Instead, the elements were the real enemy—considering the plodding curiosity of the nincompoops in our charge.

The Kozlov expedition moved half the speed of any group of sane men who shared unity of purpose. The reasons were manifold. Foremost among them were the collectors. The delays multiplied with every verst, with the painstaking care with which these scientists on the expedition captured bugs and pleaded with us to shoot small creatures off the road, and then watched from a distance as we skinned them at their exacting instruction. The collectors tagged these faunal fragments and put them in jars or carefully wrapped them in paper they marked with tiny tags. This was the purpose of the trip, they said, smiling strangely as they collected and catalogued, sorted and arranged. We must document everything we see, everything we find, they said in voices as flat and lifeless as the dead creatures amassing in their collection. Those smiles remained, unwavering. The other scouts and armed men in our party looked at them askance, laughed and lit another smoke, or went and gambled some of their advance pay away over vodka. I just watched.

I alone understood, out of this group of explorers and seekers, that true knowledge is finite. The vastness of the universe is an impossible eternity; only faith can bridge its corners. Deepest resignation—not dissection—is the only way to plumb the secrets of existence. No matter the weather, the heat, or roaring sandstorms, we stopped every verst to scrutinize the land, the plants, the dirt. The experts dismounted and unhurriedly caught bugs and butterflies in lazy nets, like children. Other times they hollered, pointing out into the grasses for us to shoot an antelope or a wild sheep or a rabbit. Invariably, we waited while they gutted and tagged it, ready for future investigation back in their European laboratories. Sometimes we slept on the trail while they sketched elaborate depictions of the specimens in their books. Sometimes I swore they were tasting the very oxygen itself, measuring its properties with their wagging tongues.

Kozlov had selected his team well, I had to give him that. He was prepared. He had accumulated fifty-four camels, eighty horses, a small flock of sheep, and we sixteen guards. The explorers, as the experts called themselves, numbered about fifty. Among these were two leaders among them: Kaznakov and Ladygin.

Kaznakov, a phlegmatic and shifty man with eyes darting across the horizon, was fascinated by insects and mollusks. Ladygin was consumed with his pursuit of plants and the people with skin darker than his own pale hide. Ladygin, setting hungry eyes on me, asked me a question the first day of the expedition.

"What army do you belong to?" he asked.

"A vengeful God's," I growled, baring my sharpest teeth, making a pistol with my forefinger and thumb, pantomiming a shot straight through his heart.

He almost cried. He quickly maneuvered his horse back toward the back of the pack, to consult with other Siberians and Chinamen from the steppe. The rest of the trip, he avoided me. The thought made me laugh for the entire excursion.

Camp was a drunken debacle from the first night of the journey, with much merriment and singing. I pulled my cap over my eyes at the edge of the firelight, listening to rustling from Boris and Vasily's shared blankets rise, go frantic, taper off, then cease altogether. Sleep overtook me unawares. And again, the dream came to me of the golden city Agharti that had so eluded me for all these years.

The dream faded into vapors and void as the sun jolted me awake. I remembered nothing of the splendor of my previous visions; I only had the overwhelming sense of their golden hugeness, their importance. But there was no time for dreams on this excursion. We were off again, most of the rest groaning about the vodka still oozing from their pores, billowing from their breath. I was the first in the line of travelers now, entrusted with one of the compasses by Kozlov himself.

Kaznakov and Ladygin broke off from the main expedition days later, in pursuit of phantoms to the south, to a landscape pockmarked with lakes and forests. Kaznakov dug into the Earth as he went, looking for creeping things in the dirt. Ladygin traveled three-hundred versts in pursuit of beavers—nothing but those dam-building little bastards that impede the natural flow of rivers and such. I was glad for them— especially since Pravitel went with Kaznakov and was out of my sight.

Kozlov kept us on a relatively straighter path than Kaznakov and Ladygin. He encouraged the scientists to stop and catalogue the natural features of the area, but with a catch: the expedition would not wait or even slow down for them. Kozlov urged the party onward: unhurried, yet as persistent as the sun arcing over the steppe. This man was in love with the horizon, and nothing would delay him in his pursuit of it.

Kozlov drove us through the city of Kobdo without so much as stopping to water and feed the horses. That decision would prove fateful in the following weeks.

When we showed up at Chanseringhi-huduk, with its rich wells and the purest water this side of the Gobi Desert, with a much-promised few days' rest ahead of us, I finally felt at ease. Especially when we were told that Ladygin in his all-consuming hunt of flora had wandered into the western part of the desert already, and Kaznakov had yet to arrive. I slept soundly for a few days, setting camp at the edge of the group. I cleaned my Winchester and loaded it, and I watched the horizon. Boris and Vasily came and broke bread with me every so often, offering some of the group's stores of vodka. But I gently refused, and instead tended to Vasily's minor maladies with my strongest tea. The merchant was never truly sick, but never truly healthy, either. Boris cared for his comrade, and their codependence deepened. They stood close together during the day; they slept closer still at night.

When Kaznakov did return, my bearded nemesis Nikto Pravitel was nowhere to be found. The party had happened upon a monastery on a mountaintop, and the monks' hospitality had required them to stay an extra few weeks. Kaznakov's meticulous nature, set in one place for such a long time, wandered in its fancies—until he indeed decided to study the air itself. He set Pravitel and three other soldiers in a shack high above everything, a first-of-its-kind meteorological station to better understand the regional weather patterns around that forsaken mountain.

Part of me was relieved that Pravitel was versts away. But another part of me was convinced it only delayed the inevitable. Because even though I did not know this man, I sensed a danger there—and his insistent glares meant there would be no avoiding him. Eventually he would return, bringing calamity or tragedy—likely both. Pravitel and those other soldiers would break camp and rejoin the rest of us. I could not know when or where such a reunion would occur. Watching my step and sleeping with my rifle at the ready would be key to my well-being.

The Gobi Desert was the next goal. The three groups split once more, dragging three trails southward across the map like claw marks: Ladygin to the west, Kaznakov to the east, and Kozlov in the center. The Ladygin party found mountains, bears, and rhubarb in a sometimes-fertile landscape, with little to no sand. Kaznakov found oases every dozen versts or so, and his group collected beetles and flies. In our central group, we found nothing but a barren landscape, sand that slowed each step of hoof and foot, and nights that were horrifically cold—a chill that brought down a half-dozen of the naturalists with frostbite. Every single horse died, one by one. The water ran low, because we had not stopped for provisions at Kobdo, and fights broke out among the troops.

Until, in that most acute moment of desperation, we came upon the first hills—and the monastery. Even the Christians among us knelt before the Buddhist structure, and thanked gods innumerable, unnamable.

The monks knew Kozlov on sight, since he'd come this way with his mentor Przhevalsky some years before. They greeted Kozlov with warm smiles and deep bows, and huge casks of water from which we drank in a frenzy. They produced a hot meal for the entire crowd, somehow pulling together the whole thing in an hour or so—an elaborate meal with vegetables and meat from the length of the Silk Road, from China, Russia, and Mongolia alike. It was as if they had been waiting for us the whole time. Before we had even digested the steaming bowls of grains and hunks of meat, they ushered us inside their thick stone walls, giving us the choicest rooms. We were glad for the shelter. The coming winter had numbed us to the very bones, and to be out of the harrowing wind was enough to lift all our spirits for the first time in weeks.

Kaznakov and Ladygin arrived, having satisfied themselves that the freezing temperatures and snows had closed their season of specimen collecting. Kozlov decreed we would spend the winter within those walls. Somehow everyone fit, as long as rooms were shared.

But Sgt. Nikto Pravitel was still stuck on that mountaintop watching the winds. It gave me immense satisfaction to picture him shivering for nights at a time amid the gale.

Boris and Vasily were with me. As I said, Vasily was never healthy, unsuited as he was to arduous travel. But it was Boris whose breaths grew short even as he continued his duties as strongman of the group. (The heaviest boulders were his to haul, the wildest beasts his to tame.) But I watched as they cared for one another, nursing their afflictions, both perceptible and intangible. Because they had come to share a bed in those walls. At first there was much sneering and hostility among the others. But as time drew on, everyone just looked the other way and pretended not to hear the occasional grunts and moans from their rustling blankets. I, for one, was amused. After my experiences on the trail, in the markets of China, in the villages of Mongolia, and not least in the most prestigious monasteries on Earth, I had come to know the illicit love that must hide in shadows and be spoken of only in whispers by candlelight. While men can hate men, men can also love men, inward and out. I myself was not of that persuasion, but I have known many who were. And none of it gave me pause. Boris and Vasily were in thrall with one another, and I felt a kind of pride that my own journey had entwined their fates as well like a beautiful knot.

Only once did Ladygin scream at them in the middle of some nocturnal activity, calling them faggots and causing a general uproar in the camp. But Kozlov was of like mind with me, pulling his trusty plants-and-savages expert aside, whispering as he jabbed his finger hard in his lieutenant's chest. And the problems ceased. Boris and Vasily became much more circumspect afterward, issuing hardly so much as a sigh during the nighttime, and barely crossing each other's paths in the light of day. Some of the Chinese still spoke in hateful hissing Mandarin about the two profane men and things of that sort—until I kicked the legs out from under one of the instigators and choked him on the ground, his arms flailing impotently against my shoulders, until he passed out. Only then did I release him. His comrades watched in shock as I dusted off my hands and smiled at them. Ladygin had been watching carefully, too—and I made the same pantomime pistol and invisibly shot him through the heart once again.

"A vengeful God," I repeated.

He shuddered and skulked away.

Needless to say, not a single word more was said about the budding romance for the remainder of the expedition. I still overheard the whispers of the rumors they said about me—almost all of them true. I still have no idea how they knew about my gun magic or my powers of the mind. I had not even told Boris my full history. Gossip has a wisdom all its own.

The winter cracked and melted away as the spring sun emerged, and we set out again. Kozlov kept his scientists in check this time, and we covered ground. At long last we came to Tibet. We passed a crystalline blue lake reflecting the spring sky, perfect like a mirror but for the occasional breath of wind—and the Russians had the audacity to name it Russian Lake, ignoring the native names that some of the guides continually intoned in their ears.

But the joke was on the Russians and their lake—because right after they made their presumptuous christening was when we encountered, right on the road to Lhasa, a band of N'Golok robbers. Even as we approached within fifty paces, we saw rifles leveled at us, the marksmen's serious brows scrunched down over the sights. We drew our own weapons and slowly marched up to them, stopping within twenty paces or so. Kozlov shouted that we were a band of Russian travelers who wished to make contact with the city of Lhasa and open new trade routes.

The robbers laughed—and one with bright yellow teeth and skin like leather, evidently a local prince, shouted back that the European dogs could bring back their bitch mothers to trade for all he cared, but they would never gain any access to the city as long as there were rifles in N'Golok hands and versts yet to cover.

Kozlov, who didn't know much beyond his native Russian, leaned to Agwan Dorzhiev, his all-important contact for the Dalai Lama, and had it translated. (Dorzhiev left out the part about our mothers.) Eventually, with a few more shouted back-and-forths that became more and more profane, Kozlov gave a wave, and we broke ranks and retreated half a verst to regroup. Agwan told the commander he had assurances from his contact back in St. Petersburg that the highest lamas had granted us permission to enter Lhasa. Kozlov nodded sagely, stupidly, and then made the momentous decision: we would travel the long way, around the Plateau of Tibet, and Agwan would talk his way in for us through that route.

An ill-tempered beaver, however, had other ideas.

Just a day before we were going to make our attempt on the main road to the east of the city, while collecting yet more specimens, Dorzhiev was bitten in the face by a wounded and half-dead rodent he had merely winged with his shot. The translator had leaned in close to collect his quarry when the beaver attacked. He ended up with an infection swelling his noggin to triple its normal size. Half the men recoiled with horror at his gross disfigurement, and the other half laughed hysterically at the translator's stupid pleading eyes. I barely had time to make up my own mind on how to react…before Kozlov drafted me as the replacement for the coming dealings with the Tibetan authorities.

"We cannot send someone to parley looking like that engorged yeti over there," he said, gesturing over at the groaning Dorzhiev. "You'll have to negotiate with them."

I nodded. The next day I set out with Kozlov himself on the last half verst to where the guard post was. It was in midst of a village on both sides of the road. Unlike the fierce N'Golok robbers, all the people cowered in fear and ran back inside their huts at the sight of Kozlov. We ignored them and marched right up to the guard post. Two soldiers wore shiny furs at either end of the barricade, staring ahead impassively.

"We would like to come through with our party," I said, in their tongue. "These idiotic white devils think they are going to march right through to shake hands with the Dalai Lama. I'm here to vouch for them. I don't think much of them, but the bastards do have money."

They stared at me. Then they both burst out laughing. Kozlov stared at me, puzzled.

"I told them about the beaver," I said. Kozlov laughed, and then all were laughing, each one about a different joke: the European about the beaver, the Asians about the Europeans, and me at everyone.

Over the next few hours, these villagers shared some local fermented beverage that tasted like rotting vegetables, and they roasted a goat and served a hearty meal. But these humble people of the land were clearly terrified of foreigners. They kept their distance and flinched whenever Kozlov reached out for a cup or a bowl. They gave him no blade to cut his meat, so I gave him the knife off my own belt. Two of the women ran off screaming, and the children disappeared.

I gave chase. Because there was no reason why they should fear this mild European who wanted simply to have his men collect butterflies, chase beavers, and count flowers—and maybe bow before the Dalai Lama. I caught one of the two females, a teenage girl, and I grabbed her by the collar. She slapped my arms in panicked desperation. Suddenly her mother was there too, cursing me in the local dialect, and they were both slapping me. I hoisted the mother with my free hand, and I barked at them.

"Listen, you silly asses! I just want to know why everyone is terrified of this mere explorer," I said, letting them down gently, holding my hands up. "What do you have against this white devil? What is there to fear of him?"

The two women caught their breath and swallowed hard. Then they broke and ran, in two directions, as if on agreement. I laughed, and I didn't even try to follow them. But I sat down on the nearest rock, and I waited. Barely ten minutes later, a man and his teenaged son—the husband and brother of the two females—approached with heavy clubs in their hands. But even as they tried to look intimidating, their terrified eyes rolled about in their skulls like whipped horses. Before they said one word, I stood, drew the Winchester from the holster on my back and raised it skyward—but held up my other hand in a pacifying gesture.

"I only want information," I said. "I am a Mongol, Kalmyk-born, and I do things my own way. This white devil is a man you need not fear. The only creatures that need fear this explorer are butterflies and beavers and other menial beasts. Why do you run in fear?"

Their mouths hung open, but the weapons lowered. The boy talked.

"Someone said they intend to invade Lhasa. But we were more worried they had come to avenge the other European. The man with the spectacles and questions and his worship of demon science."

We broke bread. And gradually it was revealed: this was the village responsible for the infamous death of Dutreuil de Rhins, the Frenchman killed two years earlier.

Everyone across Asia had heard of this nosy bastard who stuck his Gallic snout too far up the skirts of the Himalayans for anyone's comfort and lost his life for it. More than a few felt de Rhins had deserved it. But I nodded and assured them all that all was forgiven and forgotten, that the fate of a single life had been swallowed up so completely amid the teemings of a vast continent, that they need fear nothing.

As we commiserated, I basked in that human connection I had not felt in more than ten years. And I knew my willpower had returned. It surged through my veins. I felt along my body the boundaries of my senses, and then I reached out to the teenager with only my mind, only my innate power. And I saw him jerk once, like a fish suddenly hooked right through its jaw. Then I reached out and I corralled his father too, and they were both in my power. Kozlov appeared, without any weapon at all. He sat there in the silence, not understanding anything, occasionally glancing at me with a curiosity, approximating fear. But I focused on my quarry. Without words, just using my eyes and my senses, I assuaged their fears about the Europeans—and I told them my purpose in coming to their little settlement at the apex of the world. They nodded and went back to their people. At my behest, they brought me two of their leaders: an old priest and a young priest, both with clean robes. The talks began.

"Does this European really think he can enter the city of the gods with his unwashed brethren?" asked the older one.

"They ask what you want from Lhasa," I translated for Kozlov.

"Tell them that we just want to extend a hand of friendship and learn about their people and faith in a respectful way," he said.

I nodded.

"Their intention is to survey the defenses of the city, the weaknesses, as part of the plan for further military advances into the Himalayas," I told the Tibetans. "The Russians are looking to push all the way through to India. They want the whole of Asia to knuckle under the staff of their king, one they call the Czar."

The Tibetans scoffed. Then they laughed.

"Does this maniac know that he is surrounded on all sides by guards watching, fingers on their triggers?" said the younger monk.

"What did they say? What are they saying?" blurted Kozlov.

I smirked, and I winked at the holy men. Then I turned to my European commanding officer.

"They say we wait," I said. "And we petition through the leadership of Lhasa all the way to the Dalai Lama himself."

And so, back at camp, we waited. The decree from Lhasa never seemed to come. The European camp was restless. Kozlov watched from afar as most of the other men grabbed their rifles and blasted any beast straying within a quarter verst of the encampment. After one of the drunken Russians had taken aim at a butterfly and shot wildly, grazing the shoulder of one of his inebriated comrades, Kozlov punished them by seizing all the liquors.

The commander then shook his head and pulled me toward a fire roaring at the edge of camp. He sat in the billowing smoke, and I sat at the opposite side. He set a kettle over the fire, and brewed tea. He spoke of his previous travels for hours as we drank the stuff, as the days began and ended around us. These were all places I had never been. He gave me detailed accounts of his trips through the heart of the continent with his mentor, down to each valley and bend in the river, and the tilt of each mountain peak.

As lengthy as they were, by the third day I was still not bored. That man's love for adventure flashed in his eyes as he spoke, the stories of mapping lakes and rivers, freezing in mountaintop blizzards, and of marching for days on end without water in the desert. For Kozlov, it was all adventure—and it was all he knew or wanted to know of life. That third day, he finished his story with the death of his mentor Przhevalsky from tuberculosis during their last journey. The tears welled in Kozlov's eyes, but he wiped at them with his sleeve, shook his head, and then turned to me, his eyes clearing.

"That is what has led me to this camp on the outskirts of Lhasa," he said. "But you, friend—I have heard nothing of your tale. Someone said you were a monk once upon a time? How does a holy man become so skilled with weaponry? What synchronicities of God's grace brings about a lama with a gun?"

I stopped myself from laughing at his turn of phrase. I smiled and shook my head.

"I can only tell you, Kozlov," I said, "that the ascetic life was not for me. Like you, I crave the open road and the horizon, the ground passing beneath a horses' hooves. A sky wheeling by."

His eyes narrowed at me, those squeaking levers and pulleys working somewhere within that blond head of his.

"Sometimes I wonder," he said. "Sometimes I wonder about any of us, whether those touched by wanderlust are not also a little touched with madness. An incurable craving for the unseen, unto death."

I had grown to like this man. He had a desperation I could respect. Enough respect that I felt some kind of misgivings, or I dare say a bit of guilt, over what I was planning.

But only a bit.

During one of our talks, I asked him his own reasons for his breakneck travels. After all, one does not take the one millionth step of a journey out of sheer curiosity, or wanderlust, or even insanity. There must also be something at the end, some gold or goal, which drives one onward. I asked Kozlov what made him so passionate for the unknown spaces of Asia, far beyond the horizon.

"The glory of the Czar, the glory of Russia, of course," he said. "The Empire is destined to rule over all the East. My country will soon envelop the globe, as it is meant to."

I grimaced.

"And what of the peoples in these lands you are discovering?" I asked. "What of the Tibetans? What of my peoples, the Mongols?"

He slapped me on the back, the imperial hand stinging me even through my thick jacket.

"Come now, Lama," he said. "You are no more Mongol than I. You may look Mongol, you may know the language…but you were born in Russia, and you were tossed out of Mongolia, if my memory serves. You must understand, these peoples we discover along our travels are simple. They need the guiding hand of civilization, the working of machines, the light of Christ. Only then will they rise out of their savage ignorance."

I smiled venomously at him. At first I only wanted to stymie their efforts to get into Lhasa. But at that moment I changed my plans. Henceforth I would exact an even steeper toll on these buffoons. These imperialists who hoped to swallow the heart of Asia would have to be destroyed.

Indeed, Boris and Vasily watched it all with skepticism.

"You know he's just using you to get entrance to the city," said Vasily, running his hand over Boris' newly shaven head, which lay in his lap. "If that idiot Agwan hadn't been mauled by that beaver, he would not have given you a second look."

"Be careful, once you've outlived your usefulness," added Boris. "On previous journeys, most guides and translators were dead by the end of the trip."

I nodded, wiping clean the pieces of my Winchester before reassembling it.

"I am not the one who needs to proceed with caution," I said.

After two weeks, the priests returned. The older one coughed continually. The younger one informed us that one messenger could travel to the lamas in the city.

That messenger was me. This was the final phase of my plan.

Kozlov slapped me on the back again, but this time it was almost gentle— wistful, somehow.

"Put in a good word for us, and for the Czar," he said, grinning. "Let me outfit you with the gifts and such we have for the Most High."

He pressed into my arms three bags of gold coins, an extra revolver, and four paper documents. He signed the parchments and blew the ink dry, before rolling them into a neat tube for me to carry into the city. I stuffed it all into a knapsack for my few versts' travel into the city with the priests. We set off, but before we left the edge of camp, I told the holy men to wait for just a few minutes while I set my camp in order and said goodbye to two of my few friends in this life.

"Hail and farewell, friends," I said to Boris and Vasily, as I pushed through the flap of their tent. They had been kissing and quickly pulled apart when I arrived. But I held up my hands. "I don't care about any of that, my friends. I just wanted you to have this."

I tossed a bag of gold to Vasily. He and Boris took the clanking contents in disbelief, their eyes boggling.

"But how did you…?" Vasily said.

"Did you steal this?" asked Boris, in disbelief.

I held up my hand, shaking my head.

"I wish you nothing but a happy life together, friends. But don't ask me anything more about where that came from," I said. "Just keep it hidden for the remainder of your travels."

I went toward the tent flap, but I turned back at the threshold.

"And if you wish to avoid a good deal of trouble, leave the party and head west before sundown. Nothing good will come of this expedition after that. Of that you can be assured."

Their eyes widened in alarm. But I pushed outside before they could speak. I walked briskly toward Lhasa.

"Lama! Lama!" echoed Boris' booming voice from behind. "Go with God! And may He bless you!"

I waved my hand without turning and continued on. Before long, I reached the waiting priests, who led me past the guard post and down the wide road south toward the city.

The walk was short, and the road was covered in shit. A few monks walked the thoroughfare, heading into or out of the city of the gods. But it was a pleasant enough walk, even with the incessant babble from these self-serious lamas at my shoulders.

"We are so glad that you warned us of their evil plans," gushed the older one. "We are always unsure about the Europeans, and their intentions. But you laid bare their exact motivations. And for that we will be eternally grateful."

I waved my hand skyward.

"They are not evil. They are just a disease that cannot help but spread in every direction, consuming everything in its path," I said. "The only thing to be done with such a cancer is to avoid it entirely—or excise it as quickly as possible once it takes hold."

They laughed. They spoke of the unconquerable spirit of the peoples of Asia. I rolled my eyes. Our footsteps crunched on the stones and the crusted dirt of the road. We saw a group ahead of us, coming out of the city. They were a trio, and I saw immediately that two were unarmed holy men. After a moment, I recognized the third as Sgt. Nikto Pravitel.

He wore a wool cap and seemed to be darker and thinner after his stint on the mountain watching the clouds pass over his weather station. The staring lazy eye glowed lifeless, like a cold gem in a bright ray of the sun.

Coming closer, I finally saw it was glass.

And his face was totally shaven—revealing a hard jawline.

He stared at me. He grinned. I gasped.

I recognized this Nikto Pravitel truly for the first time.

It was that wayward acolyte, Fang's friend, the grinning fiend, the would-be assassin, who had so plagued my journeys. I had been unaware, perhaps in denial, until that moment. But he had known me for who I was, the entire time.

We stared each other down as we passed. I braced the Winchester against my hip, under my cloak but ready for action, until we were a quarter-verst down the road. My hands trembled with rage and fear. When we were around the bend I spoke to my companions.

"When will the welcoming party make the first encounter?" I asked.

"The men set out at the same time we did. They should arrive any time now," said the younger priest, just as we reached the first hovels at the outskirts of the city.

As if on cue, shots cracked across the valley. I told the priests to wait back at one of the first structures, a falling-down shack, assuring their concerned faces I wouldn't be long. I waved a bag of gold at them, clinking it for good measure. I tossed it to them. And for all the years of spiritual pursuit that may have guided their lives, a look of avarice twisted the faces of those two ascetics, the same as any man's. They promised they would wait, and I stopped myself from laughing at their crystalline duplicity, their obvious lies.

I turned heel and jogged back toward the Kozlov camp. No one was there, but the fires still smoldered, and the gunshots were much louder. I spotted flashes despite the daylight toward the southern road. I harnessed a horse, then I rode on the ridge overlooking the pass. It was a hard climb, taking an hour to go the distance it would have taken fifteen minutes at a flat trot on foot. The gunfire grew louder and louder—and then when I crested the ridge, I saw it.

The Tibetans had mounted a stand against the Russians' boundless curiosity at a side road into Lhasa. Just as I had directed, they had not allowed some of Kozlov's other scouts to continue pushing along the eastern perimeter of the city. Emboldened by my tales of their purpose and their fighting capacity, they had decided to muster all their fighting men along the route. But I had told them expressly not to engage the entire expeditionary group. Because as was immediately clear, the Russians had better guns—and they had better aim. Five Tibetan bodies in their gaudy uniforms of gold and blue already lay lifeless in the dirt. The other dozen or so who could be seen were shooting out from behind cliffsides and boulders at the Russians, who were positioned behind the expedition's wagons and supply barrels.

Kozlov had deceived everyone. He'd used me as a diversionary tactic while he sent his contingency plan along the other side of the city of the gods. Anger swelled in my veins, and my fists went white at the thought of the double cross. But I fought down my rage and calculated my next move.

I dismounted and tied the horse to a nearby outcropping. I extended my telescope, and I scanned the battlefield. That's when I saw the man calling himself a Russian sergeant, this Nikto Pravitel. He was in the vanguard of the attacking force, a few dozen including my fellow mercenaries and some of the collectors, once reinforcements had arrived. Nikto was laughing, waving his arm up in the air to attract bullets, and even once dangling his hat on the end of his rifle to taunt the feckless Tibetans.

Pravitel reached in his jacket and pulled out something round. He jerked at it, and then threw it with a long high arc toward the Tibetans. A flash, and the earth shook, sending clods of dirt in every direction and a dust cloud billowing in the direction of the Russians. I knew my chance had come.

I crouched. I set the Winchester in a notch in the rock. I breathed steadily and aimed down the iron sights, as my target hooped and hollered and danced in celebration. A hundred yards down my scope, Pravitel crept out and advanced toward the Tibetans stunned by the grenade blast. But he was moving with cocky exaggerated steps—and not fast at all. I aimed, leading him by a yard or so, and squeezed the trigger.

Nikto whirled to the side, falling with a great spinning motion. He clutched at his groin, right where I had targeted, and where a crimson flower quickly bloomed in his pants. With his other hand, he pointed up vaguely in my direction and tried to call out something, but his voice broke high, like a terrified little boy's.

The gunfire erupted again, and the Tibetans threw something explosive of their own at the Russians, which completely clouded over the battlefield. I mounted the horse, trotted down the ridge again and back into camp, where I requisitioned what I could before beating it north, away from Lhasa.

CHAPTER 15
CAVE OF THE ANCIENT ONES

That bag of gold I stole from Kozlov and his intrepid doofuses was worth way more than any of the Czar's secret police would have you believe. They were certainly keen on reacquiring it, as I discovered during a series of running gun battles against bounty hunters lasting hundreds of versts.

I staggered westward across the plain and the steppe and the Silk Road, watching for the next trap, and the next. The occasional highway robber gang I dodged or ambushed at strategic locations with my Winchester. Terrain and weather determined my tactics. I was as careful as a doctor slicing open a patient as I sniped down each and every member of three groups of Manchurian marauders as they jerked their horses in zigzags of terror to try and avoid my bullets. None of them succeeded. So instead of being robbed, I picked their corpses clean of all valuables, and even some of their clothing. From one group I stole a drab-green military uniform just like my old one; from another I requisitioned a long knife in a green scabbard just like I once had. I even snuck up to a monks' encampment and pilfered a yellow deel. I took enough ammunition to supply an army for a short war. By these practices, I also earned the best pair of boots I would ever have, which would take me through my next years of isolation.

Back in Mongolia, I rounded the city of Kobdo, but I did not approach it. The time was not yet perfect. I had long since stopped counting the days and could not be sure without any human contact in those highest of all Mongolia's Altai mountains. I had missed another Year of the Dragon three years earlier, and I would have a mere decade before the next one.

One twilight I stumbled up to the mouth of a blackened cave. I immediately saw its promise. It was a stone womb in which I would find the repose I needed to reach my destined time for action. I did not believe in predestination on this account; I merely had to be consistent with my prophecy of years before, in order to keep the faith of the keepers of my legend, and the shepherds and horsemen who would inevitably fill my ranks when I reappeared.

This cave, as I said—it was there since before history. It was there in the cruel seasons of grunts and blood and bone and animal murder and unfathomable chasms, and long before there was an Agharti to aspire to. Long before words and language and true meaning, it was there—so it was totally pure. It had always been, and always would be.

The Ancient Ones had made it home.

The cave was deep and high. It extended more than 250 paces and a steep climb to its absolute back and rose to the height of ten men in places. The stalactites and stalagmites hid creatures teeming beyond the light of my first fire. After I hunted and foraged a bit outside the confines of the cave, the flickering flame light played across some images on one of the far walls. I went over to investigate—and I gasped.

Artwork covered the stone. Strange elephants with fur and huge curved tusks were surrounded by tiny hunters with spears. Birds flew, the sun burned, the stars winked out of the black, humans danced around the fires. My torchlight showed the strokes of blackened carbon and the delicate touch of the ancient artists. I ran my finger over the charcoal, and it came off on the tip of my flesh, flaky and brittle. I raised the torch, illuminating strange creatures I'd only seen in books about prehistoric Africa; camels and deer and a kind of horned goat I'd never seen before.

The Ancient Ones, I knew the artists to be immediately. These were our predecessors who had blazed the subterranean way into what would become Agharti. They had been primitive, that much was clear from their drawings. But there was an elegant simplicity there, in the lines, and the sure hand creating complex fearsome beasts out of simple scratches of soft mineral upon unforgiving rock, all of it predating civilization. This was the first scream of the past echoing into the future; the attempt to wrest back the moment from ever-marching time. It was brave and foolhardy, and I ran another of my fingers through the tail of the beast, laughing a little as I considered the naivete of our forebears and their hopes for immortality in objects and thoughts.

The Ancient Ones who made that artwork came to me in my dream that very night. The drawings, the traces of long-lost ancestors of us all who had burned fires and smoked their bloody kill and stripped clean the vegetation for miles around that cave, were surrounded in a golden light. These ancestors, of the wide huge heads and the flared noses and sloping brows, all had the same eyes. Eyes watched without ever truly seeing—or as if seeing the universe as one whole, and no detail. The group of them grew in stature as I watched, from a small group into dozens, and then hundreds, all raising their hands, their luminous fingertips, up to the darkened sky of the abyss above. Then they plunged downward—and dug. With shovels, with heels, with hands. They burrowed with a frenzy, as if searching for water in the desert, or warmth in the freeze. As if they were trying to reach the bottom of everything.

They delved until they were so far into the Earth that the Sun was forgotten as mere rumor. And then they built—they poured molten gold, and they shaped it into buildings. The Ancient Ones called out in some language that had no real words—it was only shrieks into the nothingness without form—a mere unity of will against the nature of chaos. Their Agharti was a bulwark against the mayhem beyond their golden fires, and beyond their hearts' yearning. But nothing more.

I awoke to a wolf licking my face, its hot stinking breath stinging my nostrils. It growled as my eyes opened. Without a moment's pause, I grasped it by the throat and squeezed. It roared with huge teeth and tried to claw me with its forepaws, but I rolled to the side, throwing it with my momentum to the side of the cave. It hit the ground and bounded back at me, but I used its own momentum to throw it back behind me, back toward the other wall. This time I heard it groan in pain, and it was two seconds slower to get back up on its paws. Just enough time for me to grab the Winchester. The wolf coiled back for a leap. I pumped the lever once. And it froze. We stared in each other's eyes, man and beast, and the gods somewhere in between.

This wolf had recognized the action of the Winchester.

And I realized for the first time that this beast had human eyes.

It had blue eyes. Like the fakir. Like my father.

The wolf sat. After a long moment, I set my rifle down and sat, too.

In the years that followed, I came to believe that Nugai the wolf was indeed my father, the protecting voice and spirit. Even if this was not another shape assumed by him, it was clearly more than just some random beast that had strayed to my cave. For one, it lived side-by-side with me for all those years in the cave. The animal also knew weapons of the hunters of the steppe—and it knew enough to help me hunt, to circle around the prey, to keep them within range of the Winchester, and to fetch the birds as they fell out of the sky. We shared our kill. The wolf also assisted me when I spoke to it, hauling crops back up from our little plot at the base of the ridge, and even dragging tools down when I needed them. It slept at the opposite edge of the firelight at night in the summers, its ear unfailingly cocked for intruders. As the days grew shorter and the winter arrived, the beast crept closer, until it was huddled against me, this wild creature sharing my warmth as the wind roared outside the Cave of the Ancient Ones. When the snow piled up outside the entrance, it was the wolf who dug the tunnel to free us both.

My dreams of Agharti were capricious, visiting once every few days, or weeks—or sometimes not for an entire year. But when the visions did arrive, they followed the history of the place. From a subterranean outpost of the Ancient Ones, it became a self-sustaining colony, and then a thriving metropolis all its own. Buildings rose into the darkness of the hollow center of the Earth, and then illuminated the black. The golden rivers flowed wider and stronger on currents powered by the denizens' spirits alone. Then I heard the roar of the chanting millions, those generations of descendants who had followed the Ancient Ones. It was in a tongue I could not recognize, and that had not been spoken on the surface of the Earth for thousands of years. But still I could understand it.

> *Heavenly holy,*
> *Down here Below,*
> *The Tides and Winds Don't Fret Us,*
> *Where the Gold does Flow.*

It went like that, extolling their paradise in their darkness at the center of the Earth. I grabbed some of the softer rocks in the cave, and I diligently recorded these dreams on faces of the cliff walls, elaborating around the ancient depictions of life they had left behind. I felt as if I was finishing the story for them, those who were so long gone and would never return to do it themselves.

> *Heavenly holy,*
> *Down here Below,*
> *The Tides and Winds Don't Fret Us,*
> *Where the Gold does Flow.*

I mimicked their style, using careful slow loops of yellow ochre to represent Agharti in its many golden twists and turns I'd seen in my fleeting glimpses. I recalled it better than any religious text or mantra I had ever encountered in my life. I went around the simple ancient drawings, careful not to smear what had come before. The work inched along, as I only spent an hour or two each night, my hand doing such slow tracing by the flickering light of the fire, before I turned in.

Years and years, meal after meal, breath after breath, the heart stolidly beating on, the work continued.

Through the work of those years, the story became clear. Gradually I filled up the entire wall around the art of the Ancient Ones with my own visions of that distant place.

Near the end, the girl with the swishing raven hair visited me in my dreams. She was beautiful and she draped herself over me, and she started to grasp at my manhood. When she saw the scar that was left in its place, she laughed and laughed. But her mocking cackles turned quickly to howling sobs, and protestations of love for whenever we would next meet in the flesh. We kissed, and I awoke in throbbing pain. Nugai whimpered and licked my face.

The very night of finishing the work I had just a single vision: the golden tangle of Agharti sinking into the blackness, the teeming currents becoming less and less visible, as the massive superstructure faded into a knot of thread, impossibly far off.

I awoke to Nugai's howls. It was just before the dawn. He glanced at me with those human eyes, and then he streaked off into the innermost darknesses of the cave. I was about to pursue when I heard human footsteps, and cursing, from behind.

Stumbling to my feet, groggy but grabbing the Winchester, I crept down the slope toward the mouth of the cave. Setting up at the final overhang before the main chamber, I aimed my piece down the slope.

Within a few moments, a figure shuffled into view, doggedly trying to ascend toward me. It was hunched and it staggered up, step by step, sliding down a bit every few paces. But still it climbed. Just as the person reached within a handhold of the top, I cocked the rifle.

"Wrong cave, friend," I said, my voice a mere grunt after so many years of disuse.

The person looked up.

It was Jimbe.

He looked far older than the years that had passed. His hair was gray, and time had fractured his face with wrinkles. His muscles had shrunk around his skeleton. His look of shock quickly faded as I set the rifle aside and offered him help. He slapped my hand away and dusted himself off.

"You sure picked a stupid place to live," he said, kicking a cascade of rocks down the slope.

"I haven't seen any people for a long, long time," I said, my voice strange. "But I am honored that you are my first guest. How did you find me?"

Jimbe took off his hat, and he wiped at his sweaty brow. I passed him my skin of water. He took it and drank it all down. He tossed it back to me, and then stood, stretched, and gestured all around at the walls and the drawings and the shadows, my companions all.

"Everyone in Kobdo speaks of the Mad Lama, a hermit in the Cave of the Ancient Ones," he said. "But no one was willing to come and see, for fear of being killed. They say this Mad Lama is a cannibal."

I laughed for the first time in years, and the booming echoes sent a flock of bats skittering off deep in the distance.

"I haven't yet eaten anything on two legs," I said. "You, friend Jimbe, look a little withered on the vine after all these years."

Jimbe scowled at me.

"Don't call me friend, Lama," he said. "I have spent years just scratching at the barren dirt to feed my family. Whatever I grow and whatever I kill is requisitioned by the goddamned Chinese."

He suddenly lunged at me, grabbing my deel. I was pushed back against the wall. I grabbed his wrists before he grasped my throat.

"You goddamned coward—you goddamned cheat," he said. "You decide to hide in an old cave while the people are suffering. You let the Year of the Dragon pass by, and the Chinese boot only grinds the Mongols deeper into the dirt and stones. I didn't even want to come to find you. It was the idiotic villagers who say you're our last hope. I tried to convince them of your lies, but they would not listen to me. So here I am."

I threw his hands off. Although he was still powerful, and I was not in peak condition, I was still the stronger. I poked him hard, once, in the chest.

"What year is it?"

"It's the Year of the Dog," he said, handing me a piece of paper. "That is the entire message I was instructed to give you. And now my duty is fulfilled."

And he turned around and slid back down the slope to the cave's entrance. The paper in my hands was blank white.

CHAPTER 16
VIOLENT MIRACLES

After Jimbe left my cave, I did not pursue him as he half-fell and half-rolled down the slope out of the cave. Instead, I made the fire hot, and I sharpened my knife—and then I set to work cutting every hair off my overgrown head and face.

Shaved clean, I packed up everything I had. It wasn't much. I pulled on my European military uniform, and my yellow deel over it. I gave one last glance up at the drawings of the Ancient Ones, and my own interpretations of their perfect subterranean civilization among them. The yellow ochre shone in the firelight, and I wondered whether another pair of human eyes would ever see them. With a snort I kicked dirt over the hot coals that had kept me alive for so many years.

As I walked out of the cave, I saw no sign of Nugai. He had vanished into the darkness. But I had my suspicions I would see him again, whether he was on four paws, or two legs—or even slithering along the ground. The thought tickled me, and as I trotted down and out of my refuge, my laughter echoed and then vanished in the great expanse of sky before me.

The spring wind was so cool on my shorn face, it was like the universe's caress on my bare lips. It flowed over my bald head, too.

One hundred versts to Kobdo took me a week on foot. I talked to myself the entire time, and I wondered if I had lost any connection to reality over the course of my years in the cave. I described the sun and the clouds to myself, and I looked across the landscape for any traces of the golden city. I kept my feet moving. Along the way I shot rabbits and fed myself. No people crossed my path. I tended small fires at night and listened to the wolves and wondered if I was being watched by Nugai somewhere near. But somehow I knew only the common beasts of the land were watching my encampment.

I arrived in Kobdo, and I saw an unruly crowd from afar. Their uproarious laughter was the cackle of joyous vultures. A ringleader before them urged them onward with some story, some kind of strange chant.

As I crept closer, some of the faces in the crowd slackened. Others looked away. The laughter died. The crowd's eyes boggled. The ringleader carried on. He had his back to me. It was Jimbe.

Jimbe exhorted the crowd.

"What is the matter with you?" he shouted. "Do you need to know anything more about your Mad Lama, the cannibal of the caves? And how he eats bones and bugs, and talks to animals?"

I stood just a step behind him at this singular moment, and there was utter silence. He continued his harangue.

"Don't you understand?" he screamed, gesturing over his head. "The man has given up. He has nothing to bring Mongolia, and Mongolia owes him nothing. It's best to just leave him be."

Everything was still. He stiffened, and slowly turned to face me. His eyes were wide. I smiled.

"At the very least, Jimbe," I said, "I had hoped to count you as a believer in this lead up to the Year of the Dragon."

His lips trembled. And as I held out my hand, he reached out tentatively and clasped it in his own. And though I felt a tremor in his arm, I yanked him toward me and into an embrace. We held it for only an unsure moment. But then I pulled away and I faced the crowd.

"I am the Lama. You may think me mad, or even a cannibal." At this I glanced with a frown at Jimbe before continuing. "But I tell you: now is our time. Our enemies have taken too many pieces of us which we can never get back.

"We can now take revenge. We must take back our destiny by any means necessary. By any cost of gold, by any debt of blood," I said.

I pointed at the sky.

"Whatever the sun and the stars may contend, the Year of the Dragon approaches. This will be the year we, as a people, rise up as a dragon from its lair— and set the past to rights."

Sure enough, the crowd cheered. They were mine, after that crucial moment from the heart. The crowd swarmed around me. Some of the men rubbed my bald head as if I were a charm suddenly reversing entire generations of ill fortune. The women fingered admiringly the yellow fabric of the blue sash I had tied around my middle. The children ran hands over the green scabbard that held my knife. I glared down at their wondering faces, and they scattered like birds.

Thus began my campaign. The gold I'd stolen from the Russians outside Lhasa got me far in the city. Crowds never before mustered in the history of Western Mongolia followed me wherever I went. By day children heard my stories of adventure and travel, men asked to ride along to the mountains for a bit of sport, and the women presented me with new clean clothes. By night the children dreamt of my exploits, the men contented themselves with songs of the Chinese drowning in blood, and the women attempted to crawl, one after the other, under the sheets with me. I sang the songs, but I did not keep the company.

It was like a fever of pride had spread through the populace. All who had been alive twenty years before remembered me. The younger ones took to me right away, the teenagers hanging on my every word and the children crawling over my prostrate form. But there were no baths this time, owing to my physical condition. Something else was a little different this time, too. My severe and shorn appearance, bald head and stark yellow robes, gave them pause. But it only seemed to strengthen their faith in me and the cause. Everything about my reappearance was a call to arms. They shouted it from the hills and they whispered it in the alleyways. Weapons were mustered, preparations started.

After a week, I spirited Jimbe out of Kobdo, after we'd doled out about half my gold. I discovered, through simple inquiries in town, the Kozlov expedition had hightailed it out of Tibet and escaped back to Russia with their hides intact. But they'd kept nothing else—not even their precious specimens.

Their retreat was the stuff of legend along the backlands of Asia. The various versions of the tale held that an ambush on the troops from Lhasa had prevented the European imperialists from conquering Tibet. Rumor had it the heavens themselves (perhaps a lightning bolt from a blue sky) had struck down the Russian squad leader, a cyclops from the East, right at the crucial moment of a decisive charge. I kept a straight face as this was relayed to me, I don't hesitate to tell you, but my heart swooned a bit at the thought my plan had been executed perfectly. Jimbe raised an eyebrow at my evident interest in this sordid saga.

"You were with those Russians in Tibet on that trip, weren't you?" he asked later, flailing the reins on his horse five versts farther down the road outside Kobdo.

"I was their guide for some time," I said, gulping down some water as the sun beat down on our heads. "How did you know, friend Jimbe?"

"When I hear about bullets from heaven and other violent miracles," he said, "I recognize your handiwork from half a world away, Lama."

I laughed and I slung my calfskin canteen at him.

"You may very well be part of the next few violent miracles," I said.

He flinched, looking at me with apprehension.

"Fret not, friend Jimbe. I am merely joking. This time the winds and the rains and even the dirt will be with us," I said.

That very same day we started our new campaign, the new strategy. Through my spyglass, at the top of a ridge about fifty miles distant, we saw a convoy of a cart and four horses. But there was only a single man riding out in front, and it appeared otherwise undefended. Jimbe looked at me in fear as I explained my plan and laid a new rifle in his hands. I stationed him on the ridge at the best vantage point over the plateau, and I rode down to greet our prey.

The single man slowed his horse and drew his revolver on me as I approached. He motioned for the cart behind him to slow and stop. The scout was Chinese, and two Chinese faces were atop the cart, too. Based on the finery they wore, these were not mere settlers, but people of distinction. I thanked the heavens above and smiled at him with my hands high overhead.

"Sir—let me give you my warmest welcome to the free lands of the Mongols, shackled for centuries—but now no longer!" I shouted.

I dropped my hands to my sides, and a shot rang out on cue. And just as I had hoped, though Jimbe's hands on the rifle doubtlessly trembled, the bullet from his unseen perch on a nearby ridge sailed clear and true—right into the dirt, not a yard in front of the scout's horse, which bucked and reared. The echo caused a woman to shriek from the back of the cart. The scout regained his horse with some effort and was about to level his piece again at me, but I reached out with my mind, convulsing his hand violently so that it dropped from his hand. Shock paralyzed him as I sauntered forward on my horse, right up next to him. I patted him on the shoulder.

"Give us all your money, your gold and your jewels," I said, very softly, voice seething with meaning. "We will leave your women and food alone, if you turn back around to your homeland. You will not find a fairer deal in all of Asia, friend."

Needless to say, these Chinese interlopers gave over a pile of riches they had brought with them. The man in the cart was a rich bureaucrat, and he tried to escape out of the cart as I approached, leaving his family behind to face the threat alone. I took aim and winged him, leaving him in the dirt, howling. Jimbe came down, and we tied up the scout. The three females—the wife and two daughters—we simply kept inside the cart. We unloaded the shiny things, the expensive things—the things this Chinese family had expected to use as collateral to dominate the poor Mongols who would work as their servants in Kobdo.

Rage built within me. They had two choices, I said: to head back to China, or take a one-way trip to the afterlife and whatever it may bring. The wife and daughters nodded, not crying, and turned the cart around. The three of them dismounted a few yards back down the road and struggled to haul up the patriarch's cowering, bleeding form. That was the last we saw of them. We left the scout, tied up, still mounted on his horse, riding off to the west. He could not have made it more than a few versts before breaking his neck, we were fairly sure. But that was not what horrified Jimbe.

"What can highway robbery get us?" he said over the campfire that night. "What can it possibly do for Mongolia, for the cause for independence?"

Shaking the bag of coins and jewels and holding up the empty tins we had just eaten from, I mumbled through a mouthful of caviar.

"It can help win the hearts and minds of the people, buy weapons, and bribe some of the key Qing officials," I said. I swallowed the salty sustenance down and chased it with just a mouthful of the elegant wine we'd stolen. "You peasants all need to learn: when it comes to the world of human affairs, there is nothing more important than money. Nothing. It can get you love, happiness, security, respect, and power. Nothing else—not even beauty—can do half of that."

CHAPTER 17
THE CITY OF KOBDO

The Chinese, those innumerable sons of Han who spread like a weed across Asia, build walls. These walls are made of stone, they aren't always high, and they don't have any spectacular names. Just look at their "Great Wall"—which despite the lackluster name is actually quite exceptional in some ways. Their compulsion is to build out, encompass, and then erect their barriers, like a crushing embrace.

We Mongols do no such thing, of course. We move through space. We wrestle the horizon, chase the sun and the moon to the edge. If we plan to conquer, we do so honestly, on horseback, down the sights of our bows, and at the tips of our scimitars. It is in this way that the whole of Asia knuckled under the Greatest Khan's wrath—and why the Han cowered within their walls, during the Jinn Dynasty.

All this was well before my time, of course. It was centuries before the Manchus brought Mongolia to heel. But for my hundreds galloping toward the city of Kobdo that summer with the fires of revenge in their eyes, it may as well have happened the week prior.

My army formed around me, emerging from a hundred villages across the landscape. From the chaos of poverty, they emerged in military formation at my shoulders, like a flock of sky scavengers, bya gtor.

Kobdo, the westernmost point of the Chinese yoke, was barely ten versts ahead. Our war cries echoed out across the valley. The city appeared over a hill.

But when we crested that hill, the depression opened for two miles before us—and we saw lines upon lines of mounted troops.

We charged all the harder, screaming louder—until we realized with several hundred yards to go that these cavalry were not moving.

And they were Mongol.

I gave the sign to slow to a halt, and it took half a verst for the hooves to stop. The dust cloud enveloped us as I rode to the front of the line. From the other side's ranks emerged a bald man with a thin dab of a moustache in the center of his lip, a military uniform which had nonetheless been stripped of all Qing imperial regalia. His eyes were hard, set over a steely frown bent downward. But his voice rang out as we approached.

"Mongols! Lama!" he bellowed. "Do not proceed farther until we have staked out a plan to coordinate our attack! We wish to take Kobdo intact!"

Murmurs rippled across both camps, his and mine. I cleared my throat.

"We wish to eradicate the Chinese menace from Mongolia forever," I hollered. "Kindly clear the way so we may tear down those Chinese walls."

Some cheers erupted from both sides at my words. The opposite commander and I had pulled to within five yards of one another at this point. He bowed first, and I reciprocated quickly, the impatience and agitation of our military stances hastening our movements.

"Ja Lama! Your reputation and strength precede you!" he said, bowing once more. "I am Magsarjav, a local commander of the resistance."

"I've heard of you too, Magsarjav. What happened to your Qing medals?" I said, sneering at the bare lapels on his coat. "Were you drummed out of Chinese service? Is that why you've decided to join the winning team?"

My adversary shrugged.

"I have been corrupting the Qing from within for some years. It's better than being permanently mutilated as a result of some fruitless gesture, don't you think?"

The barest hint of a smile tilted up the corners of his mouth, as he relished the horrible memories washing through me. My face grew hot. How could this pompous fool know? At that moment, I focused all my anger into my willpower, sharpened like a rapier aimed at the space right between his eyes. But his smile only widened.

"You have just arrived in the middle of the campaign," he said. "Why don't you just come make camp with us for one night so you can hear our grand strategy?"

I redoubled my effort, squinting hard at him. But then he reached out and gripped my elbow. Nodding, he spoke so only I could hear.

"There is so much you don't know about how we plan to liberate our homeland, Lama," he said. "I insist you join us and meet some of the leadership. Just so we won't end up killing one another, once the shooting starts."

His grip was tighter on my arm than any hand had ever been before. And I felt his own willpower, pushing back against mine. We reached a kind of stalemate; I clutched his hand in a taut Western handshake. We grimaced at each other in the false approximation of a friendly smile. Both our sides cheered, even as beads of sweat trickled down our brows, our flushed cheeks.

"I hope we can all just get along," said Jimbe meekly.

Both I and this Magsarjav laughed deeply at that. And for the moment, the armies relaxed grips on their weapons.

We roasted a leg of lamb on a spit over the fire just as dusk shuttered the sky. Magsarjav was a good head taller than me, a massive man who spoke with clear confidence and a graceful vocabulary. But he was not the overall commander. The real leader of their group had been east, drumming up some support troops from Uliastai a week before. Damdinsuren would be arriving any hour, under the cover of night, with the information allowing a total takeover of the city from within, according to the advance messengers.

"Damdinsuren?" I asked of my counterpart, the one they called Magsarjav. "The nobleman I've heard the villagers all speak of? The negotiator with the quicksilver tongue?"

"He is one and the same," said Magsarjav. "Damdinsuren has a certain currency with the Qing, having dealt with them at court for so many years. He is reputed to have a hold on their sensibilities that most of us Mongols do not. Take me—I served in their garrison for a long time, but they never promoted me high enough to give me access that would allow us any further advantage to our cause. The Chinese bastards are not all that smart, but they are shrewd in their caution, is my belief."

Magsarjav pulled out a bottle, uncorked it, and tipped back a deep draught of whatever was inside. He held it out to me, and I got a whiff of some infernal rotgut I had smelled on so many of the Russians during the trip to Tibet. I held up my hand, refusing.

"Years at the monastery left me without a taste for the stuff," I said.

"Yes—I've been meaning to ask about that. At which monastery did you study?" he said, corking the bottle again, smiling slyly at me. "And how on Earth did you become a freedom fighter?"

The verbal traps he was setting for me were plain. This man always sought an angle—even over his allies. Thus I chose to answer just one question and answer it as untruthfully as possible.

"In my youth I studied at the Drigung Monastery," I lied, nodding earnestly. "And I left the pursuit because Mongolia cries out for warriors, not another lama among thousands."

"It's funny," he said, barely waiting for me to finish speaking, "I would have thought with the way you wear that deel, and your history, that you would have instead studied at the Drepung Monastery."

I blinked. But then I forced a smile.

"Such things are so far in the past," I said. "And we live in such a different and dangerous world, what does it matter where a single acolyte spent some of his lonely formative years? What matters more is the questionable loyalty of Qing lackeys who claim they've come to rescue their homeland."

Neither of us blinked as we stared each other down. Finally, an underling came and knelt to Magsarjav, whispering close into his ear. Magsarjav shut his eyes for a moment. Then he clapped his hands once and stood.

"Damdinsuren has arrived from Uliastai," he hollered out to the crowd, and there was a short cheer. He turned to me. "Lama—please join us for our strategy meeting."

We followed Magsarjav toward the biggest structure in the center of the encampment, a yurt shaped the same as all the others, but double the height and three times the size. When we pushed inside, a middle-aged man in the clean black robes of a Chinese nobleman stood hunched over a table where the solitary candle burned. The sides of this man's head were shaved, and the back of the hair was grown long and prematurely gray, a lopsided take on the Qing queue. But the angry angular face, sweaty and scowling in the low light, was clearly Mongolian. The figure rifled through the sheaf of parchments with agitation, ripping two of the pieces by accident. He took a deep breath, trying to calm himself. He scratched at his moustache, which looked like a hairy ferret lounged atop his mouth, fairly dwarfing Magsarjav's.

"Damdinsuren, as I'm sure you've heard," whispered Magsarjav, "is from Inner Mongolia and spent a lifetime working for the Qing. But he swears his loyalty now to the greater Mongol peoples, whom he hopes to unite from Hailar in the East, all the way west here to Kobdo. I find his plans…ambitious, to say the least."

"Of course, you would say the least," croaked Damdinsuren, with an accent not quite Mongol and not quite Chinese. He stood up straight, or at least straighter than he had been, but he walked over to us with a hunch, bowing without much trouble at me. "You must be the eminent Lama everyone's talked about for the last twenty years here in the west. Everyone wondered where you've been. What took you so long to make your move."

I did not bow, but I walked past him to look at the parchments. They strolled up behind me as I ran my hands over the biggest stack.

"I was busy lighting fires of freedom in Mongol hearts all across Asia," I said, brandishing the papers, then dropping them back down onto the surface. "I did not have time for bureaucratic wrangling and words piled upon words, stacked within papers on papers."

Magsarjav's lips rose in a tight smile, and Damdinsuren held up his finger. He went around to the other side of the table, and picked up a sheaf thicker than the rest, with seals and signatures strung out across the bottom like colonies of ants marching.

"The Bogd Khan convened a secret congress last year in Urga featuring all the leaders of the movement," he said, chest puffing with pride. "We successfully put together a plan. Earlier this year we took Hailar, as my friend mentioned, and we have marshaled all our political capital in support of the Bogd Khan. And it all starts with this document—it's like the Americans' Declaration of Independence."

"That's well and good," I said, turning away to the sections of maps that showed troop movements, numbers, and strengths. "But the Americans had to fight a war for eight years on their own soil—on territory they started with. You have yet to take little Kobdo, let alone Urga."

Damdinsuren touched his temple with his index finger, and then pointed at Magsarjav.

"That is why we are so glad the legendary Ja Lama has joined us, right at this most auspicious moment, to lend his powers to the fray," said Damdinsuren. "We can hardly lose when we have the invincible monk, the scourge of the Chinese and the Russians, the bandit with Buddha at his back, the eternal hope of the Mongols, working alongside us."

"Who said I will fight alongside you?" I said, sneering, half smiling. "I could take this tiny town and rule as khan of all Western Mongolia. I have all the troops I need to take and embed myself in this place, like a tick. The Chinese and even the Russians would be powerless to stop me."

Damdinsuren shook, his head, and scratched at his politician's moustache with fingernails long and sharp like the claws of a predator. He was strategizing. But Magsarjav laughed, a hearty soldier's laugh.

"Because there is still a warrant out for the arrest of the acolyte who murdered his roommate in Drepung Monastery some years ago," Magsarjav said, blackened eyes twinkling. "We wouldn't want the Dalai Lama and the authorities to catch up with that student, if he was crucial to our cause."

"And," added Damdinsuren, "the Russians are still looking for the mutilated exile who's supposed to be quietly living out his days in Astrakhan, his true place of birth. He may know something about the murders of two of the Czar's secret police. We all must hope they are never so informed."

They knew much. Almost everything.

But what did I care? When one has nothing left to lose—that is freedom. I smiled at them.

"That acolyte and exile stands before you after years of fighting for the survival of Mongolia," I said, slowly placing my hand on the Colt at my side, underneath the deel. "I would tread carefully with even a humble holy man from the steppe. Threats alone are powerless in this life. You must back them with death. Nothing else carries weight."

Magsarjav pointed at me as if to shoot me with his index finger. But Damdinsuren grunted and reached forward, pulling his hand down.

"No need for further bravado," said the nobleman. "We just want you to know we are here to support one another. We are prepared to give you autonomy over Kobdo and the western reaches of the Altai Mountains, pending the Bogd Khan's approval. He has soured on the Khenbish Khan, so there's no worry there. I trust you've met the Bogd Khan on your travels?"

"I have never had the pleasure," I said, of the Bogd Khan, ignoring the reference to this Khenbish Khan figure whose name so continually echoed through my journeys.

The Bogd Khan I well knew from the stories circulating throughout all of Asia of the huge slob with a taste for supple young flesh—and a predilection for poisoning his enemies, as I have mentioned before. I had promised myself some time before I would never sit down with the man for a cup of strychnine tea.

"No matter—you will meet the Bogd Khan in due time," said Damdinsuren, waving his hand in the air. "But more important is ridding Kobdo and Mongolia of the Chinese menace."

"And especially their crimes," added Magsarjav, rubbing his bald head slowly.

"What crimes?" I said, curiosity momentarily overcoming my strategizing.

Damdinsuren held his face in his hands.

Magsarjav took a deep breath.

"The Chinese merchants have set up a trading post in their part of the city," he said. "They are selling livestock."

"Okay. What animals?" I asked. "Sheep? Goats?"

"Children," said Magsarjav, face hardening. "Little boys dressed as girls, to be exact."

"You jest."

"We do not joke about such things. Not when rape and murder are their currency."

My heart beat hard. I staggered away toward the opening of the yurt, clenching my right fist within my left until my fingers nearly broke. I glared out at the bustle among the tents, the Mongol troops mingling, comparing their flintlocks, rifles, and swords.

My head reeled. Can it be that the Chinese were engaging in such horror? And the same horror that had so totally knocked me off the pathway to enlightenment, throwing me off onto a journey so utterly all my own?

The young of Mongolia, and the future of the motherland, were in danger.

"We have plenty of evidence of their disgusting trade network," said Damdinsuren, nodding.

Damdinsuren snapped his fingers. I turned to see a boy stepping forward from the shadows at the edge of the tent, who had been invisible before. The boy stepped right up to me. He was a Mongol child but delicate, with hair grown down past his ears, thick lips and an effeminate softness to the cheeks and neck. His lips and cheeks were painted to a flushed red. I crouched so we could see each other's eyes, and I placed my hands on his shoulders.

"Is this true, boy?" I asked. "Are the children being sold by the Chinese?"

"Yes, sir," he said, sniffling, scratching at his eyes—and I saw the dark mascara around them, adorning the lashes.

"What do they do to the boys?" I asked.

"They do the unthinkable, Lama," interrupted Magsarjav. "They sell them to Russians, who have their way with them, and then slaughter them. The others they simply mutilate for their amusement, then set free. This one is like that."

Magsarjav's hand lifted up the front of the boy's tunic, and I saw something very familiar: the boy had been mutilated like myself. After a moment, I turned my head, and he dropped the tunic down again. I hugged the boy for just a moment. I stood, and gently ruffled the boy's hair. Thus dismissed, the boy walked out of the yurt. I turned and contemplated the darkness for a long time. Then Magsarjav was close behind.

"We figured you could personally understand the atrocities wrought by the Russians and the Chinese, owing to your condition," he whispered, his voice barely a breath. "Not to mention the horror that pederasts can perpetrate, whether they are in a Mongol city, or in a revered Tibetan monastery."

I turned, and I knew my face could not betray the shock I had in his knowing the two most depraved crimes of which I'd been victim. But this shrewd man, so clearly in possession of himself and his believed destiny, did not smirk at me. He simply put a hand on my shoulder and squeezed.

"This is why we figured you were just the man we needed to help us throw these bastards out of our homeland. To take back what is ours," Magsarjav said. "Our land, our children."

"Our pride," added Damdinsuren, nodding. "Our destiny."

I glanced from one to the other. And since I knew my voice would not be working, I only nodded. And our agreement was struck.

The raid commenced at dusk. We lit fires all around the valley, each of our two thousand men set up four standing torches on the surrounding ridge, making our forces in the gathering darkness look as plentiful as fish in the Caspian Sea.

Jimbe led this part of the preparations, and the horizon in every direction was ominous. As the flames burned, and we forced our excited soldiers to keep quiet for a few minutes, we heard the far-off wailing and shouts of the people inside the city. It sounded like the lamentations of women crying over children lost forever to time. But in truth, it could be none other than the cowardly violators inside the city. They had believed our ruse, and their panicked terror echoed across the plain as justice closed in. As Magsarjav looked on, I rode up and down the lines of mounted cavalry, the men quaking with anticipation, their steeds chomping at their bits.

I attempted something I had never tried before: I reached out to the whole group, stretching my willpower as thin as a string-sized lasso to reach all of them. And as I shouted out, I knew both my voice and my mind were in their heads, knocking around their hearts.

"You must not fear death, and you must not retreat!" I shouted. "You are fighting for Mongolia, which the gods have already anointed. Do not fear death! It is only a release from our struggles here on the earthly plane. Death is the quickest path to paradise. Look there, to the East!"

I pointed, and the two thousand faces turned in that direction. Jaws dropped. Because there I produced a vision for all of them: a phantasmal scene of what could have been and what should have been—and what may yet still be. It was a bustling city, not this frontier village of Kobdo, but a powerful and elegant city of dignified homes and sturdy yurts, with solid temples in between. Riches of silk and gold, soft pillows, and candelabras of shining metals. Succulent dishes covered the tables, from steaming lamb legs to tall jugs of wine, to overflowing bowls of cheese and dates and nuts. A handful of golden pipes sat in trays, smoking, waiting for hands and mouths. I made it resemble the Agharti of my visions and dreams, yet here above the Earth. The armies quivered in excitement as they saw a Mongolia that was again a power around the hearth, as well as on horseback. Some shouted as I let the vision fall from their eyes and settle back into the darkening landscape of the plain.

"This is our destiny! To the battle! None of us return without victory!" I hollered, hoisting a rifle in my hand toward the moon overhead. "I am with you, and we cannot lose."

No general order was given—instead, I reined my mount toward Kobdo, and the thunder of two thousand men, eight thousand hooves, followed close behind. Rage rose within me as I discerned the humps of dark Mongol yurts clustered together like beggars along the edge of the city...and the soft warm lights of the comfortable Chinese homes stretched out luxuriously within their walls. To the west I rode harder, and the men galloped faster still, catching up and surrounding, making me the center of the advancing line.

Jimbe was right by my side, teeth gritted, head down, sprinting forward into the future with everything in his being. He was laughing.

"This is it, Lama!" he hollered. "This is finally it!"

I didn't have time to admire his insane resolve. Because the black line of the wall in the moonlight grew before us—and a verst ahead were the closed gates, locked tight. We were heading right for a collision, on breakneck speed and a momentum of faith that the plan would work.

I strained my eyes.

The blackened wall loomed...

...closer...

...closer...

...dangerously closer...

...no time to turn...

...and there it was! The signal!

The two torches burst into flame atop the gates. And the doors swung inward, just in time. Our saboteurs had done their job.

The Mongol cry of seven hundred years roared across the valley, from my heart and mouth and from two thousand more besides. The horses' hooves roared, as we streamed inside the Chinese merchants' section of the city of Kobdo.

CHAPTER 18
VENGEANCE

Mahakala is the true reason for what you've heard about Kobdo: the massacres, the mutilations, the flaying, the heart extraction, and the frenzied crowds bathed in blood. Mahakala—the fiercest protector of faithful righteousness— suffers neither fools nor the faithless gladly. The extreme depravity in Kobdo by the child killers of The Cartel of the Emperors was met with an extreme vengeance— an unthinkable backlash against the unspeakable evils. This was the guidance of Mahakala himself—which made the stuff of legend you may have heard.

The reality is no more virtuous than the stories.

I was shot three times during the battle for Kobdo. Or at least I found three bullets in my uniform, nestled in little holes blasted through the thin fabric of my deel. I picked them out and shook them in my hands, and they made a little clatter. A small crowd of my newest supporters fell to their knees at the sight.

"The Lama is invincible!" said one.

"The Lama cannot be harmed by mortal weapons!" said another.

"The Lama is a shrewd operator," murmured Magsarjav, elbowing me in the ribs and winking at me with a grin, through a cloud of cigarette smoke.

Total surrender came two hours after we breached the walls. A quarter of the Chinese garrison was mowed down. The survivors hung on for a bit longer. But as the shouts and shots closed in on the last occupied buildings in the middle of their settlement, the call for capitulation was sounded out in Mongolian, Chinese, and Russian. Screams of surrender resounded.

The enemy survivors were disarmed and herded into the courtyard between three of the biggest administrative buildings. Celebrating started, and so did the looting. A group of five lamas emerged from one of the local temples and started issuing effusive blessings. Magsarjav took the honorific "Firm Hero"— Khatanbataar—while Damdinsuren gleefully nodded along with the ceremony to humbly dub himself the "First Hero"—Manlaibataar. (And these exalted titles for the pair who had only ridden into town once the last shots were fired.) The lamas came to me, and started their water purification rituals to honor me, but I grabbed the wrists of two of them.

"There's no need of that," I scoffed. "I don't need to be a hero today. Everyone here is a 'hero,' already—except the disgusting pederasts."

They scurried off. Jimbe appeared out of the darkness, and into the firelight.

"Why did you send them away? They were going to consecrate me next— I was going to become 'Horse Hero,'" he whined.

"'Pig Hero' would be more fitting," I said. "But never mind that. What we have to do is find the Mongol children. Finding them justifies any means."

Jimbe and I walked around the Chinese section of the city, tracing the other wall from west to south to east. The pillaging commenced all around, by firelight. A few dozen foreign houses were burnt. I stopped rapes and assaults—at the end of my blade. I gave the firm command that all the children were to be rounded up in the building nearest the courtyard with the captive soldiers. I say all this to illustrate there was indeed method amid all the madness. I was trying to keep the insanity from fully fermenting.

But what I discovered was, there were few if any children to round up, throughout the entire city. The few eventually located were Chinese, and a few Russians. The Mongol youths were all gone. It was as if they had disappeared in advance of our arrival. Jimbe and I interrogated the terrified women and doddering old men we saw on the street, asking whether there was a place where the children had gone to. Each and every one stammered and could not answer, until we came to a fat little Chinese merchant, whom we caught slinking in the shadows along the northeast nook of the wall. I caught the little man by the collar and lifted him off the ground. His feet scuttled in the air like a bug's, and he made little squeals.

"Where are the children?" I asked. "Where are the Mongol youths?"

He stopped flailing, and his eyes rolled so hard I saw the bright whites shot through with blood vessels. I pulled out my Colt, cocked it, and pressed it to his skull. Urine promptly soaked through his robes and pooled onto the ground.

"It's The Cartel of the Emperors—it's all of them! It's not just the Chinese or the Russians! It's the Mongols, too!" he bleated.

"What are you talking about?" spat Jimbe.

"I…will show you…the one I…have in…my home," he stammered.

I nodded and dropped him. He crawled on his knees, then sprung up to his feet, trotting a bit faster than I would have expected. Jimbe and I glanced at one another, and then pursued him. It wasn't hard to keep up with his little legs. After a minute of walking, he pushed into a home and spun around, thinking to close the door on us. I simply strode forward and kicked it in on him, and he went sprawling backward. I strode inside, followed by Jimbe, and we were stopped in our tracks by a tiny figure.

The person looked like a little harlot, with a painted face and a gaudy golden dress, and bright red high-heel shoes. Dark hair hung over the shoulders. I stepped forward and yanked upward at the tresses.

The wig came straight off in my hand, revealing a shaven head. I took a rag and scrubbed this person's cheeks. It was a boy, a Mongol. He fell to the ground and cringed. Underneath the finery, he was nude. I helped him to his feet. I patted him on the shoulder.

I turned to the groveling merchant.

"It's not what it seems!" the merchant yelped, trying to scramble backward on the ground away from me, like a beast of the dirt. "It's The Cartel—it's not me!"

I kicked him sharply in the ribs, and he cried out, rolled over, and went limp. I peeled off my deel, threw it aside, and holstered my sidearm. Crouching next to his head, I struggled to control my voice—and my fists.

"How many of the children have been treated like this?" I asked evenly. "Answer me honestly, and I promise I will limit the pain you are about to experience."

His lip trembled. His whole body shook. I reached down for his throat. And then he told me everything.

You must realize, I tell you this entire tale, all these sordid episodes, even from this furthest vantage point, so you may understand a bit of the truth behind the rumors, and the many lies. The excesses of Kobdo that night and the days to follow, although some have screamed about their extremity, were really just the setting to rights of the balance in western Mongolia, our homeland that we love. It was a balancing of the scale, after centuries of abuse, rape, and murder and pillaging. Violent it was, surely, but it was just as surely a reaction to the atrocities that came before as anything else.

Vengeance. In a word.

This Cartel of imperialists needed to pay for what they had done to our motherland.

Our investigation started with Jimbe and me, but soon was joined by a dozen stalwart Mongolian raiders as we crisscrossed the merchants' stronghold within the city. The hysteria grew with each door we smashed inward. We knew where to go: the first merchant confessed everything, he groveled and asked for forgiveness, and he even drew us a map. We traveled to the red Xs he had slashed reddish-brown with his own blood on the thick parchment.

It wasn't just Chinese homes we invaded. It was also the Russian ones and some Sensibly Western homes besides. It seems The Cartel of the Emperors was not limited to any one people. It was the entire ruling class who had been victimizing the Mongolian people—and absolutely everyone was complicit. Mongolia had become a colony, a playground, for the depraved. The conspiracy was covered up. The work of the local Chamber of Commerce, as we discovered.

At each and every X, we found a little Mongol boy who was dressed up as a little woman. Some of them were dressed resplendently, like the princess of the first house. But others were dressed like gaudy whores. All had bruises and the signs of trauma on their little bodies. All had far-off stares which showed an existence beyond caring about their fate. I spoke to them in soft words, I shook them, I swore at them—and I embraced them. Nothing seemed to have an effect. Their eyes were like those of little corpses, each and every one of them. Of course, I tortured all of the members of the Chamber of Commerce who owned the homes where these children were found. But it wasn't until the seventh house that one of the cowards spilled his guts entirely, with barely a slap on the cheek. The frail bookish little man gasped, and shrunk to a ball on the ground, with just a single droplet of blood trickling from his nose.

"No! Please don't hurt me!" he cried. "Look in the Chamber of Commerce! Dig in their earth! Prosecute those liars! They are the true criminals!"

I bent down to beat some more answers out of him, but he had passed out. And the little boy who was dressed as a woman—like a little prostitute—appeared at my side like an apparition and laid a small hand on my clenched fist.

"You waste your time on him," said the boy. "He is a weakling, and there are other villains still trying to make good their escape."

"But what about you?" I barked, motioning as the crimson painted lips and his blue powdered eyelids. "What about what has been done to you and the other children?"

"We will survive," said the boy. "But you have no time to lose. Ask your questions. Go to the Chamber of Commerce and dig as you see fit. There are true victims here in Kobdo…but I am not one of them. You will find answers at the Chamber of Commerce."

I nodded and motioned at Jimbe, but not before kicking the unconscious pervert in the crotch, hard.

The Chamber of Commerce was at the center of town, where piles of extinguished torches littered the ground. We approached in the darkness, and I gave the dozen Mongols signals to completely surround the place, stationed four apiece at each of the three doors. At a quick whoop from me, we all kicked in the doors, with guns drawn. But what we saw froze us momentarily in our tracks.

Because there was no need to dig. The bodies were piled right up to the ceiling, about fifty of them, mostly nude, splashes of blood everywhere. Some corpses still bled afresh. Two dozen Chinese and Russian and Indian and even

German and British imperial officials were standing a few feet away from the macabre funereal mound. They spun around like tops from one doorway to the next. Vengeance in our weather-beaten faces advanced on them like an angry Mongol horde of old.

Their lamentations, their wails, and their pain-wracked squeals held no pleasure for me—though it sated the thirst for revenge among some of my mob. With the lash of the whip and the prod of the sword, and two quick-shot executions, we rounded up this Cartel of villains in the courtyard of the Chamber of Commerce. And there the Mongol forces surrounded them, waiting. I went inside to again consider the evidence, all those little massacred bodies.

One of the merchants was brought to me, apparently the leader. He was actually the first one we had encountered, in the first house, with the ladyboy.

But a transformation had come over this repugnant pervert. In the hours since I had beaten the partial confession out him, he had either been drugged, or perhaps plunged himself into the depths of an opium binge, knowing the inexorable fist of justice would come. I had noticed that all these merchants and diplomats infesting Kobdo were decadent and loathsome—emissaries of tyrannical crowns from across the globe. But this one's skin had now waned to the color of ashes. His eyes had dulled to the hue of ancient glass. And he smiled dreamily.

"What have you to say for yourself?" I asked. "What have you to say for these children? How did they die? What were their crimes?"

Rubbing at his cheek narcotically, he shook his head.

"They did not obey everything…that was asked of them," he said, a lecherous smile spreading across his face like a rot. "We all agreed. They were unable to willingly provide…joy."

He laughed at his own use of the vile word. And I smiled at him, even as the venom poured from my eyes.

But I held back the full power of my will, waiting for the right moment. I needed more from this man first.

"You admit that these children were the victims of rape and murder?" I asked, like a Russian policeman would.

"That and more besides, to be truthful," said the merchant, his eyes lolling back in his head. "The Mongol hordes only understand one thing, and that is barbarity. We gave their little boys some barbarity they could not mistake…and would never forget."

I pulled out the hidden razor from my robes, and, quick as you please, slit off the lobe of his right ear. He howled, still half in his drugged stupor, and the blood flowed.

But I was not any closer to a solution.

I walked away, nearing the nauseating pile of flesh. I straightened my military uniform so that it was crisp, the belt and pistol holster snug and in place.

In this life—amid this pandemonium, this abattoir of a world—there can be no equivocation. No wavering. Maybe in some other universe, and some other time, you can reason and have a version of justice that is gentle and patient and kind and wise. But for the rest of us out in this slaughterhouse, there is no time for those kinds of lofty sentiments and nose-in-the-air idealism, these soft modern ideas of mercy.

Because in this life there is no resolution.

Because in this life finality is all.

In our few years breathing and walking around on this cosmic pebble hurtling past the stars, there can only be resolve.

And resolve I did.

I drew my sword, and I nodded at Jimbe. Our cadre grabbed the collars of the Cartel criminals as if we were one and dragged them to the street, and then out of the Chinese section of town and half a verst down, to a bend in the middle of the main road overlooking the Buyant River. The Cartel eyes saw our stern looks of resolve—the utter hatred—at our lips and brows. When one tried to run, he was hacked to pieces by two of our strongmen. The hands, arms, legs, and part of the torso were scattered across the ground before the screaming head was cut clean from the body.

No one else tried to run after this. They lined up on their knees dutifully amid our shoves and blows, their eyes rolling in their skulls like terrified cattle.

But they had made a mistake: not resisting until the end. What was to come would be, for them, the worst horrors ever imagined. I drew from its green scabbard my trusty knife, which split a morning sunbeam from the dawning horizon. And we started to set things to rights.

CHAPTER 19
A WHOLE NEW ERA IN
WESTERN MONGOLIA

The messenger was not yet a man, with just a little black fungus sprouting on his upper lip. He'd tried to stylize it into tendrils, like the Chinese emperors of old. I was not surprised to see the Qing send some emissary after I'd broken up the disgusting Cartel, and I was sharpening my blade at the front of my yurt when he arrived, half-carried along by two of my strongest men. When this messenger was dropped on the ground, trembling and stammering, I did not hold back my laughter. I whetted the blade with the rough stone, grinding away in a slow rhythm. The man-child in front of me fell to his knees as I threw aside the rock and sheathed the knife in my green scabbard.

So this is how it will be—this is how the imperialists will send death to me, I thought. True comedians, those Chinese. What arch jokesters!

"The Qing have sent a child, thinking I will take pity on an emissary who hasn't lived long enough to have his testicles descend?" I said.

The boy attempted to stand, but stepped on the hem of his own robe, and faltered. I stepped forward and dragged him to his feet. He was light—just a skinny expendable Chinese youth. I understood their reasoning: it would be no great matter to send some foundling to his certain death among the barbarians of the west. I slapped him on the back, and he practically folded in two.

"Come walk in our new paradise, my new friend," I said. "We are creating things here which will outlast your forbidden cities, your great walls."

He did as he was told, walking a half-step behind me and to my right. I motioned at my assistants and lackeys, and they dispersed. I could at last be alone with this representative of the Qing whores, so I could test the mettle of these imperialists.

Early on in our jaunt, the boy started breathing heavily with a kind of exertion, clearly some strain. But I persisted with questions requiring his response, spitefully wasting more of his precious breath as we walked the streets of my city.

"I take it you have heard of what happened with the peacekeeping action after Kobdo was liberated from under the boot of your people," I said.

He nodded. But he said no more.

"Tell me what you heard about me, and the Khanate I was given to rule alone by his holiness the Bogd Khan," I said. "I can tell you what is true, and what has become mere myth, spreading like a fire across the wilds of Asia."

The boy stopped, and he tremored where he stood. The trembling grew to the point his quaking feet kicked up dust from underneath the soles of his feet. It was then that he pissed himself, the stream hot and steaming down the leg of his trousers. I shook my head, but I felt the corners of my mouth turn up just a bit, of their own accord. Truly, in my months as the Khan, the honored Tushegoun Lama of Western Mongolia as decreed by the Bogd Khan, dozens of men pissed themselves in just this way before me. Their eyes tried to blink away their fear...but their bladders betrayed terror every time. I laid my hand on his shoulder and squeezed with just a fraction of my inner strength—and I focused some of my most positive thoughts on his psyche. It was enough to calm his fluttering heartbeat, which I felt within his spindly flesh.

"You can tell me what you've heard," I said, softly. "Truly, I have heard it all before."

He took a deep breath, shuddering, and then he held his hands over his eyes. It was such a look of despair that I almost felt sorry for this Chinese errand boy with his own knife hidden so clumsily in the folds of his coat.

Almost.

"Everyone has h-h-heard—about the s-s-sacrifice," he said. "The b-b-b-blood."

I shook my head. I needed him to say it. I wouldn't let him simply think he could get away with allusions, the merest hints of atrocious terror.

Details are where the secrets of life are hidden, after all.

"Sacrifice? Whatever do you mean? Blood?"

Tremoring and stammering, his fear started to shake him.

"The h-h-h-hearts," he said. "The Chinese merchants of K-K-Kobdo were all sacrificed, one after the other, by having their hearts cut out...and their gushing blood d-d-drunk from the cups made of the skulls of ch-ch-children."

I wagged my finger, clucking my tongue disapprovingly like a teacher would at a child.

"They were not the skulls of children," I said. "And this is all exaggeration. The Cartel of pederasts were all killed, sure. But did any of the rumors coming east to China mention how they had raped and mutilated and murdered the children of Mongolia, I ask you?"

The Chinese errand boy's jaw hung slack. He was unsure of what to say. He only shook his head. I saw deep within him the secret—the mission that had brought him here. But I knew it would not come out until it was time. Well, time was something I had in those days of my total rule in Kobdo. So, I smiled, and I let him work himself up toward that inevitability.

"See? You are told by your boy emperor whatever he wants you to hear," I said. "Your crowded cities only generate rumors and lies about Mongolia, where people yearn to be free."

"But Lama," he said, his voice steadying, "it's said that you used the blood of the executed Chinese to consecrate the celebrating Mongol horde, splashing it from the skull cups on the revelers, and blessing them with Buddhist rites. The entire mob was painted red."

"Once again, most hallowed dignitary," I said, "no skulls were used as cups. Some rites to Mahakala were performed in the first blush of victory. It was not just Chinese. We killed Mongols who were complicit in the conspiracy, too. But I can assure you, nothing unjust was done at any time. The people decided on justice, and I consented to their will."

"I also heard that you flayed alive the leader of the Kazakh villages in the Altai," he said, regaining his composure. "I have heard that the skin was stripped from his body, starting at his feet, and it was torn asunder until all his lifeblood had leaked onto the hard-packed earth."

"There is some truth in that, my friend," I conceded. "But those were the same Kazakhs responsible for untold slaughter of women and children throughout the Altai. They were brigands who raped and killed and destroyed everything in their path. They too worked with The Cartel of the Emperors, supplying victims to their whims. I ask you: what sense is there in civilized dealings with savages?"

"Might not someone in another place and another time call you a savage, and deal with you accordingly?" said the boy emissary, suddenly haughty, challenging me.

His scowl showed true malice. I smiled at him. He was warming to his purpose, closing in on his ultimate mission. But there was still a bit of time. I slapped him on the back and pointed at a huddled crowd. We had arrived at the stocks, and I pulled him through the throng to the front of the pack. A bald-headed lama was doubled forward, with his head and splayed-out hands emerging from three holes in the heavy jaws of wood.

"See these, my esteemed guest?" I said, sneering. "A group of Russians told me about the use of this device in England and America centuries ago. One of my first orders in Kobdo was to set these up in the center of town. We use them as a corrective measure to make sure our city progresses in the right direction."

My guest did not remark on the table with dark stains on it, which was crisscrossed with thick ropes that lay unknotted. I did not remark upon them, either.

We pushed through most of the crowd and stood before the punished. The monk's head was sunburnt, and his cheeks were dirty and streaked with long-since-dried tears. But as his yellowed eyes flicked up at me, they sparked ever so slightly with a strange mix of hope and fear. He dared not speak to me first. I went over and patted the top of his head, like I would a dog.

"It's been two whole days already, hasn't it?" I asked.

"Yes, teacher," he croaked. "And the last whole day without food or water."

"We must remedy that," I said.

I reached for the dull iron latch shutting the stocks, and I sensed his body tremble with an anticipation bordering on the last twinges of despair. My hand paused, and the monk's eyes stared at it wide, unblinking and terrorized again.

"We have learned this time around, have we not?" I asked.

He nodded so furiously I thought the creaking wood of the stock would break.

"Oh yes, teacher. Oh yes, Tushegoun Lama," he said. "Never again will I commit so grievous an infraction, such an injustice to myself and my community. You can count on me."

I nodded, and then I released the latch. He sprung up, rubbing his wrists, and shaking his head. Promptly he bowed deep before me, going prostrate on the ground for a moment before springing up and running away, like a gazelle.

We continued walking, my guest and me. I had become aware of a scent—something of a perfume—emanating from his flesh. It was floral and decadent and maddening. I focused on breathing through my mouth. I missed what he was saying to me.

"…and what did he do?" the delegate was asking.

"Who?" I asked.

"That tortured monk," he said. "What did he do to deserve the stocks?"

"Oh—that," I said. "That monk was caught drinking and smoking during Shagai last Saturday night."

"Is that a crime?" he asked.

"For true lamas here in Kobdo it is," I said. "Listen, esteemed diplomat friend. My plans have been explained to everyone. They are posted in the temples. We have a vision of order in Mongolia, the likes of which haven't been seen since the army of the Greatest Khan. I want fewer lamas—but I want better ones. They have a choice. Those who want to indulge can do so, but they also have to abandon the spiritual pursuits—and start digging ditches."

We had approached a line of young lanky workers smashing rocks, amid great clouds of dust and debris. They swung their pickaxes up, nearly losing balance in their exhausted arms, then swung them down with sharp clangs on the rocks, which split and crumbled away.

"And we see here some of the basic productivity," I said. I hollered to the exhausted men, and they attempted to bow in deference, but two fell over. The others helped them up, and they all stood at attention until I waved them off and they returned to their herculean efforts.

"These men were monastics in training. But as acolytes they showed more aptitude for a life of the body rather than a life of the mind and spirit," I said. "So, I gave them what they wanted. I set them free to work their limbs and their lungs as they see fit. If they leave the holy life, they can have wine and women and tobacco. That is the trade off."

As I talked, I stepped nearer to the closest one, the largest of the bunch, a good head taller than me, who was also the strongest. They had started calling him The Horse, because of his huge attributes, which included an enormous swinging cock that everyone saw when he got drunk and ran naked around the yard. (I found it amusing, so I permitted this.) In spite of his intransigence, I liked The Horse. But he could not hide his dislike of me; he looked at me strangely as he swung down again and again with the sharp blade, picking up the pace, as I drifted closer. His rage flowed from the sweat on the burning hot muscles of his arms. Right at the peak of his arc, I stepped in and stopped him, with my hand on his shoulder. He glared at me with a mix of fatigue and derision. Despite his massive strength, he might have collapsed.

"My friend, does this life make you happy?" I asked.

I did not pressure him with willpower, I assure you. I can only tell you that I challenged him with his eyes, directly confronting him, man to man. And he blinked. He lowered the pickaxe softly to the ground and wiped his brow. He was defeated.

"Lama, you know we are all working toward a better future in Kobdo, and the rest of Mongolia," he said. He turned to the Chinese delegate. "We are building the next great empire of Asia. As our guest, you should realize this too."

I patted The Horse's shoulder and turned to our Chinese delegate, who cringed when I put my arm around him.

"See?" I said. "It is a testament to what we are doing here that even a former priest understands the need for hard work in the dirt, to raise us toward the skies."

"But Lama," said my guest, glancing back as we walked away, "what exactly is the point of breaking rocks in a field?"

I laughed and led us farther down the dusty thoroughfare.

"That is for me to know, and for them to find out," I said. "Come, I'll show you more."

Next we saw the long rows being planted by the women in irrigated ditches, swinging great bags of seeds on their hips. Some slung Mongol children like small rifles across their backs. A group of men on the side of the field were tending to the creation of a huge latrine. Already they had piled bricks three feet high toward making the building I had ordered just the day before.

"Ah—see this?" I said, slapping my guest on the back. "This is what I am referring to. No more defecating on the ground near the wells where children drink. No more wallowing in filth like beasts. We Mongols will combine the free life of the herds and the yurt, along with the modern trappings. It will bring us up to the standards of not just our cousins in the East—but also those of the European powers."

The emissary simply nodded his smooth face, but a measure of approval was in his eyes as he stared at these people creating a whole new society. My heart beat hard with pride as I walked him back toward the administrative center of town.

But the route took us again past the center where the stocks were. And it was there that another of the punishments was just starting. This was one I had ordered halted until the diplomat had left our town—but I had left Jimbe and the rest to decide the time to begin.

The timing was completely wrong, as so often happens in this life. They were starting the punitive actions just as we neared.

There next to the empty stocks, upon the table splashed with the dark stains, was a large Mongolian, completely nude. He howled into his gag, barely making a sound. At his feet were two of my best lieutenants, a stocky Mongolian named Tömör and a tall European—a newcomer whose hatred burned perpetually in his mad eyes.

They were flaying him alive, removing the skin amid his screams. The small knives they were working with had made precise incisions around the heels, and the toes, and they gradually sliced and peeled upward. The sheet of skin had made it as far as the mid-shin. The blood flowed freely. The gag ripped—torn by the man's teeth—and his howls of horror pierced the air unfettered. The European madman raised his bloody fist and punched him with a resounding blow on the temple, which knocked him unconscious. The man sagged, limp. And the two went back to carefully yanking at the living rind. Off to the side, Jimbe vomited at the sight. My little Chinese messenger doubled over onto the ground and retched.

"And this," I said. "Is a terrible case. Something that could not be avoided."

Just as soon as I had said something the man regained consciousness and started screaming again. The Chinese diplomat looked up at me and wiped at his mouth.

"How could you ever justify something so cruel be done to another human being?" he spat.

I brushed past him and grabbed a handful of the flayed man's hair, lifting the head so the screaming became just a little bit choked. Then I struck his face forehand and backhand, and dropped his skull with a thud back onto the wood.

"This man is no human being," I said, lashing the gag back tight between his gnashing teeth, and the flailing head. "He violated fourteen children—he killed ten of them. The other four we could not find. Nothing, neither bones nor ashes. And it was not just Mongol children. It was little boys and girls of your countrymen, as well, oh most esteemed dignitary of mine. The youngest of his victims was a two-year-old girl. How else can we prevent this from happening again, unless we make the punishment so unimaginably awful it deters the mere thoughts of such evils?"

He stood, and his jaw tightened. He wiped with his sleeve at his mouth. My story had meant nothing. His resolve had flowered. From the look in his eyes, now no longer fearful or innocent, I knew now was the time. We had reached that singular moment of truth for this messenger and me.

"Tyrant!" he screamed. "Killer!"

My guest the assassin pulled a knife from his hidden sheath and ran at me.

I did not move, but at the last moment, I got down low and leaned forward with all my weight, and just as the knife was plunging toward my breastbone, I thrust my heel into his knee, and bone cracked.

The assassin crumpled immediately, screaming, the knife bouncing a few feet away. He tried with one hand to grab his hidden derringer, but I swatted it away. As he clutched at his broken leg, I swept the knife handle away carefully with my foot. I crouched down next to him, taking the small gun into my possession, too.

"I'm going to ask you several questions," I said calmly, tapping the barrel of the tiny pistol against my palm. "And if you tell me what I need to know, I will make sure everything to come will proceed quickly, and there will be relatively little pain.

"But if you do not, I will give you to my friends here," I continued. "They will take their time and make your death as slow as the change of the season. And when it is over, the last thing you see with your dying eyes will be your skin nailed to the outside of my yurt."

The widened eyes told me I had made my case effectively. The trembling hands beseeched me. And the mouth told me everything else, quickly, and without any delay at all. And the execution was the quick flash of his own derringer behind the ear, just as I had promised.

Later on, the mad European was wiping down some of his blood-stained knives with a white handkerchief, soaking them in a bucket, wringing the red stuff out.

The man was barely out of boyhood himself, and he was tall, with a huge forehead and a strange fire in his eyes. But the man's taste for violence set him apart, ever since he had appeared in Kobdo the month before. At first I had thought him a foreign spy, but it was clear from his tenacity that this man had a higher purpose in that enormous, distended skull of his, those hard dark orbs set wide in the middle of them.

I approached him as the dusk faded over the horizon, holding the whip I had taken to carrying around the city so I could urge on the workers more effectively.

"You do well, soldier," I said, in Russian. "I have seen you around Kobdo for some time now. What is your name, and where do you come from?"

The man stood at attention, saluting me in the German and Russian fashion, like trained animals doing tricks. I waved him off, but he still stood there, rigid.

"Lama, my name is Ungern-Sternberg," he replied. "I came to learn from the people of Mongolia. The might and the legacy."

"Oh really," I said. "What do you mean—lessons on how to live in filth and be subjected to the whims of decadent empires from every side? The might of the downtrodden—the legacy of the vanquished?"

Ungern shook his head thoughtfully, wiping one of the wet blades dry on his cloak, then returning it to a sheath at his waist with a sound like a quick hiss of a snake.

"No," he said. "I want to know how to conquer the world. Only one people has ever done that, under your Greatest Khan. I would like to help make that happen again, someday."

I beckoned him up, and I put my arm around his shoulders as we walked past the stocks, which had another lama imprisoned there—this supposed holy man had impregnated a Chinese woman, mixing his holy pure essence with the invaders' impure blood. Before I could speak, this European started talking again.

"There is so much to learn from your rule of law, and your leadership," he said. "If justice is to be absolute, and the fate of Mongolia is for greatness, no quarter can be given. Nothing can be held back—no measure too extreme, and no weapon or torture spared, in the pursuit of victory."

I nodded.

"I believe you will someday take your own stab at greatness," I said.

He stopped in his tracks, so my arm slid out from around him, and we stood apart.

"I did have one question," he said.

"Please, ask away," I said. "I will answer as best I can."

"I understood killing those murdering and rapist Cartel criminals," he said, scratching at an enormous pulsating blood vessel in his temple. "Disgusting fellows, they were. But I still do not understand cutting out their still-beating hearts and drinking their blood from the skulls? What does that accomplish?"

I patted him on the head, then I put my arm around him and started walking slowly, step by step, toward the administrative center of the city we were transforming into the center of the Buddhist world.

"You're from the West," I said, patting him on the back like a true longtime friend, feeling his sinewy, desperate muscle beneath all that clothing intended to make him look more intimidating. "The West, with its Western Sensibilities. You can't truly understand the unforgiving land, the cruel air of Asia. The beasts and men—and the gods in between.

"You have courts of law in Moscow and Berlin, and you have policemen that walk the flat and paved streets at night," I added. "You have pipes to bring water right to your cooking pots, and others to take away the waste.

"We have dirt paths that trip you up while you walk. We have mob rule. We have wells, we have foul ditches.

"We have vengeance, and endless memory."

I squeezed his shoulder as hard as I could, gritting my teeth, and he squirmed away from my grasp.

"You see, this is what we have in Mongolia," I said. "We have this legacy in our blood of total world conquest, of the birthright we have never seen. And yet now we wallow in our own filth and lick the boots of our former slaves. It's a fate worse than death.

"So, you see, the only thing that can match their cruelty to us is barbarity to them in turn," I continued. "It's a cycle that will never end and will drag on for generations that will never quite know where it started, and yet will pursue it without end."

I nodded at him.

"As for the ones who were rapists and killers of children," I said. "Sometimes justice can never be cruel enough."

This Ungern-Sternberg nodded, and he closed his eyes. He placed his sleeves within one another and processed with assured steps, like he was himself a bodhisattva, patiently delaying his own nirvana. All the slaughter, and the talk of bloodshed, had sated his tempestuous soul.

"I believe I understand," he said. "After all, I am a Baron. I come from the nobility. And in Europe, we nobles are a dying breed. We once ruled the whole of the world, hand in hand, from dynasty to dynasty, and century to century. But no longer. It is now the gutter-dwellers who are making trouble and hoping to destroy us all."

I nodded. But I never really understood too much about European castes, their clans and kings and so forth, so I was unsure of what he was speaking. But he spoke of it with conviction, and an assurance so few of the maniacs among us are blessed with.

"I will watch your bid to become Khan," he said. "And if ever you run into trouble with the Russians or the Chinese, I will be sure to support the Mongolian cause to the end. Whatever the cost."

He bowed to me. I bowed to him. Then we turned and went our separate ways.

"That boy is a lunatic," I said to myself a few paces away, not caring to really speak softly. "But maybe that's just the kind of man this century calls for."

CHAPTER 20
ORDER AND THE ABYSS

The fear in the eyes of the people of Kobdo marked my fortunes spinning out of control, like a line of prayer wheels whirled by maniacal children. Even as I lay in the still of the night, I heard the far-off whispers of mutiny and rebellion against me. I never slept, you see; it's always been one of my greatest advantages against my enemies. They all must rest; but I need not.

I rounded up the mutineers and put an end to them. The horror in their faces was identical, as Jimbe and his cadre of warriors I personally selected to keep order in western Mongolia whisked them away.

"I will never understand your foolishness," I told one of them, a howling young man who had been a spy for the Qing. "We are trying to turn the tide here. We are trying to interrupt the cycle of history and set it back on the right track. But it isn't easy, like it isn't easy to move the moon. But it's inevitable, and it is our charge. Your betrayal of that charge leaves me no choice."

The blood thus shed, things quieted down after that. The projects proceeded. We dug three wells in as many months. We repositioned yurts to make straight thoroughfares through the rest of Kobdo beyond the Chinese walls. We tore down those walls, too. An agricultural schedule was begun by some of the experts, splitting the land between cash crops and food, with acres left fallow beside. I gave some of the international merchants who had not been pederasts assurance of my protection, in exchange for better interest rates to the Mongolian people. Within weeks, I had toilet trained the people of the city to leave their waste in the designated pits at strategic locations at the edges of the newly hewn streets.

Still—you must not become haughty, said the voice, that of fakir or father, or both, to me. *The whispers may fade, but they remain.*

I simply could not believe the voice, for once. I dressed up in a disguise, with a long wig atop my head and different clothes and walked the streets incognito. While I heard complaints about the difficulties of making the changes, there was real hope in the words I heard, speaking with tones unaware their leader moved among them.

The Bogd Khan sent a letter and a gift. The letter said he blessed my mission in the Altai west. He gave me advice, written in a mix of Mongolian and Tibetan, to let my spiritual lessons guide me in the tug of war between the Russians and Chinese.

The gift…well, that was a pig.

A prized little pet, cute and adorned with a blue bow on its ear, which came from the Bogd's own menagerie. The messenger told me the pig could do tricks and was one of the holy man's favorites. The Bogd felt he could finally part with it because of the auspicious rise of the Mongols of Kobdo.

Within a half hour of sending the messenger back on his way to Urga, I had that pig turning on a spit over a low fire. I fed it to the poorest of Kobdo, and some cheered. But many others were silent, in the shadows.

While I understood the Chinese sending their boy-assassin after me, and the networks of Cartel spies they and the Russians had embedded in my city like so many fleas in a mongrel's fur, I could not understand the insubordination of the Mongolian people themselves.

I had come to believe we as a people had become lazy in the centuries since we swept across the plain. Our warrior spirit had withered at so many roots that once held fast the soils of Asia. And I was now more certain than ever before that I was the shears to prune the dead branches and make the whole family tree healthy again.

"Do you want to put out another call for volunteers to construct the armory this week?" Jimbe asked me one Sunday, while we shared a leg of lamb in the flickering firelight.

"Just requisition some of the families from the next valley," I said, chewing a bloody tendon.

"If you say so, Lama," he said. "I just want to be sure that we're enlisting enough strength to be able to haul the stones. Those are mostly women over there, you know."

"They can pitch in, just the same as the rest of us," I said. "The children can play, but the men and the women work side by side."

Jimbe stared at me for a second, and then bit into the rare meat, the juice cascading down his chin.

"Whatever happened to Amursanaa?" he asked in a flat voice—not loud, but not soft, either.

"What do you mean?" I asked, actually taken aback by the name which had not passed my lips in so long, perhaps a year or more.

"I mean, you once told the people that you were the reincarnation of the strongest Mongol since the Greatest Khan," he said. "But yet you have not mentioned it once since the taking of Kobdo and the greatest victories yet for our cause. Is there a reason for this?"

I gripped his shoulder, hard.

"I am proving that I am the second coming of the great prince through my deeds and actions, dear Jimbe," I said. "Words can only say so much, and they do even less. They only take up air, they only distort the very oxygen you breathe. You have to learn this, Jimbe, my friend."

He blinked, but he did not wince as I squeezed the muscle there and stared him down.

Beware your own reason, Lama, said the voice from nowhere, yet again. *Words have as much magic in them as gunpowder these days.*

The next day was when the summons came from Urga, carried by a messenger in gray robes, a middle-aged man with the look of a predatory hawk, sharp eyes, and a pinched nose like a razored beak. He strode up to the front of my yurt, where I waited with a hunk of goat cheese oozing between my fingers.

"I have already received word from the Bogd," I said, bowing to him. "I hope he has not sent more gifts. We are all out of spits."

The messenger bowed, but his face was fixed in a businesslike mask. He held out a parchment. Once I took it, he had the impudence to turn on his heel and walk away. I was so affronted by his presumption to turn his back on me, I nearly gave Jimbe and the guards the order to slit his throat. But something held my hand. Instead, I stuffed the goat cheese in my mouth and unrolled the document.

The missive was from Damdinsuren and Magsarjav, my former allies in the conquest of Kobdo just a year before. As I read, a queasy feeling rippled through my innards. Toward the end of the communiqué, I almost choked on the cheese. I spat it all out and had to steady myself and I sat down on the ground, right in the dirt outside the yurt entrance. I read it again.

Dear Lama,

We humbly greet you. We congratulate you on your supremacy in the West. Not since the time of the Greatest Khan have the Mongols been so feared by our neighbors. We now consider the Altai Mountains to be a stronghold against Chinese and Russian invaders alike.

Accordingly, we hereby invite you to meet us in Urga as soon as possible. We have to coordinate our response to some of the incursions by the Qing and the Romanovs, as well as some of the highwaymen who still stalk the open roads of our fine land despite your iron-handed crackdowns. Your reporting directly back to the capital will be the best way to get back some unity of purpose to our future campaigns. It will also help establish a strong state government based on government for the Mongolian people, based on our faith.

Please come forthwith to Urga. Take with you as much security as you need, but within the city they will not be necessary, and will be disarmed before coming within the walls.

We look forward to seeing you, Lama.

Sincerely,
Manlaibataar
and
Khatanbataar

I dropped the document and cursed my enemies with language unfit for the lowliest brothels of Asia. To think that Damdinsuren and Magsarjav—now the pompous Manlaibataar, "First Hero," and the even more ridiculous Khatanbataar, "Firm Hero"—had these honorific names enraged me in that moment. I sprung to my feet and went inside my yurt. Jimbe's footsteps followed me inside. I didn't turn to greet him; I was too busy furiously drafting a response message to those traitorous whelps.

My recall to Urga was simply an invitation to death. And they knew I knew, too. That's what made it all the worse, the wretched impertinence of the gesture by these "Heroes."

"What's wrong, Lama?" said Jimbe. "What did the letter say?"

I did not answer. I harnessed all the bile rising in my throat for the missive I was drafting at that moment.

Estimable Heroes,

After reading your letter, and meditating on your effusive praise, I realize I have been working too hard out here in the borderlands. I have come down with an illness of the foot the doctors have not yet found a way to name, let alone cure. Thus, I must stay here in Kobdo. I will relinquish my duties until I am recovered enough to again assume command of the military and material needs of the region. My trusty colleague Jimbe will be assuming the interim leadership post here, in both name and reputation.

And Damdinsuren and Magsarjav, please accept my most sincere congratulations on your "Hero" titles. Please give the Bogd my regards, as well. He sent me a pet pig that arrived here just a short while ago, and I welcomed him like you might a friend and ally.

Sincerely,
Ja Lama

I handed Jimbe the note. A strange smile crossed his face. I had taught him a rudimentary literacy while we were out on the trail, so he had read the note over my shoulder. And he clearly was concerned and elated in equal measure.

"Illness of the foot, Lama?" he said. "Are you really putting me in charge? That would be such a smart strategy! Brilliant! I can work from within, planning all the while to bring you back to your rightful place of power against those ruffians."

I stared at him. He had never been more elated than at that moment, the promise of power. I flicked him hard in the ear with my finger, and he yelped.

"No, Jimbe," I said, "I do not mean to actually put you in charge. And my only illness is how damned sick I am of these turncoats trying to impede our progress. My progress."

His jaw was slack, as the piece of paper dangled low in his hand. I reached forward, helped him fold it and then tuck it into his pack.

"I want you to take this pack and load it up with a few hunks of the cured pork from the Bogd's pig. Put the blue bow on the fattiest chunk. I want those bastards to see what I'm capable of," I said. "Give the package to the fastest rider there is in the city—probably that Batu boy from the stables. And then come back here, and we will plot our next move."

I patted his face with my palm, hard enough just to break him out of his stupor. Then he wiped his eyes and carried out my orders. In the meantime, I realized it would only be a matter of time before I would be challenged. I quickly cleaned and loaded my two Colts and prepared for the inevitable.

The voice arrived unbidden, as it always did.

Don't eat the pig, said the voice.

But I did, eating the last of the roasted ribs from the Bogd's pig, one bone of which lodged itself in my windpipe. And as I choked, inevitability arrived in the form of eighty drunk and armed Russians right at that remarkable moment.

That very moment.

At this crucial crux of history, I was virtually helpless.

As I flailed around, driving my sternum down into the edge-point of a trunk in my yurt to dislodge the blockage, the thunder of hoofbeats resounded—long before their shouts, or their dust, or their rifles. They simply appeared out of the northern foothills. The sentries had not warned anyone, and that was something I later decided had been purposeful mutiny. It felt like my heart had stopped, my lungs had seized.

The marauders slashed at a few of the delirious half-asleep Mongol men as they passed, killing only a half dozen of them outright, but it was enough to set everyone back on their heels. So there was no resistance—not a single shot fired—as they encircled my city of Kobdo.

A hundred yards out, I knew they were close. Still choking, unable to breathe, I grabbed the two Colts and crept out of the flap. I cocked the weapons and listened to the hoofbeats grow in terrorizing thunder. At this point, you realize, I assumed these were Chinese imperial cavalry, and I was convinced there would be a thousand of them to topple our independence. But still I assured myself I would take as many to the grave with me as I could.

My air ran out. As consciousness faded, I fell to the ground, a stone punching up into my midsection.

Just as I coughed up the bone, they were upon me. Rifles pointed, they were all around—and in the split-second before I could aim my weapons at them, I saw their uniforms.

"Goddamned godless Russians!" I rasped, gasping. "Die!"

I pulled the triggers again and again, cocking and emptying the cylinders in rage.

And that's when everything, once again, went black.

You have so much yet to learn, said the voice into my void, from which I could not escape.

CHAPTER 21
SIBERIA, EXILE, BEYOND

The Russians would never let me pick the hell of my own choosing. Nothing about hell is voluntary, after all. The torture is in being bound, constrained. The Czar's secret police were experts at all sorts of prisons, of course.

They were ecstatic with capturing me with so little fuss, just three of them dead, and their quarry badly wounded, relatively defenseless. I had been shot in the left arm, and they endlessly prodded the wound to keep it bleeding as we journeyed westward. I gritted my teeth and thought about using my willpower, but I was simply too physically drained and bloodless to try.

The wagon clattered, once again away from the homeland where I had finally found intermittent happiness and purpose. I remember nothing those first days. I drifted out of consciousness continually, and it was day and night in moments. I may have been drugged, and it felt as if my heart ceased beating for hours, maybe weeks, at a time. All I recall is the baleful barking of the Russian language all around, the crack of whips, the moans of the slow trudging horses.

Only once did a familiar smell wake me from this reverie, after what seemed like an eternity. It was the familiar fetid stench of the asafoetida, that horrible resin tree of Kazakhstan. Beyond that was the empty space of water not far off. I knew at that moment I was again passing Lake Balkhash. I shook myself and slowly stretched my shackled limbs as far as they would extend. I rolled onto my side and angled myself upward to look over the side of the cart.

It was high noon. The great curve of the lake extended off into the horizon, pointing back east like a gnarled finger toward Mongolia. I sighed, closing my eyes, knowing fate was wrapping its vines around me tightly once again. The cart clattered like an epileptic chicken over that primitive Kazakh road, and sickness rose in my gullet. But I held it down, and I gestured to the nearest Russian guard in the cart to bring me some water. He laughed and spit square in my face.

Anger rose in my chest, but I only shook my head. I had very little willpower left in me, but with my remaining energy I reached out with my mind and I felt how weak and drunk this cretin's soul was. I gently nudged him to tip a flask of something up to my mouth. It was vodka, and I nearly spit its acrid taste out, but I immediately realized how the poison blotted both my pain and the filthy scent of the Kazakh trees, so I greedily took a second swallow. I nodded at the guard, and he set it aside and returned to his place. I forced him to smile. Then, with just a slightly stronger nudge to his frail psyche, he stuck the muzzle of his rifle under his chin, cocked the action, and pulled the trigger.

The cart stopped for a few minutes while the Russians investigated the apparent suicide of their compatriot, mopping up chunks of brain and brushing skull fragments off the cart. They worked around me, scowling and occasionally snarling at me. But I was totally immobile at this point from loss of blood, and they saw I was physically unable to have attacked their fellow idiot. Even as they rummaged around me, I angled my exhausted head to look through a hole in the side of the cart, one just wide enough to peer through, in the direction of that foul lake in that godforsaken land.

But a crowd blocked my view. It was a mob of Kazakhs milling around. A wind howled, and it blew dust in wheeling gusts around them. Their faces were covered, their arms raised to shield them from the worst of the advancing dust storm.

Except two of them. The pair was totally mismatched: one gargantuan, the other thin and fey in comparison. They stood there, their eyes staring from little slits in their face coverings, their arms hanging limp at their sides. They stared. The skin around their eyes, though dirty, was as light as Europeans. And I had a pressing feeling I knew the pair.

"Alexei killed himself, no doubt about it," said one of the Russians. "He blew his brains out, by his own hand."

"The question is: why," said another. "He was always so happy. He sang. Something must have happened."

The two of them looked down at me. I blinked at them.

"Your man gave me a drink while we were talking of our homes," I said. "He kept saying how terrible he felt about being a murderer and a rapist before he shot himself. The guilt must have done him in."

"You lie!" shouted the leader, stooping, and smacking my face. "Alexei was a good and brave man, and he would never have done any of those things you describe—least of all kill himself. If you don't tell me, so help me, I'll beat the truth out of you, False Lama."

He lunged toward me, but the other one restrained him. I smiled, because even if he had broken free I would have killed him with a sharp shard of metal tucked up my sleeve. I promise you: no matter how weak I am, I will always find a way to gut one last lackluster mercenary, a final secret policeman. The other one dragged him away, his boot heels scraping along the wood floor of the cart.

"You will pay, False Lama," he spat back at me, six others hauling him away. "You will get exactly what you deserve, even if it's while you sleep."

Moments later, a few more Russians hoisted the headless body away. I heard the bones crash against the hard dirt below. And moments after that, the cart moved. I peered through my hole in the wood, and I saw the crowd of Kazakhs descend on the body like a flock of vultures, stripping the clothing, flinging the effects in every direction, struggling over each stitch. Except the two strange Europeans. Each simply held a hand up in salute as the cart pulled away.

The trip after that was a grueling one—for the Russians.

One morning there was a great general cry when they awoke. The first few had awakened to find the wagon barreling on—without a rider at the reins. It had been the turn of the leader, the one who had spit at me, at the front. He had simply disappeared from his perch overnight. Panicked, the other Russians stopped the cart to a clattering halt. They sent one of their number back on one of the horses a few versts to see if there was any sign of their compatriot back down the trail, if the drunken bastard had nodded off in the middle of the night and fallen out of the cart. The scout returned, reporting he'd found…nothing. To a man they looked at me with terror. I smiled.

I can tell you, the rest of the trip passed without incident, even though in the night I heard some of them whispering about throwing me off the wagon and speeding west as fast as they could. The terrified hissings I heard in response dismissing such thoughts made it clear my travels would be safe all the way back to the Caspian Sea—simply because they feared what I might do before they could get rid of me. Still, when we neared the Aral Sea, just as they relaxed a bit, I made sure that another of their number vanished in the middle of the night. They found a single torn kidney in his place on the wagon. This truly horrified them.

For the last seven hundred versts or so we made double time all the way back to…the same damnable view of the Volga, where they kicked me out of the cart—right back on Pestelya Street. Three of them shoved me in the door of the same damnable apartment building with the same damnable courtyard where I had already wasted away a good part of my life, with only a sack of some of my blood-stained clothes. Men at three windows overhead stood in shadows and clouds of cigarette smoking, watching this, my homecoming. The Czar's secret police lit cigarettes in shadowy windows down the street, resuming their surveillance.

Three floors, seventeen rooms, and crooked floorboards. I staggered into the door and toward the stairs of this my once and future prison house, compliments of the disgusting emperors from the Cartel of Russia and China and beyond. But I dropped my bag and fell to my knees at the threshold of the courtyard. I rubbed my eyes in disbelief.

Because in the chair where I had spent so many of my prime years, legs crossed and daintily smoking a cigarette, sat the girl with the black swishing hair.

"I thought you'd never make it," she said, voice sultry, the streaks of gray in her hair catching the light for a moment.

And with that, I collapsed to the ground.

I awoke in a bed to my former fiancé doing some dexterous stitchwork on the hole in my arm. The needle and thread were twisted in her delicate fingers. I was in my old bedroom. It was dark and filled with the identical wooden furniture and piles of paper junk. Not a single item had moved, other than the extra layers of dust.

"It's been years since I've done this," she said, noticing I was awake, smiling down at me. "If you want to just pull this taut, you should heal up pretty nicely."

I took the thread and pulled. She tied it off close to my skin. In truth, she had done a masterful job.

But I was more focused, of course, on her—this long unrequited love of mine. Even by the standards of bizarre backlands Asian and subterranean worlds I'd traveled, seeing her again was remarkable. I wondered if my downfall in Mongolia had precipitated a final break with true reality. Had my mind finally broken? Was she really there? *Was I still alive?* Her eyes gazed into mine with a withering intensity.

"Don't worry too much; you're not insane. You've seen crazier in your time anyway, haven't you, Palden?" she said lighting a cigarette.

She remembered my true name. I still did not remember hers. She ran the backs of her fingers across my cheek. I grabbed her hand. But she just laughed.

"You still have some of that Mongolian spirit in you, after all," she said. "And you still don't remember my name."

She clucked her tongue and sat down on the edge of the bed. She ran her hand over my arm.

"What happened—did you lose the battle back in your motherland?" she said. "It's hard, fighting the Russians and the Chinese at the same time. Caught between a rock and a hard place, you know."

She sliced off the ends of the thread. I crawled out of bed and paced around the perimeter of the bedroom. She smoked her cigarette, then lit another one.

"No, I did not lose any battle," I spat at her, after a time. "I won every fight. I conquered every foe before me."

"But what about the ones behind you?" she asked.

"Those bastards knew just where to stick the knife," I hissed, nodding.

I stepped behind her, admiring that beautiful black head of hair. But in that half-light, I saw new silver streaks in her mane—and the wrinkles in the skin at the nape of her neck. Time had caught up with both this erstwhile girl of past fantasy—and also with me.

I hobbled from the room and went down to the courtyard. She followed. I paced, and she sat as twilight started to fall. I did revolutions around the open space, under that sky. I took stock of it. A new rocking chair waited in the corner. New growth had appeared in some nooks: weeds sprung out of the dirt in some of the corners, and some of the skeletal bushes had miraculously bloomed green once again.

The goat was gone from this prison. And here, in his place, was this girl from my past. Her features were utterly stark, as beautiful as they were horrific in that twilight.

She wouldn't shut up. Often it wasn't words. Sometimes she sang in some Chinese dialect I didn't know. It sounded vaguely familiar—did I hear some pidgin Kazakh in there?—but I couldn't make it out. I kept pacing, and even as my feet kept bringing me around and around in that circle of dirt and sprouts, I found myself meditating.

Mongolia. My one true love. She had turned out to be such an utter disappointment. It was something that I had never known—that my beloved homeland had completely and utterly let me down.

My first failures and my personal disfigurement had been the product of hostile foreigners, the Russians and Chinese and even some of those Kazakhs conspiring to keep Mongolia fractured, hobbled, weakened. They knew in their blood the terror of the past, the raids of the Greatest Khan ever to ride across the vast expanses and lay waste to everything that opposed him, armies and cities, even forests and mountains. They feared such a resurgence of our national pride, our inherent superiority on horse, and at war.

But the second time it was the treachery of my own Mongols which had let the enemy in. Traitors in our midst. Some of our own had opened the gates, and they'd welcomed in the invaders. And while I knew there was dissatisfaction among some of the troublemakers and malcontents, I had no intimation how deep it was buried within ourselves—until it had been too late.

Truly, if one struggles one's whole life to achieve something, only to discover their quest is an utter failure, what options are left?

The girl's voice had stopped. And I realized she had been singing. It had not been spoken words at all. The sound had been strangely like that of...a singing bowl. But now she cleared her throat.

"If you're going to move back permanently into your old room," she intoned, coughing out the smoke from another cigarette, "you'll have to stop dwelling on all the lost chances in your past. And for all that is holy, stop that infernal pacing."

I stopped my steps. My rage rose.

"And you who are so wise, just a girl from Dolonnuur, what kind of insights are you offering me?" I said. "Can you peer into the soul of Mongolia, or the hearts of men? What do you know, other than seducing monks or smoking your filthy cigarettes?"

Her eyes narrowed as she took a deep drag of tobacco. She leaned back and blew the smoke straight up at the sky, where it vanished immediately into the very clouds above.

"Nothing but doom," she said, laughing, "You always were doomed, Palden. But we all are, aren't we? The only end for everything is to be tossed into the abyss from whence we came. And not your golden city, mind you—but the all-consuming darkness which is the foundation of the entire universe."

She doubled over, coughing. I leapt forward and raised her chin, inspecting her beauty. Her hair was more silver than black, on closest inspection. The years had taken their toll, indeed.

"How do you know about Agharti?" I asked. "How can a merchant's daughter know about paradise?"

She smiled, knowing and sly.

"I know much only because I long ago embraced my doom, my ineffable fate. That means I know everything," she said. "After my dowry was lost, I tracked you down. I wanted you to know how it felt to be left powerless. I traveled all of Asia, and I found you. I took you, that one night. Then I went and saw the rest of the world."

She snickered.

"How about you, Lama? Have you yet found a way to let go of the cares and whims of the world, and discovered a way to float along with the unseen tide of things? To revel in the doom, as it were?"

"If that's all there is, then why would any of us continue to do anything at all?" I asked. "Why would we even continue to go about each day, or eat, or even breathe? Why would you or I even be talking here?"

"I get hungry," she said, stubbing out her cigarette, nodding. "Got to eat. I get grouchy otherwise."

She rose with a moan from her seat, and she stretched her arms high overhead. And she herself paced, step by step by step in front of me.

"I find that life is infinitely easier than death," she said. "But to make life go, we need to at least work at it a little, don't you think?"

The talk went on like that for hours. Finally, I was just too tired from blood loss and my weeks of travel, so that I simply crawled up to my old room and collapsed on the dust-covered bed. My sleep was utterly dreamless.

I awoke with the smell of something burning. I jolted upright. She was sitting in the corner, smoking.

"I know you are no longer capable of loving me the way you once did," she said.

Groggily I wiped my eyes and turned over.

"The world has taken much from me," I said. "But it has given me other things in trade. I apologize for any youthful transgressions against you. I was an unruly youth. I can see that now."

She smiled and flicked the cigarette in my sheets. With a yelp, I kicked the flaring ember to the floorboards.

"You've slept long enough," she said, clapping her hands once. "Time to get to work."

The girl with the swishing silver hair led me downstairs. And just as her heels clattered at the bottom of the flight, there came a knock at the entrance of the building. We walked toward the door, but she slipped me a strip of paper and slid into the shadows before the passageway.

"Hand them this, and have them bring the shipment into the courtyard," she whispered, sliding into the darkness behind the door.

Although my suspicions warned me against obeying the strange directions from this woman in the shadows, I nonetheless answered the knock.

A man with the weather-beaten face and thick clothes of a mariner stood there, unsmiling. Behind him was a motley crew of hirsute men. He held out his hand. Into it I placed the slip. Without averting his eyes from mine, he folded the paper in half, slid it in a breast pocket, nodded once, turned, and motioned to the crowd behind him. He then pushed through the threshold, dragging the front of a huge train of carts.

Behind him came a procession of a dozen other strong serious men, all the huge containers covered with sheets. The odor of the sea wafted to my nose. They wheeled the line to a spot in the courtyard, and then turned on their heels. The leader waited until the last one had filed out, and then slipped me a piece of paper in return—it was a hundred-ruble note with the face of a dead Czar on it. He pulled the door shut behind him. The moment it closed, the woman sprung forward from her hiding spot and clicked the latch to lock it. She clapped again, once.

"Well now, let's get to it," she said, sashaying toward the courtyard.

"Get to what?" I asked.

Pulling the first cloth, she revealed huge mounds of fish. Ugly, scaly, pungent fish with bloody staring eyes. The salty smell rose feverishly. The other containers were unveiled. Dozens of the leviathans. The size of sea monsters, they were—some had to weigh a ton or more.

"What are we supposed to do with all these fish?"

"Not just any fish. Beluga sturgeon," she corrected, patting me on the back. "The most valuable fish in the entire Caspian. Their caviar and meat are the envy of the entire world."

"So what?" I said, turning and sniffing at the brackish scales of three of the biggest ones. "Are we going to eat them?"

The metallic scrape of knives sharpening came from behind. I wheeled around, and she gripped a knife in each hand, her eyes fixed strangely on me. But before I could assume a defensive posture against her blade, she offered me the handle of one of them.

"No, these aren't for us to eat. They are for us to clean and gut and get ready for market," she said, nodding slowly, as if I was simple. "For money. This is your job now."

A job it was. She demonstrated deft maneuvers with her blade. The horrendous fins and spikes had to be sliced off. Then two cuts behind the head and toward the tail. Running the blade up the length of the spinal cord and across the ribcage loosened the meaty flanks just enough to have them come apart, with some strong effort. The filets were then stacked on a nearby table and wrapped in wax paper. All the wasted guts and gore went into an enormous bin at the center, which quickly overflowed with blood and waste that ran out onto the ground, fertilizing the hard-packed dirt.

Hours flew by, and the shadows grew long in the courtyard. I had reached the final few males when my mentor completed the final female's egg sac, carefully collecting all the rich caviar into an enormous jar.

"This," she said to me, tapping a long fingernail on the side of the glass jar, "is worth a king's ransom. You could buy the finest of anything in Astrakhan with such a motherlode."

"Let's keep it for ourselves," I said, flinging a fish head atop the waste pile.

"God, no," she said. "It wouldn't do to cheat our employer of his goods. Our legal remuneration is enough, you'll see."

"Who is our employer?" I asked, slicing into more guts.

But she never answered me—not in that moment, or ever.

The girl with the swishing silver hair helped me dissect the last of the males, and then we stacked all the filets and the enormous caviar jar on two of the carts.

The heads, guts, and viscera overflowed the bin. We had barely five minutes before sundown when another knock came at the door. My companion assumed her secret spot behind the door, and I opened it. In streamed the fish merchant and his crew. Without a word, they went to the carts and the refuse bin, and wheeled them out of the building the same way they'd entered. As the last one disappeared beyond the threshold, the merchant stepped toward me and slung a huge bag into my arms. It clinked with coins. He nodded and left, pulling the door shut behind him.

My partner stepped forward and caught the bag of money, just as my wounded arm gave way underneath its weight.

"Riches await those who wait," she croaked, lighting a cigarette. "Let's celebrate."

My unrequited fiancé was a drunk, as it turns out.

She pulled out a huge jar of vodka and drank heartily as I tended to a fire I built in the courtyard. Over it I prepared a potato and onion soup as the darkness gathered overhead. My companion swilled her stuff with a thirst that was superhuman. As she talked her words loosened, and she bleated in between her pidgin Mongolian and smoother Chinese. She told me about her time as a rejected woman out on the Asian steppe. She had one true love in all her life, in Inner Mongolia. It was not me; it was an even sadder tale.

"They're all sad tales, as you know," she said.

The farmer, she recounted, was a fiercely efficient man who had every part of every season notched into a calendar on his wall. He would not stray from it for anything, no matter what germs or blight or weather had befallen his house and fields. The girl with the swishing black hair, being still young, had come on as a field hand. The farmer had a son, and this son was her true love. The girl and the son exchanged glances over the hay and the reaping—then smiles over the seeds. When the day was over, the farmer swore in hissed whispers and warnings at his son at the far corners of the land—but the girl still heard every word. The son would return with lowered eyes and would not look at the girl the rest of that evening. But the next morning, as the sun drew high and the sweat really began to flow, the son and the girl locked eyes and it would start all over again.

Until one summer night, the girl crept into the family's yurt. She needed to kiss the son; it was an itch that must be scratched. She could not stop herself, consequences be damned. One step after another, she snuck across the family's snoring forms to the son at the back of the yurt. She got on all fours and lowered her lips to his. He kissed her back, and his hands roved over her body. She stripped off her clothes, she peeled off the blankets, grasped the son's rigid manhood, and lowered herself down onto him. When all was finished, she kissed her lover and then crawled her way out of the yurt, step by step...until she stepped on a finger of the sleeper nearest the flap. A yelp of pain startled her, and she leapt out the yurt and ran back to her bed.

The next day, as she bent over one of the troughs, she felt a rough hand on her ass. She turned around with a deep breath and a smile.

The smile fell. The farmer-father stood there, grinning and nodding. And behind him was the son, scowling, with a splint on his finger.

She stole a horse and went west that very night.

"That story sounds very familiar," I said.

"With a much different ending," she said, jabbing the bottle at me.

"Was it me?" I said, stoking the fire, and stirring the cauldron. "Was I the one that set you on the wrong path?"

She smiled briefly, shaking her head.

"Perhaps," she said. "Or maybe not. Perhaps we're all just prayer wheels in an endless line spinning forever at one another."

"Perhaps that's it," I conceded. "One can never be sure of anything in the heart of Asia, where the climate and fate are each as fickle as a human soul."

She tapped the bottle to her brow, in a sign of salute, then swigged more vodka.

"What is your name?" I asked. "Long ago you told me...but I never truly knew."

"Does it truly matter?" she said. "Will my name change anything? We could have loved. I could have been a wife. You could still have a cock. But here we are, unmarried and sexless."

A moment of stillness. But then I laughed. She laughed. We clinked glasses.

Years went by like that, with questions for questions that meant nothing in this life. And to an extent, we were happy. We professed love, but its true physical nature was obviously impossible. We slept nestled together in my musty bedroom, through the cold of winter and the scald of summer and everything in between. Our kisses were tender and pure.

During days we filleted what must have been all the fish of the Caspian Sea. Hundreds of bins filled with the wasted heads, gills, and guts. We harvested millions of eggs and enough hearty beluga meat to market to feed all of Mongolia, perhaps all of Kazakhstan, too. Not that any such delicacy would ever reach those impoverished mouths so far away.

My heart was there every time I slept, however—in these dreams I fought the Chinese and the Russians all alone, slashing at an endless horde for hours while I jerked around like a beached fish in the bed. In some of these dreams I was cut down mercilessly, chopped to bloody pieces quivering out the last spasms of life in the dirt. But there were other visions of crystalline perfection: memories of playing with the little Mongol children, as they crawled all over me in a swarm, and where I rode dear Chingis on the endless steppe toward the absolute edge of the world.

I dreamt too of making love all those years ago to the young girl with the swishing black hair, back when such things were not only possible, but life lived itself.

Only once, in my one thousand days in Astrakhan, did I dream of Agharti. It was no longer the paradise shown to me in fleeting glimpses. The streets of gold were not liquid anymore. They were viscous; they supported neither foot nor boat. And I sank. Even as my heart leapt up to find myself back in the perfect place, the horror rose in my stomach, chest, shoulders—my very being. Burning smells rose all around me, as if my flesh was being incinerated from the feet on up. Only then did I sense something hard and unforgiving on my shoulder, hammering me down harder and faster into the drowning richness. I opened my eyes.

And it was she tapping me hard on the shoulder, trying to wake me. The smoke from her cigarette had enveloped my head on the pillow. The odor, once repugnant to me, had become comforting. I turned over, away from awareness. It was the beginning of winter, and still darkest morning.

"Wake, my love," she whispered. "The sun will soon rise. More work is on its way. Sharpen your knife and come to the courtyard."

More days flew by. Yet more years passed. As they do. I never determined how this woman had set up a lucrative seafood business, let alone captured my hardened heart. I never knew our employer—though I suspected it was really her insatiable liver which reaped all the profits. Her hair shined totally silver, all streaks of black melted away in the time we had shared.

One day, she did not wake me. I stumbled out of bed when the sun was high in the sky. When I got down the stairs, my girl with the swaying silver hair paced back and forth, waving her knife around like she was in mortal combat with an invisible enemy. After a while she flung the blade into a wood wall with exceptional accuracy, right at head height. She sauntered over, collected it, went back across the courtyard, and threw it again. And again. And again.

We sat like that until late afternoon. Finally, just as the sun was beginning its final arc down the western sky, there came a little rapping on the front door— nothing like the hard pounding at the door of the beefy mariner's hand. Nonetheless, the woman leapt up and started yammering, cursing about how late they were and how the work would last through the night. I grabbed her and corralled her into her normal hiding spot, and I opened the door.

The tiny figure was still cloaked in dusky shadow. But even after all those years I knew it at once as Vasily, the little merchant I'd last seen in the outer reaches of Lhasa. I laughed happily. He stepped forward into the stray light from a torch nearby, and I recoiled.

Vasily's face was a pockmarked horror, looking for all the world like he'd been struck with leprosy, syphilis, and a half-dozen flesh-eating maladies besides. What was left of his nose was blackened and pitted. He shuffled forward and started to fall, reaching a diseased hand out to my shoulder. I caught it and hauled his wraithlike arm around my shoulders.

"Come, friend," I said, "it's been too many years. Let me make you some food. We will catch up."

"Uhnnnhnnmm," he moaned, the only sound he could make.

I fixed some fish-head soup, mixing in onions and potatoes. When I placed the steaming bowl in front of our guest, he greedily slurped down the scalding concoction. The searing of his flesh from the still-boiling soup made me cringe, but my disfigured guest seemed not to notice. Devouring the entire brew in a minute, he belched and gestured upward with the bowl. I ladled out another helping. This happened twice more. The woman watched with bemused detachment, as she smoked and delicately sipped from a label-less bottle. Vasily drained the fourth helping, and he dropped the empty metal bowl on the ground, which clattered and rolled in a circle as he reclined back in the chair. He belched, sounding for all the world like he would choke.

"I have not eaten in two weeks," he said, sighing. "I have not had a moment's rest since Irkutsk."

"What were you doing there?" I said. "I last saw you and Boris in Tibet. I hoped you had found a place just for you."

His hideous face crinkled at the mention of the other Russian, his lover. The pain rippled across his face until he brought it under control, boils, sores, and all.

"Wrong—you had seen us once more since," said Vasily, scratching at his eyes with his gnarled fingertips.

"We had some beautiful years together," he continued. "You saw the beginning of what would become the best time of our lives, Lama.

"In Tibet we broke away from the other Russians, and we used that gold you gave us to travel. We rode trains and horses to corners of Asia we had never heard of before, let alone seen. We journeyed throughout the highlands of the Himalayas. We walked the bazaars of India, the crowded cities there, and the abandoned stone dwellings of Cambodia and Thailand. We saw the splendor and chaos in China, from the starving peasants of Canton to the frozen streets of Harbin and right up to the ramparts of the Great Wall."

"Did the money last?" I asked, nodding.

"The money never ran out," Vasily said. "But our luck surely did."

The erstwhile merchant sighed and leaned back. The woman leaned forward and offered her lit cigarette. Vasily grabbed it from her with two withered fingers without so much as batting an eye and puffed on it greedily. He sank in his chair, limp, like the story he was about to unload had defeated him utterly.

"Travel across the strange lands of Asia has never been safe for most. For some, it brings nothing short of mortal danger. With Boris and I having our particular…way of life…it was inevitable that we would run afoul of some hateful person out there. We just never expected it to be the Czar's secret police in what some call Poland.

"You see, after we had settled down, we sank the money we had left into a little shop outside Krakow," he said. "We had heard from people who'd shared similar forbidden love as ours that this one town in southeastern Poland was a place where two men could live free together, if discreetly. We took over a general store, with my hand on the money and the numbers, and Boris using his still-impressive strength to do the lifting and stocking of the dry goods and supplies. We worked long days and weeks, and the locals were all unanimously friendly and punctual with payments. Within a few weeks, we had nearly doubled the business on the previous owner's books. Everything proceeded better than our plan—until The Incident.

"One of the most frequent customers was a big burly Ukrainian, the local butcher," he continued. "But the butcher moonlighted as the local constable, as well. One day when business was slow, Boris came over to me behind the counter and encircled me around the waist and we started kissing. It was just a tender, spur-of-the-moment thing. But at that particular moment the door burst open, and there stood this butcher. Boris and I quickly pushed away from one another, straightening out our shirts and the like. But the butcher's face was twisted in hate as he backed out the door. Boris and I laughed, knowing some of the Jewish ladies in the town thought we made a good couple. We were living in such progressive, good times— if it was only the local pigheaded butcher horrified by our true love, who cared? What could he do?

"The Czar's secret police came at the cock's crow at the cold of the next dawn. They beat on the door until they kicked it down—just as we stirred in our bed. The arrest and the conviction in the nearest court took mere hours. From there, a quick judgment sent us packing on a train eastward to a prison camp outside Lake Balkhash. And it was there that my dear Boris, already in decline for so many years, suffered to the end. His powerful frame vanished by days into the unforgiving Siberian atmosphere.

"I didn't fare much better," Vasily continued, gesturing at his ruined face, "but I did survive all the years of cold, and privations, and meaningless work. It was the Revolution, you see. The Bolsheviks cast out all the killers, robbers, and rapists out of the Czar's old prisons. But they also cast out all the old homosexuals, too.

"The last walk Boris and I took around Lake Balkhash, during a dust storm no less, will forever be sealed within my soul. We didn't move fast, and the wind kicked up right as we reached the farthest point from our camp. But who did we see imprisoned in the back of a Russian cart full of soldiers? Our old friend the Lama!

"Boris gripped my arm in that huge viselike hand of his, which was nonetheless always so gentle. He whispered, 'We must give him eternal thanks for the life he allowed us to have out on the road for the time we had.'

"But your cart left to the west before we could reach you. Boris succumbed the very next day. Siberia had been too much for him, as it is for almost all men," Vasily said.

He stifled a little sob.

"But what little time we had, what meager peace we shared… You enabled it all to happen, Lama. And for that I am eternally grateful.

"When Boris had said to seek you out I merely nodded, not really understanding what he was saying. At that time, I was merely concerned with his survival in that hellish place," said Vasily. "But when the gates of the prison camp were thrown open by marauding Reds one blustery day in the Spring of revolution, I thought only of tracking down the Lama. I had no family or friends left to speak of, after so many years on the road. Boris had been my all. I needed to find you. I needed to tell you that you can again roam freely your native Mongolian steppe, since the Bolshevik chaos has set all of the Czar's enemies loose again on the land. The outlaws are once again free."

He nodded at my love, then continued.

"It wasn't easy. But your legend has grown. Eventually I reached Astrakhan, and I came directly to this building on Pestelya Street you always cursed on the trail. I must say, I didn't expect you to have a beautiful companion," he said, smiling at her. "But then, you have always collected the best ones around yourself, Lama."

I scratched at the roots of my beard, now a foot in length, and I ladled him more soup.

"I am so glad to see you, old friend," I said, patting him on the back as I set the bowl down on his lap. "You can stay here in Astrakhan as long as you may need, and we will nurse you back to health. I have gun magic and other tools at my disposal."

But Vasily shook his head, setting aside the soup bowl, rising. The day by now had grown long in shadow, and his sores and rotted limbs looked even worse than before.

"I cannot," he said. "I cannot stay for even a brief meal and the shortest conversation. Because ever since my escape from Transbaikalia, I have been followed. I am marked for death by man and by time."

"Nonsense, merchant," I said. "Wherever a murderer's hand lunges out, it can be chopped off before it pulls the trigger or grasps a blade. This has been part of my philosophy out amongst the killers of all Asia."

Vasily shook his head.

"But when there is not one hand, but the endless hands of Mahakala, never sleeping, never resting, always pursuing?" he said, sighing. "No, Lama—there are some inevitabilities which can only be delayed for a short while, and only through the suffering of dread."

"Who is this pursuer? This would-be murderer?"

The merchant shook his head.

"The worst villain this world has ever known," he said. "A man with one eye, no balls, and a scarred brow that never unclenches. But he has a smile. The most horrible, terrible grin the universe ever produced. He is a soldier of fortune, and he has been part of the worst scourges and atrocities in Asia. He has gone by dozens of different names across the continent. But I have always referred to him by the name that he went by on our Tibet expedition: Sgt. Nikto Pravitel."

I held my face in my hands, a groan erupting from deep within me.

"Do not feel bad for having mutilated this person, Lama," said Vasily, patting my head.

"No, truly—I feel bad only for not making sure he was stone dead," I said, looking up at him.

For the first time, the merchant laughed. A raspy, diseased laugh it was— but it was beautiful. And I joined in, and the woman cackled, too. For a minute or more, we sang at the sky, the desperate heavenward soul-heaving of a businesswoman, a dying man, and a castrato all together.

But then the merchant doubled over, coughing, and I rushed over to help him to a bed, carrying him over my shoulders to one of the empty beds, which puffed with dust as I lay him down.

"Thank you for everything, Lama," he said, shivering. "I pray you will one day rule an empire that spans all of Asia."

"If that happens, you will be my trade minister," I said, kissing him on his deformed skull. He smiled as I backed out of the room.

That night he died. It was like he had waited simply to see me before expiring, waiting for that blessing of a kiss. I had heard wheezing, the labored breaths, the ragged attempts to swallow air, and I went in the room. The struggle for every breath didn't last long. With a gasp, a shudder, and a shake, everything was still. I felt under his nose and at his jugular, and all was lifeless.

I sat by the bedside for a long time, meditating. I heard the dissipation of the merchant's soul outward from the body, a slow emanation not upward, but down—a hissing down to the floor and around my ankles and past the door, down the stairs and out onto the street. I wished with all my soul his essence had a destination far beyond this Russian dirt—that instead it was the golden city far beneath us all.

But who can be sure about these things?

I took his cold hand and felt for any remaining vestige of Vasily, but the fingers were as lifeless as desiccated bones. I dropped the limb on the bed—and out of the sleeve something fell, clattering across the wood floor and then circling like a quick vulture. I stomped on it, then stooped to pick it up.

It was a Mongolian coin, stained and scuffed copper barely legible. But it showed a grimacing profile of the Greatest Khan, which was clean and seemed to shine somehow in stark relief.

My soul rose up. It was a sign that Mongolia still called out to me.

My time in Astrakhan, dicing up fish guts and toiling away my days with my damned love, was at an end.

No matter what, I would go East. Now it was destiny. Year of the Dragon be damned.

"I can see something in you," said the woman with the swaying graying hair. "Something is different...within you."

I kissed her and said nothing for a long time.

She was right; things had changed for me. But my circumstances, of fish guts and exile, were substantially the same. Because despite the so-called revolution and the chaotic reshuffling of the decks across the breadth of Russia, the monarchists and Bolsheviks would both agree that Mongolia should never rise from its knees. I would never make it beyond the Astrakhan Oblast before being shot down, since I was unarmed. The Czar's secret police would always be watching; even if there was no Czar, his secret police would always be watching, until the end of time, doing the bidding of the Bolsheviki or any other master. There will always be the secret police. They will always belong to the rulers, No matter their names or color of their crowns. I had to come up with an alternate plan.

The woman with the silver hair and I cried all night, until the dawn. But then we dried our cheeks and rose again for another day.

No goal worth taking is easy; most often the path to success is covered with unpleasant thorns and stones, any of which can cut and trip. In this case, my saving grace was the fish guts.

We buried Vasily in the courtyard, and then the day's load of beluga arrived at the door. The merchants gave no reason for their absence the day before, but some showed wounds on their arms and faces, and a few limped as they pushed their carts over our new burial plot. I asked no questions, and she and I set to work. But there was a difference. As the day ended, and we counted the stacks of filets and the jars of eggs, I embraced the woman and bid her farewell.

She said something through tears glistening in those dark eyes. It didn't make any sense—something about the end being the beginning and middle all at once, and a nothing, never-ending. I climbed into the refuse bin, and, as I held my breath, the woman shoveled the waste upon me until I was covered.

I breathed through a tiny snorkel poking through a hole we'd punched in the side of the container. Moments later, the front door opened and the thunderous feet of the fisherman gang returning.

I heard murmuring, but I could not make out the words. I felt shuffling, and the clattering of the carts. Then an animal's scream—and what sounded like the sharp clattering of hooves on stones. The loud crack of something, like a pistol, reverberated outside the cart. Then all was silence. I strained my ears, but then the bin was shoved out the door, and out onto the street. I breathed through my tube, careful to keep my nausea down. At least the guts and blood were fresh and hadn't yet had time to truly rot around me, I told myself, as we turned the corner and headed east.

CHAPTER 22
FORWARD TO THE PAST

As the cart neared the market, I burst from the fish miasma. Since the trash bin was the last in the train, only the one pushing it saw me. It was the leader, the rough mariner who had always paid me. He blinked as I lunged and punched him square across the jaw, knocking him out. The train of other carts pushed off around the corner, out of sight. Springing from the bin, I crept up to the unconscious mariner and robbed him of everything—all the money, a jar of caviar, and a Colt just like my old one. I peeled his clothes from him, and stripped off my own filthy rags, using them to clean myself of the viscera as completely as possible. Then I donned his, which were a near-perfect fit. I hauled the leader's naked body into the guts bin, which was mostly empty by this point and presented no real threat of drowning, and then pushed the whole thing into a dark alleyway. I wanted to wake him and make him tell me what happened to my love. But doing so would jeopardize my escape to Mongolia. I had to leave without knowing what became of her.

The night bloomed a swollen bruise overhead, the sun vanished far-off at the horizon. Feeling the wind whip through my beard, I knew I was again a free man heading to his destiny.

First things first, however. I backtracked and headed toward the spot where there had always been a seedy inn on the edge of the city. Sure enough, it was still there. I tied my new horse up around back of the establishment, and I went inside. The old woman saw the fish blood crusted around my knuckles and around the corners of my eyes, and she sneered at my smell. I used my considerable powers of persuasion, however. And as I pulled out my money to pay for a private room with a washroom and toilet, I finally saw how much I had robbed from that leader of the fishermen gang.

I chuckled as the gold filled my hands. I dropped one, then two, and finally three pieces into the old woman's hands, and I nodded. She smiled wide in understanding. I would have a truly peaceful night. I hacked off my beard. In the tub, I carefully washed myself free of the piscine stink, and then cleaned my new gun with a rag and brushed my clothing smooth and free of dirt. The funds would easily take me halfway across Asia, making many friends along the way. But I wanted to be sure. So I promptly dressed, extinguished the candle, and crept out of the darkened house. I walked toward the center of Astrakhan.

I heard the drunk reveler long before I saw him. His footsteps were heavy and unsteady, and he shouted and mumbled in conversation with himself like a man possessed. I waited in the dark of an alley. The moment he passed, I grabbed his throat, dragged him to my hiding spot, and pistol-whipped him across the face. Only then did I see he was another monk. Falling limp to the dirt, the holy man breathed harshly as I robbed him.

As I siphoned all the gems and coins and trinkets from his pockets into my own, I laughed for the second time that night. I had happened upon the only drunken rich man walking the streets alone at night without any protection—and a monk, no less. Sometimes the luck really does come in droves; I had perpetrated the motherlode of all muggings.

I returned back to the inn, and there I counted the gemstones and other valuables that would get me back East. I slept that night with the coins and precious jewels surrounding me on the bed, heedless of their count, speaking deliriously to myself of Agharti.

When I awoke, my mind was clearer. I did a careful numbering, and I segregated the collection by value and type into different sacks and pockets of my clothing. And I cleaned the gun again. I would not be caught unprepared by highwaymen along the roads of Innermost Asia.

And I would never be taken alive ever again.

Instead, this time…I would be the highwayman.

In the very first village I came upon, at twilight, the entire populace sat around the campfire. The tales there were breathless, about how the Red Horde rounded up everyone they could find at the borders, simply killing those who couldn't read. As they recounted what they'd heard across Asia, from the Caspian Sea across Kazakhstan to Ürümqi and beyond, I kept a blank expression on my face. They glanced at me occasionally, the only stranger in the group, but they gradually calmed when I nodded in agreement with them. After staying a single night there, I turned back around and headed north, on the well-traveled route along the Volga.

All the Russians wanted to kill me, whether they were Red or White, revolutionaries or monarchical loyalists. I knew they were watching me; they always had been, I realized. And they had clamped down on the routes I had traveled so well in the past.

Thus, instead of taking a trail they would have expected the infamous Ja Lama to travel through the central continental wastelands and the savage wilds of Kazakhstan, I decided it was time to re-route my plans.

The new route: the Trans-Siberian Railway.

My pursuers, even that wily one-eyed Sgt. Nikto Pravitel, would never think to look to the strange iron beast hurtling across the north.

Of course, nothing in this life is easy. Everything comes with complications, and even a pessimist is inevitably surprised by the vagaries this universe musters against even the simplest of plans. I had to ambush three gangs of highway robbers along my five-hundred-verst trip north. Two men ended up dead. There was no other option. I took the uniform of one of them. The rest were left without mounts in the desolation along the highway. I believed they'd survive—but I could not be sure.

Czaritsyn was arrayed on the western bank of the Volga, like phalanxes of an ancient army facing the wrong way. The bustle on the river, with heavy ships docking and unloading tons of goods, setting off again upstream and downstream, made me dizzy. I'd seen the frenetic energy of Chinese cities twice the size of Czaritsyn, but they were places long established and set in their ways. This kingly city was like a place possessed, like it was preparing to meet a terrifying future—like it was waiting for an indescribable cataclysm to come.

The wide brick edifice of the city's railway station ran down the center of the settlements like a split seam. I strode into its center hallway and bought a ticket. I slept on a bench with my feet on the floor for an hour before a sharp whistle and a shaking awoke me. It was the ticket agent, vigorously yanking me and then shoving me toward the northbound tracks. I leapt on the train just as it started to move, handed the uniformed man the pass, and ducked into what I later discovered was a sleeper car.

I tried again to sleep, but a jolt of lightning hummed through me. I had spent my entire life traversing the Earth in stride, or at most a horse's gallop. The mountains and the horizon never seemed to change. But on this mechanical beast, I felt the sheer speed of whisking across the planet. I opened the shade to the window, and in the dusk, I saw the city of Czaritsyn vanish completely, like it was being destroyed in a matter of monstrous moments as we wound along the Volga northward.

At Kazan I switched to another train which raced through the Urals before linking up with the Trans-Siberian Railway at Yekaterinburg. All this in a matter of three days. A journey like that, even on the best roads, would have been weeks, depending on the murder, robbery, and weather one encountered along the way. I laughed as I boarded the biggest train—this one bound for Siberia.

Perhaps, I told myself, there is something to this 20th century. Perhaps there's promise for the advancement of mankind, his machines, and his nature-conquering science. Perchance humanity could fly across the land and knock down mountains. Maybe a new human would emerge from the chaos of kingdoms and killing. Maybe a new era of illimitable culture and peace would sweep the world, and there would be no hunger or rape or murder or suffering or war or apostasy ever again. Perhaps a human being somewhere could truly become enlightened and perfectly attuned to the needs of the world around them and serve it to the exclusion of their own needs.

I laughed even harder. Because no such human would ever arise on this Earth.

And of course, I was speeding headlong toward Mongolia, where there would probably never be any peace at all.

The train was a marvel. We moved through space like I could not have imagined back on two feet in Astrakhan. I saw the mountains, the lakes, and the rivers and the arid plains hurtle by. It was like having wings, like outrunning the sun itself. After hours of watching Asia blur past, I had to rub my eyes, get up from my seat, and walk a bit along the machine.

Askance looks followed me up and down that train, from the engine to the dining car to the caboose, and along every stretch of the aisle connecting that enormous mechanical snake winding its way east on Asia's clattering spine. The people teemed in every corner, it seemed, from the first-class dining car and its opulent furniture and soft carpet underfoot, to the hard floor and bare chairs of the tail end of the car.

I walked the entire length in the European military uniform, which looked exactly like my uniform of old. Its green was a shade so dark it was closer to black, like it was covered by the most ancient of bloodstains. Everyone aboard shared the same disgusting toilets, holes in the slick floors of small compartments toward the back of the trains that stank of shit and vomit. But the crowd spanned the gamut of society. They were businessmen and ladies who I saw for most of the trip, the savvy merchants attempting to escape the civil chaos of Moscow and the other cities, with their well-dressed plump wives in tow, and even some bratty children.

Though the passengers were generally suspicious, I nevertheless wandered free as a ghost up and down the cars. The back of the train was a different story. These were almost all rough men aboard for just a stop or two, almost all of whom were loud and drunk, and who sought distances progressively farther from civilization and the rising Red tide. Some carried rifles over their shoulders, others sheathed blades at their belts.

I hid my own revolver in my pants pocket and was careful to make no eye contact with the barbarians for fear I would have to kill someone—and thus give myself away. I had managed to pose as a Russian soldier, and though in those chaotic times of revolution it was not good to be on any side, I carried an imposing figure dissuading most hostile intent.

So I walked the train, up and down, and used my stash of coins to buy myself simple meals from the dining car amid the strange bustle of the bourgeois exiles and the incognito revolutionaries hunting them from within the terrified mob.

Omsk is where I started to encounter problems. By the time we reached this gateway to all of Siberia I had become convinced this miracle machine, despite all its speed and magic, made the journey…boring. The thrill of travel was tamped down, like a flame on wet logs. Even the intrigues among the passengers were nothing like the wide-open space of Asia. It was nothing like tracking the landscape and watching the horizon for the first sign of other bandits sharpening their knives for the riches I had so rightfully stolen from other travelers. It was nothing like having to sleep with one eye open around the embers of your campfire for that first sign of ambush and murder. There was honesty out in the wild. In civilization, the brutality was all clandestine.

I yawned in the soft seats of the dining car and flicked out a newspaper, legs crossed, sipping tea, waiting for the train to pull away on our continued trek east. A half hour later, we departed. But as the whistle hooted, I heard the shrieks of men, and as the train ground forward, the thunder of boots on the hard metal of the vestibule.

A group of four burst into the dining car. Their quick hands slung rifles. Their tattered uniforms barely clung to their rangy forms. In their eyes was the unmistakable specter of death.

I glanced out the window. And there I saw…Sgt. Nikto Pravitel, a pistol raised in his hand. My stomach bottomed out.

As the train picked up steam, he fired some shots back at pursuers. But the train gained speed and pulled away. Pravitel disappeared under the train, and there was a slight bump in the car, and my heart leapt for the second time at the apparent death of my nemesis.

Bolsheviks, they were, fleeing from the Whites. A platoon of Whites were pursuing Pravitel and his men. The fugitives intended to escape the White capital on the last train possible. The bullets pinged and ricocheted off the side of the train. Others ducked but I read my newspaper, knowing—as is always the case—I was either doomed instantaneously, or would escape completely unscathed. Either way, there was no sense worrying—or dodging fate.

An aristocratic woman who had been eating her lunch with her husband and daughter was not so lucky. Laughing just moments before at the violent struggles of the proletariat, a stray bullet from the battle outside blew through her throat, and she fell into her bowl of soup, flailing and gargling for air. Her daughter screamed and her husband pounced toward her to administer aid, but the blood flowed thick across the tablecloth and into the soup bowl, which overflowed, red and steaming.

Safely aboard, the escaping Bolsheviks brandished their bayonets and rifle stocks at the passengers. They growled at the children and lingered to sniff the air around the well-kept women. Everyone cowered, holding their collective breath. The men, of course, were not always smart enough to just let them pass like a fleeting storm. The first well-dressed gentleman who stood up and started barking at one of the Communists was promptly smashed in the face with a rifle stock, blood splashing everywhere. Another man stood to take his place and was kicked in the groin and then beaten without mercy on the ground. No one moved to help.

Then one of the Bolsheviks came to me, the rifle raised in his one hand and ready to strike, dry spittle flecked across his lower lip, and sadism twinkling in his drunken eyes. He was a young man whose beard had barely sprouted on his face. His smirk was wide and hopeful and contemptible and full of youth. He reminded me of me, from a long time hence. I hated him on sight.

"What is this uniform?" he yelped, like a tiny dog. "Another worshiper of the Czar, are you?"

"I am not your enemy—yet," I said, raising the newspaper again. "See that I don't have to become one, sonny."

The bayonet came down through my newspaper, tearing it straight down the middle, leaving an equal half in each hand. Just as he started to advance at me with that razor-sharp tip, I nodded at him.

I squashed his mind with my willpower. I did it like you would crush a spider with your fist: hard and fast, without any chance for survival or spreading the mess. I had him lower the rifle and I was surprised how easy the puppetry was. There was enough of him left in that meat husk so he could speak if I gave him general commands, but there was nothing of individual agency or free will left. Which, of course, was perfect for my purposes. I could keep him operating, moving around like my marionette, while I went about other things. His comrades approached, gesturing madly at me, and slapping my puppet's shoulders.

"He's a soldier—why haven't you disarmed him?" asked one of his friends.

"Already did," the young Bolshevik answered woodenly, at my behest. I fingered the trigger of the Colt in my hidden pocket. The contingent glanced at me for a second, considering whether I was a threat, and carried on terrorizing the other passengers.

Minutes later I retreated into my personal sleeper car and locked the door tight. For several hours I was on guard. Sleep was not in my plans, as I clutched the revolver tight to my chest.

But the clacking of the train, the miles passing underneath, was as good a lullaby as a mother's soothing voice and the world swelled dark around my eyes and then just vanished. The mechanical beast beneath rocked me to sleep better than anything since the embrace of my own mother's arms. For the first time ever, I slept even amid the danger around me.

Yanked awake, hands jerked the gun out of my grip. The four Bolsheviks were crowded in around me, and they were grinning stupidly down. The one who now held my gun had syphilitic sores on his face, peeking out from underneath his beard. He reached out and slapped my face.

"These disgusting Mongols," the brute said, licking his lips. "Filthy bastards. We should just clear out their country in the name of The Revolution."

"Marx would have no patience for these nomads," said a second one, the biggest of the bunch, reaching down, grabbing my throat, and choking me upward. He was incredibly strong, and my feet dangled a few inches above the ground.

The syphilitic one slapped me once across the face before I could even really open my mouth to protest. The brute was choking me. The third one was grinning and gave me a quick jab in the belly with his fist. But the fourth in their quartet, my meat puppet—he hung back, with a dazed look on his face. I still had him. Disregarding the assaults being perpetrated against me, I gripped his young brain in my own, and I squeezed.

Neat as you please, the lad raised his rifle, and executed two of his comrades with shots behind the ear. Some hot spray of blood hit my face, and I dropped to the ground. The bodies collapsed, rivers of blood flowing from their skulls. The syphilitic one's jaw dropped.

I slapped him back across the face and grabbed the handgun from his holster. His eyes widened in terror, his syphilitic sores cracking open on his strained, horrified face.

"I wonder what Karl Marx would say about this," I said, smiling. "I guess I should equally distribute the means…of lead."

I shot him in the gut. Amid his screaming, my marionette shook himself awake enough to take his own rifle, raise it to his chin, and pop the top of his own skull with an enormous bloody blast.

I wiped my face with a towel and considered the sight of the boy's demolished head. I had given him just enough agency to allow him to off himself, unfortunately. I could have used him in my journey ahead, for at least another few stops on my cross-continent trek.

For another hour I sat on the small cot, with feet up off the ground, sailing across Asia aboard this impressive machine, and I prayed out to the universe for safe passage the rest of the way to my destiny, whatever it may be.

But just to hedge my bets, I picked up the Bolsheviki firearms, and all the ammunition in their pockets. Prayer and meditation are one thing; bullets and a warm gun are another. I would be ready for anything.

Because these were not times of peaceful treks across continents. These were the times of blood in the air, a whiff of salty vengeance and revolution fomenting for centuries that had finally hit the palates of violent men. My optimism for the 20th century died that night aboard the Trans-Siberian as I shoved the Bolshevik bodies out the tiny window of the sleeper car, one by one by one by one, before we reached Krasnoyarsk. The corpses were hunger-thin, but already stiff, and I found the job difficult. But it got done. And then I settled down to a short nap before the city.

Of course, as is so often in this life, the very nights you need rest the most are the nights that remain sleepless. Right as I was finally about to drift off again, I was awakened—this time by a soft knock at the broken door. I stood and pulled it open. A half-dozen passengers with worried faces stood there. I recognized most of them from the dining car. One was the man whose face had been smashed in by the Bolsheviks, his skull now totally wrapped in bandages that muffled his voice.

"Whff—happnn—to duh—bastudds," he said.

"He's asking what happened to the bastards," his wife translated, patting his cheek, making him groan in pain.

I wiped at some blood spatter on my sleeve, which only smeared further into the fabric. The passengers all saw it, and one gasped.

"They violated the Russian Imperial Travel Code, and they were thrown off," I said. "I can assure you they will no longer be bothering anyone aboard this train ever again."

I started unbuttoning the stained coat.

"Or anyone on this Earth, for that matter," I murmured.

A hand reached out and grabbed the loosened sleeve. It was the injured man's wife.

"We can wash this for you," she said, smiling softly. "It's the least we can do."

Some hours later, my entire uniform was clean and pressed crisp, and my sleeper car had been scrubbed clean of blood, brains, and hair—all evidence of the four deaths. And by the time we pulled into Krasnoyarsk, families were again relaxed in the dining car, and I was reading my newspaper as if we had never been beset by those savage young men at the prior station.

Sure, the Red authorities boarded the train, looking for enemies of the revolution—but they inquired in low voices of bureaucrats, and not the shouts of the barbarians. As they moved down the car, some cash exchanged hands quickly. When they came to me, they gave me barely a glance—partly because I was now in makeshift monks' robes fashioned from bedsheets, but mostly because I clouded their minds, directing their gaze past me. (These socialists were very easy to manipulate mentally, I found.) After a half hour, the train lurched eastward again, its final stretch toward my destination.

We reached Irkutsk at dawn. The sun set aflame the Angara River and its slow churn away from Lake Baikal. I got off the train and walked past the handful of armed Reds waiting there, unassuming in my makeshift monk's garb and with my sack over my shoulder. I walked through the train station, and just before I reached the darkened exit, I saw a Bolshevik smoking a cigarette alone in a corner. Walking straight up to him, I ran my eyes up and down his form. I smiled. He smiled back.

And I reared back and kicked him square in the shin. He screamed and howled in pain—and I bolted down a darkened hallway. He chased me down that hallway and through a darker door, within the thick walls of the building.

I emerged from the shadows of the Irkutsk train station ten minutes later with a perfectly fitting Bolshevik uniform, badges, regalia and all. I was some kind of sergeant, I think. I felt carefree for the first time in years, knowing that Mongolia was now just a short ride south across the land. I marched up to a private manning the hitching post with a full line of horses. The private was asleep on his feet. I waited there thirty seconds before I finally cleared my throat. And then he practically jumped out of his boots and saluted.

"Yes, sir!" he squeaked. "Waiting for orders, sir!"

"Show respect for that uniform," I said, flicking his buttons with my index finger. "After all, while you were sleeping at your post, you could have allowed just anybody to come and steal these horses out from under you."

"I will not forsake my duty, comrade!" he said, saluting me.

"Good," I said. "Now give me the best horse here. I have an old whore to meet across town, and I cannot be late."

I was riding away from that post on a new gleaming saddle five minutes later, on the way to meet my lover, that wronged spinster, Mongolia.

But she was no whore.

You must move through space until you know the perfect place, said the guiding voice in my mind.

"Long time no speak, you devil," I told the voice, trying to ward its words away. "Shut up with your drivel."

The travel south through Siberian Russia was met with strange troops every other valley or so. They were Communists who called each other Comrade and talked endlessly about the future world and about equality. My uniform let me pass among them, with slaps on the back and laughing, and also with generous offers of vodka that I refused utterly. Boors, all these idealists were.

The encounters were exhausting, but there were so many of them. I knew to play along—to melt into my stolen sergeant's togs. Normal soldiers also greeted me along the way, the Czarist supporters who were called Whites. Far fewer in number, they had to be killed at each and every encounter—there was no way around it. For the first few skirmishes I attempted to reason with them, tell them they were fighting a secret ally dressed as a Red, but they would not listen. And my strength of will did not work, either. Thus they had to die so they would not kill me. By these means I cut my path south.

I burned the Bolshevik disguise in a campfire a day's ride across the border into Mongolia. I knew I had reached home again—I smelled the freedom on the wind, and the very soil underfoot lent a spring to my step. Thereafter, I met a few groups of Whites, and I did not have to kill them, because I was no longer dressed as a Red. They were weary of soul and body. They were also not so insane as to talk my ear off about the coming of utopia and the perfection of the human race through worldly wealth redistribution—or the majesty and might of divine kings, either. We just drank tea. This was an utter relief. I reached Urga in a week, I rented a room, and I made careful inquiries around town about the political situation, the power structure, and the order amid the greater chaos.

You see, these times of civilized society were anything but. I never saw the Great War so many thousands of versts to the west, but I had heard all the tales second-hand, and the names stuck with me: the barbed wire and the machine guns and the piles of bodies at a river named the Somme; the thick gas burning the men from within at the strange Ypres; and the soldiers slowly drowning in the bottomless mud at some place called Passchendaele. And the Bolshevik power grab was savagery in the guise of enlightenment from the first shots fired in what they renamed Petrograd. Murder, gleeful slaughter, was everywhere. And no stage was more open than the vast expanses and lawless towns of my beloved Mongolia.

You must understand this to truly grasp what happens next.

I understood the dangers of every breath instinctively. I knew that just marching up to my old allies in Urga meant certain death. So I improvised. Disguised in a revolving arrangement of filthy robes and hats I stole, I walked the city and listened to every voice. I heard the peoples' words of fear and hope. But mostly it was strange resignation I encountered, like history was an ever-changing weather forecast, an unstoppable wind gusting over the Altai Mountains, through the homeland and beyond.

The talk was of power struggles and shifting alliances, and the appearance of emissaries and spies from Russia and China. Paranoia ruled the streets. Some even looked askance at me, as if I was one of the operatives. But I was not recognized as the former warlord of the western wastes, the second coming of Amursanaa, the Lama with a Gun. Instead, I was accepted as just another pair of eyes and ears at the mercy of the strong.

Large clans planned to leave the country, heading for the borders in every direction. Much was made of a large group of Tibetan merchants rumored to have exchanged most of their stocks for gold; most of the city watched with breathless anxiety over whether they would take all their wealth back home to Tibet.

I listened patiently to all the stories. In truth, I was still strategizing. In the years since my kidnapping, Damdinsuren and Magsarjav had become important enough figures to justify their pompous monikers. Manlaibataar and Khatanbataar—"First Hero" and "Firm Hero," how utterly ridiculous!—these were the names on everyone's lips. The tales indicated the two had an uneasy alliance with each other. But their agreement stood only as long as it took to subjugate and kill their mutual enemies. They had no intention of sharing power; instead, they vied for true, sole command.

But their parallel schemes kept hitting a snag. That snag was the wily Bogd Khan, the bon vivant and animal collector who had gifted me that most delicious of all tributes, that fat pig with the pretty bow which had ended up on my spit.

The Bogd Khan, a sex maniac and profligate spendthrift who owned the most exotic of all animal menageries in Central Asia, had a razor-like intuition for weaknesses in his rivals. It also came with no compunctions about killing those who stood in his way. Generally, these deaths were accomplished through poisoned tea during dinners, as I may have mentioned. No one knew where the bodies went. The best bet was the evidence was disposed of in the stomachs of his wolves and tigers.

Two of Khatanbataar's own lieutenants vanished this way. Manlaibataar had received several invitations to the Bogd's palace but had politely declined each and every one. The Bogd Khan himself, suffering from gout and drunk every afternoon, barely left his premises, due to security concerns. But his home was his castle. No one, not even the powerful, was safe if they ventured to pay him honors.

Into this nest of vipers, I crept stealthily. I wore all black as I stalked the city's nighttime streets. I had discovered the locations of the Two Heroes' homes.

The first one I visited was the vaunted Firm Hero's home. I waited by the wall for a few minutes, watching for the streets to empty, before vaulting over the wall into the garden. It was sparse, just a few grasses and a gnarled fruit tree lurching toward the house. It was a brick European structure, the mortar barely dry, clearly built within the last year or two. The windows were lit, and through them and a wispy curtain I saw people waltzing in circles, everyone dressed in European finery. I heard uproarious laughter, and in the corner closest to the window, Khatanbataar stood with quaking shoulders, throwing his head back and laughing deliriously as he held court with a dozen admirers. The window was opened ever so slightly to let in some breeze off the steppe. I crept closer and put my ear to the opening.

"Well, K.B.," said one man dressed in a blue uniform, "I wonder what the Russians will make of your little scheme. They have been trying to push down south through all of Asia, not just Afghanistan. They must have designs on us here."

"I'll tell you," said Khatanbataar, draining the rest of his drink, and leaving it on a tray held by one of the waitstaff, a short Mongol. "We have been planning for everything—the Qing spies, the Bolshevik partisans. The Bogd Khan has proven to be an integral force, a glue that holds all our people together for everyone's good."

"What about Manlaibataar?" asked a breathy woman. "Are you two in joint command?"

"We are," said the host, his tone turning steely. "We both fill roles. I am a warrior defending us from our enemies. He is the politician who signs papers in the blood of our dead heroes."

Snickers rippled across the room, and the woman touched his arm and looked at him so adoringly their love affair was visible from a distance, even through the curtain. A pedantic-looking man, in spectacles and a black suit, cleared his throat.

"But K.B., do you fear any other Mongolian leaders?" he asked.

"Who would I fear?" said the host. "The Bogd Khan and my ally Damdinsuren, Manlaibataar as you may call him, and myself—we are all linked unto death. We rise or are buried together as one. They'd no sooner turn on me than I would turn on them, for fear of our mutual destruction."

"Do you not fear Ja Lama?" said the academic looking man. "The rumor is he escaped from the Bolsheviks and has again set course for Mongolia. Rumor has it his return could be in a number of weeks, depending on his progress across Kazakhstan."

Khatanbataar only laughed.

"That mad monk will only get himself killed along the roads back to Urga," he said. "You see—I too heard the rumors of his escape from his exile, and I made sure that patrols are stationed along every road to the west for hundreds of miles.

They are to shoot the insane holy man on sight. He will never make it so far as Uliastai, if he even survives the guards at Kobdo."

Their laughter was general, and the band again struck up another waltz. The crowd dispersed into yet more dancing, chaotic and drunken reveling which resulted in collisions on the dancefloor and crashes into the ornate dinner tables littered with bottles. I shrank away from the window and started around the corner of the house.

The traitorous rabble had turned against me—had turned against Mongolia—for the last time. Betrayal of myself was a crime I would normally punish by dispassionate revenge; but the treachery to the homeland meant something special was required.

Stalking along the wall, searching for the back entrance so I could exact my total vengeance on the whole lot of revelers inside, my rage swelled to a feverish burn. I would slaughter as many of these parasites as I could, and gladly accept my own death in trade. In that moment, I was ready to exchange all…for vengeance.

Upon reaching the utmost darkness of the garden, I was suddenly struck in the head by something large and metal. A bright light was suddenly in my face. I rolled back with the impact and landed dazed—but crouched and ready for the next blow.

But it was only a secret back door to the house which had opened, knocking me back and spilling light from inside the dwelling out into the night. A figure strode out with a large sack of garbage in each hand and slung them into a huge barrel by one of the dead fruit trees. When he turned, it was a familiar face.

The beard was nearly down to the figure's protruding belly, but it was clearly the face of Jimbe.

"Jimbe!" I hissed.

He stopped short and squinted into the darkness. He stepped into the shadows, and I leapt up and fairly tackled him. He started to struggle, but I grasped his shoulders in an embrace.

"It's me!" I whispered. "The Lama!"

He stopped struggling. And then, after a shuddering breath, he embraced me back—and we clenched each other with the strength of men who know what they are about. He kissed my cheek and whispered to me.

"I never thought you would make it back alive," he said. "Can you really be the return of Amursanaa?"

"I'm more than that," I said, patting his cheek gently. "I am Ja Lama. I am your leader. And together, we will make China and Russia howl."

We stole into the night, creeping away from the darkened old house back to the latest room I had rented. Together we shared a cup of tea, and he showed me the vajra. It was scuffed in places, but still intact. His voice was quieter than before—and he seemed sadder and perhaps wiser, somehow.

"I believed it was gone for good," I said.

"I held out hope," he said. "And it is gold, after all. All that glitters will always hold some value and power."

I nodded, turning away to shield my glistening eyes.

We caught up. I told him all there was to know about Beluga sturgeon guts and caviar. He told me about the chaos of Urga and the open expanses of our country, and the fights raging in the open, and in secret, across its breadth. It was much the same as what I had heard on the streets—though he did have some interesting gossip.

"The Bogd Khan's enemies do not last for long," said Jimbe. "They are invited to a meal from which they never return. They say the poison is on the eating implements themselves. No matter—they never leave the palace, and their bodies disappear. The rumors are that he disposes of the remains through his menagerie. He has a lion and two tigers and even a bear there, you know. They are all fat beasts indeed."

"I have heard that the Bogd can be ruthless, as many of our most high spiritual leaders can be—as I myself can be," I said.

"I have seen it with my own eyes," said Jimbe.

I asked how the hell he had ended up as a man of servitude taking out the trash for these corrupt men in the years since I had been gone. And his face inverted, his hard scowl so horrible I winced.

"Nothing. There was nothing to believe in," he said. "The days dragged, and there were people who were in command who were unable to carry the water of any of the leaders of the past. They were no khans. But what could I do—what could anyone do?

"There are men in this world who have no idea what they're doing, they're just living meal to meal and enjoying the sound of rain on the roof, even as the leaks soak their heads. And then there are those who dream of owning towns and cities, who look to the storm clouds for infinite inspiration. How could the skywatchers not rule the sodden? It's in their very souls for it to happen. It's meant to be."

"What are you trying to say?" I said.

"I'm saying there is no option. There is no salvation in this life," said Jimbe. "I have truly learned from you, Lama. I thought you had been the coming of a new era in our world. But it's clear that there is no new era. There never is any new era. There will never be a Year of the Dragon. Everything still remains the same. There is only the same drawn-out death struggle of the rich and the poor, which is never any contest at all. Though there are a few wins this way or another in the one direction, the same balance is restored right afterward. Knowing all this, I took a job as a servant with those most likely to win without you here. At the very least, I thought I might reap some benefits from my surrender."

"You chose to make a living off of defeat."

Jimbe stared at me for long moments, without blinking, and I knew at that moment that he had become someone entirely different in our years apart. He had changed...somehow.

"I just knew that Mongolia is a strong beast that seems to only respond to a strong master," he said slowly. "Even if you truly are the return of Amursanaa, it makes no difference. Once you were gone, taken away by the Russians, I knew the only ones who could ride the beast of our nation was the Bogd and his lackeys. It was that, or the Russians and Chinese, that Cartel of abominations. And I'd rather take out Khatanbataar's trash and fill his guests' wineglasses, than lick the boots of some savage Bolsheviki or some opulent Chinese viceroy with a taste for the flesh of children."

We locked eyes. He knew my thoughts; he knew I wanted to try again. He was hesitant. This too I saw in his mind.

"We have to try again," I said, tapping the vajra with my finger.

"No. Why?"

"Because what else is there?" I said. "We have one chance left. And if we don't take it, we may as well have never taken any of the others. As you yourself said, the death dance between the poor and the rich, the Mongols and the empires all around her, is all too familiar. But perhaps, with our resolve, we can change the beat enough so that all fall to the floor. Then the downtrodden could finally have a chance."

I reached out with my willpower. But there was no need. He had already grown far beyond his meager beginnings in that respect. I was shocked to feel his was a power near that of mine, though he did not know how to truly use it. Our eyes met. We came to an understanding. And it was in that moment that our fates were locked together as surely as a door and its handle, a key, and its lock.

"Alright. We shall go," Jimbe said. "But you cannot stay in Urga. We need to leave the city. They will kill you otherwise."

"I'd like to see them try," I said.

"They would not only try," he said. "I know these men, and you may have foiled them until now, but they will not rest until they have your head in a jar, Lama."

"Alright," I said. "Best to just carry out the plan."

Jimbe's eyebrows lifted, and he smiled.

"You have a plan?" he asked.

"Yes," I said. "We are going to the desert, where we can see death coming over the horizon, and make it follow some rules."

As we prepared, I told him of my scheme to head to the desolation south of Uliastai, deep in the western wastes of the Black Gobi. His eyebrows furrowed at the mention of that legendary wasteland. But then he told me of the gang of followers we may enlist from within the city.

"There are twelve who would leave with you, sight unseen," said Jimbe. "Growing our numbers beyond that will be a matter of talent and treasure."

"We will do that along our travels," I said. "There are many versts to go, and we will win souls and hearts along our way."

We set off on foot, at first. It was still the deepest and darkest time of night, so we walked in shadows all the way to the house of "First Hero." But just as we neared an alleyway one street before our destination, a figure stepped from the shadows—straight into the sights of my Colt.

"Halt," I said. "Show yourself and you may yet survive to the dawn."

Out stepped a young man. His face was familiar, somehow—boyish and clean-shaven. But upon reaching out to his mind, I was rebuffed. That too seemed familiar.

"Don't shoot," he said, palms upraised. "I come from the Bogd Khan. He sent me to give you this."

Into my hand he dropped something small and light. It was a key. Into Jimbe's arms he hauled a heavy sack, which made a muffled jingle. Clinking coins within the bag made Jimbe exclaim a moment later.

"Do not spend it here in Urga, the Khan instructed me to tell you," said the young fellow. "He wants you to use it to drum up support out west. He wants you to raise a force to fight against Mongolia's enemies—even if they're Mongols themselves. Especially if they're Mongols. Those are his exact words."

"Why is he doing this?" I asked, scratching my scalp with the rounded end of the key. "I thought he was allied with those so-called Heroes."

"He survives merely because he is an emblem of the continuing struggle, nothing more," said the young man. "He knows Khatanbataar and Manlaibataar are allies only as long as they keep each other busy with their stupid political posturing and still need his holy blessings."

"Have we met before?" I asked, waving the key in the invisible darkness. "I seem to remember you."

He bowed. That was as much I could see in the shadows.

"Lama, you do me great honor to remember our first meeting," he said. "There was a boy who you met on your trails many years ago, one who had been left alone by his parents in a small shack filled with treasures. A boy who you tried to help a little bit. That boy survived his abandonment, though his parents never returned. I was that boy. Most now call me the Diluv Khutagt."

Jimbe reflexively knelt. I groped forward, thinking of embracing his former youth. The boy had always been somewhere in my thoughts, my mind churning the possibilities of whether he had indeed survived the next winter.

"I am so glad you survived, friend," I said, still reaching out, trying to touch the location of the voice. "I am doubly glad that you are now in the employ of the Bogd. But perhaps you might consider joining our growing army…"

But silence was the only response. And by the time I reached the spot where he had been just a moment before, only empty space remained. The little Diluv had vanished, in less than a breath.

Without losing a moment, with all the urgency of revolutionaries the world over, we ran to Manlaibataar's house. We crept around the back, stole seven horses, and opened the pen to set the rest free. We were long gone by the time the inevitable chaos erupted of the animals roaming freely across Urga. In the poorer part of town, we picked up five men, all of whose faces looked familiar to me.

"All these men were with you in Kobdo," said Jimbe.

"We are all committed to the cause," said one.

"We are all committed to you," added another.

"You say that now," I said. "But do you totally trust my vision for Mongolia? Do you pledge your lives to the business to come?"

"We all do," said a third, without hesitation.

"To a man," said the fourth and fifth together.

"Good—because the future will not make sense, at times," I said, swinging up on the saddle of my new steed. "We can only plant seeds in the soil haphazardly, in every direction. Only later will we water the ones which take root."

The six of them before me nodded solemnly, then took to their own horses. Jimbe shook his head, but his face remained impassive. And so seven of us rode off to the west, as the sun rose behind us. Into a tiny creek, I threw the Bogd's key that sank into the shallow waters without so much as a splash. Whatever deal that key represented—whatever lock it would have opened—would have been too costly for Mongolia, my followers…and me. I knew this instinctively. I cannot further explain.

You must go until you know the perfect place, said the voice in my mind again and again.

We traveled as hard as possible, trying to leave assassins and that spectral voice in my wake. We escaped one, but not the other.

The perfect place, said the voice.

The perfect place.

The month of travel took us across the breadth of our country, from mountain to plain to desert. Jimbe rode up ahead as scout every other day and was careful to identify the travelers we intercepted. We mostly avoided the bands of Reds galloping across the horizon—though we ambushed and killed the smallest groups of just three or four of them. Civilians we only robbed, leaving them with enough provisions and goods to make it to the closest settlement. Some of the guards we conscripted into our own travels. And in this way I had at my command thirty of the roughest men in all of Asia, all committed to my cause and adhering to my every whim. I wandered as a stormcloud pushed by the wind of faith, and they were my lightning bolts. I'd know the spot when I saw it.

After the weeks of hard riding, hundreds of versts south of Uliastai, I pulled the reins up short in a valley. Desolation was all. And all was promise.

"This is the place," I said.

It was a series of rolling hills, still with the darkened sands of the Black Gobi and its rock outcroppings and barren soil where only the hardiest weeds eked out an existence under the scorch of the day and the freeze of the night.

But there, trickling along at the absolute bottom, was a stream a few feet wide. It seemed to come from nowhere in the desert and lead back out to the wastes' oblivion—but at this perfect point, it manifested for just half a verst, offering life and sustenance. Jimbe fairly fell off his horse, stooped to its banks, and lowered his face straight in the water, like a common beast. He came up with a soaking beard.

"It is good—it is clean!" he shouted.

The men cheered, then tumbled off their mounts to drink, too. I walked to the north, maybe half a verst, looking at the ramparts of the hills and rocky outcroppings. The place was a tactician's dream. In the southern part of the valley a fortification would have its rear backed up against some steep cliffs, the blue beginnings of the Ma-tsung Mountains, which protected the site on nearly three sides. A narrow pass behind the fortification could easily be walled off. I glanced up the valley and its long approach from steppes heading toward Uliastai. This was like a beast's lair—a trap in which prey could be lured, and was inescapable, if a proper ambush and crossfire was set on both sides.

"What do you think, Lama?" asked Jimbe, breathless behind me, wiping his wet face with his sleeve.

"This is the place," I said. "We are going to have our biggest quarry yet come right through this place in the next fortnight. We should set up sniper's nests on both ridges, and we should dig some trenches right past the creek. We have to be done in a matter of four days, at most."

Jimbe's face screwed up into a skeptical grimace. But there was a sly knowing aspect that was in there, too.

"I always wonder how you have your premonitions, your prognostications," he said. "I doubt sometimes this willpower, this mind supreme you always claim. I wonder instead sometimes if it's the knowledge you get through careful observation of the tangible world. For instance, one could have advance knowledge of a wealthy Tibetan caravan leaving Urga and returning home passing right this way…"

"I guess it will have to remain a mystery—but just tell the men," I said, cutting him off. "Tell them we need to be prepared to fight nothing more than a handful of mercenaries, but it's a fight I want to win quickly and with as little bloodshed as possible."

Jimbe nodded, bowed, and went back to the men. Some whoops and cheers were followed by the clatter of gear as they immediately prepared for the next battle—although in truth it was nothing more than a simple robbery.

These men were committed to my every word, as I have said. I never told them the source of my powers, real or imagined. But I can tell you a bit about this—because it makes me prouder to pull back at least a part of the curtain, than to allow you to believe I simply saw the future. No indeed—I knew about the Tibetan merchants I had told you about from my careful listening in Urga. In fact, I had bribed some of their lackeys, their stable boys and henchmen and so forth, before departing. The hired help knew all—they were the ones making the preparations for the long excursion back to Lhasa. I knew very well they were expected to leave the very day after we seven souls had fled in the night. Calculating the two-thousand-verst journey, I knew we would make it at least two weeks earlier than them. All I needed was a proper base to prepare an ambush, and their treasures would be ripe for the picking. This valley, Baying Bulak, the rich spring, would provide everything we could ever need, if everything broke right.

The trenches were dug, the sniper's perches were accessed, and the valley was prepped for war in just three days. I peeled off my military uniform, leaving only my deel and my holstered revolver.

"Why aren't you wearing your soldier's clothes?" asked Jimbe.

I smiled.

"We are fighting on the behalf of a vengeful god, my friend," I said. "A vengeful god."

My timetable was just slightly off. The quarry appeared the very following day, allowing no time for true rest. The glint of a spyglass at the far northern part of the valley was the signal. Everybody assumed their positions.

The plan was executed almost perfectly. Of the dozen Chinese mercenaries whom I knew to be traveling with the group, ten fell at the first volley of shots. The other two were wounded and were finished off. The riches of the merchants were just as had been described to me, the sixteen sacks of gold and the other valuable golden trinkets and jewels. The fifty Tibetan merchants were as meek and terrified for their lives as I had been led to believe.

But what I did not count on were what the high shrieks coming from the wagons. Those screams were from...women and children. Thirty women, and at least a dozen youths were traveling along with these traders fleeing back home. I ordered half my men to round them all up near the stream, and to keep guard, and the other men I asked to finish the robbery. But before everything could be counted, I heard terrified screams.

Three of my men were groping and trying to remove the clothes of two women and a girl who hadn't even reached puberty. I walked quickly over and smacked the two groping the women, and then I pulled out my revolver and blew off the head of the man accosting the girl. The shot echoed, and everything was still.

"We will have order until chaos is approved...by me," I said. "And no matter what happens, the children are off limits."

All eyes were on me. (When you kill someone out in the open, and are still holding the weapon, the witnesses are usually very concerned what might happen next.) My men and the hostages alike watched me, with stares unflinching, unblinking. I went over to the crowd of male captives. Their leader, a short and bald-shaven man in a resplendent robe, held his hands together in front of him—as a plea to me or a prayer to some deafened god, I could not tell. But I lent him my ear, either way.

"You may join our camp, so long as you are useful," I said, bowing and blessing him with a few short words in Mongolian. "May you always remain so."

I finished giving the blessing, and as I turned away I saw the faces of the captives relax ever so slightly. Then Jimbe and the men hustled the human captives off toward the ditches, and the digging.

My hand was forced with the children and the women. As you know from my story, I am not one to trust in fate. Even if things are predestined, I will fight with every inch of my flesh and heart to alter the direction of the universe's current. But there are times where things are just inexorable, when the flow is so strong in one direction, you just have to obey the tide—like those winds that once pushed to the southern reaches of the continent. I think that's what my father was trying to tell me, in his own way, those years earlier. Looking at those terrified women and children, their Tibetan and even Chinese faces bright with horror, I knew they could not just be killed, even in those times and in that land where all bets were off, and all rules were broken. I looked around the valley, this spot in the Black Gobi, and I knew this must be the place. To begin a village. To start again.

This is the perfect place, said the voice.

"Put them all to work," I said. "They can earn their freedom through their labor."

Jimbe came over and clutched at my sleeve.

"You can't be serious," he hissed. "We can't have all these people at a robber's hideout in the middle of the desert."

"You may have become accustomed to the insanities of Urga," I said. "But we are starting something new here."

Jimbe tugged at the hem of my garment.

"How will we survive in the desert, Lama?" he said. "That's what I care about. No number of extra workers will make this sand fertile for enough crops to feed the people."

I draped my arm around him, smiled, and walked over to the creek.

"Friend Jimbe, we are going to live off the kindness of others," I said.

CHAPTER 23
MAKINGS OF EMPIRE

Of course, when I say we would live off the kindness of others, I was being amusing. You know me by now—I enjoy a bit of mischief on this plane of existence. It makes each breath worthwhile.

What I really meant by the kindness of others was: exploiting to our fullest satisfaction the docile trust most people place in the world around them. There was no true kindness in Innermost Asia in those times, as I've made clear. There were alliances of convenience and occasionally even something like friendship, yes...but the interplay of power and fear, pride, and jealousy, always coursed in the currents, the arterial spurts, of those times.

Drinking in that wealth from the crowds streaming over the trade routes of Asia, is how we'd build our state this time. Sparing the politics and sharpening the sword would be the foundation of our new society. Negotiations would be skipped in favor of the righteous blade. At least that's what I told them. And it worked.

For the first six months, the occasional caravan would near, mostly on their way from the agonies of Uliastai or Kobdo or Urga, on the way down to the promised riches and peaceful life in the Himalayas. Every week or so, a hapless group of wagons appeared at the far end of the valley, hoping to traverse our narrow pass through the mountains. Our spotter would see them. The wagons numbered always between three and twelve, carrying whole families and all their possessions, their most precious treasures. Without fail, each of these groups was guarded by mercenaries past their prime, drunken and slow to react, riding unawares straight into our ambush. None of them felt the pain of the first sniper's bullet knocking them out of the saddles, splattering their brains on the hard dirt of the earth. The attacks went seamlessly, and only one of our men was shot by a cowardly trader's handgun as we closed in. Our man, and the trader, were buried in ground marked for the planting of root vegetables. Corpses make great fertilizer, as the 20th century proved again and again.

But the rest we did not kill—even the men. Those who surrendered when they were defenseless were simply brought into the growing community, which multiplied like a mound of desert grasses. The men were put to work building the yurts and digging the fields. The women collected buckets of water from the stream and tended to the homes and the gardens. The children were free to play. None was allowed to leave, and none could deviate from these rules. With minimal punishment, everything came together with little opposition or complaint.

Even as the well-ordered lines of a village formed (this civilization emerging out of the sunburnt earth of the Black Gobi, its foundation merely willpower and some faith), I did not have to keep these hundred or so followers on a tight leash after the example I had made. The children were safe, there were no attacks or threats. Everyone knew punishment always loomed—the lash and the knife always at the ready. It was enough.

It was time to make my foray out into the wilds. I had to know the deals between these jackals who called themselves my countrymen, and the Chinese imperialists and Russian Reds. Those buffoons would not forever overlook my outpost even if it was out in the Black Gobi, and I must be prepared. Even my fortified valley could not stand fast forever against the forces of the entire world.

But it was curiosity more than anything that put a spring in my heel, a bounce in my boot.

Because three of the last wagon trains had spoken of the coming of Mahakala. But they spoke of him as the unforgiving god of war. Somehow, Mahakala was a white man who had come from somewhere to the west, perhaps Russia or Prussia.

This European had single-handedly thrown out the disgusting Chinese and liberated the Bogd Khan and his vast menagerie by slaughtering and burning the cowardly invaders on a funeral pyre. The flames differed in height in each account—the largest being some two hundred feet high. This mortal Mahakala's eyes burned like the sun. His skin stopped bullets. His bones broke stones. I laughed at the exaggerations, and the invoking of this most fearsome god's name. But still I found myself drawn in that direction, toward Urga and whatever chaos was brewing around this crazed European who aspired to be Khan.

But first I needed to know what was going on at the fringes of the country. We needed to know how far the rot had spread. If, like a piece of bread, there was mold around the edges, we would need to completely extract the affected parts. Kobdo, the site of my former rule, was foremost a foreign, imperial colony; it always would be, no matter how hard I had tried to recreate it in the vision of our forefathers and descendants-to-be.

Thus, Jimbe and I traveled due north to the desolate lake country outside the town, hoping to meet familiar faces. Virtually all the yurts and settlements had moved in the years since we had last blazed through on our holy liberation mission.

We came to the Baga Nor, a lake about halfway between Kobdo and Uliastai, where the Zavkhan River meandered alongside the enormous sand dunes like hunchbacked yaks at Elsen-Tasarkhai. This tiny oasis had been one of our stopping points in the campaign against the Chinese so many years before. We intended to settle our mounts for a night or two, among a familiar arrangement of dwellings there, up a steep slope from the banks. One of the yurts spewed smoke straight out the top. As we approached, we rode the horses' hooves hard and called out with echoes, so the inhabitants would have advance warning. An old Mongolian shepherd, one who had been a loyal follower of mine in Kobdo and for many years before, stretching back before the turn of the century, poked his head out and squinted into the sun. His face brightened, he flung open the door and came outside with arms wide.

"Our Lama has returned to us!" he hollered, falling to his knees, bowing into the dirt.

"Arise, shepherd," I said, as Jimbe pulled him up. "We are glad to be back among the country and doing destiny's work. But for now, please just put us up for the night."

A look of apology crossed his face, and he again fell to his knees.

"I have no room for tonight, most holy one!" he said. "There are two strangers, Europeans, who have already taken places around my hearth…"

"Never mind that, never mind that," I said. "There will indeed be room enough for all."

We went inside. There sat two skittish fair-skinned men, bundled up in traditional Mongolian furs and hats, smoking pipes. They resembled albino cows draped in blankets. They stood and nodded in my direction.

"Good evening," I said in Mongolian, motioning for them to return to their seats.

"Evening," they responded in unison, glancing at my new golden deel and the blue sash poking from my overcoat. But their eyes grew especially wide at the holstered Colt at my side.

"Let's speak Russian," I said, grabbing a roasted chicken leg, still steaming, from a bowl nearest the fire. "And let's talk politics. What do you fellows think of the Bogd's government in Urga? Of those vaunted Heroes around him?"

The two looked from one to the other. I immediately found an affinity in the mannerisms of the smarter of the two, a man with a strong soulful face bordering on middle age, and a nose that bulbed out at its fat tip. This was a man with whom

I could do business—even if it didn't involve money. His companion called him Ferdynand, and they said he was not a Russian, but a Pole. He turned to me with questions he asked with a straightforward, open-eyed look.

"Will the Chinese send help to Urga, to clear out the Red menace?" he asked. "We have heard many envoys were sent."

I laughed out loud, despite myself. I recalled some of these envoys, carrying riches that had been repurposed for setting up my fortress in the Black Gobi right at that very moment.

"I caught all those envoys," I said, scratching my brow. "And then I sent them back…into the ground."

I laughed loud, and Jimbe joined me with his own husky merriment, even though he never truly found my jokes funny. The shepherd also joined in, and the Europeans were forced to also add their own mirth to the mix, though I saw the mere mention of murder pained them, particularly this Ferdynand. As I said, the man had a soulful way about him. He was Western, and he had Sensibilities.

The three of them drank vodka. They talked about the happenings in the country—and beyond. The two Europeans were trying to escape the Bolsheviks by way of Tibet, but they had been turned back by the Dalai Lama's armed guards far to the south.

"I could have helped you, if you had only asked me," I said. "After all, the word of Ja Lama carries some heft south of here, if not in the West."

Their eyes grew big at the mention of my name. The smart one, this Ferdynand, asked me as coolly as he could about my travels, and my rule in Kobdo. I told them a bit of what had transpired, leaving out the human sacrifice and the other few unsavory bits. There were only so many things Europeans needed to know, lest we true Mongolians dare offend their delicate occidental beliefs.

I talked just a bit about my travels and the years behind me: the prayer wheels and slaughter and fish guts, and just a bit about the hopes and dreams of the descendants of the Greatest Khan. I was feeling wistful; you will have to pardon me. The wind wailed and roared and blasted the snow against the stretched felt of the yurt. Outside from the direction of the others came far-off laughter, almost like a wolf's howl, ethereal and almost godly, but it must be human. The two Europeans' eyes split even wider, the whites of them gleaming in the firelight. I focused all my willpower within that yurt. I waved my hand, and the laughter vanished in the air.

"Very much is unknown in all of the universe—and the skill of using the unknown, the unseen current flowing all around us and through us, can produce what you people may call miracles," I said, staring into their eyes. "But the power is only given to a few of us."

I stood and beckoned the shepherd over to me. He leapt up and came over to me. I unbuttoned his coat, and then unsheathed my knife. He stiffened but stood there.

"The universe is not always what actually is—sometimes it's simply what you see," I said.

And I plunged the blade into the shepherd's chest. With a pitiful yelp and an impressive gush of blood, he collapsed. The Europeans gasped. I knelt over the shepherd, pinning his convulsing form down with my knee on his throat. I sawed through the ribcage, making a huge, ragged circle in the meat. Blood erupted everywhere.

"What have you done?" cried Ferdynand. "My God! My God!"

But already I had reached in and yanked out the still-beating heart, which I held before them, pulsating, and spurting in my palm. The Europeans' eyeballs rolled up in their heads, and they both fainted dead away.

"Is this really necessary?" asked Jimbe, stifling a yawn with his dirty hand.

"Sometimes it is worthwhile to dazzle people as a first impression," I said. "It worked with you."

He scoffed.

Minutes later they all awoke as I was sharpening my knife on a stone. The shepherd's bare chest—intact, with neither blood nor wound—rose and fell as he snored softly on the ground. The two white men staggered to their feet and dragged the shepherd to his feet. They felt his flesh and found it intact.

"How?" said this Ferdynand, out of breath. "How? We clearly saw this poor man die, right before our eyes."

"You slaughtered him!" said the other fellow.

"There are more things around us and within us than your Western Sensibilities will ever comprehend," I said.

But I said no more, no matter the questions they continued to ask. But I made sure they saw the little splash of crimson, the last remainder of the deluge of blood, at the hem of my deel. At this, Ferdynand's companion again fainted dead away. The Pole raised his finger and opened his mouth to speak—but quickly shut it and said nothing.

Later that night, as we were tucking away the horses for the night in advance of a snowstorm coming from the north, this Ferdynand pursued his queries. This time, I acceded.

"You Europeans will not recognize that we dark-minded nomads possess the powers of mysterious science," I said.

"What do you mean?"

"Perhaps you will see."

"Where are you headed?" he asked.

"To Agharti," I said. "Eventually."

"The subterranean city of gold?" he asked.

It was my turn to be taken aback. How did this logical European, this simple Slav, know of the hallowed earth?

"You know of Agharti?" I asked.

"Only through the legends I've heard as far north as Lake Baikal," he said. "But no one on Earth has ever traveled there and returned to tell the tale."

Pounding my chest, I shook my head.

He shook his head in disbelief.

"You…you have been to…to Agharti?" he stuttered.

"I saw it twice," I said. "And that is my goal at the end of my days, to finally make the final trek there, deep within the subterranean kingdom and its thoroughfares of gold."

I slapped his shoulder.

"But I suspect I have some time yet before then. I believe what you were really asking me was where I plan to travel in Asia, here above ground?" I said. "My assistant and I are currently surveying Mongolia. We are trying to determine how best to throw out the Russians and Chinese. I believe this trip will take us to Urga before we get back to our home base of operations."

"In the Black Gobi, to the south," said Jimbe, emerging from the darkness behind us.

I smacked his head, which made a hard thump on his skull. The fool had been instructed not to give away even the slightest hint of where our base could be, until the fortress was complete.

"You do not tell anyone about our operations, even among new friends," I said. "Go prepare our places in the yurt."

Shoulders slumped, Jimbe left. The European grabbed my sleeve.

"Everyone knows about your brigade of robbers," he said. "And things in Uliastai are bad. But there is a glimmer of hope in Urga."

"And what is this glimmer of hope?"

"The Baron. Baron Ungern."

"That name is so familiar," I said. "Do I know this Baron?"

"Perhaps not, Lama—but he knows you," said Ferdynand. "They say he is Mahakala, returned."

This Pole went on to explain that the Baron had seized power in Urga by freeing the Bogd Khan, slaying the Chinese, and building roads and telegraph wires throughout the city. As he started his nascent empire, this Baron told everyone how he'd learned much about ruling from the Ja Lama's years in Kobdo, where he had been one of the faithful foot soldiers of the short-lived fiefdom. Ferdynand, who called himself by the patronymic Ossendowski, had barely escaped the Bolsheviks in Siberia with his head still atop his neck. Now he was acting as a scout and emissary for the Baron to drum up support in the west.

As the Pole spoke the memory returned. I pictured the strange European sadist with the distended head back in Kobdo, the torture artist, who spoke about the beauty of Mongolia and the need for conquest.

Would I thus have an ally in the capital to the east?

First there was the little problem of Uliastai. Ferdynand assured me things would improve once the Baron stabilized Urga and mobilized westward. But up to that time the Mongols there remained in constant danger of a pogrom, since the local Chinese had all the guns. I knew what I had to do, making the plan up in that very moment under the stars.

In the morning, Jimbe set out south in the direction of Baying Bulak, with an order to bring fifty of the best men, with the rest to remain and continue building the settlement and the fortress. I went east with the Europeans to Uliastai. Along the way, we caught and passed a caravan of three Mongol families, frozen rigid in the saddles with terror. There had been a pogrom already in Kobdo, in which the Chinese killed every Mongol and Russian caught out on the streets and set fire to half the town. Rage rose in my throat, but I kept it down. Instead, I gave the families a half-dozen gold pieces and urged them to hurry around Uliastai and go directly to Urga.

"That Baron could be the savior of our Mongolia," I shouted back as we sped away.

"Or," I muttered to only myself a moment later, "he could be its destroyer."

The Han devils were thick as weeds in Uliastai—and they were going to be just as hard to yank from the earth. Armed Chinese patrolled every street, and although we were let inside the main gate of the town, the doors were quickly closed again. There was no escape. In the ensuing confusion, in which my European friends indignantly demanded their freedom of access, I slipped away. I made my way to the opposite end of town, where I met with some of my old followers from Kobdo. And I waited until nightfall.

You see, the Chinese authorities every evening met by torchlight in the nagan hushun, the massive vegetable garden that doubled as a courtyard for meetings of the mob. This particular evening the entire town was gathering there. My Mongol kin led me to the open plain outside the garden fence. I left my pale horse at a post some ways off. Under the moonlight I crawled the half-verst of ground, hiding behind the massive piles of frozen manure to slip toward the sentries. At last, I found a hole in the fence through which to see and hear all.

A thousand, perhaps two thousand, Chinese men shouted. They hoisted medieval weapons to the sky—not just rifles, but also axes and torches and pitchforks and clubs. None of the words made any sense; they were slogans about vengeance and justice. The hatred seethed in every hissing syllable. It was the worst sound I ever heard, worse by far than even the sounds a man makes drowning in his own blood.

A huge man, neck bulging with muscle, climbed to the top of a rostrum in the center of the crowd. He stood over them and barked out a speech.

"We must do here what our brothers have done across the country!" he screamed. "We must kill the dogs before they can kill us. The Reds and the Mongols are working together, and they will never be satisfied until all the Chinese are killed. So we must kill them first! Remember Blagoveshchensk!"

This last name brought an enraged howl from the men below him. You probably don't know Blagoveshchensk. Only a few remember, but those who do are driven mad by this tortuous long name, like a horrible insane incantation. This was a mass drowning of all the thousands of Chinese being deported across the Amur River one summer night in 1900—a source of terror and revulsion even years later.

But it had happened far to the east of Mongolia.

It had nothing to do with Mongolia. It made no sense at all.

But that did not matter to the mob. Like with all mobs, its insanity carried its own momentum. That momentum grew, at that very moment.

"I am going right now to demand the Commissioner of Uliastai confiscate all Russian weapons!" the burly man shouted. "When I return, we will start our ride of revenge and settling scores!"

A cheer went up from the crowd, and the muscular man jumped down to the ground and started walking to the front gate. No time for hesitation—I sprang up and dashed back for my horse, sentries be damned. But they didn't see me, they were too caught up in the frenzied bloodlust within the garden. I mounted my horse and rode back toward the main gate of the nagan hushun. The muscular leader walked toward a tied-up horse, his axe in a sheath on his back.

Rope in hand, I rode as hard at him as I could. For the roaring of the crowd behind us, he didn't hear the thunder of the hooves until I was a yard away, and my rope was already around his throat.

I yanked, and in the blink of an eye, his body jerked across the rough road. His choked screams as I dragged him away were drowned out by the mob.

Five minutes later, I rode up to the fence. I slowed down just enough to get the best leverage to throw my package high over the fence and into the crowd. It landed with a hard thump-bounce on the wood of the rostrum.

Silence. As I galloped away, they unwrapped the bag and gazed into the dead eyes of their leader, head separated forever from that muscular body.

The screams of the crowd echoed behind me as they realized what had happened to their comrade. I laughed and laughed.

"For some reason, the mob split up!" said Ferdynand the next morning, after I had found him at the only inn in town.

"The Chinese were said to have been preparing some huge massacre," he continued, wide-eyed, "but after all the shouting and chanting and rabble-rousing, they just all went back to their homes, and there's been silence ever since. Rumors are that one of the main leaders went missing in the night."

"It's a good thing," I said, eating a piece of fruit I had stolen off that leader's remains the night before. "Never prudent to lose one's head in these situations, you know."

"Now all we need to do is get the Baron's forces in firm control of Urga, and they can march westward and join us here," said Ferdynand.

"I won't be around for that," I said, standing, tossing the fruit rind aside. "It is time for me to move through space. I am planning on making my own forays in the west, perhaps Kobdo again."

The Pole's reverie was broken. His face sagged.

"But this is right when things are starting to turn in Uliastai," he said. "And as Uliastai goes, so goes Mongolia."

I patted his shoulder.

"I will be working along the same lines as you and your Baron," I said. "You will not see me, but you will certainly see my work."

I gave him no time to answer, I turned and walked away, spitting out some bitter seeds as I went.

I left town on my pale unnamed horse mere minutes later. I had plans, and since Uliastai was now no longer in danger of erupting, it was indeed time to move through space.

I traveled two hundred versts south along the main road before I saw my forces. I was confused at first, since there were closer to two hundred men instead of the fifty I had asked for. But sure enough, the golden glint of the vajra was the sign of Jimbe leading the galloping horde. I was all set to punish him for leaving Baying Bulak without proper defenses, when he arrived at my position.

"We added more than a hundred men along the way. Volunteers. Ready to serve," he said, breathless in the saddle. "We tried to make good time, but the refugees got in our way and demanded to join us, too. I could not turn them away."

Indeed, some of the men were elderly and others were very young. But all appeared able, and of fighting age. After a cursory inspection, I nodded at their ranks.

"We are ready," I said. "Now follow me, and let's make ourselves an empire."

The cheers erupted behind me as we rode off, but they faded within a verst and only the wind and the horizon were left to us.

CHAPTER 24
MONGOLIA IN PANORAMA

We traveled fast. We traveled strong. There was no avoiding the Bolsheviki or carefully circling around bands of Chinese, this time. We had advance scouts a few versts ahead, and we simply crushed anyone in our path who was not Mongol. Tibetans, and even a group of hapless Americans simply seeking escape from our war-torn land, were not spared. We did not kill those who simply surrendered; women and children were set free as a rule, and I had to execute some of my new men due to infractions against them. But there were no real threats in our days, or in the peaceful nights sitting in rings around three fires.

"I didn't think we would ever be so unchallenged on the steppes of Mongolia," crowed Tömör, one of my newly promoted lieutenants, beating his chest. "Who on Earth can stop us now?"

"Perhaps the Year of the Dragon has come early," said Jimbe, drily, looking at me.

We reached Uliastai in a mere matter of days. My entire army arose each morning well before dawn, the thunder of our hoofbeats drumming up a dust storm that the Greatest Khan himself would have watched with approval. Jimbe rode beside me. Somewhere on the second day, he pulled out a pipe and started smoking. At our furious pace, he struggled to keep the tobacco lit.

"Since when have you smoked?" I asked.

"Since we have decided to take on the world," he said.

I laughed and flicked my hand in his direction, and the pipe flared, spurting with sudden smoke. He inhaled too much and coughed for an hour. When he finally settled down, he pointed the pipe stem at me.

"You know," he said, "I will never know how much of what I have seen in my travels with you is real, and how much of it is utter claptrap, lies abundant."

I laughed again, whipped the reins, and pulled ahead of my entire horde. We rode with purpose. We rode with speed and strength. The anticipation of a thousand sleepless nights were behind us, and the promise of a new day reached before us all.

We stopped twenty versts outside Uliastai. The men were surprised we weren't riding directly onto the town, but I quelled their consternation with a speech about patience and picking the right time for a battle. Some cheered, but when I turned my head, I saw Jimbe at the edge of the crowd shaking his head, eyes cast down, smoking that damned pipe. His eyes were dark, flashing.

I pulled him aside afterward.

"I need you to travel into town, to meet with the two Europeans again," I said.

"What for?" he said. "Aren't we just going to camp out, and wait for the Russians to come? Isn't this just another of your goddamned hesitations? Excuses?"

"Yes, the Russians are coming—they're always coming," I said. "What I need to know is if we can expect a good fight. That's what we need: a single good fight to get these men into fighting shape. And to spread word of our strength."

He glanced at me, then banged out his cold pipe on the heel of his hand, dropping the ashes down, grinding them into the dirt with his heel.

"Sure thing," he said. "I'll bring back intelligence and whatever else you need. While I'm there, need anything from the market in town? Perhaps a bushel of resolve? Maybe a bottle of courage? A tincture of derring-do?"

I stared at him.

"Just bring me back word of the next band of brigands to come through, be they Bolsheviks or Chinese," I said. "That is our next strike."

Jimbe nodded, turned, and walked away. He did not look back, but he strode with a purpose I had never seen before.

The four men, Jimbe in front, rode toward town an hour later.

Two days afterward, only three returned.

Jimbe was not among them.

"The Chahars from Inner Mongolia are in the town, raising havoc," said Tömör, who had been second in command for the mission. "Their chaos includes burglaries, assaults, and drunken orgies. There have been two reports of child rape. The Chinese Commissioner has used them to enforce his law on the people of the town."

"What became of Jimbe?"

Tömör shook his head, blinking rapidly.

"Jimbe took off in the night for parts unknown," he said. "He did not return."

I nodded. But I leaned in close, so none of the other men could hear.

"Did you plant the seeds of the rumor I told you?" I whispered.

"Yes," he murmured. "Those criminal bastards believe we are heading out of the Gobi in this direction, a full week behind."

"Perfect," I said. "Now set up the ambushes at all the designated overlooks. And tell the men we expect to win a great victory over the traitors in our midst."

We did, of course, win a great victory over these traitors in our midst: a group of Chahars, Mongol servants of the Chinese. They staggered right into our trap, and just a few minutes after the first pull of the trigger, we overran them. After that, it was all a matter of angles and shouted negotiations. The survivors surrendered after two hours, agreeing to whatever conditions I saw fit. Their leader stepped out from behind his boulder and dropped his rifle on the ground. He approached slowly, with a bowlegged walk from years of riding across the plain. He wore a strange hat with raccoon fur, like an American pioneer. Knife scars ran down over his forehead and cheek, and one of the wounds had taken his eye with it.

"We surrender," he said, slowly, like the dumbest person in all of Asia.

But his eyes were like that of a hawk, and I saw he was still planning his next move. I had my men line up him and fifty of his men who could still stand. I had my men lower their firearms.

"You surrendered," I said. "But we are not in the business of taking prisoners."

We glared at one another. The sun was setting in the west, far over the horizon past the town. His natural willpower crackled in the space between us; it was almost as strong as my own.

Almost.

"You do not need a demonstration of our resolve," I said. "I am Ja Lama. I am no longer a monk. I am a warrior and avenger. If you Chahars decide to join us against our mutual foes, the sons of Han and all their collaborator shitmongers, you can join us on our way to Urga. But you will have to swear allegiance to me."

The man in the coonskin cap chewed something and spat on the ground. One of my men raised their pistol, but I waved him off.

"And if we don't join you, swear our allegiance, and place ourselves under your yoke?" he said.

"Then you place yourselves under this ground. Right here. Right now."

The Chahar just nodded. He spat again. And he raised his arms.

"I for one know there is no way I'm going to Urga—"

But before he finished speaking, I drew the gun and shot him through the coonskin cap, blood, brains, and fur spraying on about a dozen of the men behind him. About half the Chahars tried to run away, and they were gunned down in seconds. But those who stayed and fought and were overpowered and knocked to the ground bloody were the ones we merely held captive.

When things had settled, I had them all set on their feet again, some bleeding, others groaning to support their own weight.

"You are men of spirit, I will give you that," I said, walking the line of them. "You Chahars fought valiantly against your enemies for centuries."

I stopped short, scratching my brow.

"But yet now you fight on your enemies' behalf, against your Mongol brothers and cousins."

I continued pacing the line, back and forth, back and forth, Colt still in my hand. Silence followed me between the men, some of whom trembled as I passed, as if I was the coldest gale.

"I implore you—come join your natural allies to fight your most ancient enemy," I said. "Together, we can again liberate all of Mongolia—not just Outer Mongolia, but Inner Mongolia too. We will be at the very gates of Peking itself in the time it takes to blink an eye. They will tremble."

I holstered my gun. Then I dragged my foot in the earth, making a line in the dirt separating a section from the west and the east. The Chahars were on the east side of the line, and all my men were on the west.

"What we will do here—without hysterics or panic or rebellion—is separate those who have a Mongol spirit from those who prefer the Qing life of indulgence," I said. "Those of you who wish to continue life's journey should come onto the Mongol side of this line. And those of you who wish to die on the wrong side of history, are totally free to do so."

I pointed at them.

"Freedom. That's one thing we have here in Outer Mongolia, if nothing else," I said.

Utter silence. Then—some of them limping, even two crawling—all of them came across the line to the west, with the rest of their true-blood Mongol cousins.

Together we all rode straight east, and right to Urga (some of the most wounded had to be slung sideways across the horses' bare backs). The guards at the gates aimed their guns, and one even fired an errant shot into our ranks. But my men were as afraid of me and my orders as they were of that bullet, so all our arms stayed holstered.

"Open the gates, idiot!" I hollered up at the rifleman. "Tell the Baron that his ally from the west is here to break bread with him. Tell him Ja Lama is here to parley!"

The shooter's jaw dropped even as he lowered his sights. A moment's pause, and then the city gates slowly cranked open. And I led my men inside.

"Lama!" said the Baron, on first sight. "How goes the fight?"

The Baron's skull had physically swelled even more than before. That enormous forehead shone in the early evening light and those eyes burned. His willpower tried to grapple mine, but he did not realize the full extent of my capabilities. He was like a frog jumping out of the water, thinking he could compete with the eagles of the air. His eyes shone with power; he was just finishing whipping bloody one of his subordinates for failing to bow in his presence. He saluted me in the style of a European soldier. I bowed like a Buddhist, instead, and he followed suit. We spoke in Russian.

Eventually we sat down outside his yurt, and our men left us alone—though both groups were within shouting distance. He had a handful of something that he rattled in his hand, which clattered like tiny dice he was ready to roll out on the ground. Yet he kept them hidden from sight. The campfire flames whipped the air between us.

"I understand totally what you say about Western Sensibilities," said Baron, as the darkness of the Mongolian night gathered around us. "As a member of a European noble family, and a soldier, I can tell you that civilization has grown soft and squeamish. Cowardly, at best."

Grabbing a poker, he thrust into the coals of the fire, flicking sparks up into the dark that lasted for a few moments, and then flittered away as black flecks of cold ash. Then he threw the red-tipped spear aside.

"You were my inspiration for all this, you know," he said, gesturing toward the dim lights and shadowed hulks of Urga. "If I hadn't seen your rule in Kobdo and known firsthand how strength can stamp chaos into order like a boot squashing a bug, I never would have attempted to bring about a new khanate. You showed me, Lama, that the ends can truly justify the means."

I raised a cup of tea, which scalded my mouth. I smacked my lips and cleared my throat.

"Just what do you have planned here?" I asked. "You've fled the Reds in the north, and the Chinese are to the East. In the West, I can hold off the silly Kazakhs. But how do you propose fighting all our enemies at once?"

He smiled. Out of the shadows emerged an underling, a Mongolian taller than either I or the Baron, but thin as a rail. He stopped short in front of his leader, stooped to one knee, and then presented to the Baron a cup steaming with a stench that made my eyes water, even from where I sat feet away. It was not alcohol, but was something else, brewed of roots deep in the Earth, or something from a tropical land on another world entirely. The Baron offered me a sip, and I bowed in thanks but declined. He shrugged and raised the miniature cauldron, the strange fluid splashing down his gullet all in one go. He wiped his moustache with the back of his sleeve and whistled loudly.

"The Chinese make me laugh," he said, chuckling. "Do you really think that those corrupt cowards would ever be able to swallow any part of Mongolia?"

"They are like a dog with its teeth clamped down on a bone in Inner Mongolia," I said. "And they outnumber the true Mongols five hundred to one on this Earth. Even armed with sticks, they could overrun Urga in a matter of weeks, or days."

"Nevertheless, the true enemy is the Red Horde," said the Baron, his eyes glinting in the firelight. "The Bolsheviki aim to destroy every vestige of order, of hierarchy. They aspire to nothing less than setting every estate on fire, from Siberia to the north of France. Every castle, every single fruitful field."

He spun the bowl in his hand. But it made no noise, and it did not sing. The only sound was the drunken bellowing from far-off, and the howl of a wolf farther distant in the darkness.

"In some ways, I can't blame them, honestly," he said. "On the Eastern Front, I saw things I did not believe possible. What soldiers do to each other. I was wounded five times, Lama—each time worse than the last. But I kept making the charges. And each time we broke through, there was no time to take prisoners or to show the slightest mercy..."

The Mongolian remained on his knee in front of his master. The Baron handed him his bowl, and then shoved him over with his foot. The Mongol rolled nimbly across the ground to his feet, then quickly skulked away into the darkness.

"We just shot them all," he continued. "We shot them in lines, we shot them on their knees, we shot them in their backs as they ran away, we shot the ones already dying from disease. Because in these times, Lama, there is no quarter, to be given or taken."

The Baron picked at his teeth.

"You must remember, Lama," he said, "when it comes to insanity, the Eastern Front of the Great War was just the beginning. Understand: all the machine-gun slaughters and the uneven executions are only going to get more efficient and thorough the next time around. There won't be any great enlightenment, any kind of turn toward kindness because the Europeans feign horror over some poison gas, or furor over who is leader. The white men—the Europeans and their precious thrones—will continue to hoard the power. They will not only send millions off to die in their stead, they will also kill millions of civilians, anyone who stands in their path.

"This century, Lama, will be something to behold. It will be a kaleidoscope of horrors. But it will only be seen in true definition by those depraved enough to crank it into its most terrifying configurations. The leaders of men will push and pull the masses through barbed wire and machine gun fire and holocausts of all intensities in the furtherance of their big ideas about progress."

Nightmarishly he clawed at his face, dragging his flesh down so his eyes rolled back and protruded from his skull, and his sharp wet teeth glinted in the firelight. Resembling nothing so much as Mahakala incarnate, I saw why even his most loyal people feared him.

The simple torture artist of Kobdo was no more. This Baron had transmogrified into a megalomaniac whose cruelties and murders emerged on a whim. He sighed, covering his face totally with his hands.

"The only thing separating the human race from the abyss is the strength of kings," he said. "That is why we fight these disgusting Bolsheviks, to rescue the Romanovs and the rest of the family tree rooted across Europe."

"That may be fine and well for Europe," I said, interjecting into this long harangue. "But what does it mean for Mongolia? You are considered a great khan right here and right now. We Mongols need someone who is going to put the interests of our motherland first—and not fret over the fate of German kings."

The Baron snapped his fingers, and his aide-de-camp appeared again with another strange steaming bowl for the Baron, and one of plain barley-mutton soup for me. The broth in front of me smelled odd, so I faked a few spoonfuls and set it aside. The Baron inhaled the aroma of his own elixir, and then again poured it straight down his gullet into his belly. This time he didn't wipe his face, so the foul fluid flung from his wagging jaw as he spoke.

"I will not let the Mongolian people down," the Baron said. "You remarkable people, who swept across Asia and conquered everything that stood in the way. To be outnumbered by the entire world, and still to press forward, without any retreat whatsoever. Truly, this was the kingdom of kingdoms, built by the king of kings."

"The Greatest Khan. I should know," I said. "I myself am the reincarnation of his spiritual heir Amursanaa, as you may have heard. It seems we share something more than just a ruling style, don't we, Baron?"

Glaring at one another, the challenge hung in the air. Without moving a physical muscle, we struggled. His innate strength resisted mine. But he was unable to grasp my own, which was stronger by far. I didn't want to crush him. I needed him. And so, at our deadlock, we relented. We had our stories we told our people: his tale of personifying the vengeful warrior deity Mahakala…and my past life as the prince of some centuries hence who, according to legend, had been the incarnation of that very same god.

The question of how we could both be new existences of the same divine being hung in that burning air between us.

"It seems we are at an impasse, Lama," said the Baron, baring his teeth in something like a smile.

The lackey, again waiting on his knees, accepted the empty bowl and passed yet another one up to his master. But the bowl tottered, and then dumped in the lap of the warlord Baron. The Baron leapt to his feet with a great roar, kicking at the prostrate and writhing form of his servant, who had received most of the boiling liquid straight in his eyes and mouth. But it made no difference. The Baron laid into him with the ferocity of a wild animal. His men suddenly appeared in the ring of firelight and joined in kicking and whaling on the defenseless form, which soon went totally limp. Only then did they stop. The Baron dragged his finger across his neck and sat down, breathless, removing his cap for the first time.

"Take that insubordinate son of a whore to the pit," he said. "Let the wolves mete out the appropriate punishment."

The Baron toweled off the spillage with a thick fur, and then beckoned me to follow him. We walked through the darkness, with only his voice pointing the way to a destination unknown. The howling grew louder, the growls shook the ground. I had never known the purest form of fear until that moment, and my spine felt afire.

"There was a pack of wolves feeding off the scraps at the edges of the city. We rounded them up with traps and snares," he said, his voice wavering weirdly in the dark. "Instead of killing them, we made them our allies. As it turns out, they're the perfect execution squad."

We came to two torches, at either end of a black hole in the ground. Just as we approached, the transgressing Mongol was flung into the hole. There was a thud, the cacophony of growls and roars, then a scream that did not stop for an agonizing few minutes. Throughout it all, I glanced only once down into the blackened pit. But I watched the Baron's reactions. He did not smile, and he did not grimace. He didn't even blink. He just stared at his man being brutally eaten alive by wild beasts because of spilled soup.

The scream finally stopped.

"There is either order, or chaos," the Baron said. "There is no middle ground. There is only the tradition of monarchs, and the strong jails they built, or there is the utter pandemonium of the mob and the guillotine, blood slicking the savage streets."

I released my hold on the knife sheath underneath my deel. But I didn't totally relax the tension in my limbs, as I waited for an ambush from the shadows all around us. This man was a beast, regardless of either Western Sensibilities or Eastern Sense, whether at a friendly hearth or a blood-sick abattoir.

"I am no friend of Bolsheviks, Baron. And I am no stranger to wielding the whip," I said. "But I do not believe that men need to be eaten alive by a pack of wolves to keep simple order."

From the pit came slurping and crunching sounds. The Baron turned slowly to me, and he tilted his head toward the campfire—the pinpoint of light at the other end of the darkness.

"You know, Lama," he said, slapping his cap against his thigh to free it of dust. "I think we two can exist in our different Mongolias. You out west, and my rule here."

A spell had been broken. He grinned hatefully once more—and that's when I knew returning to my lair in the Black Gobi would be no mean feat. Because even though the expanses of Mongolia were vast in every direction, there was not enough room for the both of us; there could be only one second coming of vengeance for the Greatest Khan and his reincarnations. It was between me and the swollen-headed European. And this Baron determined he would be the sole inheritor of that legacy. All this meant unavoidable death for the other claimant: me.

I informed the men on guard to be on high alert. I did not sleep in my appointed yurt that night—instead I waited in the shadows outside it with my knife drawn. The assassin appeared in the darkest point of the night, sneaky and without a word of warning. As he crept into the yurt, I grabbed him and slit his throat, right down to the vertebrae. I dragged him a hundred yards away, where I dropped him, still spurting blood, into a hole my men had dug for the purpose. The minute he hit the hard dirt beneath, four of my strongest men shoveled earth atop him until his flailing and gurgling form disappeared forever.

In the darkness of the advancing night, I braced for a second attack which never came.

The Baron, however, was not surprised to see me at the dawn as he walked up with a contingent of his guards to where we were saddling the horses for the journey. Our side warily watched their hands, waiting to draw our weapons.

"I know you are a hard man. I remember from your time ruling Kobdo," said the Baron with a smile. "But you must watch your back out there on the open roads. There's any number of Reds and Chinamen out there who would love to set upon your little group before you could ever get back to your hideaway."

I saluted him with a smirk on my face.

"I believe we are up to the challenge, Baron," I said. "I do not fear Communists or the sons of Han. I only fear the attacks from behind I don't see coming. The betrayals."

I didn't even flinch as he came at me, and embraced me, his rough beard grazing my smooth face. He breathed hard. It was like a sigh.

"I only have weeks left, that's what the oracles have all said," he whispered to me. "No matter how many Jews I hang, or how many Reds I flay alive, they are like the grains of sand on the beach, they all say. Thus, I have nothing to lose at all."

"That makes two of us."

He smiled. I pulled away, turned, and continued my preparations. My men and I rode out the same hour, on a different road than the one which took us into the city.

The Baron's attack was not long in coming, and we saw it approaching from versts away. They rode, seven hundred or more, with great clouds of dust rising behind them at the horizon like the smoke from a great machine. But we turned our group onto a ridge overlooking the steppe floor, and then they were down below us, to the east. Half of my best riflemen opened fire from the overlook, picking off the Baron's lead horsemen. The other group I sent to the bottom of the slope, and they too started firing into the crowd. Each and every shot toppled a horse and rider. Still they came.

Just as their ranks closed within striking distance, the final two volleys of shots toppled the final big wave, which collapsed in the dirt with screams of man and beast alike. Barrages of shots continued even after the throng of survivors broke away and galloped madly away in full retreat.

I thought I made out a familiar form among the cowards; I thought I saw…him.

But never mind, I told myself.

It could not be true, I assured myself.

I barked the order, and the men at the bottom of the slope hunted down most of the stragglers like diseased beasts, dragging to death the ones who weren't shot.

But a handful still survived, and there was no sign of him—the man I thought I'd seen.

It could not be true, I told myself one last time.

Such was the Baron's attempt to vanquish my rule in the west of the country. After we galloped a hundred versts, a solitary rider came galloping up behind, and I had him apprehended and tortured as an assassin. It was quickly clear that he was a messenger, and nothing more. The parchment he carried was emblazoned with the Baron's seal and had just a single command.

"Go forth and prosper in your demesne, Lama," the Baron had written in slashing handwriting like stab wounds. "Good luck after my death. But do not ever deign to consider yourself the reincarnation of Amursanaa in Urga ever again. I will haunt you to the end."

I tore the message up and scattered the pieces on the night wind. Just as the messenger pulled out his dagger and lunged at me, my men ran him through with their own blades.

And on again we rode.

CHAPTER 25
CONSPIRACY

The Baron and his pit of wolves, true to the oracles, didn't even last weeks. Any fury that burns that hot, rage fueled by a gale, has time itself as its greatest enemy. Each breath, each heartbeat, causes those embers to flare hotter and hotter—until the source fuel is consumed utterly.

We heard of Ungern-Sternberg's fate—the chase, the mutiny, the Soviet show trial, and the firing squad, quick as you please—through the travelers we robbed along our route. I allowed some of the men to celebrate that night, toasting the death of the underhanded warlord, a disheveled European nobleman no less, who had tried to kill them and their Lama. But the next morning I told them there would be no further carousing on the account of the Baron's demise.

"Because he is just a man who took measures too extreme to make it in this world," I told them. "We must use him as warning of the world tinkering in Mongol affairs. We must master our own fate."

"The crazy bastard did not shy away from death," added Tömör, my hulking lieutenant. "He rode into the jaws of doom with a kind of glee, despite all the prognostications from the oracles…"

"It was precisely—because—of the prognostications from the oracles that he rode to his damnation," I emphasized. "That man was hell-bent on selfish glory and self-destruction. The only way he could be assured of immortality was by dying as quickly as possible. We will not make that mistake. We do not seek death as a way of prolonging life. Our mission for Mongolia is much too important for such gestures. After all, what has the Baron bequeathed the world, other than a collection of sycophants in Urga now eager to please Russian Communists?"

"What do we do next?" asked another of my lieutenants.

"Let me tell you," I said, clearing my throat.

Thus they heard of my plan, and from that speech forward, our conspiracy to overthrow the powers in Urga commenced.

Poison was the method and means, of course. Everyone in the capital believed it was the Bogd Khan alone who used this political stratagem of stealthy murder. But that was exactly why it would work for our movement. It would be totally unexpected if it were used in some other venue far from the Bogd and his insane exotic zoo. The only choice to be made was the target. I had to pick a particular figure, or a group, whose annihilation would definitely topple the tenuous order, and allow the Mongols of good faith, the ones wandering the steppe, to take arms and finally seize the freedom that had always been their destiny, like a piece of fruit on a branch just out of reach from the ground.

We would shake that tree, suck that juice dry.

But which target? The usual suspects were the Two Heroes themselves, but killing just one or the other would simply throw power over to the survivor. No— it would have to be both at once, plus a bunch more besides...

And that's when I remembered the drunken ball at the home of Magsarjav, the Firm Hero. The women, the loose talk, the gossip, the revelry...and that bowl of punch. It was just too perfect.

I briefed five of my savviest men, all of whom spoke Chinese, Russian, and Mongolian, and had the skills with tongue as well as sword. They were to infiltrate the home of the "Firm Hero" by any means necessary; to attend one of the parties that included the "Hero" himself and other dignitaries; and at one of the crucial moments, to dose the food or drink of the party, wiping out the ruling elite of Urga. Any survivors would be executed by the blade, to eliminate the possibility of their talking. Finally, they would ride back as fast as possible a hundred versts to the west, where I and others would be waiting for a signal to descend on the city and liberate it at the moment of leader-less chaos. From there, the drunken Russians and stinking Sons of Han would be shoved out, once and for all.

We left on a day in late winter, verging on the spring. The snows were melting, and the occasional flimsy green sprout broke through the ice. But a chill still left our breaths hanging in the air along our eight-hundred-verst route. We did not hide, but we did not seek out those who would pursue us.

But no one crossed our path. And still we marched, north and then east. The Reds were too busy with their plans for Urga, and the Chinese had their tumult at home. Finally, Mongols traversed their own lands without ambush, without fear. There was much revelry among the troops, but I kept them from becoming irresponsible. At nights I kept watch on the appointed guards. Within mere days we had covered the ground, the planned rendezvous spot, and the five steadfast men embraced me in farewell and set off for the city.

We waited. It would take at least a week, maybe two, for them to return. We set up defenses and patrolled the terrain from mountain to plain. The men hunted for beasts and Communists, but they only found the former. We roasted the biggest over the fire each night.

Boredom set in. Target practice commenced, the rifle shots cracking across the valley. The nights were when the men would bundle up around the fire against the spring winds, and they would wait for me to talk. The strange silence started the first night and persisted through the week. These boisterous and virile warriors, these conquerors of the dirt and sky, simply waited for me to tell them something—anything—about the world in which they roamed. I told them stories from history, but I kept them short.

Each morning the camp roused itself with the sunrise, and still we waited for our small detachment of saboteurs to return. We negotiated from a local herdsman a dozen sheep, which we slaughtered and cooked, confident the meals would last us our entire encampment. And from the carcasses were pulled a surfeit of ankle bones which the men used to play Shagai, gambling away some coins and other valuables, to pass the time. I forbade anyone from using them for fortune telling.

But a week later, we had to go buy another dozen head of sheep from another shepherd—and there was a strange leer on the impatient men's faces as we waited on and on. So I added a single tiny goat to our order, and I started up the game of buzkashi. At first my Mongols were dismissive of the Kazakh game. But once they saw it would be a test of strength and speed and skill on horseback, they took to it like no one else. The next week flew by, with days spent in the heat of sport. We went through the carcasses of four more goats, which were pulverized into broken skin-sacks of meat by the end of a hard-played day.

It was at the end of one such day, as dusk was cutting short the game, that a rider emerged from the darkness in the east and scooped up the goat. The rider had not given the secret signal for our camp—and instead whipped the horse and came as fast at me as possible. Something long and dark was in his hands, perhaps a rifle. I didn't recognize the person, so I rode hard at him, drawing my sword, lining up for the perfect decapitating stroke.

The rider turned sharp and slid off his saddle at the final moment under my swung sword, tumbling into the dust, rolling, and scampering to his feet. I pulled up reins hard, leapt to the ground and sprinted hard at the interloper. The other men closed in and encircled him by the time I got there. Blades were drawn, rifles were leveled. Except for the intruder, who…smiled.

It was Jimbe.

I had him released into my custody, but my guards made sure he was disarmed of the rifle-shaped object—which was actually a wide scroll, a message from Urga. I tossed it aside to one of my lieutenants for later review. The guards followed his every move with disapproval from mere feet away.

I had no such concerns of assassination. This man had traveled so many versts with me, any distance between us due to the ensuing time apart would be like mere inches between stars in the firmament. I appraised him. My old companion was fatter—he looked healthier. It was good to see him. Jimbe smiled, but he kept his distance. Instead, I lunged forth and embraced him, asking him where he had been and—before he could even take a breath in response—telling him he was welcome back into the throng out west. Truly, I did not realize how much I had missed this one old friend of mine.

But something was off. That smile was crooked. Even though he was immune to most of my strongest willpower, I could attune myself to some of his more basic vibrations. And in this moment, as he finally began to speak over a cup of hot broth beside the fire in the gloaming, I knew this man had ceased to be my ally.

I rejected my instincts, at first. For the first time in my life, I did not want to be astute. I did not want to be all-knowing. I did not want to know the secrets within a man's heart. I'd rather not know the worst truths of the currents swirling through the abyss. I wanted to keep my friend as a friend, nothing more.

But he just...would not stop talking.

"Lama, I have come as a messenger," he said, inhaling the steam of the bowl in front of his face. "I must urge you to immediately read that missive I brought to you."

"What is so important that it can't wait for two old traveling partners to catch up properly?" I asked, eyeing him.

Jimbe's head dropped. He chuckled, his shoulders quaking. There was disdain there.

"Why don't you just read it?" he spat. "Lama, shouldn't you already have some idea of what's going on here? And what must come next?"

The tone in his voice told me all. Everything in those words. There was no denying the truth in front of me. It spurred me to action. Now I had to crack open that heart and drink up all the secrets coursing through it.

In the blink of an eye, I kicked him in the chest backward onto the ground, and I lunged down to place the blade at his throat. He tried to catch the breath I had knocked out of him, but I wouldn't allow it to happen.

"I would like to repeat," I said, "What is so important that it can't wait for two old traveling partners to catch up? Tell me. Now."

Jimbe blinked. But he showed no fear and no regret even with his back pinned to the ground, with death looming over him.

"Your spies were all sniffed out and killed," he said. "I helped the Two Heroes figure out who the intruders were, and all were rounded up and shot within days of their arriving in the city. Two escaped notice for some time, and even made it into the employ of Khatanbataar. You would have been proud of them. But in the end, they were caught dumping a concoction down a drain, and they were arrested and executed like their comrades."

I froze in place.

"You broke up the Cartel of the Emperors. And the Emperors never forget, Lama," he said.

I yanked him up to his feet. I stepped back and let him catch his breath. But right when he stood upright, I punched him in the pit of the stomach, as hard and as fast as my fist could move through space. I heard the rush of air like the escape of his very soul out of his entire body, and he collapsed to the ground again. I rubbed my knuckles, sheathed my blade, and paced around his writhing form. Rage trembled through my hands.

"I have wondered," I said, "why you abandoned the cause, Jimbe. You followed me to the ends of Asia and went through some of the hardest privations ever known in Mongolia, let alone the rest of the world. Now I have the possibility of raising a new khanate to assume the power our people deserve. Victory is only now just within reach. And yet now you forsake me. Have you always been this foolish?"

Jimbe, slowly recovering, raised himself on an elbow.

"I was a fool before, Lama. But now I've come to my senses," he said, spitting dirt. "I, unlike you, realize that Mongolia is a figment of history, an apparition of legend. It never really existed the way we want it to, the way we believe it to be. Temujin was simply a boy who grew to be a warrior fiercer than all the others around him at that time. It was not destiny. He conquered the world, sure. But what remains? The great capital Karakorum is lost to the sands. The Mongol people are a penniless and misbegotten race. The life in the dirt, the hardscrabble filth of the shitlogged streets and stinking yurts of our people can't be blamed on the Chinese, or the Russians, or the Kazakhs, Lama. The blame lies in only one direction."

He pointed at me, and then turned that crooked finger back at his own chest, where his own heart beat.

"Ourselves. We have only ourselves to blame."

I turned away from him and started to walk away into the darkness of night which had finally fallen.

Jimbe leapt up in a flash, bolted forward and his small dagger pierced my back once, twice, three times before my men could stop him.

I did not pass out. But I was in a daze as I bled profusely, and the old, scarred swordsman we'd appointed as a doctor investigated the wound. Luckily the blade had not been long enough to reach any of my most vital organs, the wounded veteran told me as he continued threading closed my cuts with a big needle lancing my ragged flesh.

"You hear that, Jimbe?" I spat. "You didn't even hit any important organs! Just skin and muscle! Next time you decide on assassinating someone, bring a bigger blade. You traitorous fool."

Jimbe had no choice but to listen. He was lashed face-down to a boulder a few yards away. The men took turns whipping him without mercy. But aside from a grimace and a few groans, he suffered it gracefully. It enraged me, this backstabber was making another attempt at betrayal; after abandoning me, ruining my Urga plot, and then trying to kill me, he had the gumption to stoically withstand my torture. It was too much to bear.

"It must...be the...Year...of the...Dragon...after...all," said Jimbe, between whip strokes. And he laughed, even as he spit up blood.

Even with the blood still running in rivulets down my back, I stood with the needle and thread dangling out of my wound, and I grabbed one of the flails and I started in at my former compatriot. But after four lashes, I flung the thing aside, and leapt forward, yanking at the knots holding him fast.

"What are you doing, Lama?" squealed one of the men.

"I will release this traitor and see if he can kill me from the front," I said, hauling Jimbe to his knees. "It's only fair the coward gets the chance to look me in the eye this time."

I pointed down at him.

"I won't owe you anything," I said slowly, "as I squeeze you out of this existence and into the next."

The men glared at me. But I nodded at Tömör, my lieutenant. He did not move at first. It was only after a few breaths that he unsheathed his knife and tossed it on the ground in front of Jimbe.

Some breaths more. No one moved.

"Take it," I said. "Take the knife, Jimbe, and try to kill me. Seal your fate."

Faster than I would have thought, he stooped down and then launched himself at me. I pressed the pain of the wounds out of my mind, and I crouched, coiled like a cobra.

With each step, with each heartbeat, time slowed. I focused my mind. I felt the current swirl around me, lugubrious and easy.

When I saw that impassive face over that blade moving through space at me, I simply let my body take over, the muscles and sinews and blood and flesh of my existence assuming the ancient stance of war.

I dropped to the ground just as the knife missed my chest, and I kicked at his feet, which sent him sprawling face down to the ground, jaw straight into the dirt.

I leapt up and stomped on his wrist, and kicked the knife away, and then I was pounding his head on the ground. I reached out with my willpower, and though he struggled, I held his being fast.

His mind was finally mine, squirm mightily as it did.

"There's…something…" he moaned.

"There is nothing," I barked, even as my hands perpetrated the unspeakable violence they were due.

With my eyes shut and my ears roaring, I pounded his head down into the Mongolia rocks and soil. Again and again and again. The tears flew off my face, so the men did not see me weeping amid all the blood.

All was silence. Mere quivers and twitches in my hands. And the blood. And then there was the pulpiness, the breakdown of the skull in my fingers. Within the collar, there shimmered the vajra. I grabbed it.

Only then did I let go of the traitor's shattered head and walk away, without so much as a glance back at what remained of my former ally, my erstwhile brother on the trail.

"Wrap the body tightly," I said. "When we get back to Baying Bulak, bury him facedown. Cover him with stones. I want him to rot slowly in the soil he betrayed."

I stopped and looked at the sky.

"Perhaps after his bones are subsumed into nothing, he will finally be loyal to the Mongolian earth."

The smell of Jimbe's blood came along. It hung on me, unrelenting. Tömör too trailed me, silent, as I wandered away from the camp and toward the nearest ridge. I didn't say anything, but I walked quicker and quicker to avoid him as we went. But his steps kept pace with mine. Finally, I stopped and collapsed on a boulder that was just the right height. The lieutenant stood at attention over me.

"Lama," Tömör said. "Permission to speak."

"Speak, speak," I said, wiping my sleeve across my face. "But what is there left to say?"

"The men do not think it wise to continue waiting for the saboteurs," he said. "If even half of what that traitor told us is true, those men are already dead, and the plot has been foiled."

I nodded.

"I have no doubt what Jimbe was saying was the whole truth," I said. "He would not have risked his life on a gambit like that for a lie. He was trying to settle his accounts once and for all, and I can respect that about him, at least."

Tömör nodded, saluted, and then turned to go.

"But one more thing," I called out.

I tossed him the vajra.

"When we get back to the camp, please throw that in the grave with the traitor. He deserves to have some token of his identity in the next life. Something to show for what he did this go-round," I said.

Tömör nodded and turned and kept walking. When his footsteps moved out of earshot, I allowed myself to cry a little, as silently as possible. But it was new to me, and I did not know how to control it in the slightest.

The smell of blood clung to me. It would not cease.

The dawn broke without warning over the east, and we galloped away from it—back to the sands of the Black Gobi, my final hideout.

CHAPTER 26
BEHIND THE MASK OF THE
KHENBISH KHAN

The trip back west was slow and there was no frivolity. The outbound warriors who celebrated and carried hopes and rough joys, instead rode back with worn boots in their stirrups across the same uncertain versts they'd come. Fights on the trail left two dead. Drunken brawls around the night fires claimed another three. I punished all. We went west.

I watched clouds. They assumed strange shapes overhead, like snakes and unshaped beasts with huge teeth. They were portents, but I could not read them. I stared up overhead and I barely remembered to breathe as I watched the universe exhale across the sky. My lieutenants, of course, were on guard against all possible threats. Tömör had seemed especially fearful of something—something I could not see. The nameless horse carried me in the same direction of the descending sun.

And we made it. The lookouts shouted down to the workers of the settlement, and they all scrambled to assemble along the creek. But I immediately knew from the guilt in their slumped shoulders and their blinking eyes they had done nothing to improve the camp in the weeks we had been away. Nothing had been built, nothing had been harvested.

"I will not punish—this time," I said quietly. "But do know that the next idle hand I see will be cut off, knuckle by knuckle, and bone by bone."

Progress picked up over the next week. Soon the place was well on its way to a productive settlement rivalling any of the ancient villages across the Gobi. The crops leapt from the earth with the extra water and attention. The fortress, which had not grown in my time away on the Urga mission, suddenly reached toward the sky.

That is when the end neared. As I said at the beginning of this tale: my trustiest lieutenant Tömör was found dead on the dirt that one singular morning at Baying Bulak. His body was blue, and his face had frozen in twisted horror of the unknown. He was not marked with any wounds. I ordered the men to quickly bury him in a neat little grave, right next to the stony hole in which the remains of Jimbe rotted, unmarked.

After offering myself prayers, I left the darkness of my yurt that morning. I climbed to the top of the ramparts. This highest point could only be reached by navigating a series of thick walls zigzagging up the northern slope of the hills. Within these walls were the yurts and camps where the men lived in peace in between our raids and robberies. At the far base, nearest the stream, the forced laborers tilled the land. Farther still down the valley, the shepherds watched the herds. The crops grew thick and high, and the sheep numbered in the thousands, the goats in the hundreds. The barren Black Gobi had been tamed, inasmuch as it might ever be. Fertility had been seduced from the parched soils.

The two strangers approached the fortress. Tömör's boy called out to me.

"Shall we shoot these two, like the other intruders, Lama?" he said. "There is a rumor one of them may be none other than the Khenbish Khan."

"Nonsense, nonsense," I said. "It cannot be the Khenbish Khan. Still—do not accost these travelers. Show them all the hospitality, the nourishment they may need. The shooting we can save for later."

Thus the two strangers skulked around the camp for that first day. I heard them: asking everyone within earshot where the Lama resided and tripping over stones at the other end of the settlement in the darkness. But they did not know where I was, on which side of the line of guards and lookouts I slept, and which yurt was mine. And they certainly could not have known that in each of my hands was a cocked revolver at all times, and that I did not sleep. They also didn't know about the tripwire connected to the tiny warning bells alerting me to anyone breaching my threshold.

The footsteps came a few minutes later, from the secret back entrance without the bells, and the lieutenant tapped four times at the flap. I lowered my guns and commanded him to come in. He was still laughing as he stepped inside, approached, and bowed.

"These fools," he said, wiping at his eyes. "They want to present you with a ceremonial scarf. But they only want to wrap it around your neck, Lama. They must be assassins. We'll take care of them immediately. Where should we bury their bodies?"

I held up my hand. When he saw the look on my face, he stopped laughing.

"Let them live until we know more," I said. "These two pilgrims could prove to have a valid mission."

The lieutenant guffawed, unable to contain his laughter.

"You can't be serious, Lama. These are imposters. Probably Bolsheviks. They want to destroy everything we're building here. They want to crush our dreams for Mongolia. They think they can do so by killing you."

It was my turn to laugh. I spit on the ground.

"Then I will take care of this threat myself," I said. "It cannot be any other way. I have always accepted challenges and faced them with my own hands, my own blood and muscle, my dint of will. I must seal my own fate. It cannot be any other way."

The lieutenant shook his head.

"At least give us a few of the guns, so we can take them out if they are about to do something drastic," he implored me.

"No guns," I said. "This place was built on visions and resolve. These are the only bulwark against the guns of this century. Humanity will live or die by these."

I walked over to a table, wiped my finger across the stock of a rifle, and picked up a thick knife, running the blade under the fingernail of my left thumb, prying out some dark Gobi sand.

"I need to rid Mongolia of these parasites one way or another," I said. "Simply executing a few of them will make no difference. They will just keep coming. No. I need to consume their minds. I need to understand their hatred, their dreams, and their bloodlust. Only I can do this."

The lieutenant trembled at my words, their apparent insanity. I did not blame him. And I don't blame you for not understanding, either. You must understand there are things that you will not understand, that you can never understand. That is the human comedy on this plane, despite Western Sensibilities, or our sheer Mongolian Sense. We can never truly understand the full extent of the universe. But we have intimations. We have glimpses. And we can hope to comprehend a bit beyond ourselves, beyond this life of faint heartbeats and fleeting breaths. A scant few of us can strive for something greater—a view of the universe and its currents above the human ephemera.

I would not subvert fate—that is what I meant to tell these my loyal footsoldiers. It is one thing to strive for dominance in this world, to fight against that which promises to destroy us, pledging never to surrender. But it is another thing entirely to reach that point where you know the universe has come calling in its debts, and you can no longer delay repayment.

I knew this because I heard the voice again. That voice that had followed me for so long on my journeys, which had come from the air and in different forms—and which I believed to have been my dead father, the fakir, the wolf called Nugai. It was all around me during these days. But it wasn't a memory or a hallucination.

Lama.

Something was different, though. Because while it was undoubtedly the same voice which had followed me on my travels across the face of the globe, nonetheless there was something—softer—about it now. Something gentler. I had not noticed this over my travels, frenetic as they were.

Was it truly my father? I asked myself for the ten-thousandth time.

The voice floated around at the periphery of my vision. Closer than ever before. I could see the aura, the energy, a cloud always just out of focus at the edge of my earthly sight. But it was there all the same—and I heard it speaking to me. The words rang true. And what else do we as humans have, other than words, and their truth, and their lies?

Palden—wake up! came the voice. I staggered to my side, lighting a lamp. And there was the brownish whitish fuzz at the corner of my eyes. It veered at the edge of my vision. It was always just out of my field of view. I turned, then whipped my head around like a dog chasing its tail, yelping in pain as I cricked my neck. Still I could not catch a glimpse. But still the voice kept on talking, talking.

These men, said the voice, *they will kill you. As long as you know that, you cannot be afraid.*

"Why would I fear death? With all the pain and suffering of this lifetime?" I asked, my voice barely a rustle in grass.

Because you will eventually realize the only lesson in existence: there are no endings, and there are no beginnings. All in all, all we are is energy. A transitory vibration. A wave in the current just waiting to rush back into the chaos of the infinite universe.

I paused. I breathed.

"You're saying I should let these assassins kill me," I said.

Not at all, said the form, quaking with laughter at the edge of my vision. *I say defend yourself to the utmost, my dearest boy. But just realize that there comes a time when the war can no longer be waged, the fight no longer fought. There is a time for resignation. You need to realize this time comes for all of us. Eventually.*

"Eventually," I said. "That eventuality can wait until Mongolia has brought Asia to heel. Only then will my heart cease to beat."

I had walked outside, the form clinging off to my side. But then the voice, the shiftless form still shivering with mirth, wheeled around behind me—and I felt its presence on the back of my neck.

You do not realize, my boy, said the voice. *There is nothing in this century left for real men of character and action. The forests of Europe, the islands of the Pacific...it will turn into an abattoir. The whole world a single slaughterhouse. A funhouse for killers. There is no room for the Mongols to try and seize their destiny. Because destiny is in the airplane, and the bloody engines and greasy gears and nuclear bombs, the burning cities and the mausoleum crematoria. The ashes of millions will smother the Earth, and the Greatest Khan's sweep across Asia will look like the old rolling of toys across a sandbox.*

"Funhouse? Nuclear bombs?" I said. "What ashes?"

Don't worry about any of this. Don't worry about anything, is my point, said the form, its ethereal touch on my shoulder, a squeeze. *There can be no worries about all that comes next. There is only death. And death is a release. The faster we can all learn this, the faster the Mongols can understand that there is only the simplicity of a breath and a heartbeat…and the ever-waiting abyss.*

"But what about Agharti?" I said.

Ah, Agharti, said the voice. *Agharti. Where the gold does flow. The paradise beneath. Yes, there is always that. But how many can ever visit that place, let alone remain there? My boy, my dearest boy, rejoice that you even caught a feverish glimpse from our simple cart with the broken axle!*

And suddenly I realized.

I realized who this presence was, that had haunted my travels for so many years.

The presence that had come with me, offering guidance in various forms and functions, in different guises and voices.

It was not my father. It had never been my father, neither in the guise of wolf nor man.

My mother—it had always been her instead.

My poor mother, who had always been too weak for the world in body, had conquered it with her indomitable spirit. My father the shitmonger had never been the strong one, for all his powers. Instead, it had been the love from my mother which had hovered over me like an ethereal shield for all these years, despite my tribulations. And my soul fairly lifted off the ground at the epiphany.

"I have been at Agharti, mother," I said. "And I know that I can once again get there. I know I will once again find that entrance, and that's where I will live out my days. But not until I have left something indestructible in Mongolia, something that will ensure that our people will never again be subject to Czars, or pederast emperors, or idealistic comrades, or warlords, or maniacs. No matter their pedigree."

Her laughing stopped.

Haven't you heard a word I said? her voice came as a whisper, fading away into the ether somewhere above my head, into the darkness. *Don't you understand the world will belong to maniacs? And you cannot behead millions of the fanatics you speak of? The mob will put their faith in leaders who crave nothing short of apotheosis. They will kill with machines, and they will kill like insatiable beasts with the powers of mechanical gods extending from every limb.*

By now her voice was but a faint whisper, as it rose up to the heavens above, and plunged to the golden streets somewhere so far beneath.

Your own strength, your own yearning for order will fail before their chaos, she said. *Just resign yourself. Less pain that way.*

I leapt up and beseeched the sky:

"I will not! I will never relinquish a single breath! Not after the struggle my life has been!" I screamed. "Rapist acolytes and murderous monks! The depraved rulers and cowardly strong men! All of them have fallen before me!"

One word came in response, nothing more.

One word:

Be.

That was all. The air emptied above me, the voice vanished. I knew it was for good. My own voice had grown hoarse. But still I growled at my dead mother's empty space in the sky, shaking my fist upward.

"I will never give up a single breath. I will never relent a single verst. I refuse to be captured alive. My corpse is the only thing the bastards will ever get. And I will leave it so rotten and diseased as to be a curse. This will be my gift to them."

The only response was a black cloud drifting across the dusk above. My fist dropped slowly to my side. And that's when I saw a half-dozen of my men gathered around in the shadows. They were rigid. Not knowing how long they had been there watching me, I dropped my hands to my sides, and I sang without song. Then I walked away.

I meditated. The ghastly scent of blood lifted from me. I left the darkness of the yurt and Tömör's son and I visited the grave of his stalwart father, and the traitorous Jimbe. It is all as I recounted to you at the beginning of this tale.

And that's when my enemy struck.

The familiar force, strong and persistent, crashed against my skull. It was my old nemesis, the one who went by the false name Nikto Pravitel. But I realized there was more to him than that.

The full realization battered me as I pressed my hands at my temples, regaining control in our struggle of will and mind.

The degenerate acolyte at Drepung.

Nikto Pravitel the Russian lackey.

The phantasmal Khenbish Khan.

All were grinning villains.

All were one and the same.

My abiding antagonist had finally caught up to me. I knew not how he was still alive, after that last gun battle along the Trans-Siberian.

But I did know there would be no running…this time.

I slapped his psychic reach away without too much trouble. But his strength had grown immensely. Truly, it was like slapping away a heavy vine, growing and writhing with life. As my steps slowly mounted the fortress and climbed up to the turret, battling back his first advances, I knew this struggle would be mightily different than the ones that came before.

But just before I reached the secret second entrance to my yurt, my foot jerked outward from some invisible force and spilled me sideways into the dirt. I tumbled halfway down the slope, rolling among a slide of rocks. Even as I regained my footing, the tug on my ankle again nearly toppled me, forcing me to brace myself.

I reached back through space and felt his presence somewhere below me. I punched him in the gut, with a force that would have knocked another man totally unconscious. He crumpled, but his will struggled mightily even as I walked back to my yurt and went inside, sat down, poured myself a glass of water...which he knocked out of my hand. I again struck him—this time in the testicles. His strength slackened. With the momentary reprieve, I cupped my hands and drank from the huge bowl of water nearest the gun rack—until I felt another shooting pain, this time in my liver. I staggered over to the front of my altar, and I sat in my normal position, and I focused. I gouged at his eye nerves—and a howl echoed from far off across the settlement.

Thus began our psychic duel. For twelve hours there was the back-and-forth of deadly stalemate. I was clearly the stronger, like I was the wrestler who could effortlessly throw his opponent on the ground and inflict any kind of contorted pain, every bent agony possible. But like a wrestler without total dominance of his foe, I could not fully pin him to the ground, to make him submit. He made me hurt, too. All I could do was progressively tire as our willpowers, our souls, struggled in the currents of the ether separating our corporeal forms.

The will of this my enemy's was one which had grown through tribulation, and scars.

It was just like mine.

I realized these similarities somewhere around the eleventh hour, when all of his force pulled back—then suddenly closed around my throat. The shock of it nearly did me in. But it took me just a few moments to regroup, refocus, and free myself. I reached out and throttled his neck.

But though he bent, he did not break. And our death clinch tightened.

We spoke evil to one another, from afar, with nothing but the words of our thoughts.

"Lama, you know that you cannot escape me for long. What did you think, you could hide out in the desert in this lopsided castle, away from the world, and expect to be left alone? When all that you represent is a threat to everything the nations of the world abhor?"

"I did not expect to be left alone. But I did expect that I would be able to see you all coming across the sands and kill you one by one and leave your carcasses out for the vultures. Bya gtor."

"Come now, you don't really believe that, do you? You don't actually believe you can beat back the fanatical Bolsheviks, and the Chinese who have more men than grains of sand on a shoreline? Your own countrymen will not stand your life for too much longer. Everyone's existence depends on your non-existence. Because Mongolia cannot defend herself any longer. It must take sides, pick a master and fight alongside. Because there is no great khan anymore to drive across the plain and plow its enemies into dust."

"I am that khan, fool. I am the one who will drive the enemies out of our lands and bring Asia to its knees."

"Oh, truly. You either have the power of a god…or the delusions of a maniac. The Baron made his gambit for glory. You will soon follow in his footsteps."

A pause.

"I, the Khenbish Khan will see to that, verily," he said. "After all, I've finally chased you down after all these years."

I blinked, nearly lost my concentration.

"I still scarcely believe you are one and the same, Pravitel," I said. "And after all these years, the phantom dogging my trail was merely a dolt who couldn't hack the monastery."

But only laughter greeted me in turn.

Reeling from pain, I staggered out of the yurt. My final battle.

I walked up to the top of the fortress, and I stared up at one of the stars or planets, one that flickered with a crimson twinkle. I never understood the heavens. I was always focused on the Earth and what lay beneath. That, to me, is the true universe—the terminal existence for which all of us lowly beings on this planet should strive.

As the sun swelled and chased the darkness westward, I relented and slowly stepped down the stairs, careful my enemy would not trip me up at a crucial moment and break my neck.

"Don't worry," he said, answering my thoughts. "I don't want to kill you in such an underhanded way. I want to see you die. I want to taste your sweat, your tears, when you fall."

"If that happens," I said, "I'll be sure to slake my final thirst with your blood, you coward."

"There's only one of us who will be bleeding when this day is through."

But the hours passed, and the day turned. I waved my away my lieutenants, who were convinced I was sick or mad. I only kept grappling because of my hatred of him and his words, his incessant jabbering that continued through that next night—the taunts and the grandiose claims for a new century. I felt his hatred was equal to mine. There would never be any peace, as long as we both walked the Earth.

Ja Lama and Khenbish Khan—the showdown was only a matter of time, even on as big a stage as the whole of Asia.

Finally, at dawn, I felt him draw back. I knew this was not a retreat. Something else entirely was planned.

And that's when my little alarm bell tinkled.

The two appeared at the door of my yurt, bearing their gift.

They walked in without sound, without footsteps, without shouts from the guards. They held out the ceremonial scarf. It had no color. It was drab, limp, creaseless.

"Tushegoun, we have come for you…" the one started to say.

"We have come to kill you," said the Khenbish Khan, face still covered like a coward.

And this is where you expect some kind of mighty struggle—that your faithful pursuit of my journeys would be rewarded by a final victory of the hero whom you have followed so far across Asia. But if you have followed my tale closely enough, you have come to realize that there is no victory. The story means nothing.

There is no final triumph, no emphatic drive of the will. You can delude yourself that mind can conquer matter, that reality can bend to the will. You could travel the length of an entire continent and conquer half of your native land. You could be imprisoned more times than you care to count. You could match wits with con men, and cross swords with warriors, spark wars between colonizers and colonized. You may even find your one true love and lose her and subsist as a fishmonger while catching the occasional glimpse of a subterranean golden paradise…and even then, you would still have to reckon with a final defeat, an ultimate end, among the dead.

And so even as the scarf came up in front of their grimacing faces, I anticipated the pistol underneath the falling cloth. I realized the grinning bastard had been clouding my mind, distracting my inner strength, the entire time they had been planning the real assassination. He had just been pretending, lulling me into a false sense of security. So even as the first three shots ripped through my throat, I was only just starting to recover my senses.

Total release. The damage, done.

Pain and blood, of course, throbbed through my fingers. I could not scream for help. The two of them leapt forward and pinned me down, and there were more shots, two magazines' worth that ripped my neck almost entirely from my body.

Then my nemesis, removing his eyepatch and winking that ugly socket in his skull at me, lifted a blade. This Khenbish Khan brought it down on my neck. It was a pressure and a pain I had never felt before. Only once the blade had entirely severed my flesh did I realize it was my own knife.

My mortal enemy reached through all my blood and picked up my head with two hands so that my eyes were level with his. I blinked.

"You are still awake! That is excellent!" he said. "Now you can listen to my parting words, you fiend."

I was still aware, somehow. My nerves were all afire, my brain was alight with death.

I actually saw the swirls, the currents of the universe, the dead and the in-between, surrounding everything.

The power and energy between each breath and fleck of dirt, the specks of dust and spittle, the moments between the thoughts and acts.

It was all there, finally, for me to see with my dying eyes.

It was the current of everything, finally laid bare around me. It was beauty and horror together.

Consciousness was still with me. I mouthed gibberish language at him—words in Russian and English and Chinese that would mean nothing to him in context. After all, it's not often that one finds oneself a disembodied head in this life.

"What is this?" said the Khenbish Khan. "Does the exalted Lama wish to impart his dying words to me? Tell me now, and perhaps I will remember them."

With a laugh, he lowered my head down toward his ear. But he could not hear me, and he brought my mouth closer, ever closer.

Closer. Closer.

Now is the time, screamed my mother's voice, out of the void.

That's when I reached out with all the willpower I would ever muster. Everything that was left within this existence. My inner strength surged out of my eyes and my flickering mind—and this time I saw it stab out with a greenish jolt—and pierce him right between the eyes.

And I threw at him the sum of all my wisdom with the final strength left in my dying brain.

The sum of my wisdom.

Just three words:

it

matters

not

Even as I started to fade from this plane, I watched this Khenbish Khan's face slacken, though his eyes betrayed his terror. Because his hands were moving against his command. His eyes clenched shut as he turned his gun on himself. And before his compatriot could stop him, this imposter khan put it to his forehead and executed himself with a great blast.

And with that, the tent was plunged into darkness. Everything fell soundless, in a deep repose, a stillness even as my mortal remains leaked my last blood into the sands of the Gobi. The last thing to meet my earthly senses was the far-off shouts of my loyal army as they surrounded the yurt. I felt nothing any longer—certainly not anything from my separated body, untethered once again from this mortal coil.

But I had killed the imposter khan. And a smile crossed my dead lips— along with three more words.

perhaps

next

time

It was maybe an eternity in those ultimate moments when everything lifted into the ineffable currents of the universe I had finally glimpsed. And so even as my soul strived downward, toward that impossible city of Agharti, I was instead picked apart, piece by piece, bone by bone, and borne aloft by beak and gullet, bya gtor.

The End

GLOSSARY

Agharti. A legendary kingdom located at the center of the Earth. Often conflated with Shambhala, the perfect kingdom which will be ruled over by the future Buddha.

Amursanaa. (1723–1757) To some, the final hero of Mongolia, who ruled over Dzungaria in the 18th century—and led an unsuccessful revolt against the Chinese. Ja Lama claims he is a reincarnation of this leader.

asafoetida. A foul-smelling perennial plant which grows in Kazakhstan. Referred to as "Devil's Dung" in English.

bataar. "Hero" in Mongolian.

black apples. A rare variety from the family of Hua Niu apples (also known as the Chinese Red Delicious). Their color is due to their growth in the mountains of Tibet, where they receive a lot of ultraviolet light during the day, but dramatic temperature drops at night cause the skin to develop the deepest hue. The flesh inside is just like any other apple.

Blagoveshchensk. The site of a horrific massacre of thousands of Chinese, who drowned in the Amur River, at the hands of Russian Cossacks in 1900.

Bogd Khan. (1869–1924) The de-facto ruler of the newly-autonomous Mongolia from 1911 until his death in 1924; a spiritual leader of Mongolian Tibetan Buddhism who was the eighth Jebtsundamba Khutuktu. As such, he ranked just below the Dalai Lama and the Panchen Lama in importance to the faith.

buzkashi. A sport in which horsemen try to throw a goat carcass into a goal. Polo with guts. Popular more in Kazakhstan than in Mongolia.

bya gtor. "Bird scattered." A Mongolian sky burial by another name, by which a body is left out in the elements, and vultures provide funerary services by the tips of their beaks, and appetites.

Czaritsyn. A city now known as Volgograd, but which was known for a long time as Stalingrad. The location of arguably the world's most important battle in 1942–1943.

deel. An item of traditional Mongolian clothing, often made of cotton or silk, which reaches below the wearer's knees.

Diluv Khutagt. (1883–1965) The reincarnated scholar of Tibetan Buddhist texts who survived the civil strife of Mongolia only to flee and live out the rest of his years in…New Jersey.

Dolonnuur. "Seven Lakes." A city in Inner Mongolia, which is a cultural center and was historically the summer capital of Kublai Khan and the Yuan Dynasty.

Dutreuil de Rhins. (1846–1894) French explorer whose 1894 murder in Eastern Tibet outraged two continents.

Dzungaria. A confederation of Mongol tribes which came together and made a powerful khanate in the 17th and 18th centuries. Dzungaria was essentially rendered extinct by genocide at the hands of the Qing Chinese, after Amursanaa's unsuccessful stand against them. The Qing murderers were supported by the Uyghurs of that time (the descendants of whom as of this writing in the 21st century are themselves subject to genocide at the hands of a different dynasty of Chinese rulers). Estimates place the Dzungarian death toll of the 18th century at nearly 800,000—or roughly 80 percent of the population. The death toll of the ongoing Uyghur genocide by the Peoples' Republic of China has yet to be determined.

Ferdynand von Ossendowski. (1876–1945) A Polish writer and explorer who escaped Communism after years of struggle. His tales were collected in several books, most notably *Beasts, Men, and Gods*.

Inner Mongolia. A portion of China (bordering Mongolia) in which Mongolians have gradually become a minority.

Karakorum. The opulent capital of Genghis Khan in the 13th century, which became a major political center of the world. Razed by the Ming Dynasty in the 14th century. The stones of the ruins were used to build a Buddhist monastery in the 16th century; little beside remains.

Khatanbataar Magsarjav. (1877–1927) "Firm Hero." Mongolian general who was a leading independence figure—even when he betrayed Baron Roman von Ungern Sternberg and essentially delivered him to the Mongolian Communists.

Mahakala. Guardian deity in Tibetan Buddhism, with four arms, three eyes, and nearly infinite power.

Manlaibataar Damdinsuren. (1871–1921) "First Hero." A diplomat born in Inner Mongolia who worked in the Mongolian independent movement, especially in the 1911 operations. Legend says he was tortured for months in a Chinese prison but refused to kneel—and so died standing up.

nagan hushun. A Chinese vegetable garden, courtyard, or enclosure in Mongolia. They can get large enough to accommodate a riotous mob.

N'Golok. An Eastern Tibetan peoples who pride themselves on being distinct from Tibetans and Chinese both.

Outer Mongolia. Mongolia that is not ruled by China and where Mongols are the majority.

Palden. Ja Lama's birth name.

P.K. Kozlov. (1863–1935) A Russian and Soviet explorer who continued the work of exploring Central Asia and Mongolia begun by his mentor, Nikolai Przhevalsky.

Przhevalsky. (1839–1888) A Russian imperial explorer and geographer who studied Central Asia.

Qing. The final imperial dynasty in China, which lasted from 1644 until 1912.

quintuple underhand constrictor hitch. A knot made of thirty-seven different turns, impossible to undo without the secret knowledge of its making; even harder to re-tie.

shagai. A traditional Mongolian game of dice, using the ankle bones of a sheep or goat. Such bones are also used in fortune telling, as well.

takhi. A kind of horse particular to Mongolia, all of whom are supposedly descended from the horses upon which Genghis Khan's armies rode to global glory.

Tian Shan. A large system of mountain ranges in Innermost Asia. The name means, variously, the "Mountains of Heaven," or the "Heavenly Mountain."

Turpan Depression. A fault-bounded basin in the far western part of China (current-day Xinjian Autonomous Region), outside Ürümqi. The third-lowest point on the Earth's surface.

Tushegoun. An honorific for Ja Lama bestowed upon him by the Bogd Khan; a noble title.

Roman von Ungern Sternberg. (1886–1921) A monarchist from European nobility who fought in World War I and the Russian Civil War before becoming a liberator of Mongolia for a few brief months in 1921. "The Bloody Baron" maintained he was another incarnation of Mahakala, but that didn't last long before he was captured and executed by the Bolsheviki.

Urga. An historical name for what is now called Ulaanbataar, the capital of Mongolia.

vajra. A mystical weapon, like a Tibetan club, which has the symbolic power of both diamond and thunderbolt.

verst. A unit of measurement used by Russians in the era of the Czars. Equivalent to a kilometer, roughly.

Yuan Dynasty. The Chinese dynasty which was essentially Mongolian. Established by Kublai Khan, the grandson of Genghis Khan, and lasting from the 13th to 14th centuries.

ACKNOWLEDGEMENTS

This novel owes a debt to many people who, wittingly and unwittingly, dead or alive, helped make it possible. Ferdynand Ossendowski, who left this life nearly eighty years ago, kicked off my psychic journey into Mongolia. Henning Haslund, Owen Lattimore, and the Diluv Khutagt cast beautiful light on a wonderful land and peoples through their writings.

More recently Andrei Znamenski and his books opened up a whole new world to me, which has been beautiful and terrible and inspirational. Also helpful were relatively new narratives by James Palmer, Don Croner, and Jack Weatherford.

For inspiration I thank Brian Evenson, Jeffrey Ford, Kate Folk, and Nathan Ballingrud, among many others.

Closer to this text, I thank Rachel Schoenbauer and Forrest Driskel and Tylee Ertel, who are editors supreme. Zara and Allan Kramer are terrific supporters of my work, as are Christine Gabriel and Elgon Williams.

All those currently battling against the ongoing Uyghur genocide, from Ilham Tohti to others of conscience who shout into the void, are of utmost inspiration to me, as well. The Dzungarian horror of the 18th century will not be repeated in full, I hope…although as I enter middle age I am more convinced that Santayana's Law is more prophecy than warning.

In my travels on this earthly plane I have invaluable interlocutors: Tom Casal, whose teachings sent me on the way to the Indian subcontinent; Sonya Kulczyckyj, who is among the best listeners I've ever heard of; and Dick Paterson, who is among the best of anyone out there.

Closer to home are all my ladies: Izzy and Addie and Amy, who let me disappear into The Treehouse in between meals.

ABOUT THE AUTHOR

Seth Augenstein is a writer of fiction and non-fiction. His debut novel, Project 137 (2019) was called "an involving, tense and visceral near-future thriller" by Kirkus. His short stories have appeared in numerous magazines and fiction podcasts. He spent a decade writing for New Jersey newspapers, lastly at The Star-Ledger. He picked up some state journalism awards, along his travels to crime scenes, hospital operating rooms, natural disasters, funerals, and quiet homes. He was also the editor of Forensic Magazine, a tour guide at the James Joyce Centre, and a student in Saul Bellow's final class. Now he lives on a rocky ridge in New Jersey with his wife, daughters, dog named Mishima, and cats.

Your purchase of *Lama With A Gun* by **Seth Augenstein** supports our growing community of talented authors.

If you enjoyed this book, please let the author know by posting your review at https://www.pandamoonpub.com and register today to receive advance notice of new book releases, special bundles, and discounts.

pandamoon
publishing

Growing good ideas into great reads…one book at a time.

Visit http://www.pandamoonpublishing.com to learn about other works by our talented authors.

Mystery/Thriller/Suspense
- A Rocky Series of Mysteries Book 1: *A Rocky Divorce* by Matt Coleman
- Ballpark Mysteries Book 1: *Murder at First Pitch* by Nicole Asselin
- Ballpark Mysteries Book 2: *Concession Stand Crimes* by Nicole Asselin
- Bodie Anderson Series Book 1: *Code Gray* by Benny Sims
- David Knight Thrillers Book 1: *The Amsterdam Deception* by Tony Ollivier
- David Knight Thrillers Book 2: *The Tokyo Diversion* by Tony Ollivier
- Dee Rommel Mysteries Book 1: *10 DAYS* by Jule Selbo
- Dee Rommel Mysteries Book 2: *9 Days* by Jule Selbo
- *Fate's Past* by Jason Huebinger
- *Graffiti Creek* by Matt Coleman
- *Killer Secrets* by Sherrie Orvik
- *Knights of the Shield* by Jeff Messick
- *Kricket* by Penni Jones
- *Lama With A Gun* by Seth Augensein
- *Mile Marker Zero by Benny Sims*
- *On the Bricks* by Penni Jones
- *Project 137* by Seth Augenstein
- *Rogue Alliance* by Michelle Bellon
- *Sinai Unhinged* by Joanna Evans
- *Southbound* by Jason Beem
- *Suicide Souls* by Penni Jones
- *The Juliet* by Laura Ellen Scott
- *The Last Detective* by Brian Cohn

- The Moses Winter Mysteries Book 1: *Made Safe* by Francis Sparks
- The New Royal Mysteries Book 1: *The Mean Bone in Her Body* by Laura Ellen Scott
- The New Royal Mysteries Book 2: *Crybaby Lane* by Laura Ellen Scott
- The New Royal Mysteries Book 3: *Blue Billy* by Laura Ellen Scott
- *The Ramadan Drummer* by Randolph Splitter
- *The Unraveling of Brendan Meeks* by Brian Cohn
- *This Darkness Got to Give* by Dave Housley
- *To Kill a Unicorn* by DC Palter

Science Fiction/Fantasy
- Children of Colonodona Book 1: *The Wizard's Apprentice* by Alisse Lee Goldenberg
- Children of Colonodona Book 2: *The Island of Mystics* by Alisse Lee Goldenberg
- Dybbuk Scrolls Trilogy Book 1: *The Song of Hadariah* by Alisse Lee Goldenberg
- Dybbuk Scrolls Trilogy Book 2: *The Song of Vengeance* by Alisse Lee Goldenberg
- Dybbuk Scrolls Trilogy Book 3: *The Song of War* by Alisse Lee Goldenberg
- Everly Series Book 1: *Everly* by Meg Bonney
- Everly Series Book 2: *Rosewood Burning* by Meg Bonney
- Finder Series Book 1: *Chimera Catalyst* by Susan Kuchinskas
- Finder Series Book 2: *Singularity Syndrome* by Susan Kuchinskas
- Fried Windows Series Book 1: *Fried Windows (In a Light White Sauce)* by Elgon Williams
- Fried Windows Series Book 2: *Ninja Bread Castles* by Elgon Williams
- *Humanity Devolved* by Greyson Ferguson
- Magehunter Saga Book 1: *Magehunter* by Jeff Messick
- Magehunter Saga Book 2: *Priesthunter* by Jeff Messick
- *The Bath Salts Journals Volume One* by Alisse Lee Goldenberg and An Tran
- The Crimson Chronicles Book 1: *Crimson Forest* by Christine Gabriel
- The Crimson Chronicles Book 2: *Crimson Moon* by Christine Gabriel
- *The Grays* by Dave Housley and Becky Barnard
- The Phaethon Series Book 1: *Phaethon* by Rachel Sharp
- The Phaethon Series Book 2: *Pharos* by Rachel Sharp
- The Phaethon Series Book 3, Phantasma by Rachel Sharp
- The Sitnalta Series Book 1: *Sitnalta* by Alisse Lee Goldenberg
- The Sitnalta Series Book 2: *The Kingdom Thief* by Alisse Lee Goldenberg
- The Sitnalta Series Book 3: *The City of Arches* by Alisse Lee Goldenberg
- The Sitnalta Series Book 4: *The Hedgewitch's Charm* by Alisse Lee Goldenberg
- The Sitnalta Series Book 5: *The False Princess* by Alisse Lee Goldenberg
- The Thuperman Trilogy Book 1: *Becoming Thuperman* by Elgon Williams

- The Thuperman Trilogy Book 2: *Homer Underby* by Elgon Williams
- The Thuperman Trilogy Book 3: *Thuperheros* by Elgon Williams
- The Wolfcat Chronicles Book 1: *Dammerwald* by Elgon Williams

Women's Fiction
- *Find Me in Florence* by Jule Selbo
- *The Long Way Home* by Regina West
- *The Shape of the Atmosphere* by Jessica Dainty

Non-Fiction
- *Marketing for Freelance Writers* by Robyn Roste
- *The Writer's Zen* by Jessica Reino